BARRY COLMAN

WILD CARD

Published by The Liberty Publishing Company

A catalogue record for this book is available from the National Library of New Zealand.

ISBN 978-1-7386083-3-1 (Paperback)
ISBN 978-1-7386083-4-8 (EPUB)
ISBN 978-1-7386083-5-5 (Audiobook)

Cover design by Jeroen ten Berge, jeroentenberge.com
Publishing services: Martin Taylor, Digital Strategies

To Kati

ONE

DR MICHAEL KOUGH SLIPPED THE GLASS PHIALS INTO ONE OF the pockets on the front of his white lab coat. He instantly felt his heart rate spurt. He had never stolen anything before.

And soon realised, he had stolen too much. The dozen glass phials bulged conspicuously from the single pocket. Worse, they clinked against each other when he moved.

He nervously transferred half of the phials into his second pocket.

He felt his hands shaking slightly, but he was happier with the new balance of contraband.

He turned away from the refrigerated laboratory cabinet and did his best to look casual as he walked back to his workstation. The big open-plan room was quiet and dimly lit by concealed light tubes, while each workstation was an oasis of light from low individual desk lamps.

His desk was cluttered with the usual array of microscopes, technical measuring instruments and computer screens that a busy virologic researcher would use. Today was the last time he would sit there.

His co-researchers took no notice of him; their heads were studiously down, as they beavered on with the laboratory's mission of enhancing the deadliness of natural viruses.

Kough watched them tentatively for a moment. His Big Brain

warned him, there was no going back after his next act. He took a breath, pulled his research files up on the screen and began deleting them.

The data files seemed to spin before his tired eyes and then vanish. They were deleted, not forwarded, so there were no easy footprints left for a later forensic search. A search that was inevitable when the laboratory bosses realised what he had stolen.

Kough had a freakishly high, one hundred and forty-eight IQ, so he routinely relied on Big Brain to memorise screeds of data, as it had done with the contents of the research files he had just deleted.

As a further protection, he had altered essential parts of the work he was deleting. Any forensic genius who did uncover his sensational discovery would eventually come to the conclusion his work was only a jumble of tangled calculations and hopeful speculations.

He looked at his cheap plastic watch, a symbol of his economic misfortune. He knew the time had come to transfer the phials to the ice packs in his briefcase. The move posed another danger: they would momentarily be in the sight of any colleague walking past his station. His stomach cramped. He had a sudden urge to rush for the john. Stealing was a harder business than he had imagined.

He resolutely grabbed the briefcase from beneath the desk and snapped it open. He reached into a lab-coat pocket and held three phials tightly together to avoid them clinking.

His peripheral vision showed no one was near him. He unloaded them three at a time and placed them among the mini ice packs in an inner zip-up pocket deep in the briefcase.

It seemed to take forever. When he finished, he glanced around the laboratory again and was sure no one had seen anything. But his nerves were still jangling when he closed the case.

It was now twelve minutes to five, and the official end of his final day. The next and most dangerous challenge still lay ahead – staff were searched by Marine guards each time they arrived or left the germ-warfare laboratory.

There was safety in numbers, he believed. So he would join the queue when most of the staff left at five. Which they would, as there would be no normal after-work drinks to mark his departure.

Why would there be? He had been sacked after several warnings.

The bosses believed his work was not advancing the lab's mission to find the world's most lethal killer germs.

His experiments had all failed. His hire had been a mistake. He had turned out, despite elite qualifications, to be an awkward loner, a bankrupt with a gambling addiction whose wife had given up on him.

Kough was habitually a dishevelled figure. His clothes were rumpled, complementing his generally hang-dog appearance. The dark lines under his eyes emphasised the sleep deprivation he suffered from countless early-morning stints at the Denver casinos.

He was a mess. But he was going to do something about it, he promised himself. His discovery amid the black arts of germ enhancement would earn him impossible riches. He would no longer be a mug punter either – he would be able to buy his own casino.

Kough had got the American job because very few others wanted to work in the germ-warfare field – and that meant good staff were rare and the salaries obscenely high.

He had originally intended to use this money to repay the gambling debts he had left behind in Australia.

Then he rationalised, with the new stake money, he could hurry things along with the winnings he would make at the local casinos. But the truth was, he could not live without the thrill of a big punt on the roulette wheel, whether he was winning or losing.

Some nights he did win big: in the six figures. But on bad nights the floor manager politely intervened and took him upstairs to a complimentary room, where he crashed for a few hours' sleep, before making another late appearance at the lab.

Now, he was heading home to Canberra, the federal capital of Australia. The city where his life had imploded two years ago and where he would now become impossibly rich.

Kough realised he looked stupid and suspicious as he sat at his desk, a leg each side of his battered briefcase, so he shoved it forward, lay it on its side and rested his feet on it. It still looked a little odd but ... Big Brain said, Stop fiddling with the damned thing.

His early career in Australia had gone well professionally and he had made good money as a virologist because of his exceptional talent. But gambling had undone him, despite his certainty, as a scientist, that luck ran in cycles. That meant quitters never won. So he never quit. He stayed and stayed while the little glass marble sped around the wheel, hyping his adrenaline rush to exquisite levels. If it clattered on to the right number, he scored a thirty-six to one return.

But there were never enough big wins.

He winced inwardly each time he recalled the night his credit finally ran out. The wheel had stopped, Lady Luck had shaken her head, and his chips were raked away. He had stood rigid in shock. He had been so sure that it was not logically possible for his bad luck to continue.

After that his friends had melted away like the ice in his once-complimentary bourbons. All his friends, that is, except for John Able.

TWO

Kough sensed the laboratory supervisor nearby. He sat up and tapped the computer keyboard. The screen lit up obediently. She assumed he was still working. She turned on her heels and strode off, puffed up with the unearned importance of lower-middle-management plonkers.

Kough pulled *The Wall Street Journal* up on his screen. He thought reading the latest news was a harmless way to kill his final minutes as an American military research contractor. He saw his homeland had made page one.

Australia was baulking at some Chinese Government corporation's plan to take over a mineral resources company.

He smiled to himself: Australia had never seemed to figure out its real place in the world. Its population was a mere twenty-five million to China's one and a half billion. Yeah, Aussie had truckloads of mineral resources and coal and gas, but it was still an indefensible island at the end of the world with just five cities scattered around its outer edges.

The story made him think of Johnny Able. He had made the big time very early, landing a job as the prime minister's chief of staff at only twenty-nine. It was a role he was very proud of, and it placed him in the political nerve centre of Australia. Johnny was meeting him at the airport.

It was Johnny who had given him his hated nickname, Boffy. The name had stuck because Kough was a boffin type who relished his time in the school labs. It was no matter that his heavy-boned physique was used successfully on the rugby field, his teammates still referred to him by his nerdy nickname.

Kough reached down for the briefcase. He opened it again. He passed his hand over the zip-up pouch inside but could not feel the frozen contraband. He jolted upright in surprise. Then he realised the phials were in a pouch deeper inside. He could feel their coldness through the thin leather. Relaxing again, he emptied a big lungful of air. Big Brain said, For God's sake, calm down or you'll blow everything.

Miss Importance appeared again, silently, seemingly from nowhere. 'Still here, Micky?'

Kough snapped the briefcase closed. A red blush smothered his guilty face: 'Yeah, yeah. Still here. No government employee leaves before their allocated time.' He tried a short laugh.

She stared at him, lips pursed: 'I don't think Uncle Sam will mind in your case.'

He bloody would if he knew what I'm taking home, thought Kough. Just the Holy Grail of virus control. He had not thought for a moment what a nightmare it would be being too rich.

Miss Importance peered over his shoulder: 'Are you reading the *Wall Street Journal*?' She stood back and shook her head dismissively: 'You're wasting your time; it's just another Murdoch rag these days.'

She turned and left. Kough checked his watch. Six minutes to the final hurdle.

As other staffers began to pack up to leave, he removed his lab coat and stuffed it into the briefcase before joining them. Several co-workers offered their hands in a final, muted farewell. Some bade him good luck. Most ignored him.

The lab had its own, recycled air supply ensuring no lab germs escaped into the outside atmosphere.

At the exit airlock two Marines patted down the staffers in a familiar, cursory fashion. The queue moved steadily forward. Kough braced himself. He saw bags and briefcases being opened and the guards snatching a glance inside.

His turn came. The sergeant nodded: 'Your last day I hear, digger?'

Kough nodded.

'You know the drill. Open the case please.'

Kough opened the case a beat later than an obedient slave. The sergeant looked inside: 'What's this?'

'It's my faithful lab coat. It's not worth anything. I'm taking it as a souvenir.'

'No way, digger; it's government property. It stays.'

'Oh, come on. That's bullshit.'

'Please don't make any trouble, sir. Just take it out and leave it on the table. We'll return it for you. Unless you want to be charged with the attempted theft of government property.'

Kough stared at the sergeant, aware a line of impatient workers was bunching up behind him.

'Get me your duty officer and we'll sort this out here and now.'

The sergeant swallowed: 'Lieutenant Collins is not here right now. But it wouldn't make any difference. He wouldn't let you keep the coat either.'

Kough half-turned to the people pressing behind: 'Are you hearing this bullshit? One old lab coat and suddenly it's precious government property.'

No one said anything.

The sergeant looked at the queuing researchers: 'Sorry folks.' He turned to Kough: 'Yes, it is government property and you ain't takin' it.'

Kough grabbed the grubby lab coat, held it upside down and shook it hard: 'See, there's nothing in it. It needs a clean. It's worth bugger all. I only want it as a keepsake, so what the hell is your problem?'

The sergeant leaned forward and looked into the briefcase: 'No other little souvenirs in there?'

Kough's heart stopped.

'No, there bloody isn't.' He shoved the lab coat into the sergeant's hands. 'Happy now?'

'Thank you, sir. You have a good night. Okay, folks, let's keep the queue moving.'

Kough shut the briefcase. He felt clammy; there would be perspiration on his forehead. Without looking back, he walked out of the air bubble and into the freezing Colorado night. Big Brain said, Well played, sir.

He took his place on the shuttle to Denver, hugging the precious leather briefcase on his lap.

Betty had taught him well. How to get your booze into any stadium on big-game days in a picnic hamper. Give the officious stewards something to find. Something little. And they would miss the high-octane stuff packed between the sandwiches. It had always worked. Betty had been a smart sheila. He wondered where his separated wife was right now.

THREE

Kough had expected the laboratory's exit search routine. But he was wholly surprised to find he faced another one, at Canberra Airport.

The name badge of the spotty-faced kid in the Border Control booth was Horatio Hadley. He was so skinny he could take three steps before his uniform moved. He regarded the bleary-eyed Kough with open distaste. Another unshaven sap from economy class, he thought. With probably a bit of dark web, weirdo porn in the briefcase or some kind of new magic powder from the Los Angeles street markets.

A second Border Force officer stood a metre behind Spotty Face, surveying the arrivals. Duty Manager Gerry Ryan had been a commando in the Australia Army back in the day. He'd knocked off a few ragheads in his time. The pre-retirement border job was a big drop in status, but it was what it was. You had to soldier on.

So, he was projecting his 'not to be messed with' persona with the last of the travellers, usually the ones to cause trouble. They were tired, grumpy and had often imbibed a little too much of the airlines' free alcoholic travelling anaesthetic.

Kough glanced at Ryan. He recognised the upright military stance, the legs slightly apart and the shoulders back. It was a stance professional soldiers never lost.

Spotty Face asked Kough for his passport. Kough handed it over. Then Spotty Face asked if he had anything to declare. Kough's face went white.

'No, no. Nothing at all.'

Spotty Face put the passport through the scanner. No issues. What was the white face about? he wondered. He had someone to play and exactly at the right time: he could impress his immediate boss, old Gerry Hardballs, who was watching nearby.

'Can you open your briefcase, please, sir?'

Kough gripped the case handle with both hands. His mind went on a wild, panic-stricken whirl.

Suddenly, on the home stretch, he was in serious danger. Why did he think he wouldn't be searched again? He was a poor bloody thief and a worse smuggler. The Big Brain said, Try a whole new tactic.

Kough coughed and stuttered something incoherent. Ryan heard and raised his eyebrows a fraction. He could sense trouble. He was still alive because of it, he prided himself.

Spotty Face cocked his head: 'Sir, can you open your briefcase, please?'

It was always the politeness of the little Hitler creeps that riled Kough. They just needed a uniform to elevate them from their generally boring tasks to creatures of power.

Spotty Face knew he was doing this stop by the book. Calmly and professionally. A half-smile of a reasonable man played at his lips. It sent the perfect passive-aggressive, silent question. He did not get the chance to do the John Wayne silent but powerful technique often. Revelling in the moment, he waited. The power of silence would go to work.

Kough cleared his throat: 'I'm sorry, I'm not allowed to show the contents of this case to anyone. It's a matter of national security.'

Spotty Face smiled. What sort of fantasist loser did he have here? But he felt Old Hardballs stir behind him.

'National security, did you say, sir?'

Kough said: 'Yes. Yes. I need to see a senior officer. As quick as you like.'

Ryan straightened and stepped forward: 'I'm the senior officer tonight, sir. What's the problem?'

'Is there somewhere private we can speak? Is there anyone here with national security clearance?'

Spotty Face gave a noisy snigger.

But Ryan said: 'Well, I had security clearance to two A in military intelligence.'

Kough thought: what the hell is a two A clearance?

'Okay. We need to talk in private, urgently.'

Ryan looked at the worn traveller. Maybe he could be a real live spy. They didn't all dress like James Bond.

Ryan said: 'If you would like to come this way, sir.' He opened the Customs barrier and Kough stepped through as if it was his everyday right and without a glance at the furious Horatio Hadley.

A RUSH of guilt seized Kough. He was really pushing a true friendship to its outer limits. He had explained his top-level mission in hushed words to an incredulous Gerry Ryan.

Kough was bearing such sensitive intelligence he was only authorised to hand it over to the Chief of Staff of the Prime Minister. The chief of staff was meeting him personally at the airport.

Ryan pushed his shoulders back. Kough thought he was going to get a salute.

'You stay here, sir, and I'll see if we can locate this man. What's his name?'

'John Able. Same height as me but thinner. But wait, before you go, can you lock this room?'

Ryan paused: 'You think you might be in some danger, sir?'

'You can never be too careful in these matters.'

Ryan nodded curtly: 'Quite right, sir. I'll lock the door and be back as fast as I can.'

Ryan left. Kough heard the door lock snap into place. He was alone. I really enjoyed all that 'coming in from the cold' stuff, he thought. Intimidating self-important officials was a rare joy. But he had probably gone too far: lock the door? Danger? What was that about? He could feel Big Brain rolling his eyes.

Maybe it was the thrill of a successful deception. Like the thrill of a roulette wheel delivering a big win. Then the wheel daring him to double up. As he had dared himself to double up the deception game with Ryan. The man clearly revelled in a frisson of danger.

Kough sat at the bare desk. He swung the swivel chair around. Checked the time. Got up to confirm the door was actually locked, walked back to the chair. He felt smug. Until suddenly he did not.

He felt the call of nature. Oh God, he thought. He put his head in his hands on the desk. The position increased the pressure on his bladder. Oh God, oh God. He had knocked back quite a few bourbons on the flight.

He sat up straight. The office was sparse. A soulless place to intimidate drug mules. He looked under the desk. No trash bin. Oh God. Spies did not pee their pants. He stood. Only three minutes had passed since the can-do former commando had left.

Kough went to the door and hammered on it. There was no response. He hammered again. Nothing. He had asked to be left safe and secure.

Time went into slow motion. His mother would say: this is God punishing you, he thought, for being a liar and a thief. He walked the few paces around the office. It seemed to help. Temporarily.

Big Brain said, There's only one receptacle in here. It is in front of you.

Kough looked down. There was a drawer in the desk. He opened it. It was empty. He shut it with unnecessary force.

The action sparked a new tension in his bursting bladder. He opened the drawer again. Unzipped his fly. Suddenly there were voices at the door. He was caught on the edge of a urine precipice. The flow could not be dammed once he started. He had to step back. He rushed to hoist the zip back up as the door behind him opened.

A voice exclaimed: 'Boffy.'

Kough swung around, held up a stern finger: 'The password is not to be used in front of third parties, Able. You should know that. Okay, let's get the hell out of here. Right now.'

He grabbed his briefcase, nodded his thanks to a startled Gerry Ryan and strode out the door. Johnny Able followed.

Ryan, mystified, walked to the desk, peered into the open drawer. Empty. Shook his head and closed it. Spooks. Well, he'd have a new story to tell his mates at the Returned Services League: his decisive role in a top-level intelligence op. He had personally saved the day. No doubt about that.

John Able half cantered to keep up with his old mate. The pair went down several brightly lit corridors. Then Kough made a sudden lurch into a male, Staff Only, toilet.

Able followed and found Kough panting at a stall, shoving his trousers and underpants down in one frantic sweep. There was a groan of relief and a Niagara Falls torrent beat against the steel wall of the latrine.

Able stood with his hands on his hips: 'What the fuck is going on, Boffy? What bloody password? Secrets for only the PM's office? A frantic piss? Geesus.'

A relieved Kough smiled at him: 'It's a long story, Johnny. Boy was I happy to see your smiling face. It's been quite a day. I'll tell you all about it – but you're not allowed to lecture me, okay?'

'Oh dear. What the hell have you been up to now?'

FOUR

ABLE HAD BORROWED ONE OF THE PRIME MINISTER'S LIMOS and chauffeurs. It was an act of corporate masturbation, but it would impress the hell out of his old, hapless rival.

Small pennants flaunted their illegality on the bonnet of the big car as it swept imperiously up the Grand Hotel concourse. Big Chinese and Australian flags on tall flagstaffs waved grandly outside, symbolically side by side.

The driver's presence had made private conversation impossible on the journey.

But Kough said he was worried that Able looked haggard and drawn.

'It's the Chinese thing,' Able said. 'It's always a Chinese thing these days.'

'I read a bit about the latest fuss in the *Wall Street Journal*. Is that why their bloody great flag is flying out there?'

Able nodded. Kough said: 'Trying to steal our stuff again, are they?'

Able laughed: 'Yeah. As usual. They are here for a big conference. They want to negotiate a law change so they can buy strategic companies we don't want them to have. But there's bugger-all negotiating, more of the old-fashioned bullying actually.'

'Tell them to get fucked.'

'Why didn't I think of that? Boffy, you would make a great diplomat.'

'Let's teach them a lesson, bring them back to earth. Here, hold this briefcase.'

The limousine stopped on the forecourt and Kough leapt out. He beat a track to the concierge and asked him if he had a Swiss Army knife. Puzzled, the concierge nodded, and produced one of the iconic all-purpose pocket knives.

Kough strode to the flagpoles. With a quick slash, the main flag-bearing cord securing the oversized Chinese flag went slack and it fluttered unceremoniously earthwards.

There was a hubbub among Chinese plainclothes toughs scattered around the forecourt. Kough ignored them and returned the concierge's knife: 'You keep it nice and sharp, mate.'

'Yeah, yeah, I do ... but mister, you've really pissed off these Chinese guys.' The doorman pocketed the knife in a practised instant.

Kough scoffed: 'Well, that's tough luck. Bullies need to be brought down to earth.'

Kough took his briefcase off a gobsmacked Able.

Able said: 'What the hell do you think you're up to?'

Kough smiled and shrugged: 'C'mon, let's check in. We've got a lot of catching up to do. Hey, don't give me that look, I remember what you did to the varsity's flag on capping day.'

Able looked at the chauffeur: 'John, can you please get the beast out of here as fast as you like? And take the bloody pennants off as soon as you get around the corner.'

The chauffeur tipped his cap and smiled: 'I like your mate's style, sir, whoever he is.'

Able grimaced: 'Let's hope you don't find out in the news tomorrow.'

The Chinese security detail looked on in confusion at the PM's gleaming limo, with its pennants, then at its two passengers and, finally, their big red flag on the ground. It seemed to be dying a slow death: its bright red cloth was rising and falling like exhausted lungs as a light breeze ruffled it.

FIVE

The swanky hotel private bar was dark and plush. The drink costs were as high as the carpet pile.

Kough and Able talked for nearly two and a half hours. It had been two years and a lot had happened. Wives had gone. Able had struck the big time in his bureaucratic political post. Kough had struck a rich vein of salary cash to fund his gambling addiction.

Able had been promoted. Kough had been sacked. Able had met a new woman. Gorgeous but from his office. In politically correct Canberra, the relationship was frowned upon. But she was too hot to ditch. Kough had not heard from his separated wife, Betty, since he flew off to Nevada to make germ cocktails.

On their ninth bourbon, Able said: 'Boffy, you don't seem to be too bothered about getting the sack.'

'Nah. I'm not. Fuck 'em. Ungrateful bastards. I got my own back on 'em, though.' He patted the briefcase he had not let out of his sight. 'And I have to say you're the one who looks really knackered, mate.'

Able slurred: 'Don't worry about me, Boffy. I'm fine. This latest flare-up with the Chinks has become almost routine.'

He pointed at the briefcase: 'Whatdaya mean, you got your own back? What's in there, 007? America's nuclear codes?'

Kough looked suddenly serious through the alcoholic haze: 'Nah. Better than that.'

Able's smile disappeared: 'Oh, fuck. Whataya been up to? You can tell me.'

'All in good time, Johnny. I have some critical intellectual property agreements to hammer out first.'

The mood changed: Able feared Kough had nicked something important from his former American military bosses. It would explain the need for him to masquerade as an Australian intelligence officer to smuggle it into Australia.

If he had purloined some hot secret, he was up for a good thirty years when the Yanks caught up with him. The Border Force officer's role in the smuggling would also create a diplomatic red face for Australia, never mind the Prime Minister's Office.

Able was trying to process the whole situation when he heard a scraping sound. He looked up. His dynamic mate had passed out and begun snoring.

THE HOTEL ROOM phone was shrilling. It cut through Kough's splitting headache. He raised his head gingerly. He had no idea where the phone was. But it was very loud and insistent. He was deciding whether to ignore it when he saw a movement.

Someone was rummaging through his briefcase. Their black silhouette was squatter and wider than Able's.

He went to yell at the figure, but he failed to produce anything from his parched throat, other than a weak croak.

But it was enough to alert the intruder. The figure straightened. The briefcase was dropped on the tiny breakfast table.

Kough staggered to his feet. Found his balance. The figure was masked. Dressed entirely in black.

Oh, shit, thought Kough. Now what?

The figure crouched, with hands held apart, and began to move towards him, silently on the ultra-thick carpet.

Kough took a breath: 'Who the fuck are you – Spider Man?'

The briefcase lay open, but the figure seemed to have nothing in his hands. The crouch was a kung fu sort of look, Kough thought.

Then Spider Man sprung at Kough, lashing out with a leg that struck Kough on the hip.

The blow seemed to momentarily unbalance the attacker not his well-built target, who absorbed the kick and was not on the floor where he was meant to be.

'Fuck you,' Kough shouted. He eschewed any fancy Asian kickboxing or karate moves. Kough instead smashed the intruder on the nose. He heard the painful crunch of nostril cartilage being flattened.

The figure cried out and flailed to keep upright. The bedroom door opened. Light from the corridor flooded in. A second man grabbed the intruder by the head and towed him backwards, through the door, and disappeared.

Mike Tyson was right, thought Kough. Everyone had a fancy fight strategy until he punched them on the nose.

Kough crossed the room, slamming and locking the door. He flicked the power switch. Fierce light savaged his bloodshot eyes.

He went to the table. The briefcase lay on its side. He felt inside for the phials pouch. It was still zipped up. He could feel the cold phials inside it.

He collapsed in a chair at the table. He had interrupted the intruder early in the search. Suddenly the room phone began to blitz his brain again. He found it beside the oversized bed.

'Boffy? Is that you?'

'Oh, Johnny. It's only me now. You just missed my burglar. Some Chinese Spider Man type with kung fu moves. He and a mate in cool black gear, but they've gone now.'

Able's tone went up a pitch: 'What the hell you're talking about? Are you still pissed?'

'How about you get your posh federal police pals to try to find this prick? A shortish Chinaman with a lot of blood under his mask. He and his mate can't have gone far.'

Kough heard Able pick up a second phone on his desk and have a short conversation. Able then asked Kough what exactly had happened. Kough explained the break-in and fight.

Able said: 'Could have been just burglars. They'd make a beeline for any briefcase left lying around.'

'Oh, come on, Johnny. This place has more security than Fort Knox.

The place is crawling with Chinese security goons. At least I stopped him from getting any of my phials.'

Able said: 'Your what? What files?'

Kough laughed. It hurt his head.

'I didn't say files. There're no bloody files. All the info I have is in my head.'

'All in your head?'

'Yeah, so it's quite safe.'

'Bullshit. It's far from safe Boffy boy. I'll call you back shortly. Don't answer the door to anyone but me, okay? Don't call room service. Make yourself some very strong coffee. Maybe have a shower, you were getting quite ripe before you flaked out.'

'Yes, sir. Yes, sir. Three bags full, sir.'

'Don't fuck me around, Boffy. The Chinese are demanding you be arrested for your attack on their flag.'

'Oh, fuck the Chinese. Another thing, when you come, Johnny boy, can you bring some Panadol with you?'

Able hung up and made for the PM's office. His own head was not exactly in good order. He had already spent the first fifteen minutes of the day being chewed out by Prime Minister Gary Stone who had made him watch hotel security video of his official car arriving at the hotel and the attack on the Chinese flag.

Able had also been told the talks with the Chinese had been postponed. Officially because of Australia's unprovoked attack on Chinese sovereignty – its flag – but mainly because its senior negotiator had fallen sick.

The Australian Secret Intelligence Office – ASIO – confirmed from its sources the diplomat had Covid symptoms. He was suffering fevers, headaches and aching limbs. The Chinese Embassy had called for a replacement to be flown out. Beijing had not responded to the recommendation but was incredulous that anyone would dare drop the Chinese flag in the dirt. The External Affairs Department had assured them that it was the work of a lone person with a history of mental-health issues.

SIX

The ASIO director-general, Frank Church, sat in front of the PM's desk and crossed his legs: 'Prime Minister, you are saying we have an Australian germ-warfare researcher being attacked in a Canberra hotel after possibly stealing top-secret American material, details of which he stores in his head while getting inebriated with your chief of staff.'

Stone looked out from under his thick, hedgerow eyebrows: 'Yes, more or less. But you did miss out the part where he singlehandedly dropped the Chinese flag and has been officially described as insane.'

'No, sir, that detail hadn't escaped me. I don't think the Chinese knew he was carrying any secrets or they would have been far more tenacious in their robbery attempt. They wouldn't have run off. So I think the Kough character was the victim of a common garden thief.'

Stone leaned his enormous frame back in his swivel chair and pointed to a chastened John Able: 'My COS says his eccentric virologist friend is batshit crazy but brilliant. He believes him: that he can keep all his research data in his brain. I take it, Frank, you know he has one other personal issue?'

Church tilted his head.

'He's got a gambling addiction,' Able said.

Church grunted: 'We've got the trifecta with this boy.'

Stone grinned: 'Yeah, so let's take make sure he's kept as far away from the talons of the Chinese or the Americans until we're certain what we're dealing with. Put him in a safe house, Frank. A very safe house. I'd like to have a chat to him later.'

Church stood: 'Yes, Prime Minister. I'll get him secured. If he gets ratty, I may have to arrest him on smuggling charges to hold him.'

John Able said: 'He won't get ratty if you make sure there's an online casino connection to the safe house.'

Church frowned. Looked at Stone who nodded: 'Yeah, that's a good idea. Keep him happy, Frank.'

Able stood: 'And give him a twenty-thousand-dollar tab, at least, to get him started. He's basically broke at the moment.'

Miss Importance knocked timidly on Colonel Bakoffs' door. He barked at her to enter.

'Have you seen the news? About our man Kough? The Aussie we sacked? I think he was a spy. Working for Australia,' she muttered.

'What? Speak up, woman. That numbskull Kough? What's he been up to? On the news, you say.'

Miss Importance nodded tentatively. 'I'm sure it was him. I saw it on the news and then YouTube this morning. He was in the Australian prime minister's car when he leapt out and attacked the Chinese flag. There's been a truly big fuss about it...'

Colonel Bakoffs turned to his computer, punched a few keys and YouTube jumped on to his screen: 'Come and show me which news service, Miss ... er, Miss.'

Miss Importance stood beside the Big Chief of the Nevada virology laboratory who couldn't remember her name and tapped a few more keys: a video of a man running to a flag mast came up. He cut the flag cord and then ran back to the main entrance. He turned and the camera froze the face shot.

'Good God. That's him all right. That's Michael Kough. What the hell's he doing?'

There was a loud knocking on the open door and a voice said: 'That's what we would like to ask you about, Colonel Bakoffs. How long have you had a spy working in your secret lab? Sorry, I'm Hank Merriless, by the way. CIA.'

'What do you mean, he's gone?' John Able listened for a moment. 'No, I don't know where the hell he is. I thought you people had a guard on his door after last night's break-in.'

Able closed his eyes. Kough was becoming a nightmare. His hotel room was empty when the ASIO team had arrived to escort him to a safe house in the Canberra suburbs.

'He has no close family in the city except for his wife Elizabeth. Betty left him two years ago. I know she hasn't spoken to Michael since. Not even sure she's still in the city. I don't think he'd go within a bull's roar of her if she is. Things ended pretty badly. Well, he is a gambling addict, maybe you should look for him at a casino or a horse-racing agency, but I don't like your chances of finding him if he's trying to evade you.'

SEVEN

ABLE DISCONNECTED THE CALL. THE PHONE BUZZED A second later. A familiar voice said: 'You may know by now, Johnny, I've gone walkabout.'

'Fuck, Boffy. What the hell are you playing at? All hell has broken loose here. Where are you, for Christ's sake?'

'I'm sorry, Johnny, but I have to find a top attorney to secure my intellectual property rights on the data I have.'

Able drummed his fingers on the desk: 'Boffy, we have to make sure you're safe, particularly after that attack on you last night. You won't be too happy if the bloody Chinks find you first for an in-depth chat.'

Kough snorted: 'Yeah, I know all that, but the buggers won't get anything out of me. I know the little shits have built an empire by stealing everyone's IP. They won't be getting mine.'

Able said: 'You'd be surprised what a little Chinese persuasion can do. So listen, will you come in if I find you the country's top IP man right now, and we go and see him together? Will you then agree to cooperate so we can put you in a safe house? It's for your own good.'

Kough said nothing.

'Did I mention you'll get a ten-thousand-dollar online casino tab at the safe house while we're guarding you?'

Kough said: 'Make it twenty.'

'You drive a hard bargain, Boffy. All right, twenty.'

Kough laughed: 'When and where will I see you?'

'I'll call you back in half an hour on this number and we'll arrange the rendezvous.'

'Half an hour? You can't get a top IP lawyer set up in half an hour.'

Able said: 'You're right, *I* couldn't. But the prime minister can. You're not his favourite person at the moment, so promise you'll behave, and I'll get him on board.'

'Okay, I promise.'

'Gary Stone used to play and coach senior rugby league. He's a tough bugger, and he doesn't like to be messed around,' Able said.

'What? He'll break my legs?' Kough laughed.

'No, no. Much worse than that. Talk in half an hour.'

Before Able could stand, his phone buzzed again. With a sigh he picked up.

'Able. Thank God. What's going on? I've just had a Chinese man banging on the door of my apartment. He was after Mikey. I told him I haven't seen him for years, but I'm sure he didn't believe me.'

Elizabeth Kough sounded scared and confused.

'Betty, has he gone now?'

'Not really. He's with another Chinese man in a car opposite my building.'

'Okay, just stay calm. I'll send someone to get you. Did the Chinese say why they wanted to talk to him?'

'No.'

'He dropped their beloved national flag in the dust last night.'

Elizabeth gasped: 'What? Why would the crazy bastard do that?'

'He just had a moment. I was with him at the time, actually.'

Elizabeth sighed: 'Oh my God. The two of you together. It always becomes a circus. Now I have an angry Chinaman watching me.'

Able made Betty promise to call him if Kough got in touch. He warned her to stay off the phone; if it wasn't being bugged it shortly would be. He thought he heard an expletive before they broke contact.

EIGHT

It was the online casino connection that gave the game away.

Chinese intelligence knew where all the Canberra safe houses were. They only had to hack in to their internet connections to discover which one was using Bigbet@aus.com.

Michael Kough was as happy as a baby in a sandpit. Four burly, overdressed men of the diplomatic protection squad crowded the modest lounge/dining area of the apartment. He sat gambling behind a console on the dining table. Their heads shot up each time Kough won and gave a cry of glee. His luck at roulette had been astonishing.

He had parlayed his twenty thousand dollars into forty-two within two hours.

It was growing dark when he arrived at the safe house. He had spent several hours at Brightson, Farttey, Lickle and Goldsmith writing from memory his anti-viral formula. The intellectual property firm would now apply for an international patent. He would then be free to approach Big Pharma to manufacture his formula under licence. Billions of dollars were about to flow in to his near-empty bank account.

Not in Australia, though. Brightson, Farttey, Lickle and Goldsmith had their tax-efficient Bermuda trusts. There would be no pesky forty-nine per cent Aussie tax rate to worry about.

Kough had reached the safe house apartment exhausted. But the sight of the computer console and the opportunity for a quick flutter re-energised him.

His winnings grew steadily, but he had begun yawning and his eyes were sore from the screen.

'Not bad, eh?' Kough loved the way the posh cops were impressed with his skills. Or luck. One of them said: 'How the hell do you get the nerve to do that? My missus would cut my balls off?'

Kough smiled: 'Mine did, mate.'

They were all enjoying the enforced camaraderie when his blinking winnings tally vanished from the screen. A second later, the apartment was pitched into darkness. The four guards leapt from their seats. Two went to the window facing the street.

The other two led Kough by his arms and felt their way into the main bedroom. They told him to lie on the floor beside the bed. It was nothing to be alarmed about. It could just be a power failure.

'My console didn't suffer a power failure, mate. It was hacked. All the winnings were siphoned off. Someone's been monitoring us,' said Kough.

The guards said nothing. The bald guard they called Hairy lay on the floor near to Kough and the other one went to rejoin the pair in the lounge. Kough could hear whispered voices and the cackle of two-way radios.

The lounge window suddenly exploded in a shower of glass and seconds later a thunder flash rocked the room. Kough saw the vivid flash in the gap under the closed bedroom door.

Then the bedroom window behind him shattered and a second thunder-flash grenade landed silently on the carpet floor. Kough kicked it under the bed.

It exploded a second later, but its blast was muffled by the bed. The smell of scorched carpet and mattress material began to fill the room.

Hairy was covering his eyes. He had been lying on the floor and part of the blast from beneath the bed had caught him on the side of the head. Kough had leapt on to the bed after kicking away the flash grenade and looked out of the smashed window.

'Give us your gun, Hairy. There's some little shit on the rear steps.'

Hairy coughed, one hand over his eyes: 'Oh fuck. I'll never live it down. Here. It's a Glock. There's no safety catch. Just point and shoot. Make sure it's not one of us.'

Kough took the weapon and crouched on the bed, peering out the window. He whispered: 'Any of your guys here tonight Asian?'

Hairy said: 'Not on this shift. If the guy outside is Asian, just shoot the bastard. We don't want another grenade lopping in here.'

Kough took two shots at the figure outside. The Glock bucked upwards in his hand. Two tear-gas cannisters came through the window in response. He lost all vision and felt his lungs explode from the acrid fumes.

He got off the bed and crawled towards where he thought the bedroom door was. He felt for the door handle, turned and pulled it open. The air on the other side was fresh, gusting in from the broken lounge window. He could see three guards stunned, sprawled on the floor.

As he dragged fresh air into his lungs and wiped streaming tears from his eyes, he saw two Chinese men in black overalls hanging from abseiling ropes, opposite the smashed lounge window.

The window was too small for both of them. But they swung in together and comically struck and bounced off each other. There was a torrent of abuse in Mandarin from one of them.

Then a sole attacker swung himself forward into the room a second time just as the apartment's front door swung open. A huge man, more than two metres tall and wide as a half truck, raced through to the lounge with a nimbleness that belied his size.

He grabbed the inbound attacker around the waist and bodily flung him back out of the window. The man howled in shock and pain as he collided with his companion hanging impatiently outside. The two hung like shocked rag dolls on their abseil lines.

Kough raised his Glock. Big Brain said, This time remember the upward kick of the pistol. Kough fired. He hit both men in the head.

Two suited men followed the half-truck guy, pistols at the ready. The three guards half-conscious from the stun grenade assault began to stir.

'Check the bedroom. Hairy is in there, half blind,' said Kough.

The suited men did a one-two act at the doorway. Hairy was the only one in the room.

Kough realised Half Truck was wearing a black suit, white shirt and dark red tie. With his hedge-sized eyebrows, he seemed familiar to Kough who was nearly as tall but only half the bulk.

The big guy held his hand out: 'You must be Michael Kough. The dragon flag slayer. That was a mean bit of shooting. Gary Stone. Nice to meet you.'

Outside, sirens wailed and rubber tyres tore at the asphalt as several cars attempted to either speed away or emergency brake. A helicopter with a search light hovered over the street. Moments later several vehicles crashed into each other or trees lining the street. The unsafe house was the centre of bedlam and excitement the neighbourhood would dine out on for years.

'Sorry about your unsafe house,' said Stone.

'Never mind the unsafe house, I was twenty-two big ones up when they hacked me.'

Stone nodded: 'No wonder you shot the buggers.'

NINE

Federal Police collected the dead bodies of the abseilers hanging over the balcony. Other police rounded up a third, black-clad Chinese man, who had lobbed the flash grenades into Kough's bedroom. He was sprinting away from the rear of the building when they tackled him.

Gary Stone instructed the police officers that the incident was to be reported as a violent burglary on a local meth dealer. A terrified elderly couple in the apartment above were freed. The attackers had used the couple's balcony to abseil into the safe house.

The prisoner was to be held in isolation. He could be charged as a terrorist if necessary to keep trouble-maker lawyers at bay.

Hairy had one side of his face scorched. Briefing the PM on the lightning raid, he pointed at Kough: 'Prime Minister, a stun grenade was thrown into our bedroom and this young bloody lunatic, or hero, kicked it under the bed before it could explode. Saved me a right shellacking. And thank you, sir, for hurling that Chinese guy clear out the window.'

Stone smiled: 'He was offside. Thought the referee wasn't watching. Had to be taken out.'

'How did the Chinese know this was a safe house?' Stone asked no one in particular.

Hairy sighed: 'The Chinese had the blueprint for our new ASIO headquarters before we'd turned the first sod, so tracing our safe houses would be doodle for them. They know everything, sir. They're everywhere – like their Confucius clubs.'

Stone stared at his feet and said nothing. Kough looked at the despondent huddle of men. A cool wind blew in from the broken windows and wafts of smoke swirled from bedroom mattress embers.

'They don't know everything,' Kough said.

Stone looked up sharply: 'Pleased to hear that, Mr Kough. It's about time you and I had a little chat. The CIA is complaining you've been spying inside one of their top-secret research labs. They want you extradited.'

'That won't fly. I've broken no laws,' said Kough.

John Able arrived and said television crews were about to descend on the scene. The PM should be gone.

Gary Stone said: 'Not just yet, John. I need a quick word with Mr Kough before the Chinese or the Yanks get to him and start another war.'

'IF YOU WANT the truth you have to promise not to laugh.'

Kough was sitting across from Gary Stone on one of the two single beds in the second, unscathed apartment bedroom.

Stone said: 'We've got a couple of dead Chinese outside. Is there something to laugh about in all this business?'

'Well, I thought it was funny at the time, Prime Minister. I'm in a germ-warfare lab and my lab mice and rabbits were the only ones that wouldn't die.'

Stone lifted his eyebrows.

Kough said: 'The Yanks thought I was shagging them around. They became very angry. They were hunting for new, improved killer germs. In the end, they sacked me.'

Stone said: 'Let me get this straight: You were in a germ-warfare laboratory and you couldn't kill anything off. All the bad viruses in your bunny rabbits and mice didn't kill them after you used your vaccine to inoculate them. Does this mean you have invented an anti-viral cure that could, like ... be a cure for the common cold?'

'Yeah. It looks like it. I haven't had a failure yet.'

Stone rubbed his chin: 'And the Yanks know about this world-shattering discovery and want the formula back?'

Kough stood to stretch his legs: 'That's the problem. They are in the dark. They don't know about the formula or what it can do. They're just guessing. That's because I deleted all my research material.'

'So you destroyed your work?'

'No, no. I kept it – in my head.'

Able looked at Stone: 'He's got a very Big Brain, sir.'

Kough said: 'I wrote it down today for my patent attorneys.'

Stone stood: 'Congratulations, Kough. If what you say is true, you have made an amazing discovery. The world will never be the same. You will save billions of lives.'

Kough held his eye: 'Not to mention, I will make billions of dollars, sir.'

'I don't want to rain on your parade, Mr Kough, but I think the Yanks would have a fair claim on the discovery. I would imagine it was made on their time at their laboratory.'

Kough took a deep breath: 'No one's getting that formula. I did all the work on it. It only exists because of me. The Yanks weren't interested in my work. The kicked me out, remember?'

Stone said: 'Who else knows about this?'

'You and me, and Johnny boy, and my patent attorney.'

Able said: 'Sir, we need to get you out of here. The place will be swarming with media at any moment.'

TEN

Kough was about to get his second shock for the night.

Able took him by the arm: 'Come with me, Boffy. It's late. You'll be safe, and I have someone that wants to see you.'

Able drove to his home. A fresh protection squad officer sat in the back. There were still lights on inside when they drew up.

He let Kough lead the way up the garden path. The front door opened. Kough stopped in his tracks and squinted.

The crows' legs were deeper on the strong face. The short blonde hair, a little tangled, but the smile was vintage Elizabeth Kough.

Fuck, thought Kough. I can't cope with Betty right now. I'm bloody exhausted. I've been in a terrorist shit storm, killed a couple of assassins and spilled the anti-virus beans to a man with the power to extradite me.'

'Well, don't just stand there gaping, Boffy,' she said crossly. 'Do I get a kiss, or a hug hello?'

John Able patted him on the shoulder: 'Betty, he's had a tough night.'

'Oh,' said Betty, 'what casino was it tonight?'

Oh, fuck, fuck, thought Kough. He mounted the doorsteps: 'Betty, not now, for Christ's sake.'

She studied his gaunt face.

'I'm sorry. John and I thought bringing you here might be a nice surprise. John's been hiding me here since some Chinese thug came searching my place looking for you.'

Kough felt he had been tossed another curve ball on a bad day. He wanted to see Betty, but only to arrange for a quickie divorce, before his zillion-dollar discovery became public.

First, the Yanks wanted the formula; the Chinese wanted to snatch him; and now his still-wife would shortly be entitled to half of his pending fortune. She could rightly claim to have been an innocent victim, left homeless by a wastrel, gambling addict.

Kough stood at the doorway, looking into her eyes. He was unconsciously calculating the untold millions his wife could claim. The Bermuda trusts were no longer the bastion they once were, able to drive off rapacious divorce lawyers.

The only sure way out would be to kill her. The thought shocked him. He dismissed it and stepped forward and forced a smile.

He leaned in and pecked her on the cheek: 'Hi, Betty. Been a long time. You're looking good.'

'Bullshit,' she said. She had two jobs to make ends meet. Canberra rents were exorbitant and the cost of living high. She had zero savings and was reduced to driving an old, rusted Mazda.

Able ushered them inside to forestall any further bickering. They sat in the lounge, drinking coffee and glasses of port that Able had found in some kitchen cupboard. They made laborious small talk. Finally, Able suggested they should turn in.

The Koughs were shown to separate rooms.

Kough lay awake. He would offer her a hundred thousand dollars in the morning. She would consider it a fortune. He would say it was his redundancy pay from the American job. She would think he was a nice guy, a generous guy.

As he began to doze off, he imagined the Chinese thugs again and their brains exploding as he shot them. They say there's a monster in everyone, he thought. He did have an unhealthy satisfaction with killing the buggers. He wondered where Betty's Chinese thug was now.

He decided he would kill him too, for her. A hundred grand and a body. It would be a good deal. He fell into a contented sleep.

ELEVEN

BY TEN THE FOLLOWING MORNING, MICHAEL KOUGH WAS back in the hideous modern offices of Brightson, Farttey, Lickle and Goldsmith.

His head ached. He had downed too much of the port. He accepted several of their strong coffees, sitting at a gleaming board table, large enough to land a jumbo jet on.

Betty had woken frosty. Offhand. She seemed unimpressed with his offer. She would think about it, she said. Her real concern was the Chinese thug who had parked outside her apartment.

The current senior partner, Orin Lickle, could barely contain his excitement when Kough arrived. He rushed to tell him the Sino International Research Corporation (SIRC), a multinational pharmaceutical outfit, based in Shanghai, wanted to make an offer on his day-old company.

Kough sat, gently rubbing his temples. The boardroom glass door opened and a man in a penguin suit bowed slightly and shuffled in. He was by himself. He carried only a slim, shiny briefcase. He sat opposite an unshaven Kough, who gave him a nod.

Mr Lickle made the introductions. The man's name was Mr Ling, but Kough forgot it straight away. The table was too wide to shake hands, but everyone nodded and small smiles blossomed briefly.

Mr Lickle said the SIRC would make an offer that would be open till five that evening. Kough frowned. Pushed his long legs out and leaned back in his chrome swivel chair.

'So, no rush then.' He looked at Lickle: 'How does this man know about us or what he's buying? We only applied for the patent yesterday.'

SIRC had seen the patent application, Mr Lickle explained. The patent process made all the applications public in case any firm wished to claim it as too similar to their own inventions.

Mr Lickle said SIRC was very, very interested in the business. Lickle did not say SIRC had privately indicated to him the night before that an offer around one billion dollars was likely. So Lickle was very, very interested too. His firm's four per cent brokerage fee would produce a tidy forty million for a half-day's work. It only happened once in a lifetime. It had never happened for him.

He fought to contain himself at the prospect of such instant riches. But he worried about his client. Kough was stretched out like a lizard, almost horizontal on his chair, and seemed distracted and fatigued.

Kough heaved himself up a fraction and the chair swivelled suddenly to the left and nearly toppled him onto the hardwood floor.

The SIRC man sat impassively as though attending to a distasteful but necessary duty. The Western entrepreneurs he had dealt with were often uncouth, ego-driven, spoiled hipsters. This one seemed to have spent the night out on the town, probably doing lines of coke.

Never mind, he thought, the prospect of a big payout always brought them to heel like the needy children they were.

Kough raised his eyebrows: 'So what are you offering, Mr ... er ...?'

Unrushed, Ling delicately opened his briefcase, like it was holding a bomb, and slowly removed three sheets of fine paper. He laid them down, evenly spaced, one by one in front of himself.

He soon accepted his theatrics were wasted on the hipster.

Kough said: 'Don't worry about the paperwork, mate, just tell me the number.' Kough knew he should be patient, but he was not in the mood. To make matters worse he was distracted by imagining what a Glock bullet would do right now to the patronising Mr Penguin Suit's brainbox.

Mr Lickle was nervously hushing him about the paperwork. The

Chinese did things in their own way, he said, a painstaking way, honed by a culture stretching back five thousand years.

Kough stared at Lickle: 'Eh? Whatareya talking about, man?'

A tic began to pulse on Lickle's right eyelid. He smiled patiently at Ling, who returned the smile, and sat back with the confidence of a man holding an ace-high flush.

Kough read the body language like a professional gambler and said: 'I trust your offer is north of one hundred billion dollars.'

Ling's smile slipped off his face. He frowned as though he was having difficulty with his hearing.

Finally, he said: 'No. We are not offering a trillion dollars, Mr Kough. But we are offering to pay you one billion dollars if you accept it by close of business today.'

Lickle sizzled on his chair.

Kough shook his head slowly. A tiny smile cracked on his face. Watching Ling's conceited smile vanish was as good as a roulette win. Kough knew he held the best hand. And it had not taken him five thousand years to figure it out.

Mr Lickle had gone pale: 'Thank you, Mr Ling. Thank you. Thank you for your offer. We'll be back to you before five.'

Kough smiled and shrugged.

Mr Ling made as if to stand but changed his mind: 'Mr Kough, this is a very generous offer. You realise that if you reject it, others are capable of replicating your work? Secrets, particularly big secrets, are impossible to keep in today's world. SIRC will be manufacturing an anti-viral product before the end of the year.'

Kough shook his head: 'Ta ma de ni, Mr Ling.'

Lickle looked puzzled but Ling abruptly pushed his chair back, gathered his papers and walked to the glass door.

Lickle rushed to reach it before him, heaving it wide open, bowing and profusely thanking Ling again.

Lickle returned to the boardroom after Mr Ling's lift doors had closed: 'What did you just say to him?'

'Have a wonderful life.'

'No, you didn't.'

'No, I didn't. He just threatened to use Chinese electronic espionage to steal my formula. You heard him.'

'What did you say to him? Tell me.'

Kough shook his head.

Lickle sat down with a thump.

Kough sighed like a patient tutor: 'He overplayed his hand. He was bluffing. I called him. He folded. Then threatened me. So I told him in Mandarin to get fucked. That's all.'

Lickle groaned: 'You turned down a billion dollars, man ... a billion.'

Kough smiled: 'Yeah, if my wife finds out she won't be happy either.'

And Betty would never agree to an early divorce if she discovered the cash bonanza he was sitting on.

Then his mind paused: unless she still loves me; or I still love her. I have missed her. More than I realised. I did put her through a lot.

But she did begin to carp on straight away when she believed he was late because he had been in a casino all day. The bitter bile inside her had erupted spontaneously. He closed his eyes. He was too tired to think straight.

TWELVE

John Able and a bodyguard were waiting outside Brightson, Farttey, Lickle and Goldsmith in a federal limo. This one had no pennants and was a nondescript light silver.

The radio news was on when Michael Kough joined them. The main story was about the eruption of a local drug war in a Canberra suburb. It had shunted the China trade crisis conference story into second place in the news.

There was little to report on the conference anyway. The Chinese had not set a restart date. A new big-wig was flying from Beijing following the sudden illness of the original delegation boss. Meanwhile China was continuing to demand an apology for the vandalistic attack on its national flag.

The third story began, another fight over Murray River water rights.

Able turned the volume down: 'So, how'd it go up there in the ivory tower?'

Kough leaned back in the plush leather seat: 'They were dicking me about. Only offered a billion.'

Able said nothing for several seconds as he digested the news. 'Okay, so what happens now?'

Kough said: 'I get divorced. Super quick. As quick as I can. I'm not taking any offers from anywhere until that happens.'

'Betty was a good catch, Boffy. A keeper. Do you think you should reconsider?'

'No woman is worth half a billion dollars, Johnny.'

Able let the matter drop. He shook out a newspaper on his lap. The Chinese crisis coverage in the serious press had taken up a lake of ink that morning.

Kough leaned over to read the headlines: 'What's behind all this crisis stuff with the Chinks?'

'We have laws that forbid the sale to foreign buyers of any company the federal government regards as a strategic asset. The Chinese are demanding we change that law and let them buy up holus-bolus anything they want, which is mainly our mineral resources, coal and lithium deposits.'

Kough nudged Able on the side: 'And Stone is following my strategic advice, isn't he, telling them to get fucked?'

'More or less, yes.'

'So what can the Chinks do about it?'

'In the worst scenario they could invade and take whatever they want. Or they could cut all trade with us and let us bleed to death slowly.'

'Oh, shit. That's pretty serious stuff. So what's Stone going to do?'

'Don't know, but China is still our biggest trading partner by far and he's under a lot of pressure to buckle for the sake of our economy. So far he's been playing for time trying to placate the enemy, which was fine until some loony jumped out of his limo and dropped their flag in the dust. Not to mention killing two of their elite assassins last night.'

Kough grinned: 'Glad to be able to help.'

'It's not funny, Boffy.'

'Neither is having Chinese men in black overalls lobbing flash grenades through my bedroom window.'

Able said the consensus of the intelligence services was that the hotel break-in was probably a run-of-the-mill burglary. But last night's safe-house attack was the Chinese showing off, wanting to prove how far their tentacles went; that no one was safe, including a weirdo boffin known mainly for his gambling debts.

Kough grinned again: 'That's good news, if it's true. It means they know nothing about what I have discovered. They just want me dead for insulting their flag. Where are we going, by the way?'

'To the prime minister's office. He wants to see you.'

'He's not going to hand me over to the Yanks, is he?'

Able nudged Kough back: 'He might do. He can't afford to have the Yanks and Chinese both offside.'

Oh, fuck, fuck, fuck, thought Kough. His mum would have had no sympathy for him. Stealing things, being nasty to his wife and buggering around with patents instead of curing millions of sick people as soon as he could. Yeah, he'd be dog tucker with her.

THIRTEEN

The prime minister was in his office with a Mr Frank Church, the hard-faced man who ran ASIO.

There were no preliminaries. Stone said: 'Mr Kough. You may be able to help us. Our spooks at ASIO are reporting that the sick man who was heading the Chinese delegation to the trade conference is someone of much greater importance than we thought.'

Kough noted that Church winced at the term 'spooks'.

Church took up the story. He spoke in a dry, off-hand manner. The sick man, Mr Dim Sim, was, in fact, the gay lover of President Fang's son, Ding Bang. It was a difficult situation for all sides because there were no gays in puritanical China and certainly none anywhere near the Central Committee of the Chinese Communist Party.

Dim Sim's health was deteriorating rapidly from his Covid illness. The respirator at the Chinese Embassy had broken down. The Chinese had been invited to transfer the patient to Canberra Hospital where there were several respirators, all functioning.

The move also placed President Fang in a quandary. He would be condemned by his unmarried son, and possibly his wife, if he refused lifesaving treatment for Dim Sim.

But if Kough's vaccine was offered to save Dim Sim's life, the president would be under family pressure to soften his hard line on

Australia's law banning the sale of strategic corporate assets to foreigners.

The room fell silent.

The thread of silence stretched on till it narrowed and threatened to snap. Kough the gambler knew the rules on the power of silence. He sat still, his poker face a mask of innocence. He relished these moments, when he held all the aces. He already knew the vaccine was worth at least a billion. Church studied the ceiling with a professional detachment. But Stone began to show nervous signs. The hedgerow eyebrows jiggled minutely.

It was Church, however, who spoke first. Softly and blandly again: 'We listened in to your negotiations this morning. Yes, we bugged them. Don't look so surprised. So, we now know how important the vaccine is to the president, with their opening offer of a cool billion.

'And we learned you know how to say fuck off in Mandarin. We also know they threatened to hack your secret formula if you didn't sell it to them. Our experience tells us that was no idle threat. They have made a national sport of hacking and stealing secrets from the West for the last forty years. Their economy was built on their mass thefts. It let them build everything from fighter jets to television sets.

'The prime minister is not sure if you are a team player, but we know the government has to bring something to the table if you want to hold out for a higher offer. So, the government is offering to protect your patent details with our top-level cyber-protection technology.'

Kough straightened: 'That's fine, but you have to bring something else to the table, something very dear to me.'

Stone's gravelly voice finally intervened: 'That something is to promise not to hand you over to the Americans, isn't it? Okay, you help us with the Chinese president and we won't let the Yanks get you, although, as you know, I am sceptical of your proprietorial claims.'

Kough felt his tension drain and he took a deep breath.

Stone held his eye: 'So, are you feeling a little more like a patriotic team player now?' A laugh rumbled from his throat and his huge body shook.

Kough smiled: 'It's a deal, Prime Minister. And I'll show you what I have with me: one of the twelve ready-to-go vaccines I imported with the help of John Able. A single injection of it would reverse Dim Sim's condition.'

Stone held up a hand. If Dim Sim was cured today, Australia would have no leverage. The process could not be rushed. China had to agree to stop its blatant blackmailing to alter foreign acquisitions laws before any vaccine was administered to save the diplomat's life.

The sick man may have to get to death's door, or even die, if the Chinese would not play ball. He believed eventually they would cave in, because Fang's only son would be pleading with him to save his lover's life.

Another advantage for Australia was the president's dictatorial powers. He could ignore the politburo puritans offended by a brief relaxing of his attitude towards homosexuality.

Kough listened in silence. He had always thought diplomacy was a gentle, humane art. But both sides were ready to kill if it suited their purpose.

Church handed some paperwork to him. The Big Brain scanned it in seconds. It gave the PM's Office permission to download the formula and put it behind an electronic ring of steel. Kough would remain the proprietor of the formula. The small print also allowed the server at Brightson, Farrtey, Lickle and Goldsmith to be hacked and the formula removed for safety's sake.

Kough signed the agreement without revealing the soon-to-be protected formula was an incomplete one. Big Brain's memory would always remain his ultimate safeguard against theft.

The prime minister thanked Kough for his cooperation. Stone said he would now call in the Chinese Ambassador and confirm what they knew from the Kough patent: that Australia had the means to save Dim Sim's life. ASIO would also contact the son directly and let him in on the secret.

The meeting broke up. Kough was following Able to the silver car when he suddenly swore.

'What is it, Boffy?'

Kough's face was white: 'I left those phials at your place, in your refrigerator. Is there still a guard there?'

Able shook his head, and they both ran for the car.

FOURTEEN

Kough pulled the fridge open in a panic. Half the phials had gone.

Kough slumped at the kitchen table, produced his burner phone and called his wife.

Betty answered immediately: 'Good morning, Mikey. I've been waiting for your call. I was thinking about your hundred-thousand-dollar offer this morning. I'm not sure if it's a good offer, but in the meantime I felt I was entitled to half your phials so I took them with me as a sort of down payment.'

Kough smashed his hand down on the table and shouted: 'Fuck.'

Able frowned. He had rarely seen Michael Kough lose his cool. And never with the long-suffering Betty. He patted him on the shoulder. Kough's eyes darted to him. Able whispered: 'Boffy, calm down, mate. At least we know where the phials are.'

Kough gripped the burner in a vice-like grip: 'Listen to me, you stupid bitch. I know you haven't opened a phial yet ... because ... because you're still alive. You need to get them back to me right now. They're dangerous.'

A long second passed.

Betty said, too calmly: 'I didn't intend to open them, Mikey. I have a friend here at Treasury who's dating a man from the Australian

Infectious Diseases Board. She's going to ask him to find out what's in them.'

Kough thumped the table again: 'Your friend's got a boyfriend who's going to open a phial and analyse it? That's crazy. Betty, you need to know the liquid in the phials comes from an American germ-warfare laboratory. It'll kill anyone it comes in contact with.'

There was another long pause.

Betty said: 'What I don't understand is how come you've got it. Did you steal it?'

Able had followed the conversation. He freed the burner from Kough's grip: 'Hi Betty. It's Johnny. We need to sort this out calmly and rationally. We are all in a dangerous situation. That Chinese man who was following you and sitting outside your apartment? He'd break your neck to get his hands on those phials. And your colleague's boyfriend would be in the same danger if you give the phials to him – and he could die very quickly if he opened a phial himself.'

Betty said nothing.

Able said: 'The content of the phials is something Boffy developed alone. The Americans were not involved in it. So it was not stolen.

'Only this morning the prime minister agreed to safeguard the phials and Boffy's intellectual property. But we must have your ones back under control before someone dies.'

Betty said: 'You're not going to bully me into returning anything, Johnny. You and Mikey have always been as thick as thieves, and I know half of the phials belong to me as a right under the Matrimonial Property Act. I've got them safely in a fridge, so they're fine. Did he tell you he offered me a miserable hundred thousand dollars to settle our divorce?'

'No, he hasn't told me anything about your affairs. But listen, Betty, if you don't bring those phials back, you're buying a power of trouble. It's possible you could end up behind bars. The government is taking this matter very seriously. The safekeeping of the phials is a matter of national security.'

'Sorry, Johnny. Everything's a matter of national security these days. Send your goons if you want to, they'll never find where I've put the phials. And I can hear you in the background Mikey, carrying on like a spoiled brat. You call me a bitch again and we'll conduct all our future dealings through my lawyer.'

Kough motioned for the phone: 'Betty, Betty. I still love you and I can't believe I've put you in danger. The viruses in the phials are deadly.'

Betty burst into sobs: 'Mikey, I can't continue this conversation right now. I have to go.' She ended the call.

Able sat at the table: 'Well, that went well.'

Kough said: 'Fuck off, Johnny. You threatening to lock her up didn't exactly help.'

'Well, we may have to lock her up before the Chinese get to her and slit her throat.'

Kough looked mortified: 'Do you think they're bugging her phone?'

'Probably. They've put a lot of effort into tracing both of you. So have the CIA for that matter.'

Able called Church, the ASIO boss, and briefed him on the phial theft. He immediately agreed to put Elizabeth Kough under twenty-four-hour protective surveillance.

FIFTEEN

The Chinese ambassador sat stony faced as he heard out the prime minister. He had nothing to say after Stone revealed an Australian scientist would be able to save the life of Dim Sim, the senior diplomat heading China's delegation at the trade talks. Dim Sim had been transferred from the Chinese Embassy and was now on a Canberra Hospital respirator. He was still struggling to breathe and in a serious condition.

Chinese intelligence had briefed the ambassador about the shock failure of SIRC's billion-dollar bid to buy an anti-viral drug patent controlled by a rogue Canberra scientist.

The ambassador told Stone he would have to consult Beijing regarding Dim Sim's future treatment.

Two hours later he was back. The news was bad for Stone. There was no appetite at the highest levels of the Chinese government to do anything about Dim Sim's fate. The man had adopted embarrassing, sexually deviant behaviour.

His government, however, was interested in acquiring the rights to Lifevac, the Australian vaccine currently awaiting patent protection. Stone had not heard the commercial name before.

And if such an acquisition was allowed, the Chinese government would be prepared to have Dim Sim's situation reviewed along with its opposition to Australia's ban on the acquisition of Australian strategic resource companies.

'We are looking for more than a review, Mr Ambassador. We want China to withdraw all its demands and stop its ongoing interference with our internal affairs; and we want a full resumption of the free-trade deals that were agreed to years ago.'

The ambassador nodded smugly: 'I am sure we can achieve a new level of cooperation if the Lifevac matter is amicably settled, Prime Minister.'

Stone rested his chin on his steepled hands: 'As matters stand right now, you are telling me China has no interest in Dim Sim's failing health, so I imagine you want him out of our hospital and back in your embassy as soon as possible?'

Stone saw the first crack appear. The ambassador gave the slightest of frowns and moved on his chair.

Stone gathered up his imaginary league football and drove up the centre of field: 'I can have him discharged from the isolation ward within the hour, although I'm told his condition is critical. He needs the Lifevac vaccine to survive. And, frankly, I'm not that keen on a senior Chinese diplomat dying in one of our hospitals. You'd understand that, wouldn't you?'

The ambassador gave a small cough: 'Our embassy's respirator hasn't been repaired yet, Prime Minister.'

'But why is that a worry if you people don't care if he lives or dies?'

The ambassador moved in his chair again.

The impasse dragged on several seconds. Finally, Stone said: 'I'm happy to let him stay another night on our respirator if that would give you time to repair your one.'

The ambassador nodded too quickly. 'My government would appreciate that.'

'Can you tell your government again that we can save Mr Dim Sim's life at any time?'

'Yes, Prime Minister, I will reiterate your offer. Thank you.'

Stone stood to end the meeting. He was certain the ambassador would be back. ASIO had, minutes before the meeting began, told him the president's son had arrived in Canberra an hour ago. He had gone directly from Border Force passport control to Dim Sim's bedside.

A fake ASIO doctor at the Canberra Hospital would reiterate to Ding Bang that Australia had a cure for his lover.

THE LIMOUSINE WAS HEADED for Canberra Hospital. Michael Kough was insisting he see the dying Dim Sim. He feared his vaccine would be useless if the man's body had already effectively shut down as it shuffled off its mortal coil.

Kough did not want his vaccine to fail under the spotlight of international diplomatic attention. A failure would wipe hundreds of millions off its open market price. And force the formula to undergo months of unnecessary trials by bureaucratic government health technicians, who would almost certainly probe and uncover its secret formula.

If he tried to treat Dim Sim, then lost him, Lifevac's efficacy would be in doubt worldwide. But if he saved Dim Sim, there was the Betty problem: she would learn of the vaccine's obscene value. Trillions of dollars worldwide were at stake.

He sat back and sighed: Betty had no right to his brilliant creation. Nor did the Yanks or the Chinese or any of Big Pharma. It was his. He wanted to be the most famous virologist in world history. He wanted to be feted for saving millions of lives. And he wanted the freedom to gamble to his heart's content.

Kough's immediate problem was to find out whether Dim Sim was now too ill to be saved. Then he would have to make a value judgement.

KOUGH and Able were dressed in full, stifling hot, protective plastics. They were led into a big room with a small bed, holding a smaller patient. Dim Sim was plugged into an array of flashing and beeping boxes and screens. He had two drips attached to his arms.

He was propped up by three large pillows. His eyes were closed. He was gasping for air despite the respirator. His skin was white and clammy.

Sitting beside the bed was a young man stroking one of the patient's arms and weeping quietly. He looked flushed and totally disconsolate.

The fake ASIO doctor beckoned them in: 'The patient is putting up a fight, especially since his mate turned up. But the doctors say he's buggered. His air absorption rate is steadily falling. He's drowning in his own mucus, poor bastard.'

He pointed at the beside figure: 'This is Ding Bang. They're an item despite China's attitude to gays. The elephant in the room is that Ding Bang is the president's son, as I'm sure you already know. The son arrived a couple of hours ago. Dim Sim seemed to recognise him. But the virus has a bloody strong grip, I'm afraid.

'Those two goons over there are Dim Sim's Public Security Office bodyguards. They follow him everywhere, even to the dunny. He tells them to fuck off every chance he gets, but they ignore him.'

Kough studied the screens. It was a depressing picture. Dim Sim would have been dead if he had stayed at the embassy with no respirator. Respirators did not save every patient. In fact, the odds of their success were fifty-fifty at best.

Kough said: 'Poor bastard, indeed. How much time do the doctors think he has left – realistically?'

The ASIO agent shrugged: 'The guy's only thirty-four and was in good health, so who knows? Maybe a few hours, or even a day.'

Ding Bang swung towards Kough: 'A few hours? Oh my God, no no, no.' A bigger flow of tears began to stream down his face: 'And the doctor says you have a treatment that could save his life. Is that true?'

Kough stepped back. He was a backroom boy. He had never had to face humans dying, drowning, their lungs full of their own fluids. Laboratory rabbits and mice succumbed quietly. Became statistics.

Ding Bang threw his arms around Kough and sobbed on his shoulder: 'Please, please save him.'

The fake ASIO doctor separated them. He took Kough and Able into a huddle on the far side of the room, out of the earshot of the goons: 'There's been another turn of events just now that would really turn our situation in a world-class cluster fuck.'

SIXTEEN

Kough and Able returned to their limousine and asked the driver and guard to leave them alone.

Able used his secure cellphone to call Stone. Stone was in a cabinet meeting. It would be wrapping up in twenty minutes or so.

Able called back after five minutes. Stone should be told to adjourn the meeting and take his call, he told an admin aide. The aide hesitated, muttering something indecipherable. Able said: 'Just do it. I'll take responsibility for the interruption.'

Able and Kough waited another six minutes. Stone came on the line. They explained the new situation. He listened, thanked Able, told him to sit tight and broke the connection.

Another six minutes passed. ASIO chief Frank Church came on the line. Able explained the situation a second time. Church listened. He told them to sit tight.

Fifty minutes ticked by. The slowest fifty minutes in Kough's life. Finally, Stone came back on the line: 'We've passed on your news that Ding Bang wants to defect to Australia if Dim Sim dies.

'The Chinese have gone mental. They say they'll drop their demands to acquire Australian resource companies if we promise to arrest Ding Bang and stop his defection; and if Michael accepts the billion-dollar offer for Lifevac. If he accepts the offer, he will be permitted to inoculate Dim Sim immediately.'

Kough said: 'Prime Minister, the Chinese are trying to steal the biggest medical development in history on the cheap. They are playing us, they're happy for someone to die to force a deal through. Tell them it's no deal. Lifevac is not for sale.'

Stone said: 'I know you're right, but I had to tell you what their demands were. I'll tell them you said no. And we won't undertake to arrest Ding Bang. You and Frank go back to the ward. I'll call if there are any developments.'

Kough said he would wait for any call at Able's home. He could not watch a man writhing as he died in slow motion. Able told the driver to take Kough and the bodyguard home.

The car pulled up outside Able's home. Kough was led up the garden path by the bodyguard. Once inside, the guard sped off to the toilet. Kough went to the kitchen. He took a syringe and one phial from the refrigerator and pocketed them.

The guard returned.

'Sorry, I've changed my mind. I want to go back to the hospital,' Kough said.

While Kough was returning, Stone and Church were in a deep debate.

'Prime Minister, it would be a huge embarrassment if the son of a Chinese president defected as he's offered to. And add the spice of his motivation, to save the life of his gay lover because his father was happy to let him die, even though there was a drug to save him.'

Stone said: 'You're right, his own son defecting would be a huge loss of face for Fang.'

Church said: 'So, do you think they'll roll over?'

'It's a fifty-fifty chance, I reckon. Saving Fang's face is the biggest thing on our side. But it might not be as big a thing as we think. The commies control all their media so events here would be an official secret; and, if they did know, quite a few of China's old folk may agree with him and say he's doing the right thing getting rid of the queers. The fact that it is his son's lover he's sacrificing would be more strength to him.'

Church said: 'That boy of his would be a massive source of

intelligence for us. He's been on the sidelines of their power elite most of his life.'

Stone screwed up his face: 'I'm not sure he'd survive if he tries to defect. He has two security thugs watching his every move at the hospital. They'd win medals if they were to put a bullet in a traitor if he tries to escape; and it's not like we have a lot of safe houses to hide him in.'

Church pursed his lips and said nothing.

THE FAKE ASIO doctor looked up: 'What are you doing back here? I thought you got squeamish.'

Kough said: 'How's the patient?'

The fake doctor shook his head. 'He's getting almost no oxygen into his lungs now. He's running on fumes. His vitals are hardly registering. His friend's almost on the verge of collapse himself.'

A real hospital doctor entered. Kough said to him: 'How much time does he have?'

'Who the hell are you?'

'How much time does he have?'

The doctor walked over to the exhausted patient. His sheets were soaked. The nurses had decided there was no point in changing them. The nurses were realistic, practical people, Kough thought.

The doctor turned: 'It's up to God now. There's nothing more we can do.'

Kough said: 'So, maybe, best guess, half an hour?'

Ding Bang dropped his head on to the bed. He had run out of tears. He had never thought understanding English would become something he regretted.

The two security goons had stood as soon as Kough returned. They were loitering with intent while the death watch played out.

Kough said: 'Johnny, we have to go back to the car.'

Ding Bang went to stand but his strength deserted him.

Able said to the fake doctor: 'If those goons try to take lover boy, shoot them. He has to stay right here for the moment.'

The Australian doctor whirled around: 'What the fuck are you saying? This is a hospital.'

Able grimaced at him: 'So another couple of dead bodies won't make much difference, will they?'

He turned and strode after Kough who was stripping off his plastic protection and half running to the lifts. The Chinese goons stood confused. The fake doctor waved them back into their seats.

STONE CAME on the line immediately and sounded impatient. There had been no further word from the Chinese. Why were they calling?

Kough tried to control his panting after running to the car: 'Prime Minister, tell the Chinese I will accept their offer and give them the Lifevac production rights for Asia for one billion dollars.'

There was a silence on the end of the phone.

'You know once they get the formula, they'll steal it. You'll get bugger all royalties or anything from them. And they'll sell it wherever they like.'

'We can debate this later, but right now sell them the legal rights to the Asian production of Lifevac. I have to go now. This poor bugger Dim Sim is about to cark it. I hope we're not too late.'

Stone's voice crackled over the phone speaker: 'John, go with him and when it's over make sure Ding Bang can get safely out of the hospital. I'll get Church to beef up his numbers there. In the boot, you'll find protective vests, bullet- and knife-proof ones. Put one on and make sure Kough does the same.'

Kough and Able re-entered the isolation room. The bulky plastic isolation garb disguised their new bulletproof vests.

Kough pulled Ding Bang away from the bed. He held up a brimming syringe. Ding Bang's eyes widened. The two goons were occupied, chatting and drinking coffee. Kough leaned over the patent. The needle went in.

Ding Bang had tears of relief in his eyes: 'Dr Kough, how long will it be before we know if the vaccine works?'

Kough had never administered the vaccine to a human being. He didn't know how long it would be. It was less than half an hour with rabbits; fifteen minutes with mice. And they were not as sick as Dim Sim was.

Play the hand as though it's a royal flush, he thought. 'We will see the first improvements in less than an hour.'

Ding Bang hugged him. The tears began to flow again.

Able's cellphone message service bleeped. It was the PM: 'Chinese signed key docs, pd $1B, and say prosperous new era of Sino-Oz relations begun.'

SEVENTEEN

Two days later Michael Kough was feted by the Federal Government in a special private ceremony in the prime minister's large office.

The Chinese had packed up and gone home full of promises to resume their free-trade agreements, and they took with them the patent and Asian production rights to Lifevac for a bargain one billion price tag; they also took with them three Chinese special forces soldiers, two of them in body bags with bullets in their foreheads and one who had charges of attempted murder and kidnapping dropped.

The Chinese withdrew demands for an apology for the flag attack.

The CIA had, meanwhile, called a truce, unable to identify any theft by Michael Kough from their germ-warfare laboratory.

Best of all, for Kough, Betty had returned the six stolen vaccine phials. The Chinese diplomat Dim Sim had made a full, and miraculous, recovery; he and his friend, the son of the president, had gone home to Beijing.

Brightson, Farttey, Lickle and Goldsmith had banked China's billion-dollar Lifevac payment in Kough's Bahamas trust account, after deducting their forty-million-dollar commission. The financial details of the agreement were not made public, and Betty and Michael Kough were on polite speaking terms again.

Betty was rewarded by Kough for returning the missing phials with an invitation to the PM's gathering. She was excited at meeting a prime minister for the first time.

The first public announcement about Kough's earth-shattering vaccine discovery, however, was imminent.

Kough lapped up the adulation from Gary Stone and decided to enjoy himself while it lasted. That would only be a few short weeks, until the Chinese tried to produce his vaccine.

Then the world's biggest bully would discover it had been conned. Kough was already planning to disappear from the Chinese and Betty, spend his one-billion-dollar windfall and produce the vaccine privately, in a scarcely regulated, corrupt, third-world shithole.

He had already paid a seven-figure 'consultancy fee' to the prime minister of Papua New Guinea, who agreed he could start his first pharmaceutical factory near Port Moresby and enjoy a ten-year taxation holiday.

If he had gone ahead with the altruistic idea to vaccinate the whole world cheaply, he would have run headlong into the hands of drug-administration officials everywhere. They would demand his vaccine undergo unnecessary, lengthy trials to prove its safety and efficacy. They would demand to know the makeup of the vaccine which would leak, as always, to thuggish governments and other shady pharmaceutical operators in places like India and Nigeria.

New Guinea would allow Safevac – its new name – to be sold to whoever wanted to buy it. It accepted Kough's assurance that it had been intensely tested and was safe.

Kough surveyed the sea of happy faces. They would soon be branding him a double-crossing con man. But his vaccine would still save lives: the wealthy or desperately ill could fly to the steamy shores of a violent dump like New Guinea, be given their jab and fly out again. Each inoculation would cost one hundred thousand US dollars.

Kough thought this was a modest charge. He rationalised the famous Memorial Sloan Kettering cancer centre in New York charged cancer patients hundreds of thousand dollars for its renowned lifesaving treatment.

The complete vaccine formula would now remain stored permanently in his Big Brain.

When the blackmailing Chinese finally woke up to his double cross, he would buy time, denying any duplicity. He would point to Dim Sim's miraculous recovery. He would question China's production processes from a plant that would have been constructed with true Chinese efficiency in just weeks.

It would help that the Chinese president would do nothing to hurry the news he had been duped. But the Chinese would come after him.

The establishment of the New Guinea operation would reach their ears quickly. They would attempt to discover the identity of the ghost investor behind it. They would fail. Big Brain had approved all the details of his disappearance and continued profit flow.

In the meantime, he would live it up. Earlier in the day he had invested in a new motor. The dealer had no idea who his new best friend was but smartly unzipped the oversized plastic condom that had protected the latest Rolls-Royce Phantom during its delivery voyage. Kough paid for it and drove it away minutes later.

He took the top-floor penthouse at the Four Seasons Hotel in Sydney's Rocks as his new pad. He dumped his worn, old clothes and spent up big on fashionable threads.

Kough looked around at the crowd attending the PM's party.

With enough bubbly on board, and enough kissing and hand shaking of the PM and other worthies, he decided to slip away. Lady Luck at the Casino Canberra was his siren. With his mega bankroll she would have to finally admit defeat when he piled on the pressure and pushed her to double up and then double up some more.

He waved across the room to John Able. He was with a stunning Asian woman. Power was an aphrodisiac and the PM's chief of staff was one the most influential people in the room. Able gave him a thumbs-up.

He feigned a move toward the toilets and then swerved to the side exit. Minutes later he was in his Rolls and being driven downtown to Binara Street – the tragic scene of his life's implosion just two years ago. They had banned him after raking in the last of his last chips. They said he may have an addiction. They asked him politely to leave. Baby, that would not be happening tonight, he thought, as he sank back in the luxury and aroma of the new leather seats.

. . .

LADY LUCK DIDN'T TRY. She gave in and let him rob, rape and pillage. The five-thousand-dollar chips on the table became a small mountain. A large crowd jostled their way around the table to watch, to be part of Kough's wild ride.

The floor manager suggested quietly he could make room on the table if he cashed in some of the chips. The casino was running short of them, he said. Kough shook his head. He loved the theatre of a high roller surrounding himself with big piles of high-value chips.

Eventually, his legs began to get stiff and his eyes raw. There is never a clock in a casino. He had to steal a look at his new Rolex President. But he could not be sure what it said. Its hands and second hand were in bright gold against the bright gold watch face. He thought it said quarter to two. He signalled to cash in his chips. The crowd sighed in protest. He now knew what gambling heaven felt like. He was a winner.

He swallowed the last of his free bourbon. The ice had not had time to melt. He turned slowly, theatrically, so his fans could see him front on. His happy spell lasted another second.

At the back of the crowd he saw the upright, military-bearing figure of a Chinese man watching him. The face was impassive. Big Brain said: They are following you, sunshine. Already.

He gave the croupier and the floor manager a five-thousand-dollar chip each. Kough turned around again: Mr Impassive instantly looked away.

Kough reflected on how much he had just won. Just when he didn't need it. Lady Luck was playing with him. He would play with Mr Impassive. The Chinese heavy casually looked back at Kough again, they locked eyes and Kough smiled broadly and nodded in his direction. The man turned and strode away among a row of poker machines.

Kough was on a high. He chuckled to himself as he went outside to where his Rolls-Royce and chauffeur were waiting to take him to John Able's house. It would be his last night there. He would be wafted in the Phantom to Sydney and his hotel penthouse in the morning.

Kough's anti-viral discovery made world headlines late that evening: 'UNKNOWN AUSTRALIAN VIROLOGIST RESEARCHER CRACKS CODE TO KILL EVER-MUTATING VIRUSES'.

The mass media reported production of the new vaccine would start in China in the next month.

Kough knew his private life was ending. Now he would be a celebrity. At least for a while. He also knew he would then have to shake off the adoring crowds and Mr Impassives and vanish.

EIGHTEEN

Kough made his way unsteadily up the path to Able's front door. It opened directly onto the lounge.

A slight movement in the room startled him. He froze for a moment, trying to focus his bloodshot eyes. There was a side table lamp creating a circle of soft light over the couch. And on the couch was the stunning Asian woman he had seen earlier with John Able at the PM's function.

She gave a wide smile. She was holding her cellphone: 'You must be Boffy.'

He was lost for words. The woman was straight off a *Vogue* cover.

'I've been reading the news.' She held the cellphone up. 'The *Women's Weekly* says you are about to become a multi-billionaire, save millions of lives *and* become Australia's most eligible bachelor.'

He beamed stupidly like a schoolboy: 'Oh. Is that all?'

She laughed: 'I'm Charlotte by the way. We didn't get a chance to meet this evening. We couldn't get near you. The adoring fans had you surrounded.'

'Oh, I get that all the time.'

She laughed again.

Kough looked around: 'Where's Johnny?'

'He took himself off to bed. He was exhausted. That's him you can hear snoring like a chainsaw down the passage.'

'And he just left you here?' No, no, said Big Brain. Settle down for God's sake. You're acting like the desperate and dateless. Kough felt his face flush.

The easy laugh again. Charlotte uncrossed her legs and sat forward: 'It's not a problem. I'm used to it. He works too hard and then crashes.'

The man's bloody mad, thought Kough. Or blind. Or impotent.

She sat forward: 'Would you like a coffee, Boffy?'

I'll have anything that will keep me here with you, he thought: 'That would be corker, thanks.' Why had he suddenly developed his old mum's language as he stood flustered before this goddess?

'How do you have it?'

I don't bloody care, he thought. The way that takes the longest to make.

'Just black, thanks. No sugar, I'm sweet enough.' Oh no. His face went even redder.

'I'm sure you are, Boffy.'

She glided to the kitchen, her hour-glass figure upright, his eyes transfixed on her low-cut cocktail dress – and those legs.

'Johnny said you probably disappeared to the casino. How did you go? Win heaps?'

'Oh, just half a million.' His words were out before he could stop them. She turned and met his eye as though she was unsure if he was being serious or flippant again. She raised one eyebrow. Then nodded her head. She believed me, he thought.

Kough swallowed: 'It might have been a bit closer to six hundred thousand. I didn't bother to count it...' Fuck. What a wanker. Big Brain shook his head furiously.

Charlotte turned for the espresso machine: 'Why would you count it? It was probably only half an hour's earnings for you.' She laughed.

Kough said nothing. He had blown it. This gorgeous woman would know he was a total tosser. How did Johnny pull talent like this? And he was busy, snoring in his bed. Good God.

Kough had not been with a woman for, like, two years. He had never been much good at the seduction thing. He remembered it had been Betty that had made the first move when they were dating, impatiently unzipping his fly while he squirmed.

He realised Charlotte was grinning at him and handing him a cup.

'I hope this is how you like it.'

'Any way, any way is fine, thanks, thanks.' He blew at the steam rising from the cup. 'I didn't expect to find anyone up at this hour.'

'Well, that's fate, isn't it?'

Kough gulped. What did that mean?

Kough decided he had to start some sort of conversation, or she would go: 'Fate ... or just good luck, as far as I'm concerned. Lady Luck was smiling on me at the casino tonight, thank heavens. I don't usually win amounts like that, not very often, anyway.' He knew he was babbling and stopped.

'Fate or luck. It doesn't matter which it is. I'm just so happy to have some company.' She stood with her back to the kitchen island.

'You're not having a cup?' he asked.

'No, I'm already wide awake, thanks.' Uh, what did that mean? Nothing. Settle down, drink your coffee. I can't, he thought, it's too hot. So is she.

'Why are you being so nervous, Boffy? Weren't there many women in your germ-warfare lab?' She laughed again and nudged his arm. He smiled and tried not to spill the coffee.

'You're beautiful,' he said. 'I'm the one that's lucky.'

She put her fingers on the knot of his tie. 'Well, you deserve to feel lucky, after what you've done.' She loosened the knot. He put his free hand behind her. She pushed gently towards him. Then gave him a light kiss. Kough's body shuddered. She took the cup off him and put her arms around his waist.

She backed up and was suddenly sitting on the edge of the island, her legs around his thighs.

This was his best mate's girl, he thought. The man is even in the house. I heard him snoring, for God's sake. She lifted her dress up. He put his right hand on her thigh. She murmured. His hand inched nervously forward. Then it stopped. He felt pubic hair. What the hell? She was not wearing panties. He shuddered again.

She leaned forward and undid his belt. His erection stopped his pants from freefall.

Charlotte eased his erection free, leaned back and guided him in. He was lost for all money. He slid in with a load moan of ecstasy. She put a hand over his mouth: 'Shhh. We don't want to wake sleeping beauty.'

Kough did not care. He was devouring this woman like a … a … She made little noises as they rocked together on the edge of the bench top.

When it was over a wave of guilt swamped him. What if Able ever found out? She reached up, cupped his face: 'Thank you, Dr Kough.' She wriggled off the island and brushed her dress down.

He stood stupidly. Pants around his ankles. His brain racing about what had just happened.

She smiled at him: 'Pull you daks up, Boffy. Your coffee will have cooled by now.'

She walked off towards the lounge. Big Brain said, Don't sweat it. Enjoy the moment. Maybe she would enjoy living on a tropical beach helping you spend your billions? Donald Trump was right. He said girls were different if you were a rich celebrity.

Kough slowly pulled his pants up. He could not wipe the smile off his face. He was a disloyal, lecherous, lying, deceitful prick, but what the hell? He was rich and famous. The world was his for the asking.

'DID YOU HAVE AN EXCITING NIGHT?' John Able had his back to him, working the espresso machine the next morning.

Kough gulped. He looked around in vain for any sign of Charlotte.

Able turned: 'The cat got your tongue, lover boy.'

Kough blanched. Able turned back to the machine: 'Well, the *Women's Weekly* says you're our most eligible bachelor.'

'Oh, that rubbish. I don't know why people buy those trashy magazines.'

'Why are you in such a sour mood this morning, Boffy? Did your night not go well?'

Kough did not know what to say. He gave a little nod and shrugged: 'The casino went well. Have you heard?'

'No. Did you break the bank?'

Kough felt his tenseness ease. Charlotte had not told him about their conversation or their other activity last night.

'I would have broken the bank if I'd kept going. Picked up close to six hundred thousand.'

Able looked around and whistled. 'Shit man, that's a fortune. Here, have a coffee. I'm sorry, it's a bit early for champagne.'

Kough took a breath as he reached for the cup: 'Charlotte not having one?'

Able frowned. 'Charlotte? No, she went home last night after I flaked.'

'Sorry I missed her. She was a bit of looker hanging off your arm last night.'

Able said: 'Yes, she's a looker alright, isn't she?'

Kough nodded: 'How did you meet her? A bit of an office romance, is it?'

Able sat at the kitchen island and sighed. She was a bit of problem, he said. Stone disapproved of him dating her. Senior staff dating the young ones was frowned on. It always led to trouble, Stone reckoned. The Cabinet rule book now officially banned cabinet ministers from shagging their staff.

Kough smiled: 'Not like the old days then? Another perk banned.'

'I've told the old boy I think she's a keeper. He says I'm just in lust and should find someone my own age.'

Able said the situation was further complicated because Charlotte was already married – to a navy intelligence officer, currently at sea with HMAS *Sydney* watching Chinese warships playing war games in the Indian Ocean.

'She says she's told him she's leaving him.'

Kough sat beside his best friend, putting his cup on the edge of the island. He was right at the scene of the crime, he thought.

'She's told him, but...' Able grimaced. She had not told him until the day before he went to sea. He was not due back for another month or so.

'So you've been cuckolding a naval officer who's on active duty surveilling our enemies and making our country safe?'

Able said: 'Fuck off, Boffy. Who's going to turn her down? Not this boy.'

'I hear what you're saying, Johnny, but I can see why Stone would be worried about a scandal.'

'Well, I think she's an asset for our office. She's smart. Worked on cyber security and firewalls before I hired her.' He paused for a moment: 'I think she loves me.'

Kough stood: 'I hope so mate. Look, I have to go. I'm off to Sydney this morning and I've got a bit of legal business to sort first.'

Kough dug in his pocket. He took out a wad of hundred-dollar bills: 'I owe you for putting me up, Johnny, and for inviting Betty here. I appreciate it and I mightn't see you for a while.'

Able looked at the wad and began to shake his head.

Kough said: 'Take it, Johnny. It's not mine. Not really. I won it earlier this week. Buy Charlotte something nice if you don't want it.'

'That's very generous of you, Boffy. Okay. But I'll tell Charlotte where it came from. I don't want her to start thinking I've got piles of cash to throw around.'

They shook hands. Kough gathered his smart new threads and went out to meet the chauffeur. The gleaming Rolls-Royce was purring at the kerbside.

What a morning, he thought. And paying a totally unsuspecting Johnny conscience money. I really deserve a Chinese bullet in the brain.

Big Brain laughed at him. Forget it. There are plenty more beautiful women in the sea. And we have a lot to do before our vanishing act.

NINETEEN

MICHAEL KOUGH DECIDED HE WOULD HIDE IN PLAIN SIGHT.
In the heart of Sydney.

Three months had passed since the Lifevac sale to the Chinese.
Kough had his hair cut and dyed grey. Began to wear contact lenses and
became a green-eyed dude. He created a false beer gut with padding he
strapped around his stomach.

He discarded most of his conspicuous, high-fashion threads and
replaced them with cheap shirts and jeans and black boots. When he had
finished, he was sure his own mother would not have recognised him at
first glance.

The Rolls was replaced with an anonymous Toyota Prius. It was a
sacrifice, but Big Brain insisted.

He drew down fifteen million from the Bahamas trust and
purchased a spacious apartment on the Woolloomooloo wharf in central
Sydney.

A white, fourteen-metre, open-cockpit sportsfisher bobbed outside
his lounge window on the apartment's private marina. The engine was
super hyped to achieve a full speed of forty-five knots. It was registered
to someone whose name and address he found in the Adelaide phone
book. The marina charges were on auto payment via the Bahamas bank
account.

He left the previous owner's plush furnishings unchanged.

He answered to a new name: what neighbours there were knew him as Michael Krump. Most of them seemed to live overseas or inter state and their apartments sat empty most months. When occupied, they were mainly used by spoilt children who had no interest in an ageing, overweight recluse.

The New Guinea production plant was complete. It was owned by a Liechtenstein entity whose trustees were based in Belize, the only English-speaking tax haven in South America. Its trust bank accounts were in the Bahamas. The tangled entity had been set up by a Singaporean legal firm with no links to Brightson, Farttey, Lickle and Goldsmith.

The New Guinea plant manager was a shady accountant. Tommy Watson was a drinker. He had fled some legal problems in Melbourne and found refuge in the wild west that was New Guinea. He was seriously overpaid and had no need to steal but, just the same, Kough had him subject to a strict auditing regime.

Using social media, Kough began to exhort the miracle cure of a vaccine made in New Guinea. No virus survived it. The medicine, now dubbed Virasafe, was derided by medical experts who described it as a blatant con because it was impossible for any vaccine to kill all viruses. They pointed out the pill was produced in a country which did not insist on any drug trials or production safeguards.

It made no difference. Desperate, dying people flew to Port Moresby, were inoculated and quickly cured. Word spread faster than a bushfire and the Virasafe plant had to run two shifts. The price for a vaccine was raised to one hundred and twenty thousand dollars. Demand was unaffected.

Michael Krump lay back in his luxury pad. His life of indolence had been hard earned, he kidded himself. There was one itch he could not scratch, though: he missed the thrill of high-stakes roulette. He connected to several online casinos. But it was not the same. There were no smiling punters to pat him on the back when some crazy wager created a boastful hill of five-thousand-dollar chips.

At night he walked the streets of Sydney's waterfront, pausing to watch the small armies of punters coming and going from the local casinos. Big Brain insisted he did not enter them.

But a man had other needs. He became a regular at a small side-street brothel in Kings Cross where he had to lose his fat belt temporarily in its pokey changing room.

Suzie's Massage Parlour promised rub downs with a happy ending. For conventional sexual intercourse, the girls insisted he use a desensitising condom. Kough objected, until one Suzie said she would put it on with her mouth. Of course, that cost an extra fifty bucks.

SMUG and comfortable in his new lifestyle, Kough was blissfully unaware of the noose tightening around his neck.

The fury of the duped Chinese took some time to fully manifest itself. At first the Chinese blamed their vaccine technicians and a possible misinterpretation of the vaccine's formula. They double checked on the good health of Dim Sim, the supposed living proof of the formula's ground-breaking efficacy.

But it soon became obvious the Virasafe vaccine was a billion-dollar pup. Unable to trace Kough, the knifes came out for Mr Ling, who had closed the deal for the Sino International Research Corporation.

The group's employees were sworn to secrecy as the politburo became alarmed at the prospect of China becoming a laughing stock, particularly as President Fang had personally endorsed the deal.

The president kept calm, however. He had the world's biggest intelligence network at his fingertips. Its tentacles went everywhere, more than any of the naive democracies ever dreamed. He decided he would find and punish the snake-oil fraudster, Dr Michael Kough, and the bring the Australian government to its economic knees at the same time.

THE FIRST PING of unease was felt by Big Brain. The online business page in *The Australian* ran a report that iron ore ships from Western Australia's Port Hedland were being held up at Chinese ports without explanation.

In the next few days, other major Australian exporters began to complain their goods were being stranded at port warehouses by Chinese Customs for no reason.

Chinese container ships scheduled for Australia were rerouted to other countries, creating a myriad of goods shortages in Australia.

A week on, the Chinese Embassy announced the new Sino–Australian free-trade deals were being reviewed. A day later they were abruptly cancelled.

A political uproar enveloped Australia.

Prime Minister Gary Stone was mystified. And scared. The Chinese Ambassador called to ask if the government knew the whereabouts of Dr Michael Kough. He was needed to tweak his virus vaccine formula. Stone reached out to John Able, but he had no idea where his best friend was.

ASIO reported Chinese Public Security undercover agents were surveilling the entrances to casinos and other, illegal, gambling dens throughout Australia – and the world.

The most far-reaching trade bombshell burst when China declared Australia officially an 'unsafe' destination. The multi-billion-dollar tourist industry went into a catastrophic spiral. The number of Chinese airlines flying to Australia fell by ninety per cent.

Michael Kough followed the developments with rising anxiety. He knew a fearsome, silent, invisible dragon had been unleashed and was circling, trying to sniff him out.

Big Brain worried his way through all the precautions that had been taken to drop off the face of the planet. There were no obvious flaws. Hiding in plain sight was still a clever, effective option.

China would have been scouring beaches and palatial homes along the tropical white sands of resorts and international tax havens. When these obvious locations failed to produce any sightings, Kough knew they would redouble their efforts closer to home.

So Kough began to eschew Suzie's Massage Parlour and the beckoning lights of the casino entrances. He feared the fruitless Chinese chase for him would lead them to illegally employ their portable facial recognition technology on Australian streets. His disguise was okay, but it hadn't changed the depth and width of his skull.

Back in China, SIRC boss Ling was under house arrest. When the intelligence services failed to come up with a quick trace on Kough, he was ordered to take the gloves off and recover, and punish, at least the vile co-conspirators at Brightson, Farttey, Lickle and Goldsmith.

TWENTY

Orin Lickle looked up. Standing in the glass doorway of the boardroom was the bossy, pink-haired leso bitch with the nose ring that they couldn't fire.

He glared at her: 'I. Am. In. A. Client Meeting.'

'Mr Ling says the matter can't wait, Mr Lickle, sir.'

'Mr Ling?'

'Yes, Mr Lickle, sir. From the Sino International Research Corporation in Shanghai. He says, if you don't take his call, he will institute legal proceedings against Brightson, Farttey, Lickle and Goldsmith today for fraud and the theft of one billion dollars.'

Lickle went ashen faced. The pinstriped clients around the table were instantly transfixed in the drama. They stared at Lickle, the go-to man in Australia for patents and royalties and tax efficiencies.

The tic on Lickle's right eyelid quivered to life.

The bossy bitch put one hand on her hip: 'What do you want me to tell him, Mr Lickle, sir?'

She was fighting to stop a sneering smile, Lickle thought. There must be a way to get rid of these bolshie bitches.

The intrigued clients waited for Lickle's response. The oldest one said: 'Sounds like you ought to take it, Orin.'

Lickle pushed his chair back, apologised for the interruption and said he would be right back.

He went to his enormous corner office to take the call. He halted in surprise when he saw there was a barrel-chested Chinaman sitting upright on his client couch.

The man said nothing but pointed to the flashing light on the desk phone. Lickle answered it with a calm, businesslike greeting: 'Lickle.'

'So sorry to call you from a meeting, Mr Lickle. I hope I haven't inconvenienced you too much.'

Lickle said nothing.

'We have experienced some unforeseen difficulties here concerning Lifevac.

'As a result, we would like our billion dollars back. Today. You need to transfer it to SIRC's account in Shanghai. As you can see, a SIRC agent has been sent to oversee the transaction. He has all the necessary forms and authority to expedite the repayment.'

Lickle dropped into his chair. The Chinese bruiser with the tight, undersized suit immediately stood. He had several sheets of paper in one hand. He placed them on the desk and pushed one of a collection of fountain pens towards Lickle. He nodded curtly, took one step back and folded his arms.

Lickle gingerly turned on the phone's record button: 'Mr Ling, even if we were to go along with your outrageous demand, the account you are referring to no longer contains one billion dollars. Expenses and costs and commissions have been incurred.'

Mr Ling gave what sounded like a small yawn or a long, bored sigh. The bruiser stood patiently in front of the desk.

'We are very disappointed you enabled the Lifevac fraud, Mr Lickle. But we have now uncovered it. What hand do you write with?'

Lickle screwed up his face: 'What hand? My right, of course. Why?'

Mr Ling gave a polite cough: 'It would be pointless breaking your writing hand, wouldn't it?'

The bruiser looked stone-faced as Lickle's body began to shake. Lickle looked through his glass walls. Nobody was in the corridor outside. The plebs were all hidden away from the big corner office behind partitions enclosing their chickencoop workstations.

'I can't transfer funds that don't exist, Mr Ling.'

'Of course not. If that particular account is short, we would accept money from your investment account.'

Lickle stuttered: 'What investment account?'

'We've been behind your firewall and know you have one. It's quite plump right now.'

Lickle said: 'I will have to consult my partners before I do anything.'

'That's your choice, Mr Lickle, but my agent has clear instructions. He will now break your left hand.'

The bruiser moved forward. A small, steel hammer had appeared in his hand. Lickle panicked and gave a scream of terror.

Mr Ling said: 'It's up to you, Mr Lickle. I would suggest you make an executive decision as the managing partner. It would prevent a lot of pain and time wasting.'

Lickle gasped. He felt his bladder give way. He tried to push back on his swivel chair's wheels. An excruciating pain shot up his left arm. He screamed and looked down to see several buckled fingers protruding at odd angles from his hand. The bruiser raised the hammer again. Lickle tried to pull the hand free, but the effort sent more fierce pain through his arm.

'Stop. Stop. For God's sake. I'll sign. I'll sign.'

Mr Ling's calm voice said: 'Very good, Mr Lickle. The agent will have placed the necessary papers before you.'

Lickle began to sob from pain and shock. He used his uninjured hand to pull the papers towards him. He noted the bloody Chinese had even placed large Xs where he was to sign. The humiliation was complete. He signed and fell back on the chair. The bruiser collected the papers and said: 'Thank you, Mr Lickle. There is now only one more thing.'

Lickle's eyes widened in horror.

'We need to find Dr Kough. How do we contact him?'

Lickle shook his head furiously. 'He sacked us. I don't know where he is.'

Tears began to pour down his face. The bruiser said something in Mandarin over the speaker phone. Ling sighed and gave a curt reply. The bruiser nodded and turned to leave, stuffing the transfer documents into a suit pocket.

Lickle suddenly became aware the bossy bitch was standing looking through the door. She opened it: 'Shall I show your visitor out, Mr Lickle, sir?'

The bruiser followed her casually to the lifts. His career was over, thought Lickle. The forty-million-dollar commission had already created an upheaval at the firm. The forty partners wanted a million each. The four senior name partners wanted ten million each.

Brightson, Farttey, Lickle and Goldsmith was imploding. The rupture would be final when the partners discovered their slush fund, better known as their Investment Account, had been almost emptied.

He began to stagger to his feet, nursing his broken hand, and remembered his soiled pants. The Bossy Bitch appeared again: 'Your boardroom clients decided to leave, Mr Lickle, sir. Would there be anything else I can do for you, Mr Lickle, sir?'

'Yes,' he roared, 'fuck off, you leso bitch. You're sacked.'

She fingered her nose ring: 'That's bullying and sexist hate speech, Mr Lickle. We have diversity and inclusion laws, you know – anyway, I cannot be sacked. I have not had three warnings, with one in writing. And you've got no grounds to dismiss me.' She turned and left. Her nose wrinkled. There was a definite pong in the air.

TWENTY-ONE

The job was proving much harder than Tommy Watson had imagined. Much harder. He looked out of his office above the now still Virasafe vaccine production line and wondered if he would be followed home again tonight.

He already had enough to worry about. He was banking more than ten million dollars a month. A colossal amount in a poverty-stricken backwater like Port Moresby. A black market had sprung up to plague him as word of the miracle drug spread. Hundreds of vaccines were disappearing off the production line every week. The illicit vaccines were offered at sixty thousand dollars each – half the official rate Watson was charging.

And the local Motu Koita Assembly chief had visited and was demanding rent money despite Michael Kough's one-million-dollar payment to the prime minister for a no-questions-asked pharmaceutical plant. Kough had not realised the Assembly controlled the land used by the plant, not the national government.

It was another headache he would have to sort. When he was sober in the morning, he would use Virasafe's encrypted email to ask Michael Kough for instructions.

The plant workers were paid the standard New Guinea rate of fifty dollars a week, but their thievery was making them rich. A long queue of greedy crooks had begun clamouring for a Virasafe job.

To create vacancies, they had called on the services of the local gangsters, or Rascals, as they were known. The bodies of Virasafe workers would regularly be found dumped with other murder victims on downtown Port Moresby streets, creating new job vacancies.

The native workforce had been a nightmare to deal with at the best of times. The population of the country's nine million citizens shared eight hundred and forty languages between them. They were mainly uneducated, subsistence farmers. Not exactly a prime workforce to draw from.

He had come to New Guinea twelve years ago, to evade awkward Accounting Society questions about his clients' trust funds. The former Australian colony was an attraction for him because of its widespread corruption.

Watson poured another scotch into a chipped glass and took a sip. Outside it was teeming its weekly inch of rain. His sweat-stained shirt clung to him as the humidity climbed to its typical ninety per cent level. His air conditioning, as usual, was broken down.

He took an anxious look outside. There was no sign in the darkening street of the battered Mercedes that had followed him home the last two evenings.

He wondered if he had gone truly troppo and had become paranoid; the booze finally rusting his remaining brain cells. No, it was not that, he decided. He had definitely spotted the Mercedes. And his driver's evasive measures had not shaken it.

Watson believed he might be a kidnap or robbery target of the Rascals. Or maybe the Motu Assembly's parliamentary thugs. He was never to suspect the Chinese Public Security Bureau.

He downed the scotch and poured another generous dram, then dialled his driver cum bodyguard to bring his GM Holden around to the front entrance.

The city streets were so dangerous no one ever dared to walk them at night. At downtown intersections where a rare traffic light still worked, his driver would not stop. Everyone knew gangs of Rascals lurked ready to hijack any car that came to a halt.

Watson locked his office, went down the rickety stairs to the assembly-line floor and made for the front entrance where his driver was waiting. The car set off for his fortified home in the suburbs. All professional white people took refuge behind high fences, often topped by electrified barbed wire. Some of the fences were solid steel. There were more security cameras in the suburbs than outside a Beijing railway station. The driver tapped him on the arm: 'Our friends are back, Mr Watson.'

Watson lowered the passenger vanity mirror: The Mercedes was trailing about three hundred metres away. He said: 'Hey sport, shall we stop? Let them get out, and then shoot the bastards?'

The driver seemed to contemplate the request seriously.

Watson laughed: 'Only joking, sport.'

The driver curled out his bottom lip and shook his head: 'Someone called me yesterday, Mr Watson. Said they would pay me five hundred dollars if I would stop the car outside your house and not activate the gates.'

Watson sucked in a deep breath. A chill rippled through his stressed old body. The pair drove on in silence for a couple of blocks.

Watson glanced at the driver who stared straight ahead as he navigated the potholes along the deserted streets lined with abandoned commercial buildings.

Finally, the driver gave a short laugh: 'I told them it wasn't enough, Mr Watson.'

Watson joined in with his own nervous laugh: 'Good for you, sport.'

The driver turned to look him in the eye: 'I told them you paid me that much a week already.'

Watson sighed: 'Okay, okay. Five hundred a week it is.'

The driver nodded: 'And maybe a little for ... er ... danger money.'

Watson smiled: 'Okay, six hundred a week.'

'You are very generous, Mr Watson. I can now buy a third wife.'

The Mercedes maintained its distance behind them as Watson's Holden approached his high steel gate topped with coils of sharp barbed wire. He took his pistol from the glove box as the car slowed and the security gate ground slowly open. As the Holden moved into the driveway, the Mercedes passed behind and continued its steady progress down the road.

He would contact Kough tonight, not in the morning. He needed more protection quickly, if he was going to stay.

TWENTY-TWO

'BOFFY!! FOR FUCK'S SAKE, WHERE THE HELL ARE YOU?'

John Able leapt to his feet clutching the secure phone like it was a lifeline thrown to a drowning man.

There was no reply. Able stared at the receiver. Then at the incoming call number display. It was a long one. An offshore burner, he thought.

'Boffy. Is that you? Are you there? Can you hear me?'

He heard a hammering noise. Like the din a barista makes in a coffee bar. Then Kough's voice came through faintly and slightly muffled: 'Johnny boy. I had to call. I've been hearing about the shit I've caused with the Chinese. I'm so sorry. Have I got you in the shit as well?'

'Boffy, where the hell are you? Everybody's been turning the place upside down for you. Are you all right?'

'Yes, Johnny boy, I'm fine. I'm sorry but I can't tell you where I am. I know I've upset the Chinks and I don't want a visit from the little buggers. Tell me what's happening.'

Able paused. 'No, you certainly don't want a visit from the little buggers. They have already visited your solicitors. Tortured the guy Lickle in his own office. Got him to refund the billion dollars they paid you for Lifevac.

'He didn't have it of course, so the Chinese extorted the balance from the firm's so-called investment account – their slush fund.

'But Boffy, their loss is nothing. Australia has lost more than twenty billion in trade since the Chinese found out you conned them on the Lifevac formula.

'And they're saying they've heard about some sort of anti-viral vaccine being mass produced in some backyard sweat shop in the jungles of Papua New Guinea, of all places.'

'Fuck,' Kough cursed.

'Yes, fuck is right. We're up shit creek without a paddle. Our exporters are laying off staff left, right and centre while they hunt out new customers. We've had to drop our commodity prices to attract new customers, but most of them are too frightened of Chinese retaliation to take our stuff.

'Gary Stone may have to resign. The Chinese want his scalp and are banging on again about needing acquisition rights to our mineral resource companies.'

Kough said: 'Good God. I had no idea anything like this would happen. I only came up with the deal because they were going to let that guy Dim Sim just drown in his own phlegm, even though they knew I could cure him.'

'I know you were well intentioned Boffy, but you've conned Gary Stone too. He acted in good faith, selling Lifevac to solve the trade stand-off, now he's China's public enemy number one.'

Kough sighed: 'So are you going to get the boot? You have been right in the middle of this shambles too.'

Able did not reply immediately. He seemed to be searching for the right words: 'I am under suspicion because of our close friendship. ASIO suspects I might have been a willing party to the Chinese fraud and have pocketed half the billion. They know I was the one who got you through Customs in the first place with your phials. I was in the room when you insisted on letting the Chinks have the patent and set up your con job.

'It didn't help when I banked the two hundred thousand in cash you gave me.

'I'm sure my phone's being bugged now. I know Charlotte's is because ASIO has warned me officially that my beautiful girl is under pressure from China to spy for them.'

Kough said: 'Spy for China?'

'ASIO intercepted a call she got from her parents in Hong Kong. They're old, in their eighties. The Public Security goons paid them a visit. They think for some reason she may know where you are hiding. I don't know why they would even think that. You never even met her.

'Meantime the goons have declared her oldies officially "unreliable citizens" and lowered their Social Security rating.'

Kough said: 'Their rating? What does that mean?'

Able said: 'It's a huge deal in China. It's how they control the population.

'In the case of Charlotte's parents, they are banned from all air travel or catching a train to anywhere in China. And their mortgage interest rate has been bumped up. So they've been pleading with her to find out where the hell you are. They think they may get chucked in jail as enemies of the people if you're not found soon.

'The goons think because she's in the PM's department she will somehow have access to secret information on you.'

Kough felt gutted: 'Oh, my God. How is Charlotte coping with the pressure?'

'Not very well. She has been ill and late for work most mornings. She's stressed out. And she and I have been told to cool it. So we're both on our own in the middle of this.'

'What can I say, Johnny? I've created a mega fuck-up. I should have let that Dim Sim character die. What's this about a sweat shop operation making anti-virals in Port Moresby?'

There was a long silence. Finally, Able replied: 'I never mentioned Port Moresby, Boffy.'

Kough felt Big Brain punch him in the stomach: 'Oh ... when you said Papua New Guinea ... I just assumed the operation would be in Port Moresby.'

Kough felt the anger vibrating down the phone: 'That's where you are, isn't it? Port bloody Moresby. No wonder the Chinese want their pound of flesh. You've been with that sweat shop mob extorting zillions for your vaccine.'

'Johnny, I swear to you, I am not in Port Moresby. I'm not.'

'You're full of it, Boffy. And you've fucked up my life with Charlotte, and probably my career. And she's now a mess. Her parents live in fear. Then there's the PM's government tottering and the whole of the Australian economy going down the bloody drain again. Well done, you dumb prick.'

Before Kough could reply, Able said: 'While you were in your germ-warfare laboratory in the Rockies, you probably missed the fact that the Chinese now own Papua New Guinea. They have splashed billions around among the crooked politicians and officials who are meant to be running the place; and loaning the dopey buggers billions to build bridges and factories, not to mention wharves and military facilities right on our back door.'

'Johnny, I'm a virologist, not a bloody foreign affairs expert,' said Kough.

'Shame you didn't stick to it,' said Able. 'Now tell me where the hell you are so we can sort something out with the Chinese before it's too late; or bugger off and we'll let them find you. Which you know they will.'

There was no reply. Kough had broken the burner phone connection.

Able looked up to see the PM watching him, the hedgerow eyebrows raised. Beside him stood the ASIO boss Frank Church.

Church said: 'Mr Able, it is standard practice to keep a suspect talking for as long as humanly possible, not to shout and threaten and scare them off.'

Stone shook his head: 'I shouldn't have to tell you, Frank, but your phones are not being bugged. Don't get paranoid on me. No one thinks you're in league with that crook Kough, certainly not me.' He turned on his heel and left. Church followed him.

Able looked across the office. A small crowd was watching him through the glass walls. Charlotte was among them. She looked pale and worried. He waved her to come in. She shook her head. He stood and went to her. The rest of the spectators scattered.

'Tell me something, Char. I've been wondering about this for a few days: why does Chinese intelligence think you know Michael Kough or where he might be?'

Because I shagged Mikey on your kitchen island, Charlotte thought, and the Chinese know because they have been spying on me since I joined the PM's Department.

She looked Able directly in the eye: 'I wouldn't have the slightest idea, Johnny.'

TWENTY-THREE

Michael Kough was mortified. He logged into the encrypted Bahamas bank account his Singapore lawyers had created for him. It had been cleaned out.

How the hell had the Chinese discovered it? He logged into the New Guinea account and let out a sigh of relief. It still held something. Not much. But something: one hundred and twenty thousand US dollars.

He transferred it into an Australian account he had set up under Michael Krump. It now held a measly three hundred thousand dollars. He felt ill. His millions had disappeared despite all his cunning financial manoeuvres. Big Brain was silent.

He sent a fourth encrypted email to his hard-drinking expat manager, Tommy Watson. There had been no reply all day. Tommy had done a bunk, he thought, or something more sinister had befallen him.

Using his burner, he called the Port Moresby plant. It was answered by a woman with broken English.

'Mr Tommy not here. Been way two days. Maybe sick. Lot of sick in Pom City all time.' Then she hung up.

Kough tried Watson's home number. The call rang out.

Big Brain told him to pretend he was a reporter and phone the local cops. See if Watson had been in an accident or thrown in the local drunks' bin.

The cop spoke reasonable English: 'We don't get many calls from the Sydney papers. Is this Mr Tommy Watson, the big-time factory fella? Let me have a look at our overnight sheets. Nuh, not been in any car accident or admitted to hospital. Wait on. I've found him: Thomas Arthur Watson.'

Kough relaxed: 'Thank God. Is he all right? Where can I find him?'

The cop paused a beat: 'Central City morgue. Reported as a robbery victim downtown last night. Bullet hole through the forehead.'

'Fuck,' said Kough.

'His was just one of the bodies we pick up most mornings. Mr Watson should have known better than to be in that part of town by himself.'

Kough wanted help from the top. He phoned the Prime Minister's Office. He gave his name. A receptionist came back after several minutes: 'The Prime Minister says he does not know a Michael Krump. You can send him an email if you like. Do you know the address?'

Kough called the plant. The same woman answered; she sounded shaken. He asked for the new manager.

'No manager. Big fire in factory. Everyone go home. No jobs now.' The woman began crying.

'How did the fire start?' Kough wanted to know.

'Big flames just started. Lab all gone, all gone. No more jobs now.' The woman began sobbing uncontrollably.

Kough hung up and googled the non-emergency number for the Port Moresby fire brigade.

A man with an Australian accent answered. Kough explained he was a *Sydney Morning Herald* journalist seeking details on a big pharmaceutical factory fire in Port Moresby the previous night.

'Are you calling from Sydney? What's the weather like back home?'

Kough said: 'Lovely. And the humidity would be half what yours is.'

'No pain here, mate. We're air-conditioned. And just now it's actually working. Touch wood.'

'Good to hear. What happened at the factory? I understand the fire started in the labs and the place went up like a torch.'

'That's about it, mate. The cops said they arrested a couple of Chinese running away from the place after the fire started. These guys were quite badly burned. They reckoned something in the lab blew up before they could steal a few of the vaccine phials.'

'So, it's an arson job, you think?'

'No idea, mate. The burglars got nothing, so it's hard to say. Maybe something overcooked in the labs. Dunno. Just don't know. But the place was badly damaged. The owners are somewhere in Europe, Lichesterstine or somewhere.'

'Liechtenstein you mean?'

'Yeah, mate, something like that. We've sent them an email and told them the place is stuffed. Don't know what they're going to do about it. Hey. I've got to go. There's another fire out in Rascaland.'

As he hung up, Kough remembered old Tommy Watson had warned him of the crime rate and the constant break-ins. Watson had said he intended to install a special explosive device to wreck the lab if the Rascals broke in. Kough could not remember if Watson had ever reported the install had ever happened. It sounded, now, like it had.

Chinese burglars or Public Security thugs? Kough shuddered. The Public Security Bureau's noose was infamously worldwide. He felt his throat clench unconsciously.

He would have to make an effort to find Watson's Melbourne relatives and report his death. Big Brain was insisting Watson had been the victim of a hit man.

Street-hardened gangsters rarely had the finesse to put bullets cleanly into the foreheads of the hapless pedestrians they were shaking down. Kough refused to think about the implications of the murder.

He poured himself a big bourbon. He didn't worry about any ice. He sipped it: what now? The person most on his mind was now under the surveillance of the Chinese intelligence apparatus or ASIO. And there was Frank in the background. Not to mention the cuckolded Commander Dudley Hull who would now be wanting his wife back with Able out of the way.

With Kough it meant the world's most gorgeous woman had three suitors in her orbit. Give it away, Big Brain lectured. Be sensible. She was only a one-night stand. And the love of your best friend's life.

Big Brain gave up. Reasoning with the illogical love-struck was a futile exercise. Rational thinking went out the window. The only solution would be to mastermind an impossible plan to put Kough and Charlotte back in the same room.

TWENTY-FOUR

Charlotte Chen had no sense she was being tailed. Because she wasn't. The Chinese and Australian security services had separately placed GPS trackers under her Audi sports car. She never saw a vehicle following her – until tonight. A small, white Toyota had stayed in her rear-vision mirror from the moment she left her office car park.

She felt fear swell up in her swelling-up abdomen. She was on the edge of tears again. Her lover Michael Kough had vanished. Without a word. But she was pleased Johnny had been forbidden to continue their personal relationship. Her guilt when he was near her was overpowering, as was the fear she had for her aged Hong Kong parents.

The Toyota was getting very close. Her anxiety mounted as she approached her apartment building. She pulled into its underground car park, flashing her digital pass at the barrier control. It sprung up.

The Toyota behind her spurted forward, almost rear-ending her. The Toyota tailgated her down the ramp. She looked at the man behind the wheel. A hand went to her mouth and she gasped: it was Michael Kough.

He waved. It set her heart racing. She was not certain why. There were so many emotions in play. She steered the sports car into her park. The Toyota slid into one nearby, marked Maintenance Only.

Charlotte knew security cameras operated in the car park. She left the vehicle quickly. There was no time to lock it. She had to warn Kough not to acknowledge her.

He was opening his door. He looked up. She was striding towards him down a long row of vehicles towards the lifts. As she passed, she continued to look straight ahead. He heard her stage whisper: 'Don't say anything. Follow me.'

Kough took his time locking the Toyota. He pulled his cap low over dyed grey hair. He walked to the lift. It was chiming as Charlotte waited, deep inside it, holding down the Open Doors button.

He walked inside the lift without acknowledging her. The doors closed. They flung their arms around each other.

Charlotte felt tears of joy running down her face. They clung to each other and said nothing. The lift slowed at level five. Charlotte told him not to follow her. To ride the lift to the next floor and come back down the stairwell to apartment number four.

The lift doors reopened at the sixth level. When Kough stepped out, a Chinese man in a black suit confronted him: 'Ah, Dr Kough. We have been expecting you.'

Big Brain took over. Kough launched forward instantly and drove Black Suit into the opposite wall. His head struck the corner of a picture frame. Black Suit was shocked by the suddenness of the attack and the sharp blow to his skull.

He had been a picture of smugness only moments before, a gloating smile on his face and a small pistol in one hand.

Kough grabbed the hand holding the weapon and twisted sharply. Several of Black Suit's fingers, around the trigger guard, cracked loudly. Kough forced the pistol up and held it under Black Suit's chin. The man squeaked in fear.

Kough pulled the pistol free, creating more carnage with finger bones and cartilage, and smashed it across the side of Black Suit's head. His legs went out from under him and he fell heavily.

Black Suit was rolled face down and Kough sat on his spine, pinning him down. Kough removed the man's shiny shoes. He stripped off his socks and tied one pair around the would-be assailant's wrists. The second pair went around the ankles. He searched the pockets and found a bundle of tissues. He stuffed them into secret policeman's mouth.

He dragged him by the feet, face down, to the end of the corridor and onto the fire escape's concrete stairs. Thinking of Tommy Watson, he shoved Black Suit down the first flight. He then walked over the gasping, broken figure, and down to Charlotte's level. Her passageway was deserted.

Her door was open. He went inside. She was standing alone. She pointed to the ceiling. Microphones, Big Brain warned.

Kough took out his burner phone: 'I'd like to report a burglary in progress. Man on level six of the Dorian Apartments.' Kough broke the connection.

He pulled Charlotte towards him and whispered: 'The Chinese spooks are everywhere. We have to leave. Right now.'

She looked as though she was going to faint but followed him out the door and down the stairs. They reached the garage and took his car. As they emerged from the car park, they saw a tall white man in civvies running along the pavement towards them. ASIO surveillance, Kough thought. He turned in the opposite direction and accelerated away.

Charlotte sat pale-faced and silent. After a moment she put one hand lightly on his leg. A kilometre further on, the flashing lights of a squad car swept past going in the opposite direction.

'That's one Chinese spook that will have a lot of explaining to do.' Kough grinned; he was pleased with himself. He took the pistol he had grabbed from the Chinese spook from his belt. He passed it to Charlotte, who took it without comment.

The little Toyota cleared the suburbs and pointed its beak eastwards along the main highway.

Charlotte looked at the hoardings flashing past: 'Are we going to Sydney?'

'Woolloomooloo, actually.'

He gently covered the hand that she had rested on his leg.

Big Brain said: For heaven's sake, speak to her. She's worried sick about her parents. Kough took a breath: 'Don't worry about your mum and dad right now. The Chinese spooks will be very busy for a little while trying to explain to the Australian Federal Police what one of their agents is doing trussed up on The Dorian's back staircase.'

She giggled. It sounded odd that she was still able to be amused amid all the trauma: 'What did you do?'

He told her. She giggled again. Leaned over and kissed him on the cheek.

'And don't worry about Johnny and the PM's office. ASIO will assume you have been taken by the Chinese thugs.'

She sighed, put her head on his shoulder and fell asleep.

Big Brain was never happy. He was trying to scope out the next step. Kough was very happy. He had got one back for Tommy Watson and rescued his beautiful girl. And he had broken free of the noose. So far. He would worry about the next step when he needed to. Big Brain gave a weary sigh.

TWENTY-FIVE

It was a brief glimpse. Probably less than a second. The lighting was poor. But it froze Commander Dudley Hull in his tracks.

The little Toyota Prius flashed across the footpath and down to the basement garaging at the posh Woolloomooloo waterfront apartments, twenty metres from where he had been standing. He strode to the entrance, but a steel grid was already cranking down, sealing off the park.

Hull stood staring at the grid. Partly in disbelief, partly in shock. He had not seen his estranged wife while on active duty aboard HMAS *Sydney*. He was not sure the woman in the cheap car had been her. But something about her appearance ... something ... he didn't know what, made him believe it was Charlotte.

As an intelligence officer he knew accuracy was distorted by what witnesses wanted to see. And he had wanted to see Charlotte. But his heart had skipped a beat when the car sped past.

The next day his world came to a standstill. He was stood down from his duties. ASIO's liaison officer with naval intelligence reported a national search under way for his wife.

They had her listed as a possible Chinese agent because her parents had attracted the attention of the Public Security Bureau in Hong

Kong. His commanding officer said the circumstances made it impossible for him to continue his duties until Charlotte's situation was clarified.

ASIO believed rival groups of Chinese agents had clashed when they had both attempted to snatch her from her Canberra apartment.

One agent was found with a suspected broken back and neck on the rear stairwell. But there was no sign of Charlotte. Her sports car was found by police, unlocked in its apartment garage. Its engine was still warm.

ASIO believed its surveillance agent had arrived only seconds after she was whisked away. Ominously, she had gone without any personal belongings. Her phone at the PM's Office had been bugged, but her only Chinese-language conversations had been with her anxious parents.

She had told them repeatedly she had no idea where Michael Kough was. They pleaded with her to use her political contacts to find him. They feared jail.

Commander Hull was pleased with one snippet of intelligence. The blossoming relationship between Charlotte and the PM's chief of staff had been shut down.

With no duties, he began to walk the streets around Woolloomooloo. He knew them well. The navy had previously had a base in the suburb.

He never realised how many white Toyota Priuses there were in the city. They popped up to tease him with annoying frequency. Charlotte was in none of them.

In Beijing, President Fang was swallowing blood-pressure pills. His ordered autocracy was suddenly facing a shambles on several fronts. The capitalist media everywhere was mocking him over the Lifevac debacle, details of which had leaked through on to Chinese social media sites.

In response, he ordered the public sacking of several spy and diplomatic chiefs. It did not help. China remained without an effective vaccine against its Wuhan viruses and Chinese spies remained locked up in Australia and New Guinea. They faced a number of charges including attempted kidnapping and burglary.

The opportunity to reverse engineer what could have been Michael

Kough's anti-viral miracle drug had been lost when Chinese agents botched a break-in at his suspected Port Moresby pharmaceutical plant and had been arrested. Disastrously, a pistol found on one agent matched the murder weapon used to kill the plant's manager.

In Canberra, Chinese spies were under suspicion of kidnapping a senior member of the PM's Office. Details were sketchy but one bloodied Chinese agent with no diplomatic immunity was behind bars while the hunt for the missing victim redoubled.

Australians were already angry at China for sabotaging their economy through the new trade bans, which had triggered a sudden and vicious recession.

But what worried Fang the most was the sudden outbreak of a deadly new virus in the western regions. It spread fast and was more deadly than earlier Covid strains.

The rest of the country was bracing for the onslaught. China's vaccines had been next to hopeless. Fang had pinned his hopes on Lifevac. But the drunk, gambling addict Kough had duped him.

Kough had already made fools of the Americans, whose intelligence community was certain he had stolen the sensational new vaccine discovery from under their noses. Seventeen million Chinese were already caught up in the new virus tsunami and the death toll had topped two million.

The huge new vaccine factory constructed in three weeks to mass produce Lifevac was sitting idle, a testament, his critics said, to his inept leadership. The failed hunt for the fraudster Kough had been a further, exasperating embarrassment.

He now feared his son's boyfriend had been part of the fraud conspiracy. Dim Sim claimed to be totally cured of Covid after allegedly being hours from death when treated by Kough.

Ominously, his useless gay son was also under suspicion for his role in encouraging China to hand over a billion dollars for an untested drug.

The politburo was restive. He could feel his hold on power loosening.

TWENTY-SIX

Michael Kough rolled over and saw dawn was still half an hour away. He could hear Charlotte retching in the ensuite. The morning sickness had been constant.

She had refused his offers to find a doctor. She did not want to break security almost in the heart of Sydney. It had taken two days before she confessed to her pregnancy. He had been delighted and dismayed. He had had sex with her only once. But she was adamant it was his. A woman knew these things, she said.

Big Brain did not seem to care. He was working on a big, new, complicated step to freedom. And riches. The proposal popped out of the ether and on to John Able's screen. Minutes later the PM was reading it.

The proposal was in turn sent to President Fang. He signed it off. He did not bother to consult his restive politburo members. He believed the new initiative would slam-dunk them. They would be infuriated he had slipped off their sharpened hooks. He feared if he took the plan to them, they would prevaricate and the virus crisis would escalate. It was a risk he would not take.

The Sino-Australia Safevac joint venture would save millions of lives. Mass production of the miracle anti-viral vaccine would begin in both countries within three weeks.

And both countries would be authorised to supply other separate territories. China, elsewhere in Asia and Africa, Australia, the Americas, Western Europe and the Pacific.

The vaccine formula and patent would be held by the vaccine's inventor, virologist Dr Michael Kough.

The formula used to create the miracle vaccine would remain secret, and its final composition would be formulated by Kough alone, on a batch-by-batch basis.

China would only pay one dollar for each vaccine it administered to its own people. It could charge, however, whatever it chose in other countries.

Kough's royalty would be eight per cent on turnover and Kough would have his own financial auditors inside the China operation. The new vaccine would be branded Safevac. In Australia it would cost ten dollars an injection and be funded by the government. Its price offshore would be set by Kough.

All trade between Australia and China would reopen immediately. Stone and Fang would welcome another new era of peace and prosperity between their countries.

Kough had saved both leaders their jobs. And he knew it. Kough was given immunity from prosecution in Australia and China for fraud or any other possible illegal events involving Safevac activities anywhere in the world, and exemption from extradition to any country.

The small print, excluded from the public announcement, agreed Charlotte's parents would be given immediate political asylum in Australia.

In return, Australia would release, on humanitarian grounds, the injured Chinese secret agent charged over the attempted kidnapping of the vanished Charlotte Chen.

Papua New Guinea also agreed to free the Chinese thugs they held for the murder of Tommy Watson, the manager of the vaccine plant. Their release would coincide with a new one hundred-million-dollar Chinese foreign-aid package, authorised by Fang and to be supervised by the New Guinea prime minister.

John Able's career was intact, but he had been humiliated. The asylum clause for Charlotte's parents confirmed, to his friends and Stone, that he had been cuckolded. His best friend had betrayed him and stolen his woman. Literally. She had been hiding with Kough, in some secret love nest.

Able finally accepted he had lost Charlotte. He told his colleagues he had known about her situation with Kough all along. He had never had serious aspirations about her. She was too young and, well, his mother had not approved of their relationship. His mother was an old-school racist, he said.

Commander Dudley Hull also noted the clause with dismay. He seethed that he, too, had been cuckolded; his wife and her parents were all pawns in an international chess game, he thought.

A photograph of her new partner was spread over every newspaper, news site and television news programme. He was feted as a hero, the saviour of the country and millions of lives. And almost certain to be the richest man in the world. To Hull, Kough was a cunning, evil lab rat. There was only one sure way to deal with lab rats.

Charlotte Chen shed tears of joy when news of the Safevac deal broke.

Michael Kough was excited he would no longer have to live in hiding without the finer things of life. He immediately bought two big, politically incorrect, twelve-cylinder Rolls-Royce Phantoms. One for him. One for Charlotte. Big Brain rolled his eyes.

MICHAEL KOUGH CLOSED the apartment door with his foot and called out that he was home. There was no answer, but he heard movement from the master bedroom.

He dumped a large bag of groceries on the kitchen bench and began to unload some of them into the refrigerator. He had become quite domesticated since setting up home with Charlotte at Woolloomooloo.

The place was quiet. Charlotte usually had a television news channel chattering in the background. Kough went into the lounge and opened the bar. He began to make himself a bourbon and ice. He switched on the lounge television. A large photo of his face appeared along with a smiling prime minister. There was more movement from the bedroom.

Kough called out again that he was home. He sat in the deep lounge chair and sipped his drink. There was no reply. She must be in the shower, he thought.

He switched to another channel and enjoyed the taste of the bourbon. The Denver casino had converted him. He had been plied with countless free bourbons while his winning streaks lasted.

He swallowed the last of it and went back to the bar. He noticed, for the first time, Charlotte's red handbag lying open on the floor beside it. He frowned and bent down to pick it up. Several cosmetic items were strewn over the carpet next to it.

He felt the first tingling of anxiety. He listened. The burbling of the television anchors continued. The sounds from the passageway had stopped.

Outside, the last of the sun reflected on Sydney Harbour. Big steel ferries forged their way to and from the northern suburbs. He heard footsteps. Light ones. Charlotte's ones. He turned to welcome her. She was gagged and naked.

She was hurled bodily into the room. She crashed against a plant stand. It toppled, its large pot plant thudded to the floor, spilling earth on the rich, cream carpet.

Big Brain said, Leave her. Bolt for the kitchen. Get your pistol from the knife drawer.

An angry voice yelled: 'That's right. Run, you yellow prick. You won't get far. You see, Charlotte, I told you the guy's a feeble lab rat. What could you see in him?'

Kough grabbed the pistol. And a large carving knife. He yelled: 'Who the fuck are you?'

Hull guffawed: 'I'm the husband, mate. Just the husband. I've been enjoying my conjugal rights while you've been hobnobbing with your posh mates.'

Kough thought he heard Charlotte grunt through the gag. Conjugal rights? Kough thought. He's been raping her.

'So you're the brave Commander Hull.'

Kough heard another strained grunt from the lounge where she and Hull were out of line of sight.

'I didn't know you'd knocked her up. You're a fast mover, Lab Rat.'

'And you are meant to be an officer and a gentleman, Commander Hull. But you are a rapist. You'd better not have hurt Charlotte.'

'She's not hurt, Lab Rat. She likes a bit of the rough, as you would know. Wouldn't ya? Bloody surprised you've got her knocked up, though. I wouldn't have felt a casino lounge lizard like yourself would be capable.'

Decision time, Big Brain said. But we are not in New Guinea. Australia takes murder seriously. You don't want to be the richest man in prison the rest of your life. So let's use your pistol to scare him off.

Kough took a deep breath and stepped through the doorway into the lounge. Charlotte lay sprawled face down on the floor panting and weeping. Hull was standing behind her, a smirk on his arrogant face.

And a pistol in his hand.

A service gun, part of his military gear. I should have thought of that, said Big Brain. Never mind, when you put a bullet through his head it will be self-defence. If you get to shoot first.

Kough said: 'Char, are you all right?'

Hull laughed: 'Char? Char, is it? Trust a barbarian like a lab rat to ruin one of the most beautiful names in the English language. Her name is Charlotte, you fuckwit.'

Charlotte lifted her head. Tears ran down her face.

'Has he raped you, Char?'

Hull guffawed again: 'Raped? She's my bloody wife, you arse-wipe. I told you, she likes a bit of the rough.'

Kough snapped his pistol up. The bullet caught Hull in the throat. Blood pumped out of the wound like a red fountain. A look of surprise froze on his face. His legs buckled and he fell to the floor across Charlotte's legs. She screamed as she rolled away to free herself.

Kough grabbed Hull's weapon from the floor. Big Brain said, We don't want him alive.

Kough stood over him and pumped a bullet between his eyes.

But at the sound of shots, Charlotte's eyes opened like big saucers. She was still gagging from a pair of panties stuffed in her mouth.

Kough took them out and pulled her up under the armpits. He deposited her on the big sofa. She went white and began to shiver.

She's in shock, Big Brain said. Get a blanket and cover her.

Before he could leave, loud banging started at the front door. The noise the neighbours heard was a nail gun, said Big Brain. You're doing renovations. Apologise. And hurry.

The hammering on the door began again.

A small, elderly lady was standing in the doorway. Dyed blonde hair standing stiffly on her head. Kough apologised for the din and said the reno job was now over. He had put away his nail gun.

'Okay, luv. It's just that I got a fright. Sounded like one of old Bert's guns going off. Nice to meet you anyway.' She extended a skinny hand: 'I'm Martha. Just next door. You're not having a sundowner, are you?'

Kough reddened and became flustered: 'No, no Martha. My wife's pregnant so we've knocked off the booze.'

Martha beamed: 'Is your good wife in at the moment? Is she the lovely Asian lady I've seen in the garage?'

Kough shook his head too vigorously: 'No, sorry. I mean, yes. She is in ... but she's lying down right now. You know how it is?'

Kough could feel perspiration forming on his forehead. Of course, he thought, you could come in, if you would like to see the last of the blood spurting from a dying naval officer and the naked body of a rape victim.

Martha said: 'Yeah, I know what it's like. Had three of my own. Two died in a car crash, when they were eighteen. Twins they were. And my daughter married a plumber out Parramatta way, nice bloke though. It's funny how life turns out isn't...'

Kough nodded and began to close the door: 'Yes, it's funny all right. Sorry, Martha, but I really must go.'

'Okay, luv. I'll call the cops back and tell them it was just a nail gun. Bye for now, then.'

KOUGH BROUGHT a blanket from the bedroom, which looked like it had been hit by a wrecking ball. Charlotte must have put up a serious fight, he thought. He covered her body. She was still shaking and her skin had an unnatural sheen.

She put her arms around his neck: 'I'm so sorry, so sorry, Mikey. You were very brave. He deserved to die. He was the biggest mistake of my life. I thought he was a dashing officer but...'

'How did he find us?'

'I don't know but he was in here when I got back from my check-up.'

Kough carried her gently to bed in the guest room. There was another loud knock on the door. Kough jumped. His nerves were fraying. What if it was the police?

He went to the door. It was Martha, again. 'Just thought I'd let you know, luv. The police said thanks for letting them know.'

She paused in the doorway. Her neighbour was a nervous young man, she thought. His face looked familiar. Maybe he was on the telly or something. He nodded at her and gently closed the door.

There was a whiff of something in the air, she thought. Asians, they cooked funny-smelling food. She went back to her sundowner and turned the telly on. There was her neighbour filling the screen. He was a handsome cove in his own way. He was the vaccine miracle man. She had missed her big opportunity. Never mind, she'd go back tomorrow and visit him, maybe with a baby guide book.

TWENTY-SEVEN

BIG BRAIN BEGAN HIS BOSSING AGAIN. HE WANTED TO WAIT till it was dark to dispose of the body. But Kough did not want to drive his sports cruiser across the harbour in the dark, so he compromised: he would wait until twilight.

Meanwhile, he rolled the body up in a Persian carpet from a bedroom. Hull was not a big man. It made it possible to manhandle the package out on to his deck as the sun began to set, down some steps and onto his private dock.

There were certain to be security cameras, but his black coat was zipped to his neck and a softball cap covered his face.

He lowered the roll carefully across the stern passenger seats of the big, open cockpit of his boat. He feared the thin rope binding it would snap at any moment. It strained but it held.

He turned the starter key. The motor turned over but wouldn't start. He cursed and remembered the choke. He tried again. The motor turned over but still did not fire.

He looked around. A tubby, middle-aged guy in bowling whites was walking down the marina path towards him. Kough turned the key a third time. The motor spluttered but still did not start. He began to hyperventilate.

The bowler stopped at his marina berth. The boat's bow was

facing out, his duckboard only three metres from the interloper: 'Sounds like she's flooded, mate,' he offered cheerfully. Kough nodded. Fuck off, you old fool, or I'll be taking two bodies for a harbour ride.

'Just let it sit for a bit,' the bowler advised. Kough nodded again. 'New around here, are you?'

Kough nodded but said nothing. 'You're leaving it a little late to go fishing. High tide was an hour or so ago.'

Kough expelled a big lungful of air. The bowler sensed it was time to move on. It was a pity, as he wanted to ask about the rolled carpet on the stern seats. Never mind, Martha would have poured his sundowner by now. 'Righto, then. Tight lines, eh?' Kough nodded and the bowler wandered off.

Kough turned the key again. The motor coughed and started. He released the ropes and nosed out into the harbour. There were flashing buoy lights everywhere in the dusk. And yachts and ferries crisscrossing. What a bloody nightmare, he thought. Big Brain told him to cruise eastwards towards The Heads and open sea. But not to speed. There was some sort of speed limit in the inner harbour.

After five minutes of bumping and jarring over a short chop, the motor coughed, missed several times and died. The boat immediately swung beam on to the wind and chop and wallowed helplessly. Kough instantly felt queasy. He sucked in a deep breath and wondered where he had stowed his seasickness pills.

On the stern seat, the roll of Persian carpet holding Commander Hull began to rock with the boat. He turned the starter key, but knew before he did, the motor would not restart.

He saw two small cabin boats heading towards him. He became frantic. Big Brain told him to calm down. The boats were at least a kilometre away. Push the bloody body off the stern before you are caught with it.

Kough struggled for his balance as the boat bucked about. He eventually got his arms around the carpet and heaved it on to the gunwale. With a huge shove he pushed it over the side. It hit the water with a big splash – but stayed afloat. He felt a panic attack coming on and an urge to vomit.

One of the cabin boats changed course, directly towards him. It rushed up and the boatie hit reverse gear to pull up five metres short of him, sending up a spectacular fountain of prop spray.

'Ya broken down, mate?' The lone occupant wore a black, wife-beater T-shirt. There was a row of serious fishing rods in chrome holders lining the stern.

Kough said: 'Yeah. I was moseying along and hit this thing.' He pointed to the half-submerged roll. 'The engine just stalled. I nearly went through the windscreen.'

Not bad, Big Brain said.

'Okay, I'll give you a tow. We'd better put a rope around whatever that is in the water, or some other poor bugger may run into it,' T-shirt said.

Not good, Big Brain said. We have got to get rid of this do-gooder. The body would likely come out of the roll while it was being towed and, anyway, what would we do with it when we reached shore? The cops would be called. Then it would seriously hit the fan.

Get rid of the do-gooder? Kough shook his head. No way. I've already shot one person dead today. I'm not doing it again. And not to this guy, who's just stopped to help.

Big Brain sighed: I didn't say shoot him.

T-shirt flung a rope to Kough and told him to fasten it to a bow cleat. But Kough secured it to a side cleat. Then he began to pull the cabin cruiser towards him. T-shirt looked up in surprise: 'What the hell are ya doin'?'

Kough hauled the boat up beside his and said: 'Can you swim, mate?'

T-shirt frowned: 'Whataya mean?'

'I mean swim. Can you swim?'

'What the fuck are you up to, mate? Hey. What's with the gun, you crazy fuck?'

'I'm borrowing your boat. You are going for a swim. Don't make me put a bullet in you, mate. Blood will attract the sharks. They come from miles away at the smell of blood, as you would well know. You wouldn't want that, would you?'

Kough could feel the man thinking. How close was he to his throttle? Would the tow rope snap if he powered off? Could this nut case boat hijacker shoot straight?

Kough yelled: 'Time's up. Take a dive or a bullet.'

That was very macho, said Big Brain. I hope he jumps because it would be hard to shoot him with that short-barrelled pea-shooter from a rocking platform.

A stream of angry profanity poured from T-shirt. He removed his runners: 'I'll catch up with you, you mother fucker, and when I do...' Kough fired a shot over his head and the man jumped into the water and began to swim for the shore.

Kough pulled the boats close together and climbed into the cabin cruiser. The motor was still idling. He slipped the tow rope, put it in gear and headed toward Woolloomooloo, with no regard for the speed limits. The body was left, bobbing quietly in the water, as night fell.

The wind and tide swept his sports fisher swiftly seawards.

Kough beached T-shirt's boat a kilometre from his marina and ambled home, letting the stress drain from his mind and body. The apartment door was unlocked. He walked in and called out. There was no reply.

He went quickly past the bloodstained carpet to the master bedroom. It was empty. He searched every room. Charlotte was gone.

He sat on the floor beside their bed, his head in his hands, and quietly wept.

Ten minutes later there was a knock on the door. He leapt up. It was Martha: 'Oh, hello, luv. You were out, so I just came to tell you that your lady was taken to hospital a little while ago, by ambulance, poor darling.'

She paused and sighed: 'I didn't want to be the one to tell you, luv, but it seems she suffered a miscarriage. I think it happened in your lounge. The ambos said there was a lot of blood on the floor there.'

Oh God. What next in this day of trauma? Kough thought. He sagged against the wall and shook his head as he took in the news. He wished Charlotte's parents had arrived from Hong Kong, but they were still days away.

'I'm sorry, luv. You aren't looking well, luv. Shall I come in and make you a nice cup of tea, luv?'

Kough blanched: 'Oh, no. No. I mean, sorry, I mean, I'll be fine ...

no need for a cup of tea, thanks all the same. I've got to see Charlotte. What hospital did they take her to?'

'Charlotte,' said Martha, 'such a lovely name. I think it was St Vincent's in Darlinghurst, luv. Bert's back from his bowls. He could give you a lift if you like. Are you all right, luv? You just went quite white. Sure you don't want a cup of tea?'

Kough shook his head and stood up straight: 'That's a very kind offer but I'll be fine. I'll call the hospital now. Thank you, Martha, thank you.' He politely began to shut the door and Martha gave him a pitying smile before walking away.

Charlotte had lost their child. The rape by her husband and his murder by Kough shortly after had traumatised her. Not that she told the doctor any of the details. Kough brought her home the next morning. She was a pale and exhausted figure lying in their big bed. Kough was not in much better shape. And his nerves were shredded when he saw online the front page of the *Sydney Morning Herald*.

NAVY SPY MURDERED. BODY DUMPED MAFIA STYLE IN HARBOUR INSIDE ROLLED CARPET
KILLER HIJACKED RESCUE BOAT AT GUNPOINT. GOOD SAMARITAN FORCED TO SWIM FOR HIS LIFE.

Big Brain said, The lounge carpet must go. Get a big knife and rip it all up. If necessary, tell the neighbours it is part of your renovation project.

And call the police and report your boat has been stolen. Most importantly, stay the hell away from neighbour Bert, who saw you – and the carpet roll – on your boat about to head off to sea. He poses a huge threat, so he has to be dealt with. Not killed or anything dramatic. Just moved. Safevac should make him an absurdly high offer for his apartment.

TWENTY-EIGHT

The hollow voice on the intercom introduced itself as Detective Roger Rougess. Kough buzzed him in.

Moments later Rougess was at the door. He looked to be in his early sixties, his face a study of crinkles and deep lines below a balding head. A face cooked in the Australian sun, Kough thought. The deep blue eyes had probably seen enough bad stuff for several lifetimes, but they were bright and alert. He wore a brown, misshapen suit with a yellow, patterned tie. Kough's heart sank. A friendly, veteran copper was the most dangerous of his species.

He led the detective to his study, avoiding the lounge.

'You reported your fishing boat stolen, Mr Kough. Did you see anything suspicious on the marina last night?'

Here we go, thought Kough, and braced himself: 'No, nothing at all. I didn't even notice it missing until this morning.'

Rougess nodded: 'Even though it's tied up, right outside your apartment?'

'My wife and I had a traumatic night, last night. She … er … um … lost our first baby. She miscarried in our lounge. I only brought her back from hospital this morning.'

'Sorry to hear that, Mr Kough.'

Rougess folded his legs, revealing orange socks and scuffed black shoes: 'Your neighbour saw a tall man on your boat early last night. He had trouble starting it. Your neighbour said there was a carpet rolled up on the rear bench seat. So, we think it was your boat that went to sea, to dump the body of a naval intelligence officer that was in the news this morning, a Commander Hull.'

'Holy shit,' Kough said.

'Do you use the boat much yourself, Mr Kough?'

'Not as much as I thought I would, no.'

'Does it give much mechanical trouble?'

'No, it's been very reliable.'

Rougess sat back and said casually: 'I'm a little intrigued ... you haven't asked where your boat is right now and what sort of condition it's in?'

Kough swallowed. Rougess *was* dangerous.

'I've had other things, like my wife's miscarriage, on my mind, as I told you, detective.'

'Call me Roger, Mr Kough.'

'I'm Michael.'

Rougess nodded: 'Yes, I know. You've been all over the telly and the papers. Saving the world from all accounts. And there are rumours among us plods that you're very good with a pistol. Got two Chinese between the eyes.'

'I ... ah ... I'm not allowed to discuss that ... a matter of national security.'

'National security? Okay, okay. You weren't surprised when I named the victim. It hasn't been released yet. Did you know Commander Hull?' He smiled: 'Or is that a matter of national security as well? Do you own a pistol of your own, Michael?'

Kough said no. But immediately realised he had paused for a half second before answering. Big Brain sighed, you're in trouble buddy.

Rougess stretched his arms over his head and yawned: 'Do you mind if I take a look around?'

'Don't you need a warrant to do that?'

Rougess rubbed his nose: 'I can get one, if you like, Michael.'

'Why would you want to search my place?'

Rougess said: 'Because right now I'm afraid you're our chief murder suspect. We think it was your boat that had the dead man on board. And a tall man, about your height, in dark clothes and a cap was seen in your boat. Not to mention the CT cameras that picked up something being loaded on to it – but not fishing rods. The CT cameras show no one came in to the marina from the main entrance at the time in question. That means the tall man was already inside the marina, most likely a resident.'

An awkward silence grew between the two. Finally, Rougess asked quietly: 'Do you have an alibi for last night, Michael, between six and ten? Did you go in the ambulance with your wife? Did you meet the medical staff attending to your wife?'

Big Brain had deserted him. He looked out at the breathtaking harbour view.

'I think I should get a lawyer, Detective Rougess. And you should get a search warrant.'

Rougess eased himself up: 'Okay, son. I'll be back in a couple of hours with a warrant. I'll leave a constable outside your door.'

He extended a hand: 'Do you already have a lawyer, Michael?'

Big Brain reappeared with a suggestion. Kough said: 'No. I'll have to consult the PM's Office before I appoint one.'

For the first time Rougess lost his air of nonchalance. He frowned, then nodded: 'Well, I'll be getting along. I have to have a chat with your mate, Bert, next door. Then I'll be back. My commiserations to your wife. Charlotte Chen, isn't it?'

Kough went to stand up and stumbled.

'You all right, Michael?'

'Yes, yes. Bit tired after last night, that's all.'

Rougess smiled. 'That is perfectly understandable, after what you went through. I'll organise my sergeant to take down your formal statement later this afternoon. Can you show me out? This pad of yours is huge. A man could get lost.'

'Johnny, you've got to help me.'

John Able recognised Michael Kough's voice immediately. He casually put both feet on his desk and leaned back: 'Boffy, help you? I wouldn't piss on you if you were on fire.'

'I'm afraid it'd take an even bigger hose than your tigger to put out this inferno.'

Able scoffed: 'What sort of cock-up have you got yourself into now? Shot a jealous husband?'

Kough did not answer. Big Brain was no help.

'Cat got your tongue, Mikey? Well, I don't care what pile of crap you've now got yourself into. You won't be getting me involved in it this time.'

Kough still made no reply.

'Okay, nice to talk to you Mikey but I'm a busy man. Say hi to Charlotte for me, will you?' Able gave a mocking laugh. 'Still all sweetness and light on the Hong Kong front, is it?'

'Before you hang up, Johnny boy, you need to make a decision: help me – or Australia goes down the drain.'

'You are a mad bastard, Boffy. What the hell are you on about now? The China deal is done and dusted, and you'll get your billions.'

'Johnny boy, there's a Detective Roger Rougess who will be arresting me for murder, probably in the next couple of hours. And, just to jog your memory, if I'm not around to complete each Safevac vaccine consignment, supply comes to a standstill. And so does your China deal.

'Not to mention there'll be lots of bodies piling up around the world without Safevac available. Believe me, if I'm in prison I won't be making up any more batches of the vaccine. Why would I? Have I got your attention now, Johnny boy?'

Able took his feet off the desk and hunched forward: 'Why would anyone be arresting you for murder?'

'Because I shot someone last night and dumped their body in Sydney Harbour. It's in all the papers.'

Frank whistled. 'Why the hell did you do that?'

'The guy raped Charlotte. I came back to the apartment and her charming husband had just done the job and had a gun to use on me. I beat him to it and put a couple of bullets into him. The last one in the head. Charlotte saw the whole thing, went into shock and lost the baby she was carrying.'

Able sat still and processed what he had been told. He said: 'But it'll be self-defence, if the husband turned up with a gun.'

'Maybe, but I wasn't going to risk the cops, or anybody, believing our story, so I decided to get rid of Commander Hull. Even if the cops believed it was self-defence, they'd charge me for trying to dispose of the body. And Charlotte would end up inside too, on conspiracy charges. I'm not going to have that happen.'

Able said the murder investigation was a New South Wales state matter. The federal government had no jurisdiction.

'Bullshit, Johnny boy. The Federal Government has jurisdiction because we're talking about a national security matter concerning the country's critical relations with our biggest trading partner. If it's not, Gary Stone will soon make it one.'

Able said it was not the way the system worked. Any decision on Kough would be made by the NSW Police Commissioner. And there were no grounds to drop the charge against Kough for trying to dump the body. There were also charges of attempted murder to consider: Kough had fired at the man trying to rescue him, and forced him overboard, a long way from shore.

Able demanded Kough's cellphone number and said not to call anyone or discuss the case with anyone, particularly Detective Rougess.

'Okay, thanks, Johnny. I appreciate it,' said Kough.

'Fuck off,' said Able. 'I'm not doing it as a favour to you. Or your girlfriend.' He broke the connection.

NEWS that the billionaire anti-viral hero Michael Kough was the perpetrator of the Sydney Harbour mafia-style killing ran through the law enforcement and security world like a crack of lightning.

Prime Minister Gary Stone knew the thunderclap had to be managed somehow. He cursed Kough. And then decided to bypass protocol and call the NSW police commissioner, Herbert Donkin, personally.

Stone wanted Donkin to call off the dogs and accept Kough had been acting in self-defence. His attempt at a cover-up by dumping Dudley Hull's body was the act of a stressed man, pushed over the edge. A jury would free him.

But Donkin had already been fully briefed by his most experienced murder detective, Roger Rougess. The veteran painted Kough as too smart, too rich, too dishonest and too dangerous to be let loose on society. He believed Kough was a law unto himself and sheltered behind the power of men like the prime minister.

Rougess was also determined to keep arrogant, overpaid glamour-boy federal spooks from taking over his case.

Rougess did not dwell on the treatment of the 'good Samaritan' who was forced to swim several kilometres, on an outgoing tide, to survive.

Because the Samaritan was the boss of the notorious drug-distributing Dirty Dogs motorcycle gang. Most coppers would have thanked Kough for almost drowning the prick. But that was not the point. It could have been any innocent boatie.

The incident proved Kough suffered severe mental instability, Rougess believed. His attack on the Chinese flag was an example of his rash, crazy behaviour. His genius IQ was a probable clue to his living on the spectrum or with a personality disorder. He had earned and lost millions gambling and had conned and robbed a succession of victims.

It was time to hold him to account. And the Commissioner felt his much-maligned, and often corruption-tainted, NSW cops were the people to do that.

Stone finally found Donkin at a training retreat in the Blue Mountains, finding his inner, inclusive self along with a group of short-haired females who oversaw the police department's human resources team.

Stone smiled to himself trying to imagine the tough-talking, beer-swilling commissioner in such company.

'Sorry to interrupt your touchie-feelie time, Herbie, but I've got quite a situation riding on this crazy fuck Kough,' Stone said.

Donkin laughed: 'Yeah, I've been told all about your mad scientist. I hope you don't want me to pull the case; he deserves a long spell in the loony bin.'

'He probably does but the mad fuck has got the keys to the kingdom.'

Stone explained that Kough was the only individual who could concoct the Safevac vaccine. Scientists in Australia and China had been unable to reverse engineer it. Without the vaccine deal, China could pull the trade plug a third time and plunge Australia back into a depression.

Donkin was silent for some time.

'Gazza, if I shut down the case, this whole affair will blow sky high. I'm sure my best detective will take an early retirement and go public.'

Stone said: 'Herbie, you have to convince him that we hate the idea of letting Kough off, but it's for the good of the country. And convince him that his talents are urgently needed for greater things as he ends his distinguished career,' said Stone.

'What greater things?'

'The chairmanship of the National Crime Prevention Commission Inquiry. It'll be based where he lives, in Sydney, and the chairman's remuneration package will be worth seven hundred thousand. The inquiry's final report is expected to take five years to complete. And, Herbie, it will need someone with your experience to act as its consultant for, say, two hundred grand a year.'

Donkin said nothing.

Stone waited patiently.

Finally, Donkin said: 'Well, I suppose it would be in the best interests of the country...'

'Absolutely, Herbie. The cost to Australia otherwise would be measured in misery and poverty for millions of us. Tell your best detective that Kough will be quietly arrested by ASIO and kept out of harm's way.

'Rougess knows the murder was really an act of self-defence and dumping the body was to protect his partner against the publicity of her rape ordeal and the miscarriage of her baby. It will sell well among the woke you have to deal with in the leafy suburbs, and a jury will never convict him. Not to mention he's a national hero in the eyes of so many people.'

Donkin said: 'Okay, okay, enough. Leave it to me. If he doesn't agree, I'll send him on a ten-year retreat to study diversity in the workplace. But Gazza, seriously, if this entitled scumbag Kough ends up killing or robbing anyone else, I don't want to be the fall guy. You need to get him under control.'

TWENTY-NINE

THE ROARING MOTORCYCLES SUDDENLY SURROUNDED THE Rolls-Royce. The deafening roar from their exhausts shattered the cocoon of serenity in the Phantom. The bikes slowly came to a halt, trapping the Rolls on the inside lane of the busy Parramatta Highway.

Michael Kough was puzzled, not frightened, by the appearance of the filthy, bearded desperadoes and their revving polished bikes.

'Lock the doors,' Kough told the driver.

'They lock automatically when your wheels roll,' the driver said. He looked around nervously, trying to find an opening in the leather-jacketed cavalcade to escape through. There was none. He was mollified that these tattooed animals would be after his boss, not him.

Kough sat in the locked two-and-a-half tonne Rolls and dialled the emergency police number. He counted sixteen bikes. As the call was answered, an axe come through his side window.

A shower of tiny glass splinters burst into the cabin. A tattooed hand reached in and expertly unbuckled him and pulled at the internal door handle. Kough was suddenly hauled out and left sprawled and shocked on the hard road.

Two foul-smelling men dragged him a couple of metres and tossed him through the open back doors of a black Mercedes panel van. He landed unceremoniously with a crash, and the doors were slammed. The van had no back windows. He sat in total darkness.

A voice sniggered: 'Time's up. Do you want a bullet or a swim?'

Big Brain woke. This is your black T-Shirt mate, buddy. The one you sent on a marathon swim, when you stole his cabin cruiser.

The voice asked: 'How come the cops haven't locked you up and thrown away the key?'

A weak internal light came on. T-shirt, now wearing leathers, was smiling and pointing a pistol at him.

Big Brain said, You said this guy was a do-gooder. So wrong, buddy, he is a big-time crim. The Dirty Dogs patch is on all of them. The Dogs are the biggest drug distributors in NSW.

That's good, thought Kough. We'll be able to buy our way out of this little trouble. But his optimism was dispelled when T-shirt waved his gun: 'Feelin' like a little dip in the harbour, are ya? Temperature's not bad at the moment. Can you swim?' T-shirt broke into uproarious laughter.

Kough said: 'What?'

T-shirt pushed a hand through his long, greasy hair: 'I said, can you swim?'

Kough said: 'Okay, you've had your fun. How much?'

'What? We haven't had any fun at all yet. Don't get impatient, Dr Kough, Miracle Man.'

Kough went to sit up. T-shirt said: 'Stay where you are, you prick. I don't want to have to shoot you. You know how blood attracts the sharks.' He broke up in laughter again. Two other men sitting in the front seats joined in.

The van moved off. Kough could not see where it was heading. After about fifteen minutes of being slung about in the rear, the van stopped. The rear doors opened. He recognised Double Bay. And saw a fleet of moored boats bobbing with the northerly wind.

Big Brain said not to make another payoff offer. These animals wanted to extract some pain with their vengeance. Kough went numb. He thought: There must be something we can do. Big Brain said, Yeah, swim, buddy.

'I should have just put a bullet through your ugly head,' said Kough.

T-shirt nodded: 'You're right there, sunshine. When you get out, walk between us. If you try and get smart, I'll put a bullet in your left leg. Don't think any of these posh Double Bay people around here will try to rescue you. They're posh, not dumb.'

Kough was helped out. The van was facing a short wharf. A four-metre cabin boat was rocking at the end of it. The group walked to it and Kough was ordered to step aboard.

Three Dirty Dogs surrounded him in the stern. The fourth stood at the helm. The boat slipped its ropes, reversed, turned and headed out into the harbour. None of the Dogs spoke. They smoked reefers and let the wind buffet their oily hair. Kough sat terrified. Big Brain was as quiet as a hibernating grizzly.

The helmsman seemed to know where he was going. The boat sped on for what seemed an eternity. The Double Bay boats shrank in the distance.

The engine was cut. The boat edged beam on to the light northerly. The sea was calm; there were no white caps.

T-shirt opened a fishing tackle box and took out a knife. Fragments of chopped-up bait clung to its blade.

Kough glanced about. The nearest land seemed to be an impossible distance away.

'Okay, give me your right arm.'

'What the hell are you going to do. What's the knife for? Christ!' Kough tried to reel back but nearly tipped over the side. When he regained his balance, T-shirt said: 'I just thought we'd spice things up a little bit.'

T-shirt grabbed his arm. He turned it wrist up and grinned: 'Just a little cut. Just to keep you concentrating on swimming as fast as you can.'

The Dogs all laughed and did high-fives. One shared around bottles of beer.

'Better strip everything off, Dr Kough, Miracle Man. Give yourself a fighting chance,' T-shirt said, and took a slug from his bottle.

Kough stripped. The Dogs had not realised how well built Kough was. 'Okay. Doctor, time's up,' said T-shirt. 'Take a dive or a bullet.' He nearly choked laughing.

When he had wiped his eyes, he stood, pointed the bait knife at Kough: 'Okay. Off you hop.'

Big Brain said: Go. The harbour is calm, you have an incoming tide and flat water. No begging or grovelling. We fucked China over, remember? We can do this.

Kough stood on the side and made a perfect, Olympic-class dive into the water. The Dogs cheered and clapped. The cold water shocked Kough. He began to swim.

Downwind from the boat he began to smell the weed his kidnappers had lit up. The boat was drifting slowly with him in the northerly. He swam steadily on, and on, and on. No other boats came near. He tried to ignore his bleeding wrist and swam doggedly straight ahead. He took his bearings from several large apartment buildings on the shore.

He lost track of time. His lungs began to burn. His muscles ached with the ordeal.

He was close to the shoreline. He could hear and see vehicles and dog walkers. He saw an unused buoy bobbing nearby and made for it. He clung on, panting hard, exhausted.

His feet touched the seabed.

And felt a sense of exhilaration. He had survived. He looked around and his high spirits sank. His tormentors were idling up to him. They were laughing and clapping and drunk.

T-shirt reached out and grabbed an arm. A second Dog grabbed the other arm. With a lot of gasping and heaving, they hauled him over the side of the boat. He fell to the floor shivering and panting.

'Did you see the shark?' T-shirt wanted to know.

'What shark?'

The Dogs all burst into laughter.

'Don't worry about it. We got a video of it. We'll play it for you when we get back to HQ. Bloody funny. It'll give the boys a good laugh.'

Kough was given a large brandy from a filthy red plastic mug. And an oily towel which had come from under the floorboards to wipe himself down. He put his clothes back on, which eased the shivering. As he buttoned his coat, he felt something in a pocket. He kept his hands out of the pocket, but he was sure the Dogs had forgotten to toss his cellphone into the sea.

The cabin cruiser finally docked. He saw the black Mercedes van waiting on the shore by the wharf. There's more to come, he thought. Big Brain said nothing.

KOUGH'S BLINDFOLD was gently removed. As he blinked against the new light of the Dirty Dogs' HQ, he recognised the woman before him: one of the Suzies he knew so intimately from the King's Cross massage parlour.

His face lit up at the sight of the petite Chinese masseuse who could use her mouth expertly to attach a condom on her clients. She grinned, a little professional grin, and pretended not to recognise him. Suzie's Massage Parlour was obviously one of the Dogs' businesses, Kough realised.

He was in a large, ill-lit room. Large billiard tables were scattered about, very big television screens dominated the walls, framed copies of their criminal rampages that had made page-one stories took pride of place above a bar that stretched along most of one wall.

There were half a dozen green-topped card tables. And, in one corner, a full-sized roulette table. The Dogs were clearly doing well, Kough thought. A collection of small video screens were mounted near the main doorway at the end of bar, showing every approach to the building. A car park, at the rear, boasted a big collection of souped-up muscle cars and a small row of motorcycles.

T-shirt was surrounded by several oversized lieutenants. He heard them call him Daggers. Several parcels and a briefcase, packed with hundred-dollar notes, exchanged hands. He heard a bearded man ask who would be first with the Chink chick.

Daggers said he might go first, he wasn't sure, so keep it cool. The man was philosophical about waiting his turn but wanted to know if it would be done on a billiard table again, so all the boys could watch. Daggers stood up without answering. The lieutenants drifted to the bar. Daggers strolled over to Kough.

'Do ya feel like a hand of poker or a root, after that little swim?'

He pointed to the Suzie who was delivering a tray of drinks to the roulette wheel. 'We've got her for the night. Bit of a bonus for the boys. We've had a big week, so I thought...'

Sex on a billiard table, cheered on by Sydney's biggest drug gang, thought Kough. The Dogs were hospitable, if they were not trying to drown or stab you.

Kough said: 'I think I'll pass on the root, thanks. But what's the limit on your poker game?'

'Limits are for pussies. How much have you got in that suit?'

Kough said he had nothing. Had not carried cash for years: 'There're a lot of crooks about, you know.'

Daggers gave a short laugh: 'Not around here there's not. It's a crime-free area; it's very well policed.' He laughed again.

He said the Dogs played five-card stud, show poker. He led Kough to a table where three others were playing amid a cloud of smoke. Daggers peeled off a wad of hundred-dollar notes. 'I'll stake you. Here's two thousand.'

Kough shook his head: 'I won't need that much.'

Daggers lifted an eyebrow but said nothing. He cut the wad in half and handed it to Kough. They both sat at the table. Daggers introduced him to Petey, Rock and Spud.

Petey said: 'Played a bit, have ya?'

'No. I'm more a roulette sort of guy – but I like poker.'

All four grunted and Petey dealt the cards. After half a dozen hands, Big Brain had memorised and sorted the tells and the style of the four players. Daggers was a little harder to read, but he was inclined to bluff when he had next to nothing. As a good guest, with dangerous strangers, and watching and learning, Kough lost all the first hands.

Then he doubled his bet against Spud's hand. The others grinned and paid a good price to see Kough's hand. It was a straight, king high.

There was a grim hush as Kough pulled the pot in. He made a mad bluff, the next hand, to make sure he lost spectacularly. Even Daggers smiled and took his winnings. But in the next half a dozen hands, he took all their money. It was too simple.

Kough counted out a thousand dollars and repaid Daggers who took the money without comment. He had needed to top up his cash pile.

Petey sat back: 'I think we need to cut a new pack.'

'What's wrong with this one?' said Kough.

No one said anything. A new pack was opened. Big Brain said it was time to go. They think you're cheating, but they don't know how.

Kough played two more hands and won another three thousand. He looked at Daggers: 'Shall we try the roulette table?'

Daggers looked wary. Kough said: 'No pussy limit on the table, I take it?'

Daggers said nothing. He nodded to the others and stood: 'No, no limit on the table. But no credit either.'

Kough said: 'That's fine. I won't need any credit.'

Daggers' eyes narrowed. He sensed trouble. He relaxed at the thought that no one beat the table.

Kough watched the wheel carefully. The table had been professionally installed but there was a definite, minor bias to the wheel's balance revealed over a number of spins. The numbers in that quadrant were consistently paying.

They all played and Spud and Rock had a couple of good collects. Kough played the corners around the top-left numbers and collected several modest returns. The atmosphere was relaxing when Big Brain suggested all in on number seventeen.

Kough scooped up all his chips and piled them on the number. The others scratched their heads and stood back as the marble flew around the wheel at a dizzying speed. Several placed bets. Small ones. The marble spun and bounced and plopped firmly on number seventeen.

Daggers swore. The others shook their heads. The payout on such a high-risk bet was thirty-six to one. The croupier tallied Kough's chips. He had bet eight thousand dollars and won two hundred and eighty-eight thousand. The croupier looked at Daggers uncertainly.

Daggers said: 'Dr Kough, the house is happy if you want to double up.'

Kough pretended to be uncertain. Gave an 'aw shucks' shrug of the shoulders and nodded casually.

Every gangsta on the floor was drawn to the table like pieces of iron to a magnet. There was a lot of whispering and shaking of heads. Daggers was a courageous cunt, they thought. The house risked a payout of almost six hundred thousand dollars.

The croupier spun the wheel and called for bets. No one pushed any chips forward. The wheel seemed to have an energy of its own and ran on for an age. Eventually the marble lost its momentum and began its dance across the wire slots before plopping delicately onto number seventeen. Again.

The croupier looked nervously at Daggers. The grimy, bearded face of the feared crime boss reddened. He felt dozens of eyes on him.

Kough turned and said to the croupier: 'I'll go and get a drink while you sort things out.'

The bar was deserted because everyone was at the roulette table. So Kough leaned on it and looked up at the HQ's security monitors. He saw black uniformed police with automatic rifles, half crouched, picking their way silently forward. There goes my six hundred thousand, he thought. Big Brain said here comes the cavalry, just in time to save your life. Daggers was in a tense conversation with his lieutenants and the worried croupier.

KOUGH STRODE over to the Suzie. He told her to drop her tray and go to the restroom. To get out of the rear window and run like hell. Her lips wobbled and then she hurried away.

Kough went back to lean on the bar just as the doors at each end of the HQ were violently smashed open and a surge of black uniforms ran in. A rattle of automatic fire floored two Dogs who went for their handguns. The rest obeyed instructions and lay face down on the floor.

Frank Church casually sidled up to Kough, who was still standing at the bar. Kough said: 'You took your time. I wondered why they called you Flash Frankie. It's because you're so bloody slow. Another few minutes and I would have been dog tucker, forgive the pun.'

'I'm going to have to cuff you, for appearances' sake,' Church said. 'It would help your future survival chances with this ugly mob if you attempted to resist arrest and mouthed some appropriate profanities. I presume the Dogs owe you a fortune, if your recent luck is anything to go by.'

'Nearly six hundred thousand.'

Kough looked over the prostrate bodies and screamed: 'Fuckin' cops. This is a private club. Get the fuck out of here you sad motherfuckers.'

Church pushed him quickly towards the door: 'Okay, don't overdo it, Kough. Keep moving, we need to get out of here. Lady Luck was looking after you today. Your cellphone battery we were tracking went as dead as a dodo just as we arrived.'

Outside on the street there was enough light coming from the roofs of scores of police cars and vans to illuminate a night cricket match.

Kough was put in the back seat of a big limo. Church got in beside him: 'We had an easy ride in. The Dogs have cameras everywhere. Why wasn't anyone watching the monitors?'

Kough said: 'I gave them something better to watch.' Big Brain sighed, stop, stop, no one likes a show-off.

He grinned at Church: 'I was about to go first with sex on the billiard table with a girl named Suzie.'

Church rubbed his nose: 'Christ, you're full of shit. Were you? Really?'

THIRTY

Michael Kough was helming his sixty-five-metre ketch, *The Miracle*, in a light south-easterly breeze, when he got the call. It was a stunning, hot day off the Far North Queensland coast. In the two years since Safevac had been in legitimate operation, his income had gone from the millions to the tens of millions, to the hundreds of millions.

The abundance of riches had calmed Kough and Big Brain was mostly idle. Charlotte had returned from her parents' home after fleeing the trauma of her rape and miscarriage.

She was on the bow with their new son, Michael Chen, and Mei, her psychologist mother. Her elderly father, Lei, was in the vast saloon downstairs watching horse racing beamed from Hong Kong.

The Safevac plant in west Parramatta was producing hundreds of thousands of vaccines each month. The Chinese one in Shanghai was bigger and made twice as many. Their partnership had gone well after its tumultuous beginning.

Kough checked the caller identification number. It began with a plus six one. Australian. But no name displayed. Kough was too chilled out to be annoyed. So, he took the call. And his world capsized.

Mr Hai Sile was with International Underwriters and wanted to check on the insurance cover of Safevac's Parramatta factory.

Kough said he did not have a clue about things like insurance cover. Hai should call his administration department. Hai said he had. The building's cover was only one million dollars. There was no loss-of-profit insurance in case of a fire. Kough saw the foresail luff and moved the helm over a fraction to fill it.

'I am sure you would understand, Mr Hai, these are not matters that I handle directly. Can I ask how you got my number?'

Hai ignored the question. 'So, you are perfectly satisfied with your coverage, Dr Kough? Would you like to give some thought to it, and I can call you back later?'

The foresail luffed again. Kough could see the crew beginning to look at him. He needed to concentrate and keep the sail full. He had not realised the breeze was swinging more to the north-east.

'Sorry, Mr Hai, you need to call my office if you want to discuss insurance matters. Bye.' He ended the call hurriedly to concentrate. He changed the ketch's bearing and the foresail filled and smoothed out. He could feel the big vessel heel a fraction and build speed.

Just after sunset his accountant called in a fluster. An explosion had set off a fire at the northern end of the Parramatta factory. A dozen appliances were attempting to control the conflagration, and the seven hundred staff had been safely evacuated. Production had, naturally, been halted.

The fire had ripped through the vaccine's vital cold-storage facilities. It would be pointless to restart production until they were replaced because Kough insisted the vaccine be warehoused at ten degrees Celsius.

Charlotte appeared beside him. Her beautiful face was a picture of anguish: 'Mikey, your factory is on television down in the saloon. It's on fire. Smoke is billowing over half of Sydney.'

'I know, Char, I've just had a call from the office.'

Charlotte put her arms around his neck as he pointed the ketch into the bay where they would overnight. The skipper came forward: 'Dr Kough, let me take it from here. I think right now you have other matters to deal with.'

Kough gave him the helm and stepped away to hug his wife. 'Things were going so well,' she said.

Kough embraced and kissed her: 'It's only a fire, Char. We'll sort it out and be back in production soon.' She pulled back and smiled at him. His phone chimed. He opened it. It was the accountant again: 'I don't know how to tell you this, Dr Kough.'

'What?' Kough hissed.

'It seems we have no fire insurance. Someone went to our insurers yesterday and cancelled the policy. I don't know what's going on. When I called them today, the insurers said they had been sorry to lose our business, but right now they're over the moon about it, as you can imagine.'

The main meal was being served in the dining room when Kough's phone rang again. He sighed. He had asked for a full damage assessment as soon as possible so he took the call.

'Kough.'

'Ah, Dr Kough. It's Hai Sile. I promised I would call you back to see if you had given some more thought to your fire cover.'

Kough leapt to his feet. His in-laws looked startled and his new son got a fright and began to cry: 'Who the fuck are you? If you had anything to do with today's fire, I'll find you and shoot you in the balls ... your death will be slow and painful.'

Hai laughed. 'You won't have any difficulty finding me, Dr Kough. I can be at your offices anytime tomorrow and arrange for the rest of your factory to be properly covered.'

Kough strode out of the dining room: 'You come anywhere near my factory and I'll cut your balls off, you scumbag.'

Mr Hai laughed again: 'Oh, so it's knives now, not guns?'

Big Brain appeared from nowhere. It was a good idea to meet him. Get him to fly north to their Port Douglas marina.

Hai quickly agreed to the meeting. Before the call ended, he said: 'And do you have a full cover on your other property, the big place at Woolloomooloo, for instance, and your yacht?'

Big Brain told him to keep calm. Kough said: 'Maybe I should be asking you, Mr Hai. Do I?'

Hai said cheerfully: 'Don't worry, Dr Kough, I'm sure they're safe right now.' Hai broke the connection.

THIRTY-ONE

The Miracle was nosing into the marina in Far North Queensland's Port Douglas when fire alarms began their painful, high-pitch screeching without warning.

The skipper swept an eye over the fire control console beside the helm. It indicated a fire had broken out in the engine room. Video from inside the room showed billowing dark smoke and flames licking up the aft wall.

The skipper doused the blaze quickly, spraying it with fire-retardant chemicals he controlled remotely. The monitoring panel showed no other blazes anywhere. But the superyacht was powerless, fifty metres from her marina.

The skipper dropped anchor. Everyone gathered in the cockpit, shaken and ashen faced. Charlotte clutched the baby close to her. Her soothing words kept Michael Chen relaxed. Her mother, Mei, however, kept staring at Kough as though he was the cause of the fire. She had been quietly cautioning her daughter that Kough was a man who attracted bad spirits and death.

The ketch's tender was lowered to take the family the short distance to shore. Kough hated the idea. The Port Douglas estuary was infested with saltwater crocodiles.

He had nightmares of a big salty chomping into the rubber side of

126

their inflatable and devouring them. According to local myth, the marina area was home to a rarely seen six-metre monster. Rarely seen because all big salties could lurk underwater for up to an hour and a half without taking a breath.

The locals, however, knew it was more than a myth, pointing to the wide slide marks it made on the river banks as it came and went. The fierce salties were ancient evaders of evolution, surviving in the brackish estuary waters long after dinosaurs were extinct.

Kough's extended family settled in the tender and an outboard engine putted them to the wharf without incident.

Kough dispatched the family to the seven-star Marina Hotel for the night. He stayed to wait for Hai who was due to arrive any time.

As he stood on the wharf waiting, he heard something rustle behind him. He spun around and a little Chinese man wearing a ridiculous-looking fedora at a jaunty angle was there, a polite smile on his thin face. Kough wondered where the hell he had crept from. The little man put a hand out: 'Dr Kough, I presume.'

Kough said: 'And I presume you're the prick setting fire to my property.'

Hai's smile remained fixed to his face: 'No, no, Dr Kough. I am the man who wants to offer you protection from such unnecessary occurrences as the one that happened at your factory and on your boat.'

'Protection?'

'Our insurance offers you complete protection from loss of property or profits should you need it.'

Kough leaned back on the marina rail: 'So you're a gangsta wanting protection money.'

Hai shook his head politely.

Kough said: 'So how did you even know about the unnecessary occurrence on my boat? It only happened half an hour ago, while you were still in the air.'

Hai looked away and gave a slight shrug. He went to say something but felt himself suddenly lurched off the ground. Kough slung the small man over his right shoulder. The fedora fell to the wooden decking and his legs flailed wildly. He shrieked as Kough carried him slowly to the end of the wharf. Then he lifted him off his shoulder and dangled him by his legs, head first over the dark water. The briefcase was hanging by a gold chain from one of Hai's wrists, and partly submerged.

'I have a couple of simple customer questions, Mr Hai? Stop squirming; you don't want to fall in, do you?'

There was a shout from his skipper. A saltie had slipped from the far bank and was cruising silently towards them. Kough could see nothing moving on the water.

The skipper shouted: 'See him? His eyes are the only part of him above the water. He's aiming straight at you.'

Kough finally saw the protruding black, beady eyeballs creating a wash on the calm estuary water. Hai saw it at the same time and a wild scream echoed around the marina.

'My wife and son could have burned alive on my boat thanks to you. If you think I won't feed you to the croc, you're making a big mistake.'

The black eyes slid silently closer. The saltie was now more than halfway across the river. Hai went quiet and still. Kough dangled him lower to the water. The briefcase floated on the surface. Hai could feel water lapping around his hair.

'When he grabs you, he'll dive and do a back flip. That will break your back. Then he'll take you over to his bank, have a good feed and store the remains of you for later. That's what salties do, Mr Hai.'

Big Brain joined the drama: I don't want to spoil your fun, but if the little twerp's eaten for dinner, we'll have lost our best lead to the bad guys.

Tough, thought Kough. He was in no mood to be logical. He said: 'Hai, what's in the briefcase? Not any food I hope.'

Hai wriggled and started sobbing.

Kough said: 'Where do you keep the keys for the chain?'

'In pocket. In pocket.'

The saltie had put on a spurt of speed. He was now only twenty metres away. The bow wave off the eyes grew in height.

Kough held Hai by a single leg and fished in his upside-down pockets. He found a key. 'Pull your briefcase up, Hai.' Hai pulled with all his feeble might. The briefcase sprung from the water and landed beside Kough's feet.

Holding Hai with one hand, Kough stepped back and unlocked the briefcase. He upended it. Papers and some office detritus dropped on the wharf. Kough kicked the briefcase off the end of it. Enormous, crooked saltie teeth appeared in a cavernous jaw and crunched down on it with shattering force.

Kough grabbed Hai's ankles with both hands and held his head over the water again. 'Last chance, you scumbag. You can give me some names or become entrée for the nice saltie.'

Big Brain glared: We need him alive, for God's sake. Kough was still unmoved. He saw the saltie turn and head back to the wharf, pieces of leather case lodged in its teeth.

'You mad. You mad. All right, all right. Pull me up. Hurry, hurry. Now, now.' There was terror in his panicked voice.

'Not so fast, Mr Hai. First you need to tell me who your boss is. If you lie, I'll bring you back here. Now, take your time. I'd say you have about ten seconds to tell me the truth.'

Hai's eyes were bulging from his face in terror as the croc went to make his leap, jaws wide open. He screamed: 'Jia Tao. Jia Tao.'

Kough heaved Hai upwards and jumped back. Hai's body shot through the air. But not quick enough. Some of the saltie's teeth tore at the side of his scalp. Water frothed at the end of the wharf, marking the creature's frenzied frustration.

Hai's body lay still. Some blood flowed from the scalp wound and dropped through the wharf decking. A small shark appeared from nowhere and began thrashing around in it.

'Did you kill him?' The skipper was paralysed in the yacht's cockpit.

Kough kicked Hai. Hai grunted.

'No. He's still alive. Just had a bit of a shock, I suppose. He'll come round in a minute.'

The skipper sat down and nodded his head slowly: 'If you had been a half second longer...'

Kough laughed: 'It wouldn't have mattered. I had the name by then.' The skipper looked aghast.

Big Brain said, Well done. I've got something to work on before the next fire breaks out.

Kough turned and gave a start. The taxi had returned. Charlotte and her mother stood with mouths open, staring at Hai's body lying still on the dock.

Kough did not know how much they had seen. Charlotte's mother,

Mei, was jabbering something to her daughter. Hai began to groan and twitch.

Kough picked him up in his arms and walked to the taxi. He told the driver he had a near-drowning incident with a crew member. Kough sat the diminutive, bleeding Chinese man in the back seat and climbed in beside him. Charlotte took the front seat, holding the paperwork that had spilled on to the wharf. Mei joined the men in the back. No one spoke on the short drive back to the hotel.

ONCE HAI'S head was cleaned up and he was locked in a bedroom, Kough grabbed his wife by both arms: 'I don't care what you mother thinks. I'm going to do whatever is necessary to keep my family safe.' Charlotte looked at her feet and gave a slight nod.

'If she's not happy, she can go back to Hong Kong.'

He felt Charlotte tense. She shook her head and began to whimper. Kough pushed her away and headed for a shower.

THIRTY-TWO

The front door was flung open. It hit the wall behind with a crash. It would have ricocheted closed again but for the tall man standing in the doorway holding a gun.

'What the fuck are you doing here?' The Dirty Dogs boss was incredulous.

Michael Kough lowered his pistol casually: 'Well, for starters there's the six hundred thousand you owe me; and there is another thing you may be able to help me with.' Michael Kough walked to the bar and put the pistol down.

Charles Henry Daggerell had been released on parole after almost two years in jail. He was in the midst of restoring the Dirty Dogs' fortunes after the devasting police raid on their HQ.

Daggers signalled to the handful of early drinkers at the gang's HQ to sit again and strolled over to the bar, wary and curious. Was Kough so crazy and naive he thought he could just show up after wrecking the gang's operation and not get his throat cut? The shitty little pea-shooter pistol he carried would hardly have saved him.

Daggers waved to the barman for two tall beers: 'Did you just fuck up my security system again?'

Kough nodded and smiled: 'Yeah, I did, Daggers. I wasn't sure I would be welcome if I didn't come unannounced. But I didn't fuck it up the first time; I was here, remember? It was working perfectly but your guys were all watching me at the roulette table and not watching the monitors.'

Daggers grimaced. 'I was pretty lucky myself that night. The cops searched the place, but they never found the dungeon, thank Christ. There was nearly two million bucks of good stuff in there. They only found rats and mice stuff, that's why our sentences were so light. How did you hack the alarms this time?'

'It's a long story but I have friends, let's say, in high places, and they want me around for a long time ... because my Safevac business is very important to them. So, they do me favours every now and then.'

'Gettin' in's okay, but that doesn't mean you can just walk out again.'

'No, but if you get one of your gangstas to go outside, they'd tell you there is a white helicopter hovering directly above. If I don't come out within fifteen minutes, the cavalry will come in.'

'Think you're pretty smart, don't ya?'

'Not smart enough actually, Daggers. There are things I think you know that I don't.'

Daggers eyed the pistol on the bar and calculated it was out of his reach, at the moment.

Kough took a sip of his beer: 'Do the names Jia Tao or Hai Sile mean anything to you?'

A wicked smile curled on the edge of Daggers' lips: 'What if I do? What's in it for me?'

Kough laughed: 'Well, there's the six hundred big ones for a start. And, of course, I'd reboot your fail-safe security system.'

Daggers shook his head. This cocky scientist was a piece of work. But his Bunsen burner is right beneath my short and curlies, he thought.

'Okay, Doc, shall we shake hands on that?' Daggers grinned and moved forward with a hand stretched. Kough started to move towards him and realised Dagger's other hand was scooping up the pistol.

Daggers stepped quickly back and aimed it at Kough's head: 'Just to show you, you can't win every hand, Doc.'

Kough laughed: 'I didn't need a lesson on that, Daggers but, anyway, you'll find it's unloaded. Go on. Check it.'

Daggers dropped the pistol back on the bar. He grinned like a shark: 'I don't need to check it. Your word is good enough for me, Doc.'

'So do those names mean anything to you?'

'Why do you want to know?'

'Someone blew up part of my Sydney factory. And let off a bomb on my yacht while I had my wife and baby on board. I caught one of them and fed part of his head to a saltie up in Port Douglas. He told me his boss was someone called Jia Tao.'

Daggers took a deep breath. 'Was Hai a little creep Chink who wears a funny hat?'

Kough nodded.

'He's small fish, fronts up the cartel's extortion rackets. He's always nice and polite. Was he offering you an insurance policy to stop the rest of your factory and boat going up in smoke?'

Kough nodded again: 'He's small fry. So is Tao big fry?'

Daggers took a mouthful of beer: 'Well, he's bigger than Hai but he's not really the big fry. The big fry is...' Daggers opened his hands wide as though he was telling a fish story.

'Go on,' said Kough.

Daggers smiled, finished his beer and waved for a second one. He looked at his watch: 'Is your fifteen minutes up yet?'

'C'mon. Stop fucking around. Tell me about this Tao guy.'

'I'd need a shit load more than six hundred big 'uns to tell you about Tao.'

Kough emptied his glass and pushed it across the bar for a refill. 'How do you know him?'

Daggers laughed: 'He ships me half of what the Dogs sell. I really don't want anything to happen to him, Doc.'

Kough said: 'Fuck.'

Daggers nodded. 'You've got some big bloodhounds out looking to mess with you, Doc. You know what it is they want – the ten secret herbs and spices you put in that vaccine of yours.'

Kough shrugged. 'How do I find Jia Tao?'

'You still wouldn't be talking to the right guy. Hey, your fifteen minutes is up. Let me make some calls, okay?'

Big Brain appeared: Don't push it, let him make his calls.

Daggers said: 'Meanwhile, can you turn on my security again?

Please? And put plenty of guards around your factory and home. Tao won't be too happy a saltie had a taste of his man's head.'

Kough said: 'Okay. Just one last thing. Give me my pistol back. I think it may come in handy.'

'Not if it's unloaded, Doctor.'

'Unloaded? Do you think I'm stupid.'

THIRTY-THREE

Superintendent Neil Akers was waiting outside Michael Kough's office early the next day. He introduced himself courteously, which alarmed Big Brain.

Kough invited him in. Akers was a big man, wearing small glasses when they weren't dangling off a cord around his neck. He looked like a mid-level accountant, Kough thought.

'What can I do for you, Superintendent?'

'It's what I may be able to do for you, Dr Kough. I'm with the National Criminal Intelligence Commission.'

Kough waved Akers to a chair and fell into his behind the desk.

Akers looked around the glass walls of the office and its modest desk. It was plain for a billionaire, he thought. There was a photograph of a very attractive Chinese woman holding a baby in pride of place beside his phone.

Kough sat back: 'And what may you be able to do for me?'

'You are going to be arrested in the next hour or so. A Mr Hai Sile has brought charges against you of aggravated assault.'

Kough frowned: 'I should have let the saltie have the little prick while I had the chance. Did he tell you why he was nearly croc tucker?'

Akers said nothing.

'He and his mates set off a bomb in the engine room of my yacht. I had my wife and child and in-laws on board. The day before, his mates firebombed a critical part of this factory.'

Akers said: 'The man says you're crazy and he had nothing to do with those events. He says he was simply selling you an insurance policy and you had invited him to talk about this at Port Douglas. The charges are quite serious, Dr Kough. Attempted murder and kidnapping.'

Kough began to stress. Big Brain arrived: Keep your hair on. Stop talking. Let him tell you what he could do for you.

Akers said: 'If convicted you could go away for ten or fifteen years. Hai says he has a witness, the skipper of your own boat.'

Kough took a deep breath and waited.

Akers looked at his notebook: 'There was a lapse in security at the Dirty Dogs HQ yesterday. It meant our phone-tapping devices worked perfectly for about quarter of an hour. We picked up a very interesting conversation and the name of a man we have a special interest in.'

'Mr Jia Tao,' said Kough.

'Exactly. In that conversation Charles Henry Daggerell revealed Tao supplied half the Dirty Dogs' drugs. It was enough to revoke Daggerell's parole and put him behind bars again. But he's still free because, in the bigger scheme of things, the Tao evidence is more important to us. We've been chasing Tao for some time. Unfortunately, it doesn't help you. You confirmed what Hai has said in his statement.'

Kough said: 'You will know from your tape that Daggers thinks there is an even bigger fish above Tao.'

Akers nodded and closed his notebook: 'Yes, don't worry, we heard that. And that's where we may be able to help you.'

Kough leaned forward.

Akers folded his legs: 'If Hai is an underling of Tao's, you could not be charged with any of the offences levelled against you – if you were an undercover agent.'

Big Brain choked. Kough looked doubtful.

Akers said: 'We'd make sure you will be at minimal risk.'

Big Brain said, Bullshit.

'It's your decision of course,' said Akers.

'What decision? Going to jail or getting tortured and murdered as an undercover cop?'

'You would be doing the country a great service.'

Kough shook his head slowly. More great service? Am I not already keeping the peace with China and saving millions of lives? he thought.

Big Brain confirmed: You're right; it's Hobson choice but better to be an undercover cop than spend fifteen years inside with the likes of Daggers. And it should mean your factory won't be razed as soon as you've repaired it.

Kough hesitated: 'While I'm doing this, this service, will you provide personal security for my family? And protect my factory? And guarantee Hai's charges against me will be dropped?'

Akers stood and extended a hand: 'That's all been taken care of, Dr Kough.'

Kough raised his eyebrows.

Akers said: 'The Prime Minister said you'd cooperate. His chief of staff, your friend John Able, mobilised a squad of diplomatic protection officers to protect your family as soon as you left home this morning. Hai will be deported today. There are apparently some irregularities with his passport.'

Big Brain said, See how things work out if you don't lose your head?

Akers laughed: 'Your friend Able warned us that no charges against you would stick, anyway. He says you're the classic certifiable, mad scientist.'

KOUGH CHECKED on the cool storage repair work. The factory would be out of action for another ten days. He called Charlotte who said two big guys had come to the door and introduced themselves. She'd given them seats to use in the corridor. They had closed the big picture windows and advised her to turn on the air conditioning to stay cool.

Charlotte wanted to know when they could go back to a settled, safe life. Kough could not tell her. She hung up without saying goodbye. Kough felt his stomach cramp. He had never thought of Charlotte leaving him. He had given her two years of the good life. But now the wheels were coming off. Again. He called her back. Her mother, Mei, answered the phone. Kough hung up.

On his desk he could see some of the paraphernalia Akers had left him. A new cellphone answering to his usual number but fitted with an extra-sensitive recording device and an extra-powerful GPS tracker.

There was also a tiny, round transmitter he could hide in the lining of his jacket or have placed beneath his skin on the back of his neck. He told Akers he would think about that. Akers had reluctantly agreed he could keep his pistol. He said the gang would search him and take it anyway.

Kough's vaccine formula was presently safe in Big Brain and subsequently protected against theft. He knew the fate of millions would be jeopardised if he was killed in an accident, hit by a truck – or eaten by a saltie. Although he was a selfish prick, a thief and definitely a tosser, who enjoyed flaunting his wealth and intelligence over the masses of ordinary, thick plebs who occupied the planet, he had a responsibility to them.

So it was critical he found a handful of people, maybe three, he absolutely trusted to each hold a third of the formula. Together they would be able to maintain the Safevac production systems if he was taken out.

Big Brain said it was a wonderful, selfless idea. But who would the three people be?

Kough thought of John Able, even though he had cuckolded him.

And Betty? She was a straight-up girl and would welcome more income than the thirty million he had given her in their divorce settlement. Big Brain said the plan so far was very laudable, but Frank would tell him to fuck off, and Betty would slam her door in his face.

Anyway, who would the third person be? Kough could not come up with a name. God, he had so few real friends. He was pathetic. Big Brain said, That's your own fault. Kough suddenly remembered with emotion and no logic – so, without any help from Big Brain – a third person he would trust.

DAGGERS CALLED. Tao would meet them both at the Pink Pussy Bar in King's Cross at six. Kough would be frisked, so no weapons. If he was carrying a wire, they would cut it out along with his balls. So, the skin-deep microphone was old hat, thought Kough.

Kough alerted Akers and then went to the dentist.

KOUGH WONDERED, why were the world's Mr Bigs such mediocre-looking people? Hardly reaching medium height, invariably a little too fat, losing hair and in love with white shirts. The thin, black moustache finished Central Casting's Crim Look for the feared Mr Jia Tao.

Daggers was in his standard, all black.

Kough wore the Billionaire Look, an understated fifteen-thousand-dollar suit, a shirt with short, designer sleeves to reveal gold cuff links and the ubiquitous gold Rolex.

He had toothache. The tiny listening device had been a tight fit, a challenge for the reluctant dentist. It seemed to be jabbing some nerves beneath his second lower molar. The polite frisk inside the entrance had confirmed the absence of any eavesdropping wire or transmitter under the skin of his neck or hands.

The three men sat in a rear, U-shaped cubicle. The dimmed red lighting was textbook, underworld night club. Despite the anti-smoking regulations, the fug of a late-night den lingered in the air.

The too-rounded, high-heeled hostesses looked like they were still summoning the courage to take the final leap to full-time prostitution. Or were in weary retreat from it. They served the men and tottered quickly away, like small animals instinctively sensing danger.

Kough watched them go and held Jia Tao's black eyes: 'Are you as dumb as you look, or did you think I'd pay you four million a month for insurance, so my factory wouldn't be firebombed again?'

Daggers nearly choked on his beer. He lowered the glass quickly and wiped foam off his mouth.

Jia Tao was startled but refused to show it. He put his glass back on the sticky table carefully. He sat peering into Kough's eyes as though he could see Big Brain lurking: 'You know I can have you shot, just exactly where you sit, Dr Kough?'

Kough scoffed: 'But we both know you won't. It's not even your decision to make, is it? Your boss very much wants to keep me alive. He knows the secret he's after is in my head.'

Tao swallowed. He glanced at Daggers and back to Kough: 'You have been misinformed, Dr Kough. I am the main man as far as you are concerned.'

Kough smiled: 'Bullshit. You don't look like you could run a chop shop.'

Tao's eyes turned to slits. Kough continued his scornful smile. Tao moved in his seat. Big Brain said, Hell, be careful.

Kough said: 'Go and give the evil eye to someone that gives a shit. Meanwhile, I'd like to know when you will be apologising to my wife and son for terrorising them with your little bomb on my boat.'

Tao made to stand. Changed his mind and sat again.

Kough said: 'That's right. You know you can't leave yet. Just sit and have a cold beer like a cool gangsta.'

Tao said: 'Fuck you.'

Kough leaned back in the cubicle and thrust his legs out in front of him: 'All right, Mr Tao, enough of the small talk. When do I get to meet the real boss?'

'You will also pay for your insolence, Dr Kough.'

'Yeah, yeah. You going to send another weasel like Mr Hai to intimidate me? Where is he now, by the way?'

'Where he is doesn't concern you.'

'Don't worry, I know. He's being chucked out of the country as we speak. Now let's talk about our next meeting with your boss. Because we've gotten on so well, Mr Tao, I'll pick where. It won't be a pokey dive like this. I think a nice expensive waterside restaurant, with a French chef, would be best. You ring me with the date and I'll set it up, okay?'

Tao said nothing.

Kough stood and downed his glass in a single swallow: 'Daggers knows how to reach me. Nice to meet you. And know this, if anything further happens to my family, my factory or my yacht, I will come after you, little gangsta man, and shoot you in the balls and feed you to the sharks in Sydney Harbour.'

Tao's impotence was reflected in the expression of hatred that crossed his face.

Kough nodded goodbye to Daggers and walked to the door and back to his Rolls-Royce.

Big Brain said, You'd better sort out the three who'll have your vaccine formula pretty smartly.

In an anonymous meat delivery van across the street, Superintendent Akers was perspiring. He took his headphones off and looked at the recording technicians: 'Do you think we've got the right guy to do this?'

One nodded enthusiastically. One shook his head determinedly.

THIRTY-FOUR

Michael Kough nodded to the diplomatic protection police officers in the corridor and let himself into the penthouse. Inside the door, he almost tripped on a suitcase. He saw there were three suitcases in the lobby. All carried First Class labels.

Charlotte appeared. She looked as if she had been crying. She looked at the cases and then at Kough: 'I am taking my family and Michael Chen to Hong Kong again where we will be safe.'

Kough was stunned. He had never thought of Charlotte leaving him again. He stood speechless, even though there was so much to say.

'I'm sorry, Mikey, but I believe it is for the best. I think if we stay here with you, we'll all be killed. I don't know what you have done, but you have upset some mean people who will stop at nothing to kill you and our son.'

Kough felt his legs sink from under him. He slumped down and sat on one of the suitcases. Charlotte rubbed her hands on his bowed head: 'We will come back when these evil people have gone. I promise.'

The door opened and one of their chauffeurs stepped in, paused and then picked up two of the cases. He returned for the third and Kough stood to let him carry it to the lift in the corridor.

Kough said: 'Do you promise to come back when I've sorted these evil men out?'

Charlotte cupped his chin: 'I promise.'

They kissed and Kough walked to the bedroom. Michael Chen was cooing on the bed in his blanket. He cradled his son for a few minutes. Charlotte arrived and silently took the baby from him. She kissed Kough again: 'I love you. Please make our home safe soon, so we can come back.' She turned and left.

It was an hour later that the landline phone rang. Kough walked disconsolately into the lounge and picked it up. His world went into another tailspin.

It was Akers. He said the Parramatta factory was again ablaze. The midsection had thirty-metre flames shooting through the roof. A dozen fire appliances were fighting to bring it under control.

Kough thanked him for the heads-up and ended the call.

He sat on the sofa and then laid full out. He felt exhausted and beaten. He was gripped with a fear that he would never see Charlotte or Michael Chen again.

The landline rang a second time. Kough almost did not answer it. Then he thought it could be Charlotte. She had missed her plane or had changed her mind.

But the call would be another bombshell.

A foreign voice said: 'Dr Kough? I have someone that wants to talk to you.'

A moment later he recognised Betty's voice. His first wife was in a panic. Her voice was shrill. Her words tumbled over themselves: 'Mikey, Mikey. You must help me. These men have grabbed me off the street. They say they'll kill me unless you...'

Kough's mind went into overdrive. He pressed the inside of his new tooth as a new voice came quietly on the line. It had a Spanish accent: 'Dr Kough, we have warned you. You have been obstinate and arrogant. Your factory has now been razed. Now your time is up. Do as we say or you will be completely out of business.

'If you want your wife back with all her limbs intact, you will take our next call in exactly sixty minutes, and we will tell you where and when to meet us. If you call the police, we will start to dismember her. You will be able to listen in. And watch a video we will post on Safevac's site.'

Kough heard a piercing scream. Then Betty shouting: 'No, no, get away, get away...'

The voice said: 'In exactly sixty minutes, Dr Kough.'

The line was cut. Kough stood holding the phone. He felt dazed. Big Brain said quietly, Hang up the phone. Akers will call now, and he would have heard everything through your tooth mic.

But Akers was on the line before Kough had hung up. Big Brain said, He's taping your landline. Akers' voice was two octaves higher than usual: 'We heard everything, Michael. Elizabeth is your first wife, isn't she?'

Kough said: 'Yes, why the hell have they kidnapped her?'

'Because they're stupid. They've got the wrong woman. Charlotte flew out of Sydney Airport an hour ago. They may think she is only your mistress.'

'If the stupid bastards don't know I've divorced Betty, they soon will. Akers, I'm not paying a red cent for her. I'm certainly not giving them the Safevac formula.'

Akers said nothing.

'These fuckers are crazy if they think Betty is a tradeable commodity for me. It would be a lot different if it was Charlotte or my boy. But I don't love Betty. We're all over, washed up.'

Kough paused and then laughed: 'They'll get a bloody shock when I don't answer the phone in an hour. That'll really give them the stitch.'

Akers took a deep breath: 'She was your wife, Michael. Don't you care for her at all? They're saying they'll cut her arms and legs off. They sound like they mean business too. She was obviously terrified, so they must have been waving knifes or saws in front of her.'

Kough said: 'They can go fuck themselves. Thicko crims.'

Kough asked how safe his wife and child would be when they landed in Hong Kong. Akers said they would be perfectly safe. No gang would ever get through a Public Security Bureau protection cordon answerable to the Chinese Politburo.

'The whole of China is a prison camp. The party operates more than two hundred million facial recognition cameras, every city and village is festooned with them. No one can move anywhere undetected. It's frightening but absolutely effective.'

'Why the hell don't we operate the same thing here?'

Akers sighed: 'We live in a democracy, Michael. Don't worry, we'll catch these gangsters. The police gang is bigger than their gang.'

'Well, you better catch them quick. I won't be paying them anything. Right now I'm going to see what they've done to my factory.'

'Michael, is it all right if I take the call in ... er ... fifty-six minutes?'

'Sure, you can take it. Give them my best regards. You can give a message to Jia Tao as well. Tell him the Sydney sharks are waiting for him.'

JESUS JAVAS DECIDED he would make the call to Michael Kough himself. The man who controlled one-third of the world's illicit drug trade was feeling smug, powerful and untouchable.

Once he got his hands on the Safevac formula, his empire's fortunes would reach new heights. He dialled the Sydney number, put his feet up on an enormous antique desk and sat back. He did not often choose to be the front man, but Kough had become an insolent target for a man like him, who was never, ever questioned or disobeyed.

When the call was answered, his arrogance failed to alert him to even the possibility he was being eavesdropped on by the Australia National Intelligence Bureau, the FBI, Interpol, the CIA, the Beijing Ministry of Public Security – and the prime minister of Australia.

The telephone was answered in Sydney and a worldwide trace was activated by the CIA's network of surveillance satellites.

'Mr Kough?'

'Ah, no. Mr Kough isn't available at the moment.' Akers thought his voice sounded too strained.

Javas gave a start. He sat up straight at the desk. His instinct for danger was suddenly aroused. There was a long second of silence. He had never contemplated Kough not answering. He heard Akers clear his throat: 'Mr Kough has suffered a breakdown. He is currently confined to his bed.'

Javas felt a sense of relief. As his inner circle watched, he put his boots on the desk again and reached for an oversized cigar. They felt the tension in the room ease.

'I'm so sorry to hear that.'

'He told me someone would be ringing,' said Akers, sounding like the perfect butler. 'Can I take a message, tell him who called?'

Javas paused, then realised the fool Kough would not know his name or the uproar he had caused within his enormous cartel.

'My name is Mr Smith. Who are you?'

Akers said his name and explained he was Kough's confidential assistant. He asked the drug king what his role was. Javas snorted a laugh. 'I'm the man in his worst nightmare. I had his wife kidnapped last night. He needs to learn a little respect, so I'm thinking of only cutting off her arms if he can find it in himself to cooperate.'

Akers sounded shocked. 'Her arms? Oh, shit, shit. That would be … er … outrageous … er … barbaric.'

Javas gave another snort of laughter: 'It is all Dr Kough's fault. We have tried to reach out in a spirit of cooperation.'

The CIA's voice-recognition computer spat out a name: Jesus Javas. Head of the world's biggest drug cartel.

Akers said: 'What … wha … what do you want Mr Kough to do? He loves his wife very much. He would die if anything happened to her.'

'He acts as though he wants her to die, spurning our friendship.'

Akers checked his watch. He was desperate to keep Javas talking. 'I'm not sure he knows the gravity of the situation, Mr Smith. Hold on, I'll go and see if I can get him out of bed. Can you hold on a minute, please?'

Javas studied the tip of his cigar: 'All right. One minute. Or he can open his email and see a video of his Betty lose one of her arms.'

'Oh, oh, one minute, oh, oh. All right, all right, please wait on, I'll go and wake Mr Kough.' Akers put the phone down and watched the second hand on his watch run at a seemingly frantic pace through sixty seconds.

After eighty seconds he reached for it and faked breathlessness and panting: 'I couldn't get Mr Kough out of bed. He was barely conscious because he's been heavily sedated by his doctor, but he said could I please ask you what you want him to do now. He started to shake and cry. He is in a bad state, I'm afraid. I've never seen him like this.'

Javas sniggered: 'All right. Listen carefully. His cellphone will shortly receive a document. He is to download and sign it immediately. It is for the sale of his Safevac patent and business. We are not dumb Chinese,

Mr Akers; we want the full formula. We will test it before we release his wife. Is that understood?'

Akers sounded nervous: 'What, what will be the … price you are offering Dr Kough? Will you continue to supply our Shanghai factory with its full requirement of the vaccine?'

The line went silent. Javas looked at the ceiling and tapped ash from his cigar: 'I will talk directly with the Chinese when I have Dr Kough's sale document.'

'The Chinese are very … um … are totally dependent on Dr Kough's cooperation with the formula.'

'Yes, I am aware of that. That's why I'm expecting their full cooperation. Or they can try to make their own vaccine again.' He laughed loudly. 'Fucking Chinks, their potential to do anything worthwhile ended centuries ago after they'd invented gunpowder.'

He inspected the tip of his cigar again: 'All right. Just remind Dr Kough that Betty's first arm will come off if we don't receive the signed sale document by eight tonight. It is already four in the afternoon here so I suggest he should get out of bed, sign the document very quickly, before I retire for the night.'

'Yes, sir, Mr Smith. I will stress the urgency of the matter to Mr Kough. What number can I call you on if I need to reach you urgently?'

Akers heard howls of laughter. Then Mr Smith broke the connection.

Seconds later the line was full of jubilant voices from the call trackers.

The CIA had a confirmed voice recognition. The caller had been Jesus Javas himself. It was his dumbest move in more than thirty years as supremo cartel boss. The computer traced the origin of the call to a small Colombian village which had previously been unknown to international law-enforcement bodies.

Twenty minutes later a document was emailed to Kough's cellphone. But nobody knew where Kough or his cellphone was. He had left to inspect his fire-damaged factory but had not been heard of since.

THIRTY-FIVE

THE AUSTRALIAN PRIME MINISTER, GARY STONE, WAS puzzled. He asked John Able: Why was Michael Kough callously unconcerned about Betty Kough? But enamoured with Charlotte and his baby son? He could steal a world medical breakthrough, save the life of a Chinese official who was a stranger to him, but double cross and defraud millions from a Shanghai pharmaceutical firm.

'And betray his oldest friend,' John Able snapped. The pair were facing each other across the PM's desk.

'Yes, and that,' said Stone. 'You always said he was a mad bugger, but is he certifiably crazy as well as being the smartest man on the planet?'

Able took a deep breath: 'Prime Minister, I think he's what they call a savant. One slice of his brain is hellishly clever. Genius clever. He understands and remembers complex research outcomes as though he has a photographic memory. He studied virology. He knew more than the lecturers and professor in double-quick time. That's why I gave him the nickname of Boffy, because he was such a fanatical boffin in the research lab.'

Stone sat back, his forehead creased in confusion. Able sighed: 'But the thing is, he's often a loser on a lot of other fronts. He's a gambling addict for a start. And he's not too good when it comes to personal relations.

'Clearly, Charlotte is an exception and he dotes on her and his son, but she is an exception, besides me, that is, or was. Autistic people can be savants with an "island of genius" amid their other foibles. It doesn't make Michael a bad person, but he can sail off in his own little world regardless of others.'

Stone said: 'As you learned the hard way. It's as though he has no clear steer on ethical matters or ... a moral compass at times.'

Able grimaced: 'Yet he saved Dim Sim's life when he didn't have to. You, yourself, told him Dim Sim's life would be a small price to pay to stand up to the Chinese.

'When it involved the eternal triangle, with him, me and Charlotte, the circumstances were very different: the fact is, I was trying to compete with a guy with a big brain and a bigger bank account and they had chemistry.'

'I can imagine. But you've got to let that business with Charlotte go. It'll drag you under if you don't,' said Stone.

Able said: 'I've always worried he'll come a giant cropper one day. Maybe this Jesus Javas will be the man to end his run.'

Stone said: 'I doubt that. Javas has become too arrogant. He as good as gave away his hidey-hole when he chatted so long and told us what the local time was. Got to believe he could walk on water. Meanwhile, we have to rebuild that Parramatta factory asap. The build-up in demand for Safevac in America and Europe is huge. And the Chinese are going to give us big trouble again if their vaccine supply is cut off.'

Stone stood up: 'Right now, we have to find out where the hell he is.'

Able had no clue where Kough was. He knew of no close friend Kough could turn to. Able thought he knew all Kough's close friends. But he was wrong.

MICHAEL KOUGH LOOKED at the world-weary face of the young woman he would trust with part of the trillion-dollar Safevac formula.

His private detective agency confirmed she had no close relatives in Australia. She had no passport and lived under the control of a criminal gang like scores of other Asian prostitutes duped in their search for a better life in Australia. To the Dirty Dogs she was only a devaluing asset.

They would soon send her back to Hong Kong with a pittance to try to start her life over.

Suzie had come into the massage parlour's dressing room searching for her next client. Her face lit up when she saw Michael Kough sitting on the small bench inside. He was still fully clothed.

Kough smiled at her and patted the bench. She squeezed on and said: 'Thank you. I not know how reach you. Thank you letting me away from Dogs' place. I just make it.'

Kough nodded: 'And, don't forget, I saved you from an all-comers gang bang.'

Suzie looked puzzled. Kough smiled: 'You were going to be the main entertainment, shagging all the Dogs on their billiard table.'

She twisted her lips: 'What gang bang, please?'

'It's when all the boys pile on for a quick shag. I was invited to go first; I was a special guest.'

Suzie looked horrified. 'I heard other girls talk about ... they used garbage afterward ... not able work for months. Some sent home quick.'

She shook her head: 'So I have thank you, so much.' Tears formed in her eyes. Kough put his arm around her back and cuddled her.

'There is something you can do for me ... with your clothes on.' He laughed. She held his hand: 'Anything, Mikey.'

He gave her a small slip of paper. It had a series of letters and numbers. They represented a chemical formula. To a layperson it looked like ancient hieroglyphs.

'I want you to read this. And memorise it. Then write it down. Can you do that? I can stay here while you study it.'

He smiled: 'I paid for an hour.' She looked wary but took the sheet and read it. And reread it. And reread it, muttering under her breath.

When she finally looked up, Kough gave her a pen and another piece of paper: 'Okay, write it down for me.'

She took the pen: 'Sure. No troubles.'

She laughed when Kough looked surprised. Suzie took a breath and wrote out what seemed to be a long password. Her memory was near perfect. Only one decimal point in one number was wrong. Kough looked at the Asian lady of the night with new admiration.

'You're a clever lady, Suzie, and that's why you'll be leaving here tonight and starting a new life. I will be your new employer; I will get you a legal passport and work visa. And I'll pay you two hundred thousand dollars a year for a simple job I want you to do.'

Suzie looked bewildered: 'I don't understand. What I have to do?'

'You will have a very simple and very important job. Once a month you will be called on this encrypted cellphone. You will text this formula to the caller. Nobody is ever allowed to know the formula that you just memorised. Understood?'

Suzie hugged him tightly: 'I don't understand but I do it. Thank you, Mikey, thank you. You are best man in world.'

Kough separated them gently: 'Take this cellphone. If I ever need to speak to you, I will call on it. If you are asked by anyone, you never knew me. This is a bank book with your account details. Your salary will be placed in your account every month.'

Kough took her piece of paper and shifted the wrong decimal point. She nodded: 'Nearly all right. Will be all right from now.'

THIRTY-SIX

THE NATIONAL CRIMINAL INTELLIGENCE COMMISSION traced Daggers' cellphone to a house in King's Cross. The federal police swooped, shot three of the four occupants, and freed a quaking Betty Kough. Outside Michael Kough leaned on his Rolls-Royce, cellphone in hand. Daggers had answered a fateful call from Kough, revealing the kidnappers' location.

'Took your bloody time, Mikey,' Betty shouted from the front door. Akers said: 'Mrs Kough, we would never have found you if it had not been for Michael and his contacts. He was desperate to find you.'

Betty started crying: 'Oh, Mikey. Were you? So, you do still love me a little bit then?'

She walked up to the Rolls and gave him a hug; her head rested on his shoulder for a while. He said: 'I'm so happy you're safe, Betty. Do you want a lift to the cop shop for the debrief?'

She nodded quickly: 'Oooh. Yes, I've never been in a Rolls-Royce. Can I wave to people?' She pulled the rear door handle, but the door opened the wrong way out, facing forward. 'Funny car,' she said, 'but you always did like odd things.'

'That's why I married you, dear,' Kough said.

'Oooh. Do you want to try it again, Mikey?'

'Just close the door, Betty. There's a button on the door pillar. Push it and an electric motor will shut the door.'

The motor whirred quietly and the heavy door closed with a solid chunk.

'You've been gambling again, haven't ya? And not paying your debts quick enough. Mikey, those guys that the casinos sent around were really mean people. How much did you owe them this time?'

Kough sat back in the padded leather seat: 'Oh, only about half a mill.'

'Only half a mill? Well, you're getting better at your gambling then.'

Betty chatted all the way to the police station for the debrief. Just before they arrived, Michael heard his cellphone vibrate.

'Kough.'

'Have you signed the papers?'

'Nah. Go fuck yourself.'

Betty said: 'Who was that? You know, you can be very rude to people, Mikey.'

JESUS JAVAS HEARD the loud clattering of the helicopter overhead. He knew immediately he was toast. Black uniformed men swung down and smashed their boots through his big windows. He was so stunned at the turn of events he suffered a fatal stroke only minutes after being handcuffed and bundled into the police helicopter.

KOUGH APPEARED on front pages and the online news media again when the police announced the smashing of the huge Javas drug cartel.

News headlines trumpeted:

'KIDNAP ATTEMPT LEADS TO CAPTURE AND DEATH OF WORLD'S BIGGEST DRUG LORD.'

'HOSTAGE FREE AFTER SYDNEY GUN BATTLE.'

'KIDNAP TRIGGERS INTERNATIONAL MANHUNT DESTROYING GIANT DRUG CARTEL.'

Charlotte and Michael Chen flew home from Hong Kong after the arrest and death of Javas. Michael Kough was jubilant, having his family happily together again. His stand against international gangsters and the ongoing success of Safevac had reinforced his hero, celebrity status.

He completed his Safevac insurance policy by cajoling his oldest friend, John Able, and his estranged wife, Betty, to each hold a third of the critical parts of the vaccine formula.

Suzie, whom he had rescued from a life of prostitution, was already holding one-third of it.

John Able had been hostile to any further involvement with the man who had betrayed him and stolen Charlotte from under his nose. But he was talked around by the PM, saying again he had to move on for his own good.

Betty agreed but was suspicious, thinking it was another of Kough's dubious moves to dodge some legal trouble. But, as it was an excuse to stay in touch with her first love, she happily accepted the two hundred thousand dollars a year for her role. Able was paid nothing. Big Brain said any money offer would offend Johnny's pride. He would do it because it was of national importance, and it would please Stone.

Using encrypted cellphone messages, the three would separately provide their parts of the biological formula at the end of each month to the Safevac Parramatta laboratory. Their 'ingredients' and proportions were the final step for the mass production of the vaccine. The texts were auto-deleted within minutes.

A hacker attempting to discover what ingredients were ordered by Safevac's laboratory, to reverse engineer the vaccine, were confronted by a half million choices of potential inputs. And those inputs altered randomly each month. The permanent ingredients were automatically relabelled by Big Brain's security system monthly but were still correctly flagged or identified by a super computer when production was about to begin.

Kough repaired the bomb damage and enjoyed his superyacht, *The Miracle*, with his budding family. The money poured in. Safevac's value was guessed at by every financial magazine. They put it at between three and seven trillion dollars.

It was an idyllic life that Walter J. Toppman III was determined to scuttle.

THIRTY-SEVEN

Toppman Pharmaceuticals was a Big Pharma giant that Walter J. Toppman's grandfather had founded in the good old days when the addition of cocaine in Coke was still a fresh memory. Walter J had retired at seventy to a non-executive role on the Toppman board and his son had taken over the corporate reins. But in his dotage, he had become an embittered man.

Big Pharma, including his corporation, had unjustly become one of the bogeymen of the modern era, regardless of how many lives their pharmaceutical medicines saved. It was under constant assault by greedy lawyers, urging their greedy clients to sue for every imaginable wrong a medicine could have caused them. Legal costs to fend them off were mountainous and permanent.

The expense of creating a new drug was prohibitive because do-gooders demanded impossibly long safety trials for each one. The failure rate for a new, breakthrough drug was high, as always. The research was painstaking and the pay for elite researchers was eye-watering.

Walter J and his father had confronted bizarre and legally questionable tactics from greenies, virtue-signalling politicians and straight-out gangster-cum-fraudsters. To combat them he used Evaltime and Associates, who knew the dark arts he needed. Fighting bad actors was now simply a cost of business. And, he confessed to himself, he quietly enjoyed the Godfather-like power Evaltime could deploy at his command.

The pharma profits were still good, but too much had to be spent on the mega-mergers needed. Size mattered when it came to bankrolling drug development and dominating a market.

Walter J was incensed to read of the never-ending success of germ-warfare virologist Michael Kough. The crazy gambling man who had slayed the biggest drug cartel dragon and was worshipped by the great unwashed. And beloved by the evil Chinese Communist Party.

Kough had introduced an anti-viral drug amid wild claims of its success without ever being forced to conduct any conventional drug trials or disclosing its chemical makeup. The man could be injecting his millions of customers with something that would have catastrophic effects on their long-term health. That's what Walter J told every politician he met.

He was particularly livid about the flood of profits gushing into Kough's coffers.

Walter J had convinced himself that jealousy played no part in his anger with Michael Kough and Safevac's success: he had been forced to play by the rules and endure endless interference, so it was only fair that Kough should be forced to comply with the same rules. It was his virtuous duty to bring Kough to heel. It was time to call the boss at Evaltime, Eddie Croake. There had to be a crack somewhere in Kough's shiny windscreen.

LITTLE TOBY ELLIS, aged ten, fell ill. He had been vaccinated by Safevac so his doctors, in rural Kentucky's Libbyville, treated him for a throat infection. Three days later Toby was dying, gasping desperately for air. The town's medical centre had no ventilator. Toby was dead by the time his ambulance reached Lexington General Hospital, a hundred and twenty kilometres away.

Walter J read about the death. He sent the head of Evaltime, Eddie Croake, to Libbyville. Toby Ellis had been inoculated with Safevac – but had died of flu-like symptoms, his lungs failing. This had to be the opportunity.

. . .

Solo mum Lucy Ellis opened the door to her small two-bedroom home expecting another neighbour, checking on her. Her son's funeral had been the previous day. Almost all the town's population had turned out. But on the doorstep was a man with a pockmarked face, wearing a dark coat, who seemed so big he blocked out the sun. He nodded but did not try to smile. He knew his twisted teeth frightened women. And he did not want to frighten this waif of a mother. She stood tentatively at the door dressed in a thin nightgown and fluffy slippers, still grieving her boy.

'I'm sorry to intrude, Ms Ellis, I'm from the Citizens for Safe Medicines Campaign. We heard about your little Toby, and it seems his Safevac inoculation failed him tragically ... as it has done many others we're investigating.'

A hand went to Lucy's mouth. Tears swelled in her red-ringed eyes: 'My poor Toby. He didn't feel well after having the jab. Said he had headaches, felt dizzy. I was really worried, but the doctors said millions have had Safevac and it's perfectly safe.'

'Can I come in, Ms Ellis? You may be able to help us and help a lot of other mothers from going through what you are going through.'

Lucy hesitated. The big man looked more like a repossession heavy than a medical charity volunteer.

'Citizens for Safe Medicines, did you say? I've never heard of them, I'm sorry.'

'Don't apologise, Ms Ellis. The Big Pharma gang are warning the media not to report our work at CSM or they'll sue them or stop advertising with them.'

Lucy nodded. She had heard of the machinations of Big Pharma. It was in the news now and again. She opened the door and led Mr Croake inside.

They talked for some time. She made him coffee. She told him Toby's autopsy had not been completed. Toby had been in good health, although he was an asthmatic and had lived with a hole in the heart condition since birth.

Lucy had not had the money to have it treated properly. Croake took notes on the hospital Toby had been admitted to, and the doctors who had treated him, and where he went to school.

Croake shook his head as he stood to go: 'Ms Ellis, if you don't mind, CSM would like your permission to investigate Toby's premature death.' He pulled several sheets of paper from his coat. Lucy looked worried and uncertain. 'If we can show Safevac helped cause your son's death we would win millions in damages. In the meantime, CSM is prepared to make you a non-refundable advance payment of fifty thousand dollars while we see if there is a case.'

Lucy's sad eyes lit up. Croake passed her a pen and laid the papers on the coffee table. She signed. She was startled when he tugged a wad of cash from an inside pocket of his big coat. He said the sum would be deducted from any future damages payout from Safevac.

Lucy took the cash and looked around for somewhere to put it, as though it was burning her hands. Croake said: 'I look forward to seeing you again when we get some results. If you get any calls from hospitals or doctors or teachers or reporters, tell them that you have asked CSM for their help and refer them to me.' He gave her a card.

Lucy nodded and pulled her nightgown tighter around her skinny body. Croake left and she sat and slowly counted the money. It totalled exactly fifty thousand dollars. She had never had so much money. Then she thought of Toby and fresh tears began to flow. There was another knock on the door. She scurried away to hide the wad in her top bedside drawer. She went to the door: It was Beatrice. With another hotpot.

CROAKE WENT DIRECTLY to Lexington Hospital's mortuary and told the duty laboratory technician that he was with the legal department. He wanted to head off any problem with Toby Ellis's death because it was making headlines in light of the boy's Safevac inoculation.

The technician said the autopsy report had been completed only an hour earlier. Croake asked to see it. The technician handed it to him. Croake said he would return it immediately after the legal meeting upstairs. The technician shrugged and Croake left. He sat in his hire car and flipped the pages of the report. The boy had not died from any virus. He had suffered since birth with a hole in his heart. The heart had given up its struggle and an asthmatic attack had fatally compounded his condition.

Croake sent a copy of the report under the hospital's logo to

Evaltime and Associates. He then dictated a new version of the report. He took the original report back to the technician.

Croake's version of the autopsy created a feeding frenzy among the media when it was leaked the following day. It was the first confirmed case of Safevac failing. The hospital's denials were lost or disbelieved in the white noise. Lucy read that Toby had contracted a virus which attacked his asthma-weakened lungs. The Safevac inoculation had failed to counter the virus. She thought she would trade in her ancient Dodge Dart for a new model.

Walter J. Toppman was ecstatic. He pumped Croake's hand and pointed to newspaper headlines scattered across his oversized desk, along with printouts from online media services.

The world's media had devoured the story. The hospital's logo on the leaked document seemed proof of the story's authenticity. It was the first time the Safevac miracle drug had been questioned in the mass media.

Walter J beamed: 'Well done, Eddie. Now we need to play up the secrecy line of the vaccine. The fact it's so secret no one knows what's in it or what it's doing to your body. Kough could be cast as Doctor Death if we play this right.'

Croake sprayed his crooked teeth outward in a rare grin: 'I'll have to go to Sydney to do that, Mr Toppman.'

'Yes, of course, of course. Some of the mainstream media will realise they've been played in a few days but that doesn't matter; the whole affair will have sown doubts among our armies of anti-science sceptics – and sceptics can be a very noisy mob, particularly if Evaltime gets its demonstrators-for-hire out there whipping things up. Eddie, I have to say, it's nice to be on the other side stirring instead of defending. The poor hospital people, they'll never explain how that report got into circulation, ha ha.'

Coake folded his arms: 'Mr Toppman, it's going to get expensive, taking a team to Australia.'

'It could be the best investment I've made for years, Eddie. Just remember to check your guns. They're titchy about civilians carrying in Australia.'

Croake laughed. More twisted teeth emerged. 'We'll be careful, Mr Toppman. There are plenty of guns in Sydney if you know where to go.'

THIRTY-EIGHT

CHARLOTTE SIPPED HER COFFEE ON THE WIDE EXPANSE OF the Woolloomooloo apartment balcony, overlooking a calm Sydney Harbour, as the sun began to rise. Kough, yawning and stretching, joined her and gave her another good-morning kiss.

'Mikey, does that news from America worry you? That the vaccine failed to save that little boy there.'

Kough sat and poured from the coffee pot: 'Nah. The vaccine works for everyone. That boy would have had other health complications. You'll see.'

Charlotte pulled her sunhat lower and fixed her eyes on her husband. He was always so certain of himself. She had never met anyone like him. She remembered the first night they met. He was so self-conscious. So red-faced and nervous when he thought he had inadvertently put her off.

He had won half a mill in the casino. He had said it flippantly as though it was an everyday occurrence. Or, maybe it was six hundred thousand, he thought. He claimed he wasn't sure. It was, sort of, just money. He hadn't bothered to count it. He had left that to the casino staff. The more he said, the bigger the tosser hole he had dug himself into.

But there was something about him. She sensed his offhand manner was a front. He was desperate to appear charming and confident, but the agony of his past financial failures had left him struggling with doubt and few social graces.

She smiled at the memory of him trying to unscramble his words. This was the same man John Able had told her was a triple failure, having lost all his money, his wife and his home to the roulette wheel.

That night he was a winner, and completely intoxicated by her beauty. She had enjoyed teasing and seducing him. Tall and handsome, he was a bit the worse for wear from his bourbons, but his smile was the real thing. He was such a vibrant character, compared to her serious boyfriend, snoring in bed up the passage. They could both hear him. It added a sense of danger to their illicit flirtation. By the time she had made him coffee in Able's kitchen she wanted to have him. There and then.

Kough said: 'What's so funny? What are you smiling about?'

'You,' she said. 'I was thinking about the night we met.'

'Oh, God.'

'You were very hot, Boffy.'

'You were the hot one that night, Char. As we found out in due course.'

Charlotte giggled. 'My parents would be horrified if they knew what happened that first night. And on a kitchen island. Mikey, do you still love me as much as then?'

'No,' said Kough. 'I'm afraid not.'

Charlotte pushed her sunhat back on her head and sat up.

Kough looked serious: 'No. I love you ten times more than I did then.'

Charlotte leaned over and punched him on the arm: 'That was a horrible thing to say. I'm never going to ask you that question again.'

She sat back: 'Fancy marrying a man who spends his life mucking around with yukky germs and viruses. Tiny, wriggly things you can't even see.'

Kough grinned. He found the mysteries of viruses fascinating. 'You know, there's still a debate among scientists about whether viruses are actually living organisms. Their makeup does not meet the criteria of living organisms.'

Charlotte adjusted her cap and sank further into her seat: 'I didn't know that.'

'Yeah. They are so minute, just microscopic particles. At their core they have either DNA or RNA genetic material. They can't reproduce themselves so they feed off animals like us. Then they can mutate to become horrible things that can kill us all off.'

'Glad I don't have to work with them,' said Charlotte. She poured herself another cup. She used the interruption to change the subject. She knew she was taking the risk of upsetting her husband and spoiling the atmosphere.

'You know my mother worries and you get very annoyed with her ... but she really believes you attract bad karma. Since you came on the scene, lots of horrible things have happened to my mum and dad.'

'The secret police back home ordered them to use me to find out about Safevac. But, as you know, I didn't know anything about it, so they punished them. They dropped their social credit rating. Their mortgage rate went up and they were forbidden to travel anywhere by train or air..'

Kough listened with a deepening scowl.

Charlotte ignored his discomfort and rushed on: 'Mikey, you must understand why my mum is certain you're bad karma. She's always nervous, asking me what the next calamity will be.'

Kough shrugged: 'There won't be another calamity. We have everything under control now.'

'All these things worry my mother – and me, of course. I've had to leave the country to feel safe. Why do these things always seem to happen to you. I mean, us?'

Kough took a big breath: 'I can't control what other people do. You don't want me to give my patent away to bad people, do you?'

Charlotte shook her head: 'No, of course not. It's just that you seem to have too many brains for your own good.' They both laughed and the tension between them broke.

Kough said: 'Things will be good from here on out. We even have the PM himself looking out for us. He's told me he won his re-election last month because of me, after I did the Safevac deal with the Chinese and the economy began booming again. How could things be any better?'

'Okay, so is that what I tell my mum? The bad karma has gone forever?'

Big Brain said, Keep calm, do not call her mother a Chink battle-axe. She's a lovely, caring mother.

'Char, I think your mum is a lovely, caring mother and you must tell her not to worry. If she does, it will ruin our beautiful life.'

Charlotte smiled: 'All right, I'll tell her.'

Kough nodded and got up. He went to the kitchen and made another pot of coffee. Charlotte held her cup out when he returned: 'Mikey, you were saying viruses are so tiny we can't see them and may not even be living organisms, so how come you found a way to make the bad ones harmless in people?'

'If I told you I'd have to kill you.'

Charlotte laughed: 'If you told me, I'm sure I still wouldn't have a clue what you're talking about.'

Kough stretched out as the sun rose further into a clear blue sky: 'What I, and everyone else knows, is that viruses have a coat of protein around them, some have two coats, called an envelope. Sometimes these coats have spikes sticking out of them, so they can latch on inside us and feed off our cells. And sometimes they latch on and mutate into something that becomes deadly for us.'

Charlotte said: 'Okay, thanks Boffy, I don't need to know any more of the yukky stuff.'

'I'm just getting to the good part, Char. I found that if you forget trying to kill the little buggers, and just have a vaccine that will remove their coats, they're completely harmless.'

Charlotte put her cup down: 'So your invention was to unclothe them, to take their coats off?'

'Don't tell a living soul.' He grinned. Big Brain said, Quit it, you're showing off and saying far too much. She doesn't know what a protein coat is, but someone she talks to might realise the basis of your breakthrough, so drop it.

Charlotte stood and pulled her nightgown tightly around her amazing body. She looked at her husband's reaction. He sat open-mouthed. She raised her eyebrows a fraction. The poor boy was still putty in her hands. She said: 'Michael Chen is still fast asleep.'

Kough leapt to his feet: 'Oh. Okay then, um, as good fortune would have it, I'm available to demonstrate my own unclothing technique.'

Charlotte nodded seriously: 'Okay, Mikey, but I've seen your unclothing technique. It is rather a rapid affair.'

'My darling, I will show you the technique in slow motion this morning.'

Fat chance, thought Charlotte, but she smiled and nodded, took her husband's hand and led him inside.

CHARLOTTE WAS STILL SNORING QUIETLY an hour later. Kough gently removed her arm from his chest and slid out of bed. He had heard Michael Chen stirring. He went to the nursery and picked the baby up. They went to the kitchen where he could heat Michael Chen's milk.

Big Brain said, I'm worried about the dead boy in America. The mass media have gone big with the story. Two more Big Pharma outfits joined the call this morning for Safevac to be banned in America until it has undergone full-length trials.

Kough thought it did not need a trial. In the American lab he had proved Safevac will neutralise any of its coat or envelope without killing the virus, so many of which were needed, particularly the useful ones in the gut.

Big Brain said, The fact is, it is much easier to arouse fear than to overcome it. We have to stop these saboteurs. Sales will begin to crater. You have to get your head out of the clouds.

Charlotte walked in wearing a happy smile: 'How are the men in my life?'

'Mrs Kough, you're starkers – in front of the children.'

'Children? Plural? How did you know?'

The shattering of such a happy family tableau seemed an impossibility as they hugged and jigged around the kitchen, celebrating the news another child was on the way to add to their family. But their blissful life was to last just another forty-eight hours.

THIRTY-NINE

IT WAS PURE INSTINCT. SUZIE LI SCREAMED AT THE TOP OF her lungs the moment she opened her front door and saw the ghastly, twisted teeth.

Eddie Croake thrust her brutally and bodily back inside her apartment. She landed on her back, sprawled on the floor as the big man with the pockmarked face and the big, full-length black coat shut the door and marched over her, into the apartment, to check she was alone.

Her nightmare had come true, she thought. The Dirty Dogs had somehow found her after all these months. She had tried to convince herself she was finally free of them and her life of enslavement and prostitution were over. She had bought her first home, funded by her Safevac income. She had been daring to feel safe.

Her scream of terror had alarmed Croake. He returned to the front door passage and rested a scuffed leather boot on Suzie's tiny chest and waited as still as a statue listening for any reaction from her neighbours. The heavy boot made breathing difficult, but she knew better than to move.

She lay helpless as her world imploded around her. She was certain no neighbour would come to her rescue or call the police. They all worked in downtown office jobs during the day.

The minutes ticked by. Finally, Croake was convinced Suzie's scream had gone unheard. He hauled the petite woman to her feet and frog marched her into a surprisingly large lounge with its comfortable new furniture.

'If the cops come, you tell them you shrieked because you were so delighted your American boyfriend had turned up unexpectedly. Okay?'

Suzie nodded. Tears were welling up in her eyes. Her life had been too good to be true.

Croake said: 'You got any bourbon or a good bottle of rye?' Suzie said nothing. He pushed her down on the sofa and walked to the refrigerator and then the kitchen cupboard. There was no sign of any liquor.

He walked back into the lounge: 'We'll have to have this little conversation sober, Suzie girl.'

She shrank back into the sofa. She was wide-eyed as he took a long knife out of the heavy, oversized coat. Then he took the coat off and threw it on an armchair.

'This is a filleting knife, Suzie girl.' He tapped it on her leg.

She took a deep breath. He pushed a hand over her mouth: 'If you scream again, Suzie girl, I'll kill you. You understand that?'

He took his hand away. 'So you thought you were going to be living the high life, did you? Pretty nice place for a Chink slut. Don't start with the tears, sweetie, we both know you're a tough working girl. I'm not here to damage the merchandise, although I know the Dogs wouldn't care.

'I'm here because I want to know everything that happened to you since you raced away from the Dogs' HQ. You know the boys think you were in on that raid, you were the snitch who got away. They'd be happy I if slit your throat.'

Charlotte found her voice: 'I no snitch.'

Croake nodded: 'Okay, I believe you. That means you can save your own skin, if you wanna.'

'Of course, wanna. Who you? What you want?'

'You can call me Eddie. And, as I said, I want to know how and why you are living here. Everything. Think you can explain that?'

He tapped the knife lightly against her leg again.

'I can no work if you cut me. You promise not cut me?'

'I promise.'

Croake got up and went to his coat. He produced a cellphone and pushed the record mode. 'Okay, from the start.'

'Will you take me back to Dogs?'

Croake smiled and the buckled teeth protruded. It was a face of evil, Suzie thought. Coake scoffed. 'No, I won't be taking you back to the Dogs. The Dog who had traced your cellphone and gave me this address won't be coming after you either, I guarantee that. I shoved this knife in his neck. I didn't want the Dogs coming here and complicating my life, either. So, Suzie girl, start talking. If I think you are shitting me, I'll cut you. Is that fair?'

She sighed and began her tale, from the moment she was warned by Kough about the police raid until she signed for her apartment mortgage. She said she was paid by Kough for keying in a password code every month so the Safevac formula was completed and new batches of the vaccine could be manufactured. She did not have all the code, so there was no point in torturing her. She was one of three people with different parts of the code. She had no idea who the others were. Kough was desperate to keep the code secret and away from his enemies.

At the end of her story, Croake said: 'You swear that's the whole story? You know I can find you, wherever you go, if you've told me a line of bullshit?'

Suzie said: 'I tell you everything. You never need come again.'

Croake said: 'There's one more detail, Suzie girl. How did you know Michael Kough? The guy's a billionaire.'

Suzie paused. Croake tapped the knife on her leg again. 'That not important. The story I tell you is all one hundred per cent trueful.'

'Suzie girl, I'll decide what's important. How did you meet the superstar, glamour boy Kough?'

'He was client.'

'What? Speak up, Suzie girl.'

She raised her voice: 'He was client.'

Croake shook his head: 'Don't start telling me bullshit at this late stage, Suzie girl. You're a good-looking gal, but you wouldn't make it in the billionaires' stakes.'

'I don't think he rich then.'

'So, where did he go for sex when he was poor?'

Suzie studied the floor. She finally took a deep breath: 'He come Suzie's Massage Parlour. King's Cross.'

Croake burst out laughing: 'King's Cross? With all the other sad johns?' He saw Suzie's reluctance to betray the personal confidences of the man who had transformed her life.

'He was a regular? Why did he choose you?'

'He was problem at start. Would not wear condom but wanted more than massage.'

Croake waited. Suzie inhaled another big breath: 'I use my mouth to put condom on him.'

'Wow. That's above and beyond the usual service,' Croake showed his shark face smile. 'No wonder he was a regular.'

Suzie swallowed: 'He nice man. Generous. No funny stuff. Just nice.'

Croake stood and walked to the picture window. He put the cellphone to his face: 'All right, Benny. We got what we want. Print a transcript and bring it up here before any of the neighbours start coming home.'

Croake told Suzie there would be a knock on the door shortly. She was to open it in case it was one of her friends. If it was, she had to pretend to be ill and get rid of them. He was expecting a colleague with a printout of their conversation. She was to date and sign it. Then he would leave. He would take her phone. He had to be sure she would make no calls to anyone, including the police or Kough.

He produced a small plastic box with a watch strap. It was a locator. She had to wear it around the clock. He would know if she removed it. She was not to go to any place she had not visited in the last thirty days.

Fifteen minutes later there was a polite knock on the door. Suzie opened it. There was a man in a white shirt holding a briefcase with Evaltime and Associates in gold letters on its side. He produced a small pile of A4-size papers covered in close-type print. Croake looked over the papers and nodded: 'Got a pen, Suzie girl? Sign the last page and initial the others, please.' She sat at the kitchen table and did what she was told. Croake put his oversized coat back on.

Benny Bland checked the papers like a diligent lawyer and put them back in his briefcase. Croake put the locator on Suzie's left arm, above her watch. He held her eye: 'Goodbye, Suzie girl. Please don't make me come back. You have a lovely face.'

He walked to the front door. Benny followed him. She heard the door shut. Suddenly she was alone in the apartment, at the table. She put her head on her arms and began sobbing. She had not been raped, stabbed or robbed. But she felt violated. She had betrayed the only man who had ever been kind to her. And tomorrow was the last day of the month. Her phone and its Safevac code were gone. She went to the bathroom and rustled through her medicine cabinet, pulling out a large box of prescription sleeping pills.

MICHAEL KOUGH WAS IMMEDIATELY ALARMED. His head of production reported Suzie was late to call with her Safevac code so production was being delayed.

Suzie Li had been the epitome of reliability. She had never missed a deadline. Big Brain said it did not matter. Production would not be delayed because he had the entire code in his head.

But it mattered to Kough. He imagined a thousand minor things that could have led to the delay, but he also worried about the Dirty Dogs hunting her.

Kough finally took the risk of calling her mobile. It was his only emergency link to her. He did not know, or want to know, where she lived. It went to voicemail. Big Brain chided his call could have revealed his number to some unfriendly person.

An hour after her deadline, time seemed to rush. She was soon two, then three, then four hours late. Kough began calling Sydney hospitals. Li Suzie, her surname was written first in the Chinese style, had not been admitted to any of them. Nor was she being held at any police station.

Charlotte could sense there was a big problem at Safevac but could get nothing from her frantic husband, who claimed he was just dealing with a production matter.

Big Brain supplied the code and Safevac production got under way for another thirty days. Kough took Charlotte by the hand and they went to bed early. He told her all was well; the production issue had been resolved. Their happy, routine family life would go on peacefully as he had promised.

He was wrong. His wife would leave him early the following morning.

FORTY

When the news broke it created a sensation. It was lead story in most countries because the miracle Safevac product had, itself, been a scarcely believable international miracle.

Big Pharma pounced, demanding production of it be halted immediately until full details of its secret properties and long-term effects had been scientifically studied.

The lurid headlines shouted:

SECRET FORMULA OF MIRACLE DRUG HELD BY CHINESE PROSTITUTE

BROTHEL CLIENT KOUGH GIVES SEX WORKER ACCESS TO TRILLION-DOLLAR VIRUS DISCOVERY

REGULAR DRUG TRIALS REJECTED BY ENTREPRENEUR BUT SHARED WITH $200-A-VISIT MASSEUSE.

TOPPMAN PHARMACEUTICAL CORPORATION CHAIRMAN, WALTER J. TOPPMAN, DEMANDS BAN AND SENATE INQUIRY. UPROAR BUILDS OVER DEATH OF INOCULATED KENTUCKY CHILD.

The Koughs' unlisted bedside landline phone shrilled at half-past six. It would have to be the bloody mother-in-law from hell calling, Kough thought. Despite living close by, Mei seemed to exist in another time zone. He rubbed his eyes open and handed the ringing phone across the bed to Charlotte.

She said a groggy hello and Kough immediately heard Mei's voice screeching from the other side of the bed.

Seconds later, Charlotte had flung off the blankets and was out of bed, heading for the lounge. Moments later, Kough heard the lounge television come on. Then a wail from his wife. He sprung out of bed. As he reached the lounge she was standing, watching the big screen. It was showing newspaper headlines from around the world and locally. They all carried the same message. Prostitute Suzie Li had given an American lawyer an affidavit saying her regular client, Michael Kough, billionaire scientist, had given her the top-secret Safevac formula.

Charlotte walked past Kough to the bedroom, without meeting his eye, and dressed. She called their chauffeur and took Michael Chen from his bassinet. Without a word, she walked out.

Kough sat and watched with deepening horror as his life's work and marriage imploded before his eyes.

Big Brain appeared. It was time to quit Woolloomooloo before teams of media turned up. The story was partly true and substantiated by the affidavit so there was no sense in issuing a denial and threatening libel action.

It made no sense, Kough thought. Why would Suzie do such a thing? The attack on him was too sophisticated to have originated from the Dirty Dogs.

The Dogs were mentioned in a later story. The body of one of them had been found in a rent-by-the-hour hotel room with his throat slit.

There would be no scandal in China, Big Brain said. The Chinese dictatorship would ensure the news would be censored and vaccine production would continue as normal.

Kough's cellphone chimed with a text. It was from a distraught Charlotte: 'You have betrayed me and disgraced my family. Please do not try to contact me. My mother said you attracted bad karma. I should have listened to her and not you, you rat. I am carrying your second child, but I don't know if I care to bring it into the world now. You sicken me. I will call the police and the media if you try to come near to me. Ta ma de ni.'

Big Brain laughed, I'm sorry but 'fuck you' from sweet little Charlotte is quite funny. Who would have thought? All right, what do we do? You have done nothing wrong except to try to protect your patent from crooks and copycats. Talk to the PM, tell him that John Able, his COS, also has part of your formula. The PM trusts you. And make a personal call to the Chinese president. Both owe their political success to you, and your talents.

We need to get rid of this crazy vaccine death story in Kentucky, because it has become an emotional anchor on this whole public relations mess.

Kough nodded to himself and then burst into tears: but what about Charlotte? And Michael Chen? And ... Suzie?

Suzie Li had spent the night staring at the big packet of sleeping pills. She felt curiously wide awake by six the next morning when the Safevac story broke.

She had almost no knowledge of international affairs, or something called Big Pharma, but she watched talking heads relentlessly condemning Michael Kough as a dangerous maverick, possibly poisoning millions of people with an unproven vaccine. They seemed to have forgotten the millions that he had saved.

The affidavit and her name and the brothel were mentioned repeatedly. Luckily, they had no photograph of her.

She picked up the packet of sleeping pills and toyed with it. Dropped it back on the table and went to the kitchen for a caffeine fix. She shut the television off. She had no cellphone, but she expected it would be full of messages from her small circle of friends, most of whom were still trapped in Sydney's gang-operated brothels or clothing sweat shops.

She sat and sipped her coffee – and thought of Mikey. He would feel betrayed and, well, raped, in a way. She refused to cry any more. After a while she realised the emotion building in her was anger. In her profession she was rarely allowed to display any anger. It felt quite good now she was.

She looked at her watch and was reminded of the locator strapped above it. And Eddie Croake. In a swift movement she undid the strap, rushed to the toilet and hurled it in. She stared at it for a minute, watching its flashing green light begin to blink erratically and then stop.

It was an empty gesture, but she had enjoyed making it. She looked around her ensuite. She had never had digs anything like this apartment. She looked at her vanity mirrors, the big shower cubicle, the heated towel rails, and the rows of cleaners stacked on an open shelf.

An idea popped into her head.

She left the apartment and went to her local convenience store where she bought two burner phones. Both had recording capability. Next door she purchased a large bottle of bourbon.

It was forty minutes since the locator beacon had met its death by drowning. There was no sign of Croake. But he would come. She was certain. She worried if he would bother to knock this time.

Suzie ground half a dozen of the sleeping pills into a fine powder and put it in a coffee mug. From the ensuite, she collected a bottle of bleach and drain cleaner. She added a large spoon of bleach and a teaspoon of drain cleaner to the sleeping pill mixture and stirred them together.

She retrieved the locator from the toilet bowl. She washed and wiped it carefully. She put it back on her wrist.

Fifty-five minutes after the locator beacon stopped pulsing, there was a loud hammering on the door. Suzie thought she felt the whole unit vibrate.

'Coming, coming,' she called. The hammering stopped. She opened the door as far as the security chain would allow. The big coat stood outside, the frightening shark teeth were glinting inside it.

'Eddie,' she said. She forced a smile: 'What you doing here? I thought we all done.'

Croake's forehead furrowed as he worked to slow his breathing.

Suzie's smile had confused him. It was shining innocently. These girls. They could act happy even while they lived at the bottom of the heap.

Croake looked at her left arm. The locator was still firmly attached. What the fuck? he thought. He knew they occasionally malfunctioned. Not often, though. He felt foolish standing there trying not to pant. He had feared the worst, but Suzie looked relaxed. She had probably not seen the news coverage. These girls, their world was tiny.

She was staring at him waiting for him to speak. Croake cleared his throat: 'I'm glad you're here, Suzie girl, your locator stopped transmitting about an hour ago.'

'Oh, it stop?' She held her left hand up and studied the square of plastic.

Croake nodded: 'Yeah, it stopped.'

Suzie stood back and undid the security chain: 'Well, now you here, come in. You try fix.'

Croake followed the woman down the passageway into the lounge. She had a nice figure. Good enough to attract and keep the billionaire Kough's attention, he thought.

'I take it off?'

Croake brought himself back into the moment: 'Ah ... yes, please.'

'No problem,' said Suzie.

He took the locator. The green indicator light was dead. He cursed to himself. The spare locator was back at his hotel. He had been in such a rush he had never thought to bring it.

'You tired, Eddie. Take seat. Was big boss happy with you?'

'Old Walter J? Yeah, he was happy.' Why the fuck did I mention his name, thought Croake.

She appeared to take no notice of the name, only that he was happy. These girls. If Walter J was happy and he was happy, Suzie would be relaxed. And fair enough, any danger to her had passed.

Croake turned the locator over in his big hands. He looked up at Suzie's friendly face: 'Ya know ... I'm sort of sorry about yesterday but I had a job to do, or I would have been the one getting a knife in me.'

Suzie's smile widened: 'Oh, I know. We all have job to do. Sometimes even when we don't like. That all over now, yes?'

Croake moved his body on the sofa: 'Yeah, yeah, that's all over, all over.'

'I know you professional. Not beating, raping. Nothing. I very grateful. Some of men I have to obey...'

Suzie stood suddenly: 'Sorry, no manner. Let me take coat. Hang it. Then can sit down comfortable.' The shark grin appeared before Croake could stop it. He stood and removed his coat. Suzie laid it over an armchair but folded it outward so its big inside pockets were exposed, though not their contents.

Croake sat down on the sofa and crossed his legs. He was wearing the same black, scuffed boots that yesterday had held her on the floor.

'It early but … I buy big bottle of bourbon. I didn't think you be back but realised I rude not keeping any refreshment.'

She went to the kitchen cupboard and took down the bottle: 'No mix, sorry, but ice.'

Croake felt conflicted. These girls, threatened with death one day and playing the smiling hostess the next. What was a boy to do? What would Michael Kough do? She didn't seem freaked out about the twisted teeth today either. She did not stare at them like yesterday.

'Yes, it is a bit early but it's five o'clock somewhere in the world.' He tried a laugh, but it was so unnatural for him it came out like a donkey braying. So, he nodded his head enthusiastically. Suzie smiled and turned to the cupboard, took out two glasses and her burner phone. She flicked the recorder button on. She poured a generous nip for him and a more ladylike one for herself.

She needed to position the cellphone closer. She took both glasses, gave him one and they clinked them together like old pals. She noticed he tasted it carefully. She said: 'This America bourbon.'

'Yeah, sure is. There's no substitute for the real thing.'

Suzie went back for the bottle and placed it on the coffee table. She could see nowhere safe to put the recorder. There was a knock on the door: 'Eddie, do you want me to go?'

'No, no. That's all right. That'll be Benny if you're not expecting anyone.' He stood.

Suzie said: 'Invite in if like.'

Croake paused in midstride: 'Nah. Three's a crowd, they say.' Fuck, he thought, what did I just say? 'Anyway, I'll have to send him back to the hotel to get the spare locator.' He turned away and Suzie heard the door open. She got up, took the recorder and positioned it out of sight in a magazine rack at the end of the sofa where Croake would sit.

She heard murmurs at the door. It closed again and Croake came back. 'Benny's gone. He'll be an hour or so.'

She filled their glasses again. Croake's almost to the top. He did not complain and tipped back a third of it in his first gulp.

Suzie put the bottle back on the coffee table and took a seat on the sofa beside him. Still apart. But beside him. He turned to get a better look at her. She started chatting about America and how wonderful it always sounded. The straight bourbon was making him feel warm and mellow.

She asked what his boss, Walter J, was like. He rubbed his pocked face: 'Walter J isn't too bad. As long as he gets what he wants. He's a billionaire. His old grandpa started a medicine company way back and he's the chairman now. Not that he does much except obsess over your friend Kough.'

Croake felt he was talking too much. But it did not matter, these girls, they lived in a universe far away from the Walter Js.

Suzie moved a fraction closer and looked innocently at Croake: 'Why he upset with Mikey?'

Croake manoeuvred one of his legs closer to hers: 'Kough's made him jealous, truth be known. Hates the idea of someone else doing well and takin' all the attention. He's a spoiled turd. Been brung up with evrathing.'

Suzie pushed her cute lips together: 'Why you work for him?'

'He needs people like me to do his dirty work. A couple of weeks ago, he wanted everyone to think a little Kentucky boy had died and it was the fault of Kough's vaccine. That the vaccine hadn't worked. People are greedy, Suzie. The boy's mum took our money and was as happy as a hamster to blame Safevac.'

Suzie looked upward as though trying hard to follow the logic: 'You mean dead boy not Safevac's fault?'

'Nah, the kid was a bloody wreck. Lucky to have lived as long as he did, had a hole in his heart, his mother said, and a crook liver. Do you have anything like a hole in your heart, Suzie?'

She smiled shyly. She was healthy girl, clean girl, she said.

He patted her on the leg: 'Healthy and clean, eh? I'm healthy and clean too.'

Suzie giggled: 'Ah, ah. No. I know you thinking. You much big for little Suzie. I need stitches after you. You very big man. Lots of muscles.'

Croake realised his breathing had quickened. He felt an erection growing in his pants. He saw Suzie had seen it as well.

She sighed: 'You no hurt me yesterday. I grateful. I pleasure you, if want.' She giggled again: 'Need two hands for you, I think.'

Croake's heart rate galloped. He began to quickly unbuckle his belt. She leaned over to help him. As he began to pull his pants down and expose a two-hand whopper, she grabbed the bottle and poured him another whopper shot. He had the ugliest grin in the world, she thought.

His need was apparently great. She took less than two minutes to accomplish her mission. While he mopped up, she kissed him on the forehead and stood. She went to the kitchen and boiled some water for coffee. She poured boiling water into his special brew and her plain one. The gangster-cum-hired gun was sitting back and smiling self-consciously. These girls, he thought. They had it when it came to making a man happy.

He took another swig at the bourbon while waiting for the coffee to cool. They chatted. He told her how he was an ugly kid and bullied all the time at school. Then became the students' go-to boy for the drugs they dare not go downtown to buy. Then he learned to be a bully. He had to collect the money when they got into his debt.

Eventually, Suzie passed him his coffee: 'Not American coffee. Our is different. Very strong. For strong men, not latte men.' He laughed and had a sip. She smiled and so he had another. He was thinking, I hope Benny is not hurrying. She also drank her coffee. He had swallowed half a cup when he went white and began trembling. She told him to put his feet up and lie down on the sofa. He was tired. He lay down and rubbed his eyes to focus. Then everything went black.

Suzie washed out the cups thoroughly. Took the recorder and hid it under her mattress. Benny knocked on the door. Suzie said: 'Please hurry. Eddie sick. Need call ambulance. Too much bourbon.'

Benny looked down at the grey-faced fixer and noticed his belt undone. Suzie said: 'Please, he need go. Might had heart attack.'

A cynical smile curved Benny's lips: 'What would have caused that, Suzie? A little too much exertion for the old guy? No ambulance. Give me a hand. We'll put him in my car.'

They struggled to half lift, half drag Croake to the elevator and then across the forecourt to the car. They poured him into the small back seat.

Benny gave a sigh of relief. He suddenly looked Suzie in the eye: 'There was no backup locator at the hotel. But we have a man watching you. So, you make sure you stay here, okay? We don't want to come hunting for you; or giving the Dogs your address. Okay?'

Suzie looked like a helpless, frightened little girl: 'I stay, I stay. Want no trouble. No trouble.'

Benny nodded and drove off. When he reached their King's Cross hotel, Croake had stopped snoring. Benny checked: Coake had stopped breathing as well. He had gone cold. He had extorted his last victim. Benny cursed him, then decided to leave him in the car. To a passer-by he would be just another drunk sleeping it off. He grabbed his luggage, passport and taxied to the airport, catching the first flight to anywhere in America.

FORTY-ONE

With Charlotte gone, Michael Kough reverted to type. Depressed and friendless, he went to the city's biggest casino. He bet in five-thousand-dollar chips. He won big. And lost big. By three in the morning, he was a little ahead but decided it was time to go. He had allowed his chauffeur to go home at midnight.

Hardly able to stand from bourbon and fatigue, he stumbled out to the taxi rank. The first driver would not take him. He was too drunk.

The second one hardly turned her tattooed face towards him as he fell into the back seat. She had to ask him twice for his address. He told her the Woolloomooloo apartments. She disbelieved him but turned the meter on and drove. She turned on to Darlinghurst Road heading south-east. It was deserted at that hour apart from the odd giant, groaning, eighteen-wheeler semi-trailer on its early morning delivery mission.

She never saw the one that T-boned her. She died instantly, crushed against the buckled steering wheel. The front of the taxi and its engine were sheared off in the impact. Her backseat passenger was left sitting, open to the elements, when the front of the car and its seats were torn away. Kough was thrown ten metres on to an empty footpath. His head clipped a lamppost.

He lay unconscious for twenty-three minutes, unattended until a late-duty paramedical crew scraped him off the ground. He stank of booze. His vital signs were struggling to register.

The paras were sure he was a goner. One found ten thousand dollars in a tight roll of notes and a five-thousand-dollar casino chip lying beside him. They saw two homeless guys sitting nearby, clutching brown paper bags which held sherry bottles and the dregs of their night's booze-up. Their rheumy eyes suddenly came alive but died again as the paras swooped to clean up the cash and crash debris.

Detective Wallace Best sighed. He was disappointed to find a small, timid, nervous Chinese woman open the door to the apartment. He was hoping for a big, swarthy, tattooed punk worthy of a decent underworld killing.

But it was her Summer Hill apartment that was displayed as the destination on the cellphone GPS they found on the body of Edward Croake.

Best said: 'Sorry to bother you, ma'am. Is this your apartment? Do you live here alone?'

Suzie nodded: 'Yes, my apartment. Just me.'

Best showed her his police card. The card seemed to make her more nervous not less. He introduced Detective Sergeant Jordan Catch and asked if he and Catch could come in and talk to her. She turned and led them inside to the spacious lounge and its attractive new furniture.

Best said: 'Can I have your name please?' She told him. She explained she had purchased the apartment several months ago. It was her first home since she migrated. The sergeant wandered off to the kitchen area. He cast his eye over its new white goods. The place was tidy and clean.

'Do you know why we are here?' Best asked quietly.

'Yes. I know.'

Both detectives stared at her. 'What do you know, Ms Li?' She let out a long breath and sat down on the sofa but said nothing. She seemed to be on the verge of tears.

Best said gently: 'How long have you known Mr Edward Croake?'

She shook her head and stared at the carpet. Best said: 'We know he visited you twice recently. Once yesterday. Your address is on his phone's GPS.'

She stared defiantly at Best: 'He very bad man.'

Best sat on the facing armchair and said nothing. The silence drew out for a long minute: 'He made me sign papers about Safevac. Tell him I was prostitute – I not any more. Have job with Michael Kough.'

Catch whistled: 'Holy shit. Are you one of the women walking around with Kough's secret formula? Wally, this is the Chinese lady who's been in all the news.'

Best sat up straight: 'Is this true, Ms Li?'

She nodded: 'My name Suzie.'

'What was this character Croake doing here yesterday, Suzie?'

She got up and went to the bedroom. She came back with the plastic locator and a burner phone.

'I turn off locator. I know Croake would come. He angry but showed him, it on my wrist. So he believed locator faulty. It was: I throw it in toilet first. I invite him in. Gave him some bourbon. Later pleasured him on sofa where you sitting.'

Best moved his body unconsciously.

'When he finish, gave him coffee. He passed out. Another man in white shirt arrived. We got him downstairs. Man drove him away, on back seat. Not seen man since. Do you think Croake come back? I very scared of him.'

Best shook his head: 'Edward Croake will not be coming back. He'll never bother you again, Suzie.'

She raised her eyebrows: 'He dead?'

Best nodded. Suzie smiled and sat again. 'That good. Very good. He bad man. His big boss bad man too. Badder, I think.'

Best was having trouble processing all of Suzie's candid information and its implications.

'Can prove him badder.' Suzie held up her burner. She pressed the play button. The detectives both sat on the edge of the couch and leaned forward, listening intently. The recorder was difficult to hear initially, then there was an audible knock on the door. Croake went to answer it. When he returned the recorder was clearer and louder.

The conversation between the sex worker and Croake took a familiar path as Suzie worked to seduce the gullible American. It finished almost an hour later. The detectives could hear cups being washed and the apartment being tidied up. A cupboard opened and shut before the man in the white shirt returned and lugged his drunken boss away downstairs with the help of the Chinese woman.

Catch pursed his lips: 'That Walter J is the billionaire that wants Safevac banned. This tape is enough to stick him in prison for conspiracy. The shit will hit the fan in America when this gets out.'

Best looked at Suzie: 'You're a brave lady. Does anyone else have a copy of this recording?'

She shook her head: 'Just me.'

'Do you know the name of the second man with the white shirt?'

'Just Benny. Not dressed like gangster, not like Croake.'

Best stood up and put the cellphone recorder in his pocket: 'There is one last question, Suzie. Croake died after he left here. Do you know what killed him?'

Suzie shrugged her shoulders and shook her head innocently: 'He left, very tired. Snoring. Drunk. Had massage with happy ending. Maybe heart attack?'

Catch smiled: 'If we were to look around your apartment, would we find cleaning stuff in plastic bottles?'

Suzie smiled and shook her head.

Best had known great liars. Suzie was not one of them. He exchanged looks with Catch, who gave a wink. Best nodded back. Suzie was not the criminal in this scenario. Croake's death was no bad thing.

Best changed direction. Was it true she held the vital key to the Safevac formula? Suzie said it was. But now she could no longer communicate with the Safevac. Croake had taken her encrypted cellphone with her password. Best said there was no sign of any cellphone on Croake or in his King's Cross hotel room.

Suzie looked at him in despair. She looked on the point of breaking down. He noticed how pale she was. There were dark patches under her eyes which began to spill tears.

'I have let Dr Kough down. I hope he will forgive me,' she said.

Another tear spilled: 'Safevac stop. No more vaccine. Anywhere.'

Best said he would return to the motel and conduct a second search. But knew no cellphone to be found. Their first search had been so thorough, the hotel owner was threatening to make an official complaint about damage they had caused to the motel's ceilings, walls, carpets and air conditioning ducts.

WALTER J. Toppman's wife rushed into his salubrious home study in a fluster. The woman was always in a fluster, he thought. Always a drama going on somewhere in her pampered life.

'Walt, there are men here to see you.' Mary Jane's voice was high pitched and urgent.

'What men? From where? I don't have any appointments this morning, you know that. I've got Nick coming for tennis later. Tell them to make an appointment, and, for God's sake, don't rush in here like the place is on fire.'

'Walt, listen to me, they're already at the front door. There's five or six of them. They're insisting they see you right now. And, and ... a Channel Six satellite truck pulled up behind them.'

'Mary Jane, I'm going on Channel Six tomorrow. Those dopey clowns already know that. I should have bought the bloody channel when I had the chance.'

Suddenly Walter J heard a loud hammering. 'Is that someone banging on my front door? What the hell? No one just arrives here and starts banging on my door.'

'Walt, I told you they were insisting they see you at once.'

'Oh, for God's sake, Mary Jane, pull yourself together. Why aren't you at your yoga class or something?'

She looked pained: 'Yoga's not till tomorrow, Walt.'

Walter J rolled his eyes: 'For pity's sake woman, never mind ... go and tell whoever it is to make an appointment.'

She looked around the study with its photos of Walter J shaking hands with the US president, accepting a tennis veterans cup, posing with Aretha Franklin and making a speech behind a Harvard University podium. She knew. These men with their blue windbreakers were not going to go away. Why had the Channel Six truck appeared at the rear of their convoy?

'Well, go on woman. What are you standing about here for?' Walter J went behind his desk and flicked on his surveillance cameras. His eyes widened as he leaned forward to watch a small crowd forming at his roadside entrance. It was closed off by tall, ornate iron gates the Élysée Palace would have been proud of.

He switched to the camera outside his main, formal entrance. His blood began to boil as he saw a group of men brush past his house maid. Moments later the study door swung open and five men strode in. The lead man said: 'Mr Toppman, please stand away from your computer.'

'What?' Walter J shouted. But he had seen the huge gold FBI letters on their blue wind jackets.

The lead man came behind his desk and took him firmly by the arm and led him away from his seat.

'What the hell is going on?'

The lead man began reading the astonished billionaire his rights. The charges included extortion and fraud. Mary Jane fainted and fell heavily against a wall, dislodging the framed photograph of the president greeting Walter J. It struck her on the head. A trickle of blood crept through the dyed blonde hair and down her forehead. Walter J looked at her. Always a drama, he thought.

Outside the Big Pharma billionaire was led away in handcuffs. Channel Six recorded their scoop.

WALTER J. Toppman III plea bargained the charges. He was sentenced to seven years and hurriedly replaced as the chairman of Toppman Pharmaceuticals.

Walter J folded after he heard the tape of his henchman Eddie Croake's conversation with a prostitute in Sydney. Croake confessed he worked for Toppman because 'he needs people to do the dirty work for him'.

Croake exposed the rort between Walter J and Toby Ellis's mother, Lucy. The claim was that the boy had died because a Safevac vaccination had failed. But the mother was given fifty thousand dollars by a bogus organisation to say her son was in good health. The tape, however, debunked her claim, with Croake saying: 'The kid was a wreck. Lucky to have lived as long as he did. His mother said he had a hole in his heart and a crook liver.'

Lucy was sentenced to two years' jail but released on parole after a month on mental health grounds.

The prosecutors withdrew conspiracy charges, for lack of evidence, against Walter J for an attempt to have Croake extort the Safevac formula from the prostitute, and to then greenmail Michael Kough. Croake did, however, coerce a signed statement from the woman confirming she had access to the formula.

The impact of Walter J's arrest led to a boom in Safevac sales internationally.

But rumours the Australian scientist who had made the discovery was dying and taking his secret formula with him pushed prices sky high.

FORTY-TWO

Michael Kough finally gained consciousness eight days after he was admitted, drunk, to a Sydney hospital with serious head injuries. Doctors had put him in an induced coma.

When he began to focus his eyes, he smiled at the apparition before him. The two most important women in his life, Charlotte and Suzie, were standing together at his bedside.

I am hallucinating again, Kough thought. Charlotte had taken Michael Chen and left him in disgust the morning the Walter J-generated Chinese prostitute story broke. So it couldn't be the two of them together. He squeezed his eyes closed against the pitiless glare of the ward lighting. He could hear steady beeps from a bank of equipment beside him. Their small lights flashed in a sort of unsteady rhythm. He had no idea where he was.

He felt what he thought was Charlotte's lips on his forehead. She had her own way of doing little kissy kisses. Then everything went wonderfully cosy as he slipped back into a painless unconsciousness. Beside his bed the two women hugged each other and tried not to sob. But Kough's doctor was ecstatic.

The patient was showing the first, tentative signs of recovery. Kough's brain had swollen dangerously after his head had hit a light pole as his body had been flung from a disintegrating taxi cab.

The cab driver had died instantly. The truck driver had gone to sleep at the wheel. He was cut free but lost both his legs. He was six miles from his depot and home after fourteen hours at the wheel. It took emergency workers five hours to clear the wreckage and reopen the Darlinghurst road just before peak-hour traffic began in earnest.

The bigger news of the horrendous crash came later in the morning, when the injured man was identified as the vaccine hero, Michael Kough.

Grateful Covid survivors inundated the hospital with flowers. Scores prayed for him outside on the pavement. A candlelit vigil went on for several days and more bouquets piled up alongside the hospital's front fence. The outpouring of grief was met with grim, unchanging medical bulletins. It was not known if Kough would recover. Or how much of his brilliant brain would survive if he did.

News that he briefly gained consciousness was greeted with a second tsunami of flowers and cards. People everywhere were on tenterhooks, not daring to celebrate too soon. A special patient online information service was created. Tens of thousands of visits from throughout the world flooded it for the latest information on Kough's condition.

While his life hung in the balance, Suzie Li decided she had to speak directly with Kough's wife. She summoned her courage and went to the Woolloomooloo apartment, but the intercom remained silent when she announced her name.

So she waited for hours outside the basement car park until Charlotte's Rolls-Royce nosed its way to street level. She jumped in front of the monster and refused to move. Its raised back seats enabled her to see Charlotte's small figure clearly through the windscreen. There was an impasse for several minutes. Another exiting vehicle moved up the ramp. It waited patiently. The chauffeur knew from experience Rolls have a deference factor. Motorists behind a stationary Rolls after traffic lights go green will wait quietly twice as long as they would behind any other car before honking.

The chauffeur turned to Charlotte: 'Shall I let her in, ma'am?' Charlotte nodded. The chauffeur got out, beckoned to her, opened the back-to-front rear passenger door and Suzie got in without having to duck her head.

He drove quietly off. Suzie turned to Charlotte. They were sitting next to each other in the expansive leather armchair-cum-seats: 'Any news on Mr Mikey?' Charlotte looked at her hands: 'No. No news.'

Charlotte had been humiliated to learn in the mass media that her husband had been a 'client' of Suzie Li at a gang-run King's Cross brothel. When the news broke, she had flown to Hong Kong and stayed at her mother's tiny apartment. She flew home immediately when she learned of Michael's horror accident. Now Charlotte was torn. The lady of the night had forced herself on her. But Charlotte knew Suzie's bravery had led to the fall of a corrupt American billionaire who had set out to destroy her husband.

Suzie broke the stiff silence: 'Mikey very good man. Very honourable. He no see me after you returned. Then saved me, saved me from the Dogs and sex worker life. He gave me job. At Safevac. Everyone know that now.'

Charlotte nodded. Her eyes were full of tears and she suddenly reached out and took Suzie's hand. Suzie gripped it tightly. They rode most of the way to the hospital in a sad silence.

As they approached the main entrance, Charlotte said: 'I have heard you lost your encrypted phone and now ... nothing can be signalled to Safevac to let its computer make the vaccine.'

Suzie said nothing.

'I know Michael went to extreme lengths to protect his formula, so this is not all your fault. Even if you know what the ingredients are, I know they can only be signalled to the Safevac computer from the encrypted cellphone.'

Suzie drew a deep breath: 'I learn my part formula. It in my head. But ... very impossible to tell computer without encrypted phone.'

'Don't worry. Michael will recover. When he does, he'll get you a new one, one the computer will recognise to allow your data to download.'

Suzie looked worried and doubtful. 'If he not get better, many die. Because of me.'

'Don't you think he'll get better?'

Suzie said nothing.

'C'mon. We're here now. Let's go up and see him, both of us together. We might be the good luck charm he needs to wake up properly.'

The chauffeur opened the back-to-front door for Suzie. She stepped down. It was a long way; the chauffeur had forgotten to lower the body. He went to the opposite door and held Charlotte's hand, to help her to the ground. 'Sorry about the height, ma'am.'

'That's all right. We all have bigger things on our mind at the moment,' Charlotte said.

They sat by the bed amid the blinking lights, breathing tubes and drip towers for nearly two hours. Kough breathed quietly, and occasionally a limb would jerk slightly. But that day the good luck moment did not arrive. Charlotte insisted Suzie stay at Woolloomooloo. They passed two long rows of cut flowers lining the driveway as they left the hospital.

It had been nine days since Kough had last breathed on his own, but the fresh flowers continued to arrive. The two women held hands on the bleak trip home.

They would have to wait another twenty-four hours before they both saw his first flicker of life.

FORTY-THREE

Horatio Hadley had worked at the junior counter level of the Australian Border Force at Sydney Airport for eight years. He had the misfortune to suffer from acne long after his early teenage years. His nastier colleagues referred to him as Spotty Face.

He also had the misfortune to grow to a height of only one hundred and sixty centimetres and never to have filled out. He was so skinny he became the butt of jokes about having to run around in the shower to get wet. His Border Force uniform hung off him like a loose blue tent. His large Adam's apple ensured his tie was permanently crooked. He was twenty-six and still lived with his parents in Ambervale, fifty kilometres from central Sydney.

Still on the basic salary – fifty thousand dollars a year – he could not afford his own home. His last girlfriend – only the second he had ever had – had dropped him a fortnight ago when he told her he had applied for a higher-paying Border Force job based in Darwin. She was a Sydney girl and leaving her family for a life in the sweltering wild west of the Northern Territory was a deal breaker. She said sorry and left.

But Hadley pushed ahead. He wanted a senior job in the force's maritime border command. The pay would be a fifty per cent rise. The force declined his application. No reason was given.

But they did offer him the job of Investigation and Evidence Support Officer. The pay was only moderately better, and the opening was in Perth, which he knew was closer to Jakarta than Sydney. And what the devil was an evidence support officer? It sounded like a poshed-up Boy Friday position.

His life had reached a low ebb. He was alone in the staff room eating the sandwiches his mother had made for his lunch when he saw a large newspaper photograph of Dr Michael Kough. Kough was the rude prick who had refused Hadley's legitimate demand he open his briefcase back when the germ-warfare virologist had first arrived back from America.

He had never forgotten the arrogant face and his humiliation when he was undermined by Gerry Ryan, his supervisor, nicknamed Old Hardballs because of his military background with the Commandos. Ryan had been pathetic: grovelling, bowing like a sycophantic butler, waving Kough through Customs unchecked.

Kough had claimed some bullshit about the case's contents being a matter of national security. The case could only be opened after being delivered to the Prime Minister's Office. Any fool could see it was bullshit.

And look how life had turned out for Kough the smuggler. He was now a billionaire with a beautiful wife, luxury cars, a superyacht and an inner-city penthouse.

Hadley produced his cellphone calculator and further depressed himself. With an income of a billion a year, Kough earned forty-eight thousand dollars an hour, as much in an hour as Hadley did in a whole year.

The staff room door flew open. Ryan, with his ramrod back and immaculately pressed uniform, barked: 'There you are pus face. What the hell are you doing here? Your shift started six minutes ago and passengers are already queuing. Get your skinny arse in your booth.'

Hadley put down the newspaper: 'Did you call me "pus face", sir?'

'I'll call you worse than that if you don't move your skinny arse. Now, get going, boy.'

Hadley stood and faced Ryan: 'Would you like to apologise for using that language?'

'What?' Ryan exploded.

'Are you going to apologise for your language?'

'The fuck I am. Now move your arse or I'll be reporting your failure to meet your work timetable commitments.'

Hadley pushed his chair under the lunch room table, picked up his cellphone and the newspaper. He ignored Ryan's glaring eyes and walked out, back to his booth.

The next morning, Ryan was called into his border commander's office. He was shown a formal letter from the Community and Public Sector Union accusing him of staff abuse and unacceptable bullying. A written apology was demanded followed by compulsory attendance at the Force's Inclusion and Diversity course the following week.

'Horatio Hadley was late for his afternoon shift. I found him in the lunch room reading a newspaper. I ordered him to get to his booth immediately. I threatened to report his unprofessional conduct to you,' Ryan said.

The commander lifted his eyebrows: 'Well, you didn't report him, did you? Does that mean it wasn't such a big infringement of our standards? He has been with us for the last eight years – and he has been reliable. No sick days. No stirring up trouble with the union over rosters or staff shortages.'

Ryan pushed his shoulders back: 'Hadley is a man-boy, a total tosser. I don't know how he got into the force. He's absolutely unsuitable for the job. He's far too officious with the public. He's a right little Hitler when he puts his uniform on. He's also too puny to take on some of our work, like physically overpowering the thugs that we have to deal with from time to time. And he *is* still covered in pus pimples most boys grew out of when they left high school. His nickname with the staff is "pimple face".'

The commander eased back in his chair: 'That's all very well, but how is our department going to handle this particular problem? I suggest you apologise, go to the inclusion seminar or request a hearing with the union and deny Hadley's allegations.'

'This is ridiculous. Hadley should be doing the apologising for missing the start of his shift, making others do his share of the work.'

The commander swung his swivel chair back and forth and said: 'I don't want union problems here, Gerry. Tell the man you're sorry. And watch your language in the future. We are all living in politically correct times.'

Ryan stood red-faced and said nothing. The commander said: 'All right, that's all.'

Ryan did not move. He took a deep breath: 'There have been rumours that Officer Hadley is looking at a job in Perth. Some admin position. Perhaps we could have a word to Perth and encourage him to move?'

'Maybe. But let's get this union matter out of the road first, okay?'

Ryan could hardly believe he was being dismissed for a second time. This commander was meant to support his team leaders, not kowtow to the bloody unions and pathetic losers like Hadley. Ryan snapped his heels together: 'Yes, sir.'

He stormed back to his office. An email message was flashing on his computer screen: 'Just confirming your apology today will be in writing. And best wishes for a positive report from your Inclusion seminar on Monday. Yours etc., Horatio Hadley.'

Ryan slammed his fist down on the desk. The tittering secretaries in the open-plan office watching him seemed to find something very amusing to smile about. He closed the venetian blinds with a sharp tug on the cord. It came away in his hand.

HORATIO HADLEY FELT EMPOWERED. Jubilant. He had thrown sand in the eyes of the bully. He read the written apology several times and was unable to wipe the grin from his face. He printed out a dozen copies and left them in the lunch room and pinned others on several official Border Force notice boards. Hadley did not see Ryan all day. Old Hardballs had beaten a retreat to his office, he thought.

The last passenger had passed through his booth. It had been an old, limping lady who had smuggled a couple of Fijian mangoes into her luggage. He gave her a wink and shut the suitcase for her. She beamed and kissed him on the cheek. He had enjoyed the best day of his life.

He went to the staff lunch room to retrieve his sandwich container. His mood was dampened when he saw the discarded morning newspaper on the table. Kough's grinning, overconfident and arrogant photograph was still staring from its front page.

A tiny hint of an idea restored his happiness. He thought about it the whole time he drove to his commuter train station and then as it rattled and shook its way to Ambervale, the distant, cheapest suburb in Sydney.

FORTY-FOUR

MICHAEL KOUGH WAS LYING IN A SERENE, DARK, PAIN-FREE universe. But he could hear voices.

There had been hallucinations earlier but now he could make out the voices of Charlotte, a man they referred to as Dr Heddle, and, distantly, Suzie. They were discussing him. Kough tried to rouse Big Brain but he was missing.

Heddle was explaining he had performed a decompressive hemicraniectomy soon after Kough's admission.

'A what?' said Suzie.

'They cut a bone flap in his skull,' said Charlotte.

'That's right,' said Heddle, 'we had to remove part of his skull because Michael's brain was swelling so much.'

'Oh, yuk,' said Suzie. 'So when he wake up he have a big hole in head?' The other two laughed. Laughter sounded odd to Kough. There had been none in his life for so long.

'No, no. We stitch the bone flap back in place,' said Heddle, 'but we have other, more serious concerns than his flap.' There was a grim silence.

'If a coma lasts more than eight days it can mean the patient has suffered structural brain stem damage. Michael has been in a coma for nine.'

'Oh,' said both women together. Kough thought he heard a quiet sob from Charlotte.

Heddle said the induced coma allowed Michael to heal by suppressing the speed of his brain function. This suppression was interrupted with short bursts of activity.

Suzie said: 'He had big brain. Very clever man. Will brain work when coma finished?'

'It's impossible to know what condition or what functional impairment someone will have when they come out of a coma. You need to be prepared to accept Michael may suffer a personality change, suddenly shouting at you, or hallucinating or having vivid nightmares. He may have periods of confusion. Or, worst case, permanent brain damage.'

Heddle said the amount of anaesthetic administered to Kough was being gradually reduced to end the coma.

'But, cheer up, ninety-four per cent of coma patients survive to go home.'

Charlotte was not mollified: 'Yes, but we don't know if his big brain will work properly.'

'That's right. We don't. There's no way to tell what impairment he will suffer, if any. But I can see he will get a lot of love and attention from you two. And a few million other people. Have you seen the acres of flowers spread all over the hospital grounds? He has a lot of people out there pulling for him.'

Suzie said: 'You right. Everyone wants Mikey get well.' She paused: 'And he will. No god can ignore so many prayers.'

Charlotte burst into tears.

The flow of anaesthetic eased and Kough found the darkness clearing. But he began to feel some pain. He assumed he had broken bones along with his broken head. He began to wonder where the hell Big Brain had gone. Maybe he had escaped when they opened his skull? At least my sense of humour is intact, he thought.

FORTY-FIVE

Deputy Prime Minister David Hicks had a well-tuned political nose. When the Cabinet meeting ended, after only thirty-three minutes, the nose was wrinkling. Cabinet usually found enough business to last at least two and a half hours – long enough for someone to suggest a late-afternoon scotch would be appropriate.

But PM Gary Stone had hurried through the agenda, forestalling debate, sidelining thorny issues. The PM seemed distracted. And he forswore a scotch. He rushed off with his chief of staff, John Able, in tow. There was something up. Maybe it was personal. His wife, Elaine, or another family member, could be ill. He would put some feelers out, Hicks decided.

Stone had led the government to a small, increased majority in the general election after steering the nation through a couple of economic crises with the Chinese. His popularity in the polls was at a career high. Hicks was beginning to worry whether he would ever get a run at the premiership. At fifty-eight he was ten years younger than Stone, but the old rugby league war horse seemed indefatigable.

Hicks had been a major when he retired from the Australian Army nine years ago for a safe seat in the Federal Parliament.

He returned to his Defence Minister's office. Its reception was festooned with war memorabilia and models of destroyers, tanks and vintage faded battalion flags.

Also, unexpectedly, in the reception was Ms Audrey Tibble, arms and legs crossed impatiently. The chief investigator for the Commonwealth Ombudsman had no appointment he knew of. His political antenna went up.

The go-anywhere, investigate-everything Ombudsman's independent office was a natural enemy of every minister, civil servant and corporate CEO. Ms Tibble had taken more than her share of scalps from among the corrupt and unethical.

Employing more than a hundred thousand people, the Defence Department always had some sort of complaint being lodged against it. Nearly all were thrown out.

'Audrey, what an unexpected surprise.' Hicks offered his hand and the pair shook after Tibble had unfolded all her limbs and got to her feet. The hair tied behind her head gave her a stern, school-mam look. There was never a skerrick of makeup. She smiled a greeting. It instantly unsettled Hicks.

'I think we may have a little spot of trouble on our hands,' she said. 'Can we talk confidentially? It involves your Border Force portfolio.'

People smuggling, drug cartels or someone's wife running an import sideline with little bags of blood diamonds, thought Hicks.

'You're lucky to get me this afternoon. Cabinet meetings usually take a lot longer,' he said, leading the way to his office.

'I had a suspicion that meeting wouldn't take long today. The big boys have other things on their mind at the moment.'

Hicks swung around to face Tibble: 'What? What's going on?'

'In your office, if you don't mind, Minister.'

They sat at the small conference table in Hick's office. 'This doesn't involve me, personally, does it?'

Ms Tibble gave a knowing smile and shook her head: 'No, not you personally, but as the deputy PM, I thought I should brief you first. Do you remember the old line about the tiniest nick in a nylon leading to the whole stocking unwinding?'

'Christ, Audrey, what the hell is going on?'

'It appears that a tiny malcontent at the bottom of the Border Force ranks has potentially enough dirt on the Prime Minister's Office to end Gary Stone's career.'

Hicks forced himself not to smile. I bloody knew something was up, he thought. My wait for the Big Job may be shorter than I dared hope.

'It must be explosive stuff to cause a ruction big enough to topple Gary.'

Ms Tibble opened a file: 'See what you think. My investigation so far has led down some dark and murky paths.'

The investigation had uncovered an alleged conspiracy at the top levels of the federal government to facilitate the smuggling of top-secret material from a US germ-warfare plant. This had involved the prime minister and his chief of staff and had allowed entrepreneur Michael Kough, an alcoholic, gambling addict and bankrupt, to steal the miracle Safevac vaccine. And, then, to exploit it to rob hundreds of millions of dollars from the Chinese government before licensing them a second time to produce it.

The smuggling was facilitated by a senior Border Control officer. He had overruled the whistle-blower, overseen the arrival of the PM's COS and allowed the contraband through Customs unchecked. The PM's official limousine festooned with his official flags had been waiting outside the airport to spirit the COS and Kough from the airport.

The limousine and its passengers were caught on Border Force's security cameras. The PM's Office had then temporarily stored the vaccine data in the government's super-secure database. It was later removed and transferred to Kough.

Kough had a liaison with a Hong Kong Chinese woman suspected of being a Chinese spy, who had been hired by the chief of staff, who had also carried on an affair with her. She had left him and Kough was now married to her.

'Holy shit, forgive my French, that's quite a saga. And all from a low-level passport stamper,' Hicks said. 'Do you think it, or any of it, is true? What's the whistle-blower's gripe?'

Ms Tibble pushed up her pencil-thin eyebrows: 'Ask your department. The whistle-blower got a written apology from his supervisor after an alleged bullying incident a couple of weeks ago.'

Hicks grunted: 'Discovered the power of the pen, has he?'

'I think the bullying incident was the last straw. The guy's never complained about anything before and he's been at the passport desk for eight years without ever being promoted.'

Hicks said: 'The last straw turned out to be the nick in the nylon?'

Ms Tibble nodded.

Hicks said: 'Okay, what now? What's the next step? Do you want me to go and see Gary and get him to fall on his sword?'

Ms Tibble looked surprised: 'Oh, no. Nothing like that, at this stage. My investigation hasn't finished. Kough is one of the key figures and I haven't been able to interview him. He's been in a famous coma until yesterday.'

'With half the world's population praying for his recovery,' said Hicks.

'And all of the Chinese government praying he will recover enough to give them the full formula for Safevac,' said Ms Tibble.

She said as the investigation widened, the chances of the accusations leaking grew exponentially. She was concerned at the stability of the government if the Opposition party began asking questions. Hicks said he would be more concerned with the Americans and the CIA asking questions.

'So, you want to keep these matters under wraps until your inquiries are complete?' he said.

Ms Tibble said: 'I am not suggesting a cover-up.'

'No, no. I wasn't suggesting that. Absolutely not. There has to be a clean-out at the top of our political ranks. I meant, once you are satisfied your conspiracy pact is true, how do we handle it?'

'That's maybe when you go and see the PM. Let's not get ahead of ourselves. I just wanted to brief you, so this will not be a huge shock and arrangements for the continuance of smooth government are in hand when the matter becomes public.'

'Audrey, that is most appreciated. You wouldn't like a scotch, would you?'

'Good heavens, no. I have to drive home. And, frankly, I don't believe in office drinking practices. It's been the cause of a lot of problems in our government departments and the big corporations' boardrooms.' Ms Tibble placed the file back in her briefcase and stood: 'Minister, thank you for your time. I'll let you know when I've interviewed Michael Kough. In the meantime, I needn't tell the

Minister of Defence. Loose lips sink ships.' She blessed him with one of her smiles and left.

Hicks had not been so excited since his horse ran second in the Melbourne Cup. He bounced around in small circles. He was bursting to tell someone the news. He picked up his phone. Put it down. Picked it up again. Put it down again. The early end to the Cabinet meeting had left a hole in his day. He decided he would go to the city and buy a new dark suit. One befitting a prime minister. After all, he had been briefed to be ready.

THE PRIME MINISTER'S WIFE, Elaine, was a study of concentration as she read the Commonwealth Ombudsman's preliminary report. She had been at Gary Stone's side during every political crisis and triumph. The pair had met as law students at Sydney University and her mother had regarded him with a faint distaste. He was a big, barbarian sort who relished his bruising rugby league games each Saturday. She was won over when she saw how much in love he was with her daughter.

They both left university after only two years because Gary's father died suddenly and he was needed to run the family's transport business in Lismore. Their two sons began to run the company after their father was elected to Parliament ten years ago. His success meant Elaine had to uproot herself and move to Canberra, a city she regarded as an artificial island of red tape and warring ambitions.

She had made the effort to fit in and was there to celebrate Gary's sudden, and unexpected, election to party leadership and then prime minister.

He had faced several critical challenges over the years, from foreign powers and political rivals. She detested the patronising description of her being the 'power behind the throne', but the pair did trust each other's judgement.

This political threat from Horatio Hadley's complaint to the Ombudsman's Office was like nothing they had confronted before. As she read it, she started to shake her head slowly. The report read like a script for a political horror show.

She finally finished the last page, alleging illegal and serious 'disclosable conduct' by the prime minister and John Able.

She put the papers down quietly. She squared them neatly on the coffee table. She removed her reading glasses and looked at the two men facing her: 'You've both been incredibly stupid. And naive. Theft, fraud, conspiracy to smuggle an ally's secrets into the country. You've been seduced by this Michael Kough character – and Gazza, all your work and success would be hanging on a thread if this ever gets out, whether it's true or not.'

Gary Stone glared at her under his hedgerow eyebrows but said nothing. He knew she was right. John Able sat next to him on the couch in The Lodge's formal lounge like a nervous sixth former being reprimanded by the headmaster for bad behaviour.

'What on earth were you both thinking?'

Stone cleared his throat and began to say something, but Elaine held up a hand: 'The solution, the way out of this hideous mess, is simple: Michael Kough must be sent to the sin bin once and for all. He has had his run and needs to be taken off the field, eliminated, once and for all.'

Eliminated? To save the government? What the hell did she mean? thought Able.

'Kough has held everyone to ransom, including you two. This nonsense about keeping the Safevac formula as an encrypted secret, that has to be renewed every thirty days, has to stop. It will immediately eliminate his power to control things. If his memory doesn't come back, problem solved. If it does come back, you two need to persuade him to give you the full formula pronto,' she said.

Stone found his voice: 'Darling, thank you for your full and frank appraisal, but if he doesn't play ball, what do we do? Shoot him?'

'No, Gazza. I have a much better idea,' she said. They sat silently as she explained her plan. Able was appalled. Stone sat glumly looking at his shoes.

Watching their reactions, she said: 'Before either of you start to protest, remember you both brought this on yourselves and, now, our whole government.'

Elaine pointed a finger at her husband: 'I don't need to remind you, Gazza, you said yourself you believed the US would have a strong claim on the vaccine because it was obviously discovered by Kough when he worked in their Colorado lab.'

Stone sighed: 'Well, even if I was right, we can hardly give it back to them this late in the game. We've been denying their claim for years and they haven't been able to turn up any evidence it was developed there.'

'No, they haven't, Gazza, because Kough is too clever to leave them any. He took his mega salary, exploited their facilities, wiped all his research files, stole his sample vaccines and smuggled them back here with the help of his best mate, right John?'

Able shrugged.

'Right, John?' Elaine repeated.

'I had no idea he was smuggling anything. I just went to the airport as a very old friend to pick him up. Next thing this officer takes me into their inner sanctum, saying Boffy wouldn't allow his briefcase to be searched because its contents were a matter of national security,' said Able.

Elaine shook her head: 'There you are, by your own admission, you could have stopped the whole business right there and then: told the officer there was no national security reason you knew about.'

'That would have dropped Boffy right in it,' said Able.

'Exactly. And none of this mess with ... what's his name...? Horatio someone, would ever have been an issue.'

Stone squirmed on the sofa: 'Sorry, darling, I'm not sure, in similar circumstances, I would have dropped one of my mates in it either.'

'Well, that proves the leadership ethics you impart to your staff are partly responsible for this mess.'

She picked up her glasses and stood. 'All right. You know what I think. I can't see any other solution to this. Can either of you?'

The men said nothing.

Elaine nodded: 'All right. I'll leave you to it. I've got a reception to organise; the King of Norway is coming to dinner tonight. Is your black tie and suit all drycleaned for it, Gazza? David Hicks told me he went out and bought one especially to wear, as The Lodge is the venue.'

Stone sat up: 'Hicks? Why's he invited?'

'He happens to be the deputy prime minister, my dear. And that's the position you'd like him to stay in, isn't it?'

She strode out. Stone turned to Able: 'Bloody women. We should never have given them the vote. Look at us, like chastened schoolboys. And Hicks never wants to attend state banquets. What's that about? Do you think he may have heard a whisper about our little friend Horatio and has thoughts above his station?'

Able said: 'I don't know, sir, but your lady wife never mixes words, does she? As one chastened schoolboy to another, I think I need to get on my bike and go and see my very best friend in his hospital bed.'

Stone stayed seated, rubbing a large hand down his cheeks: 'Naive and stupid? Dunno what's she complaining about. I've always been bloody naive and stupid. Anyway, yes, yes, John, get on your bike. Be careful. Kough's going to get the shock of his life.'

ABLE FLEW TO SYDNEY. He worried that the run of political luck he and Stone had enjoyed for so many years was running out. The Ombudsman's Office received more than twenty-four thousand complaints every year. Most never saw the light of day.

There were six hundred serious complaints each year. That was twelve every week. What were the chances that Horatio Hadley's complaint would rise to the surface?

The gravest complaints were referred to as allegations of 'serious disclosable conduct'. Many of those were also discarded because they were not sufficiently serious. 'Serious disclosable conduct' was the category he and Stone faced. But Horatio's complaint had made it to the surface on very sensational but slim hearsay evidence and rumour. The Ombudsman's Office was clearly flexing its politically independent muscles and looking forward to some righteous virtue signalling.

It was early evening when Able reached the intensive care ward. Visiting hours were over but no one was objecting to the PM's chief of staff paying an unscheduled visit. He arrived flanked by two large men in dark suits with obvious wriggly cords sneaking from their earplugs.

Kough's eyes were closed when the trio was ushered in to the ward. It was strewn with flowers and cards, as the entrance and footpaths downstairs had been.

'Evening, Boffy. How are you feeling?'

Kough blinked both eyes open and grinned: 'Johnny boy. How the hell are you?'

'I see your memory is still working, then.'

Kough said: 'Yes, Johnny boy, it's working, getting a bit better each day. I was hoping you'd come, and peace might break out between us. Who are the heavies?'

Able nodded: 'I'm sorry, it's an official visit with an official purpose.'

Kough took a deep breath: 'Official? Official purpose? What's going on?'

'Your wife is being arrested and deported on suspicion of spying for China.'

Kough said nothing as he struggled to understand. Then he sat slightly forward: 'You fucking prick. You're deporting Charlotte? The woman who dumped you because you're a loser, a nobody public service pen pusher?'

Able nodded: 'Yeah, that's pretty much it.' He made a fuss about looking at his watch. 'Yeah, right about now she'll be getting a knock on the door of your waterfront penthouse.'

'You'll pay for this, you prick. You'll never get away with it. You know she hates the Chinese government. She'd never be a spy for them.'

'That's not what ASIO thinks, Boffy. They've got phone taps of her being urged to use her connections in the PM's office to spy for them.'

'What about our son?'

'If she doesn't make any fuss, we'll let her take him with her.'

'To where, for Christ's sake?'

'Back to her home – in Hong Kong, I suppose.'

Spittle flew from Kough's mouth and a bedside monitor began emitting soft bleeping noises: 'Hong Kong? Christ, and what do you think the bloody commie cops will do with her?'

Able leaned against the bed tray: 'No idea, Boffy. Give her a medal? Throw her in prison? I'd say prison, if you don't remember the encrypted Safevac number for your prostitute's cellphone, the one that was robbed by an American gangster. I know you provided last month's supply from the info in your head, but that runs out every thirty days. Since your full memory has evidently not returned, all production will come to a standstill again.'

There was a long period of silence. The beeping continued. A nurse arrived and took Kough's pulse and looked at the monitoring equipment. 'You're fine, Dr Kough. I think you just got a bit overexcited seeing your visitors.' She smiled and left.

Kough said: 'You're mad, you and Stone. I'll be out of here soon and you won't know what's struck you if you try to take my wife and son away. You'll be dog tucker.'

Able stood and moved casually to lean on the shelf holding the flashing monitors: 'Oh, that's the other thing: you won't be getting out.'

A look of fear twisted Kough's face.

'Your condition requires complete and total rest while you recover from your brain damage.'

'What the hell are you talking about? My memory is recovering very well. The doctors have been very pleased with my progress,' Kough said.

'Oh, it won't matter what they say. You are being transferred tomorrow to a government sanitorium in the Blue Mountains, to maximise your prospects of getting back to full health. Just country air, no stressful cellphones, computers or visitors from the outside world to disturb your progress.'

Able pulled up the visitor's chair and moved closer to Kough's face, where he whispered: 'But while your memory will recover quickly to allow a change in the encrypted vaccine code, it will not fully recover.'

'Why the hell not? Are you bastards going to poison me? Send me to some lunatic asylum?'

'Best you keep your voice down, Boffy. The reason you will not fully recover from your amnesia is because the government does not want you to give evidence to an inquiry.'

'What inquiry? What the hell are you talking about now?'

The volume on the beeping monitor changed up a gear.

'Please, Boffy, keep your voice down. Lie back and take some deep breaths.'

'Fuck you, Johnny boy. Just what the hell is all this about? What's really going on?'

Able smiled: 'Not much, just trying to save the government.'

Kough looked confused.

Able said: 'I'll explain the whole thing if you keep calm. The government is in the shit up to its eyeballs and the whole mess has been of your making: starting with all the vaccine smuggling nonsense at the airport, you tangled Gary Stone and me up with that little escapade.'

The nurse came back in. Kough brusquely waved her away. But she ignored him, took some notes from the monitors and left. Able told his two ASIO agents to find the hospital canteen and have a coffee. They were reluctant, but Able assured them he would take responsibility for their leaving temporarily.

Alone with his former best friend, Able explained the saga, beginning with Kough's arrogant behaviour at passport control towards a certain Horatio Hadley. When he had finished, Kough was shaking his bandaged head and muttering under his breath.

Able stood up and stared at the flashing monitors: 'You want your wife and son back, don't you?'

Kough said nothing.

'You can get them back if you provide the full Safevac code to the Australian government. Then allow our doctors to find your brain has a permanent impairment, preventing any likelihood of you giving evidence in an Ombudsman's inquiry.

'Charlotte and Michael Chen will be free to live at Woolloomooloo until you leave the Blue Mountains sanitorium in twelve months.

'Then all three of you can leave the country, migrate to anywhere you choose and live happily ever after – or for as long as your gambling addiction can be contained.'

Kough gave a big sigh: 'You righteous government goons ... you make me sick. Stone and you had no moral or ethical difficulty letting that gay Chinese diplomat die of Covid even though I had the cure. Stone, your hero, said his death would be a small price in the big scheme of things.

'I only bullshitted the Chinese into believing they would get the full formula because I wanted their permission to save that guy's life. Which I bloody did.

'And you make accusations that I was unscrupulous after discovering Safevac. You conveniently forget I was working to enhance killer viruses, to make them even more deadly to kill off human enemies. When I came across a method of neutralising viruses, the lab bosses made fun of me. So, what was I to do? Dump my breakthrough discovery? Is that what you and Stone are saying I should have done?

'There was no bloody way I was ever going to do that. So, I memorised the formula and deleted my research files. Then I took some phials of the completed vaccine and brought them back here. Where's the ethical dilemma there?

'And you high-and-mighty rulers wouldn't even be aware I'm giving millions of vaccine doses to Third World countries at cost. I'm saving lives everywhere. A lot of them.'

Kough sat up and fumed: 'And for all my efforts, I'm going to be the one locked away in a sanitorium, away from my wife and son, and forced to reveal my vaccine formula, all because you losers can't control one petty, wimp whistle-blower, who you know, dare I say it, would be a small price if he died from a bullet in the head.'

Kough sat back exhausted.

Able nodded his head: 'I think your brain's performance is definitely impaired. You're sounding deranged and dangerous, wanting to kill some innocent whistle-blower who's sticking up for his rights.'

Kough laughed: 'Can't win with you buggers.'

'You're dead right. So long as you understand that, you'll be fine.'

Kough snorted: 'By the way, whose idea was this little plan to kidnap me, ransom me for my family? Stone's? Yours?'

Able smiled: 'I can't tell you who it came from, but I can say the person is one of our toughest political operators.'

He saw the two heavies coming back through the nurses' station: 'My idea would be to turn you over to the CIA. They would leap at the chance to extradite you if they ever heard poor little Horatio's version of your smuggling modus operandi.

'You could kiss goodbye to ever seeing Char and your son again for thirty years if the CIA gets involved. They reckon they could get you immediately on attempted theft of government property. Remember the contaminated laboratory clothing you stuffed into your briefcase and tried to nick?'

The nurse hovered in the doorway looking at her watch. Able said he was just leaving. The two security men, however, would stay to safeguard the patient.

Kough cried out: 'Wait on, you prick. How do I know you'll keep your side of the bargain? What's happening with Charlotte?'

'Just relax and do what we've asked you to do and Charlotte will be fine, and in a year you'll be free to live happily ever after. Don't look a gift horse in the mouth, Boffy.'

Kough nodded slowly. 'And when do you want the full formula?'

'We're over all your formula con tricks. So it has to be sooner rather than later.'

Kough looked bitter and angry but nodded his head.

'Well, that's it then,' said Able, 'your government thanks you for your cooperation in this matter of national security.'

Charlotte Kough was told she was subject to an espionage inquiry. She had to surrender her passport. She was allowed to live with her son at Woolloomooloo. She was left a little puzzled. She wanted to discuss the unexpected development with her husband, but the next day when she visited St Vincent's Hospital he was gone. The head sister gave her an address at a facility in the Blue Mountains National Park, an hour-long trip from Sydney. Visitors were allowed once a week on Fridays. They had to call first for permission.

FORTY-SIX

Little Horatio Hadley's elation at bringing his bullying tormentor, and immediate boss, Gerry Ryan, to heel had long dissipated.

He was rostered, it seemed permanently, on the latest shifts. He knew it was pointless to protest.

He had received an official verbal rebuke for unauthorised use of the Force's notice boards and a written warning that this behaviour would lead to serious disciplinary measures should it reoccur.

His allocated car park was moved to a distant part of the airport. It was a long trudge in bad weather before the drive to his commuter train station. He was banned from eating his mother's sandwiches for lunch in the recreation room and told to use the cafeteria, where he had a cool reception for not buying its food or drink. He was seriously intimidated when ordered to conduct almost all the anal searches on suspected drug smugglers during his shift.

The late passenger arrivals were often half drunk, tired and aggressive. They were worse when his passport scanner failed and his repeated attempts to have it repaired were ignored. Life had become a drudgery, but he lived in hope someone, sooner or later, would listen to him.

A ray of sunshine broke through the personal gloom when he

received a letter from Ms Audrey Tibble of the Commonwealth Ombudsman's Office. It was a form letter thanking him for his letter and telling him someone would be in touch in due course. Weeks went by without any further correspondence. He invited a girl he met on his commuter train to the movies, but she was a no-show. He saw the film anyway and ate both ice creams.

He got off his train one day and saw a man on the platform addressing a small crowd. The man had run to fat and wore a tired blue suit and a loose tie. On his jacket was a red rosette.

It had large letters in its centre: ALP. He joined the crowd surrounding the man and listened. The man said he was an Australian Labor Party Member of Parliament and was urging everyone to join the people's party to promote the rights of the exploited, underprivileged and low-paid workers. He said these people were important, forming the backbone of the country's workforce. Horatio joined.

Jack Ramshaw, MP, thought the pimply-faced bloke was a dwarf. But he was not quite that small, and he was wearing what appeared to be a badly fitting Border Force uniform. Ramshaw watched him fill in the membership form and pay the five-dollar fee, demanding a receipt like all minor bureaucrats did. He was not the sort to strike in passport control after a long trip, Ramshaw thought. He shook the young man's hand and thanked him. Gave him a pamphlet explaining when the next ALP branch would meet.

He had a posh name that slipped Ramshaw's mind seconds after he heard it but seemed delighted to get the invite. An MP who had spent unnoticed decades on the back bench, representing a shabby working-class electorate, Ramshaw was about to be given an opportunity to make the national news media. The dwarfish guy, with the posh name, had taken his receipt and handed Ramshaw several pages of paper. One carried the logo of the Commonwealth Ombudsman's Office. He took them home to read later.

Backbencher Jack Ramshaw spoke so rarely in Parliament, he was overlooked by the Speaker during Question Time. He had stood repeatedly and waved the sheaf of papers he knew were a wick to his political bombshell.

The priority to quiz ministers was given to senior party spokespeople. He could get on the list quicker if he put his question in writing, but that would divulge his allegations and alert the prime minister his career could be about to end.

Ramshaw was determined to be front and centre in the looming controversy. It would be the biggest moment in his career. He considered sharing his secret with his own frontbench leaders but quickly dismissed it. The glamour boys would want the publicity fanfare for themselves.

He accepted he would have to wait until the next Question Time to ask Border Control Minister David Hicks about battler Horatio Hadley's treatment amid the secret sleaze and corruption that was rampant in the Stone administration.

Feeling dejected, he set out for the cab rank. He would taxi downtown and cheer himself up with a few beers with some mates at the Thirsty Ostrich.

The taxi pulled up outside the bar. Ramshaw paid the cabbie and stepped out on to the road thinking of the Horatio papers he was carrying. There was a shriek of locked brakes. Ramshaw's body was hurled twenty metres up the road.

The impact stalled eighty-one-year-old Myrtle Dodgeman's silent BMW EV when it struck the large man with his papers. People said the electric cars were too quiet, but the man had not been looking where he was going, she thought. And look at the front of her little car: it was all smashed in.

The man was lying still on the roadway. A small group of people talking on cellphones began to surround him. Some took photos of the victim. Mrs Dodgeman hoped she had renewed her insurance policy. Insurers were so nervy these days when dealing with old people.

The half a dozen sheets of paper Ramshaw had been carrying were scattered in the wind. Several were retrieved by onlookers. Others were blown into the dirty gutter and ignored.

One woman noticed the House of Representatives logo on the top of one of the flapping sheets. She knelt to pick it up. It was handwritten and the first line raised her eyebrows. The writing was a scrawl, but she made out the underlined words 'conspiracy' and 'corruption'.

She saw the road victim was unconscious or dead. She could not hand his notes back to him. So, she tucked the sheet in her handbag. She would show it to Syd when he came home from *The Telegraph*. He only covered the league, but she was sure he would still be interested. The victim was probably an MP, and he may even have been an important man.

Horatio Hadley was having another depressing day at the Border Force's Canberra airport anal-search cubicle. He wore an earphone and had listened, while attending his duties to protect the nation's borders, to the national parliamentary coverage on ABC RADIO.

Question Time had come and gone and his new MP friend, Jack Ramshaw, had not raised his case as he had promised.

Only women officers were supposed to carry out internal searches of suspected female drug smugglers. But none had been rostered on this grave shift. It was all up to Horatio Hadley again.

He told the young woman he was searching to stand up straight again. The woman stood and turned to him. He held up a plastic-covered, gloved hand and showed her the two shiny, cylindrical steel capsules his anal search had discovered.

'What's in these?' he said.

'They're not mine. They belong to my boyfriend. He got busted yesterday at Buenos Aires. He'd put them in my suitcase because he was already carrying four. I just thought I might as well bring them with me.'

Horatio could not work out her age, but she was young. She had none of the hideous tattoos the mules usually had. He glanced at her passport. She was a Glenda Stropeshire, age eighteen. She looked attractive even in her passport photo. The short black hair had gone. She now had shoulder-length blonde hair. Almost certainly a wig.

'I didn't ask you whose they were. I asked you, what's in them?'

She looked exhausted and was fighting back tears as she looked down at him: 'Just coke.'

'Just coke?'

She nodded unhappily.

Horatio said: 'Been busted before?'

She nodded again.

'So it could be the slammer this time?'

Glenda paused and looked at the short little sap properly for the first time: 'I don't want to go to prison, not for just carrying a tiny bit of a recreational drug. Don't you think...' she looked at his name tag... 'Horatio, I would be wasted in prison.'

Horatio gulped.

Glenda took his ungloved hand and stroked it gently: 'I like to live life to the full, Horatio, and I'm sure you do too. And it's not as if you don't already know me ... er ... intimately.'

Horatio went to reply but was certain he would have stammered.

'Come on, I'm not a cartel boss. And my dumb partner is in clink and out of action. Give a girl a break ... we can go back to my place? There's no one there at the moment. We can live a little, don't you think?'

Horatio nodded. He felt his face flushing, his little legs trembling and ... something else down there was trembling as well.

He handed the small steel capsules back to her: 'You'll have to wait here for an hour, till my shift ends.'

Glenda beamed a huge smile: 'Of course, of course. Oh, thank you, Horatio. The last woman that busted me was a real bitch, just hard as nails. Not like you. Not like you at all.'

Horatio pointed to a chair: 'Just take a seat over there. I'll be back in a few minutes. I just have to make sure this camera on the wall is ... um ... rewound.'

Glenda almost squealed: 'Oh, Horatio, you are so clever. You think of everything.'

Horatio smiled and his sunken chest swelled a millimetre. He left and went to the control room. It was empty, as it mostly was for the late shifts. He climbed on to a stool to reach the video cupboard, leaned in and flicked several switches. One was a delete on Camera Five.

Fuck the Border Force, he thought. And fuck Parliament. Horatio Hadley would take care of himself.

FORTY-SEVEN

Michael Kough climbed gingerly into the helicopter, helped by the pilot and Charlotte. All pretence at stealth had ended when it had set down in a clattering whirlwind on the sanatorium roof.

Kough calculated that they would have just thirty precious seconds to get airborne and escape. That was the amount of time he reckoned the guards would take to discover his nurse had vanished and his bed was empty. The guards were quicker than he thought. He heard the first shot from a Glock before they had time to secure their seatbelts. The bullet pinged off the big Sikorsky fuselage and ricocheted harmlessly away.

The bony, bearded, sixty-eight-year-old retired pilot, Charlie Slipper, calmly pulled back the stick and a bulky three tonnes of executive SK Sikorsky rose slightly into the air. He powered it dead ahead and dropped it over the side of the twelve-storey government sanatorium. This concealed the chopper temporarily from roof-top gunfire. And dramatically boosted its air speed. He whooped as the ground came up to meet them. He pulled up at the last moment and swung the powerful machine to head due south, back over the Blue Mountains National Park, away from Sydney.

Kough had given him no flight plans other than that first manoeuvre. He had said the coordinates were with Big Brain, whatever that meant. He did not mind. He was having the time of his old life and he had a cool million bucks sitting in his bank account for his services.

He cranked up the revs and the Sikorsky was soon bolting along only one hundred metres above ground at its top speed, four hundred and sixty kilometres an hour.

Kough was panting, but he had no headache and only minor pain from the three breaks in his legs. Charlotte had laid him down on the luxury leather couch directly behind the pilot and tucked a silk pillow under his heavily bandaged head. Michael Chen peered wide-eyed and excited out of a passenger window.

After ten minutes, Kough sat up and leaned over Slipper's shoulder. He gave him a course that would take them in almost the opposite direction, north-east, to cross the coast slightly north of Sydney.

Amid the vibrations and din from the engine, and its four huge rotor blades, Kough sat back and smiled to himself. He had beaten the bastards.

He had no headache. Big Brain said it was because he was still doped up. But he would be fine. Anything would be better than accepting Able's ultimatum, locking him down in the sanatorium for a year, and forcing the handover of the Safevac formula.

It was all a desperate plan to save Stone's government from the Horatio Hadley corruption allegations. Kough was to be diagnosed as too mentally impaired to give evidence to the Ombudsman's Office in its smuggling allegations inquiries.

He stretched and could feel stiffness and some pain where his legs had been broken in the Sydney car crash. He was glad he had stolen enough medication to last him a month.

He had spent the last week working successfully to reconnect Suzie's new encrypted cellphone with the Safevac production computer.

Slipper half turned and told him to put his headphones on. Kough shook his head; his bone flap was still not properly healed.

'Sorry, Charlie, we'll just have to yell,' Kough said. He pointed to his bandages.

'Fine by me, Mr Kough. I'm used to shouting. The headphones in the New Guinea choppers were as reliable as their weather forecasts. We've crossed the coast now and, you do know, don't you, we're being picked up by every radar in the south of the country? The sheriff's posse knows exactly where we are. I can drop us down to wave height and below the radars if you want.'

Kough said: 'No thanks, this height is good.'

'Okay, if you say so. We're now fifty kilometres off the coast. How far out are we going?'

'Not much further. Stay on this heading and you'll soon see where we're going.'

Kough turned to see Charlotte nursing their son. He was gurgling and looking out at the sea, apparently unconcerned about the trauma of their escape.

Charlotte, however, looked shaken. She gave him a weak smile.

A few minutes later, Slipper pointed ahead and yelled: 'Is that your dinghy down there? Is that where you want to be dropped?'

Kough's superyacht, *The Miracle*, was heaved to in a slight swell and gleaming like a sapphire in the vast ocean.

'Charlie, just hover here at mast height above the boat. In eight minutes, head due north.'

Slipper looked puzzled as he held the Sikorsky in place.

'You're not gettin' off? Are we going to winch someone up?'

'Nope.'

'I don't get it.'

'All those people in the sheriff's posse, what will they be thinking, watching us hover this low here?'

Slipper stroked his beard: 'They'd be thinking we're getting off here.' He laughed.

'Very clever.'

The eight minutes elapsed. It was the time Big Brain calculated it would take to winch down the three members of the Kough family.

Kough then ordered the Sikorsky to fly at a sedate two hundred miles an hour, due north. Its heading would take it to Coffs Harbour in northern New South Wales. Fifty kilometres from the town, Kough told Slipper to turn off his transponder. Slipper smiled: 'I was wondering when we were going to make it more difficult for the radar boys.'

Kough nodded: 'Now we go due west. Here's the new coordinates for our last leg.' Slipper looked at his new instructions and altered course back towards the mainland. The coordinates marked the helipad at the Coolleegood Peace and Wellness Centre. The isolated centre would be their first refuge.

The centre's woke name made old Charlie Slipper worry about his own fate. He was flying 'dark' with no transponder and had, in reality, been part of what looked like a daring prison bust amid gunfire.

Till this assignment, he had been retired at Bondi living on his memories of aviation amid Papua New Guinea's mountain ranges. He had been a hero pilot known for his skill in the air, rescuing people and ferrying the injured to various hospitals – and, on the side, carrying all sorts of illicit cargo for dubious clients.

CHARLOTTE USED SUZIE, who had no ASIO agents tailing her, to offer Charlie the million-dollar fee if he could charter the biggest and fastest helicopter in New South Wales, then land it on the roof of a Blue Mountains sanitorium.

He would not be told his final destination until they were airborne. The charter requirements were puzzling. The Sikorsky was a luxury chopper designed to take fourteen executive guests and two pilots. His payload would be a family of three. It was all very mysterious, like the old days, he thought. He had not been warned about hostile fire, but it was no surprise when it happened.

As he checked his instruments, a Border Force Bay Class patrol boat was ordered from Sydney Harbour at its thirty-seven-kilometre full speed and vectored towards *The Miracle*. Radar had tracked the Sikorsky and identified the big yacht in its path.

The chopper had stopped over the yacht and then flown off northwards. As it left, *The Miracle* unfurled its sails and headed east, away from the Australian mainland.

As it closed in on *The Miracle*, the Border Force vessel radioed the vessel to heave to. The yacht's skipper refused, saying his yacht was in international waters. But he was told unless he hove to, the yacht would be traced to whatever port it visited and be arrested by local police.

The Miracle seemed to initially ignore the heave-to order. It sailed on at its twelve-knot cruising speed for another thirty minutes and then suddenly lowered its sails and hove to.

There was an air of excitement at Border Force HQ and on the patrol boat. The skipper stripped the cover off the machine gun on the bow as he closed on billionaire Michael Kough's lavish vessel.

The skipper hailed *The Miracle* for permission to board. Permission was granted. An armed search party boarded the boat's inflatable and crossed to the yacht.

Lieutenant Max Eves had never been involved in a hot pursuit. He was first over the side onto the yacht's teak deck: 'We're searching for Dr Michael Kough. We believe he may be on board.'

The Miracle skipper frowned: 'Michael? No, you won't find him here, mate. He's in a hospital somewhere in the Blue Mountains. We're checking the boat out after the fire we had in the engine room up in Port Douglas.'

Eves' crew would search the yacht, but he knew Kough would not be on board. They had been led on a wild goose chase. *The Miracle* crew said a hovering helicopter had just paused for a nosy and to probably take some holiday photos, and then gone on its way.

FORTY-EIGHT

Horatio Hadley was late to work. He did not give a rat's. He had been in no hurry to leave Glenda Stropeshire, the best-looking girl in the world. They had enjoyed a party. Just the two of them. He had learned how to snort the white powder. She had laughed at him as his inhibitions melted. He had boogied to some hard rock. She had undressed his small body, he thought. Yes, she had. He could remember that bit, for sure. But he was a bit hazy about what exactly happened after that. This morning she dressed him in his uniform and said he was very good in bed and she would never forget that he had saved her from jail.

His supervising officer, Gerry Ryan, was waiting at Horatio's passport control booth. He was holding a plastic container. 'Thanks for finally turning up, Hadley. I've been hunting for you; your number came up today for a random drug test. Let's get going.' Ryan turned and walked away.

Horatio slumped into his chair. It was not possible he was chosen for a drug test today. Did cocaine show up on these tests? He did not know. They must do, he thought.

Ryan turned when he realised Horatio was not following him: 'C'mon, Hadley, move it. The tests are compulsory, you know.'

Ryan was shocked when the little man folded his arms in defiance:

'Bullshit. This is just more bullying. I want to see my public service rep before I go off with you. You've already been warned once. Your behaviour is not acceptable.'

Ryan was speechless.

He noted Horatio's smirk. The little fucker, he thought. He looked him up and down: 'You're also in breach of the uniform code. Where's your belt? And your badge?'

Horatio lost his smirk as he felt for his badge, and then belt. Both were missing. He knew what had happened: Glenda must have taken them as a souvenir of her amazing night with him.

Ryan borrowed the smirk: 'You're having quite a morning, aren't you? Late for your shift again, breaching uniform standards and refusing a drug test. You're facing the sack, Horry boy. What a shame.'

Horatio stood, hitched up his shapeless trousers, and said: 'You're the one already on a written warning, Ryan. Why don't you go harass some other poor mug before I call my rep? You know he'll sort you out quick smart.'

Ryan turned and left.

Horatio stapled his pants tighter and sat as his first travellers of the day arrived. He smiled at them. Nothing was going to spoil his day. Then something did.

The Force had received a glowing note from an old lady. It said how kindly she had been treated by Officer H. Hadley. He had allowed her to keep the Fijian mangoes she had hid in her suitcase. Officer H. Hadley had been friendly, generous and helpful. It was a pity there were not more like him in the Force.

An hour after he started his shift, Horatio was shown the letter and sacked. Any outstanding holiday pay would be forwarded to him in due course. He used extra pins to hold his pants up and made for the car park.

His cellphone rang. It was Glenda. She had called Buenos Aires and told her boyfriend she was breaking it off. Horatio was elated and sat on an airport bench to take in the news.

Glenda said: 'You did mean what you said last night, didn't you?'

Horatio's mind spun. How much of last night could he remember? He remembered they had a great party with the white powder, but the rest was a happy haze.

'We said a lot of things last night,' he stuttered.

'I know we did. It was just great. I never thought you'd be such a hipster dude ... so good ... so cool.'

He laughed: 'Yeah, yeah, it was so good.'

Glenda's tone became serious: 'When I asked if you meant what you said, I meant what you said when you said you were in love with me ... and that we'd start to bring in some decent amounts of Charlie when you were on duty. And you said I could just leave the cylinders in my luggage so I wouldn't have to stuff it up my bum any more.'

While Horatio's mind spun, she went on: 'I hope you got on all right today without your badge. I took it off because you got so excited it was scratching me on the titties before I got your shirt off. It's on the bedside table if you want to come over tonight and pick it up and ... and you know...?'

'Do you know where my belt is? It's got the Border Force logo on the buckle. It was the only one the fat buggers could find that would fit me.'

She giggled again: 'I found it when I made the bed. It was right down at the bottom. How did it get down there, lover boy?'

He coughed to fill the void and avoid having to admit he could not recall much, or anything, of what happened in the bed.

'So, Horatio, darling, I was thinking of flying back to Buenos Aires on Wednesday. I just wanted to make sure you would be on the last shift on Friday to meet me on the way back?'

He looked wildly around. His little body shook. No one had this much bad luck. Just when he thought...

Stalling for time, he said: 'How much were you thinking of bringing in?'

'You mean "we", my darling.'

'Yes, yes, we.'

'I have lined up a cool ten kilos.'

Horatio whistled.

'Is that okay? You were okay with it last night. Do you think we should get more while we have you in place? If we did that, I'd have to make less trips.'

What the fuck have I done? Horatio thought. I had the best-looking girl in the world, I was going to make some decent money, buy a car and get an apartment in downtown Sydney.

Glenda said: 'Are you all right, darling? You've gone quiet. Are you having second thoughts? You know how easy it will be.'

'Glenny, I'm not having second thoughts, I would do anything for you, but...'

'But what, my darling?'

'It's just that I won't be working on Friday night. I won't be working any night. I got the sack today.'

There was dead silence.

Glenda cleared her throat finally. She spoke icily and slowly: 'You useless piece of shit. I'm bloody glad I didn't let you put that tiny weenie you call a cock inside me last night. You are pathetic.'

She broke the connection. Horatio stared at the dead cellphone.

He stood and continued to trudge to his distant car park, his pants threatening constantly to fall down, and slowly drove to his train-station car park. Left the meter unpaid. Went to Platform One and jumped in front of the first arriving train.

225

FORTY-NINE

Any inquiry about the page of handwritten notes recovered by his girlfriend from the MP Jack Ramshaw, while he was lying injured on the roadway outside the Thirsty Ostrich, had been delayed. The premier rugby league Stallions team had kept him flat out. The grassroots battlers' team had scored another shock win.

Its players had celebrated at their club rooms and then gone on to Harry's Bar, got plastered and shagged several of their groupies upstairs. A girl's parent complained about his daughter's state the next morning, and the episode became the hottest story on his league round for days.

Claims of high-level corruption in the Stone administration had to wait until the club players involved apologised, wept on television, paid fines and were banned for three playing days.

So it was some days before Syd Wildboare dug Ramshaw's page out and tried to figure what the appalling handwriting said. He sort of got the gist but he wasn't sure. But if he involved the political reporters, they would steal his scoop if the info was any good. He chafed at the reality that sports writers enjoyed the biggest readership but the lowest status in the newsroom.

Syd had been stuck in a very enjoyable, boozy rut for six years. He thought Ramshaw's bad luck might give him a break in his routine and a chance of promotion. I mean, how hard could political reporting be?

So he typed out what he thought the scribble meant. It seemed a Border Force guy had told an ombudsman about high-level corruption and smuggling at Canberra Airport.

The PM was involved, his chief of staff, a conniving senior Force officer, and the world's most famous scientist, Dr Michael Kough. He had allegedly slipped something through passport control when he returned home from working in an American germ-warfare laboratory.

Well, the story did have all the ingredients for page one. Not as good as the Stallions uproar after an impossible win, with its elements of debauchery, booze, sex, outraged parents and the consequent fallout. But...

Syd started by calling the Ombudsman's Office. He was surprised how quickly he found a boss lady high up in the outfit, who demanded to know where he got his information from. A Ms Audrey Tibble, that was her real name, finally agreed to see him. But not on the record.

Syd was not worried because it seemed political reporters never had real people to quote; they just had anonymous sources. So, he would too.

Syd was shown into a large office. Ms Tibble was clearly someone very important. He felt awkward. He was wearing his best jeans and a green shirt under a rumpled sports jacket. He realised, in this environment, the knot in the tie he had reused for the last week to allow for speedy dressing was not an elegant touch.

Ms Tibble looked fierce and grim. Her hair was pulled back tight, some long ethnic-looking earrings hung low from her lobes. Her pinched face was a makeup-free zone.

He sat politely deciding what his first question would be, when she suddenly began to cry, quietly at first, but soon ramping up to a full waterworks show. He had no idea what his response should be. He pushed his cellphone record button and sat embarrassed and motionless.

Eventually Ms Tibble dried her eyes and blew her nose: 'I'm sorry, I'm sorry, Mr Wildboare, I never get emotional over cases.' Looking at her appearance, Syd believed her.

'But I've been bullied out of doing my job properly and now someone has died, and I think if I'd acted properly and promptly he would still be alive.' She began to sob quietly again.

Wildboare waited in silence. After a short time, she composed her stern-looking self: 'The junior officer, the whistle-blower in this affair, was killed yesterday, hit by a train; the MP Ramshaw who found out about the whistle-blower's allegations was knocked down by a car in broad daylight, and the man at the centre of the affair, Dr Michael Kough, you would have heard of him, has vanished from his hospital bed.'

Syd cleared his throat: 'What does all this mean, Ms Tibble? It sounds just...'

'Oh, it is. I can't believe it. The key people I wanted to interview have disappeared. I'm at my wits' end. And that poor little man, Horatio Hadley, who started everything ... well, I can't believe he's suddenly ended up dead under a commuter train.'

Syd took a breath: 'Well, have you interviewed the Force guy who facilitated the smuggling? Or the prime minister who must have known about it as his chief of staff was there at the airport?'

Ms Tibble shuffled some papers on her desk and took another tissue from a box decorated with red roses.

'I don't do leaks, Mr Wildboare, never have ... but I feel what's happening needs to be brought out, brought out into the open somehow. Something's rotten in the state of...'

Syd crossed his legs and asked if Ms Tibble could start at the top and tell the whole story. He noticed her stare oddly at his shoes and realised he had picked up different-coloured socks in his hurry this morning. He put both feet firmly back on the ground and looked at her like a serious political journalist.

She looked up and met his eye: 'Yes. I'll start at the start and tell you the whole, sorry saga.'

FIFTY

The Sikorsky dropped to wave height as it bore down on the northern New South Wales coast. Charlie Slipper glanced over his instruments routinely. Everything was normal, almost normal. The tail rotor oil pressure needle had fallen a fraction. But the controls were responding normally as he flew on.

He did not want to alarm the passengers, so he decided he would not ask them to put their lifejackets on. They were only about five kilometres off the coast and on unofficial 'finals' as far as he was concerned.

He flew, glancing repeatedly at the oil gauge. Big Brain noticed. Kough said: 'Do we have a problem?' Charlie Slipper sat up surprised at the question. He had been very discreet. The Kough guy had eyes in the back of his damaged head.

He stalled as he chose his words: 'I don't think so. One oil pressure gauge ... it's probably just the gauge itself playing up ... they do from time to time ... it's showing reduced oil pressure to the rotor engine. But we're only ... er, let's see ... seven minutes out and she's flying just fine.'

Kough sat back and looked at Charlotte. She had seen the white, surf-rimmed coastline and strapped Michael Chen into her front carry pack ready for disembarking. He was chattering to himself. She was looking fatigued.

Big Brain had become aware of every vibration in the machine, but it sounded perfectly smooth. He relaxed and went back to playing chess in his head. He was just taking the queen off Garry Kasparov at the world champs, when he sensed a small wobble in the airframe.

Kough leaned over to Charlotte: 'Honey, the lifejacket for you and Michael Chen is under your seat. Pull it out and put it on, just as a precaution. Passengers are meant to wear them whenever they're flying over the sea.'

Charlotte looked at him seriously: 'It would have to be a big lifejacket to go around this.' She patted her stomach and Michael Chen sitting in her front pack.

Kough said: 'I can adjust the straps for you.' He bent further over and pulled the jacket from its Velcro fastening and handed it to her.

Charlotte grimaced: 'Mikey, what's going on? Why do we suddenly have to put these on at this stage? Tell me.'

'Honey, I just have a feeling. I want to keep you safe.'

She stared at him. She said nothing. Then sighed and put arms through the jacket and over her head. Kough loosened the straps to make it fit.

Michael Chen started to kick and complain as the straps were tightened. The jacket was obscuring part of his view.

Kough then put his jacket on. Big Brain was too distracted to go back to the chess game. He watched Slipper pensively.

Kough said to Slipper: 'Nearly there?'

Slipper did not reply. He felt the machine wobble again as its tail began to lose its grip and the machine began to turn side on.

Kough held Charlotte's hand: 'We may start to spin. The rear rotor blade is losing power.' She looked straight ahead and put her hands around each side of the baby. Her face was white with fear. She patted Michael Chen's little head. He swatted playfully at her hands. She smiled at him through an invisible veil of terror.

Kough said: 'What happens if the tail rotor stops?' Big Brain went to provide the answer, but Slipper growled: 'The chopper begins to spin around without the rotor blade at the back working. We'll lose direction. But Dr Kough, you're paying me a million bucks to fly this thing and if we do have to splash down, I'll keep this fat bird upright. She'll float for long enough for us all to get out okay...'

He looked at Kough, and then at Charlotte. He raised his voice over the engine noise: 'I've put birds down in worse condition than this over the years. We're going to be fine.' He laughed: 'I'm not leaving a million bucks behind unspent.'

'So we'll be able to get out, the same way we came in?'

'Pretty much ... when we hit, slide the door open on the lee side, facing the shore. I'll get the emergency life raft out. We'll go for a boat ride to finish our trip.'

Big Brain said, She won't sink like a stone with this guy at the controls. This big cabin will float. There'll be plenty of time for all of us to get off. But we've got no transponder working so no one will know where we have gone down.

The rear rotor began to screech as its oil-starved mechanism started to seize up. The main cabin began to go in a dizzying circle. Slipper said: 'Dr Kough, there is one thing: after we splash down, these big blades, they're very long, and they'll flop down over the main cabin. We'll have to push the inflatable through them. We don't want to end up stuck below them or we'll all go under.' He gave Kough a grim smile: 'This is a lot better than going down on the side of a New Guinea mountain.'

Kough said: 'That's good to know.'

Slipper wrestled with the controls as the wind buffeted the cockpit: 'C'mon, you big baby. We're nearly there.'

He flipped the radio switch: 'Mayday, Mayday. Oscar Hotel Charlie ditching.' He read out a set of coordinates as the machine spun faster and faster and finally struck the sea with a jarring crash.

The cabin rocked violently in the waves. Michael Chen began screaming in fright. Kough unbuckled his harness, stood, holding the back of Slipper's seat for balance. He crawled to the front passenger door and pulled its release. It slid smoothly open.

Outside, the small waves slopped against the lee side of the cockpit. Slipper went to the rear bench seat of the machine. He lifted its cushions and hauled out a large plastic box. The emergency inflatable. He dragged it to the front door, held the rope attached to its bow and pushed it out. There was a loud hiss and the boat automatically inflated in seconds.

'Kough, I'll hold the inflatable. You get your wife and son in it.

Then I'll jump in. Then it's plain sailing. The wind will blow us ashore. We're only about four klicks out.'

The old man's confidence and calm instructions made it sound like ditching was an everyday occurrence, thought Kough.

The chopper was settling in the sea as pregnant Charlotte sat on the door ledge. She felt water splashing around her feet. Slipper and Kough held her under the armpits and tried to lower her and the baby into the bobbing inflatable. It was pressing to break free. She fell forward and pitched on to the floor, on top of Michael Chen.

Cold sea water washed around the baby's head. He did not scream but clung to his mother who rolled over to free him. The two men scrambled in. Slipper knew the chances of survival were not good. The Sikorsky's four rotors had a mega, thirteen-metre span and drooped like a handful of solid but floppy spaghetti over the fuselage, threatening to trap the inflatable beneath them as the chopper sank.

'Michael, we'll have to stand up and pull ourselves along one of the blades so we can get free. The further out we can get the wider apart the blades will be, and we may be able to get out from under.'

Kough thought: What do you mean, may be?

The waves were only half a metre high but bounced the small inflatable about, making it nearly impossible to stand.

'This is better than my last splashdown in New Guinea. I was more worried about the bloody crocs than drowning,' Slipper said.

'Well, that's good to know,' said Kough.

'Yeah. Unless we tip over and the sharks get us.'

Charlotte laughed.

Charlie Slipper grinned: 'Where did you find her?'

'At a late supper,' said Kough.

'Lucky man. Okay, now, can you reach that blade? It's a bit high for me this close up.'

Kough put his hands up and clung on to the nearest blade. Standing astride, he pulled on the blade and the inflatable inched away from the fuselage.

A metre further out and Slipper managed to reach the sloping blade and the pair began to pull the rocking vessel forward, hand over hand. Finally, they cleared the chopper. They looked back. Water was halfway up the cabin. Then it rolled on a wave and sank in seconds.

Kough and Slipper sat panting from the exertion and fear.

'Do you think anyone would have heard your Mayday?' said Kough.

'Nah. We were only a few feet off the ground, I mean, water. The signal wouldn't have gone anywhere. But you never know.'

'You did a great job in getting her down flat on the surface.'

Slipper shrugged: 'You paid for the best, and this old bush pilot is still killing it.'

Charlotte laughed: 'Great choice of words, Charlie. Any brandy in the emergency first-aid box?'

'Not sure, I haven't been in a crash landing for three weeks.'

They all smiled. Kough held a hand up to silence the banter. Above the noise of the waves and wind, Kough heard a growling, throbbing noise. He tried to balance himself and half stood. Only two hundred metres away, a dishevelled prawn boat was slowly slopping its way through the sea towards them.

'There's a boat only a stone's throw from us. It can see us. It's heading towards us,' said Kough.

Charlotte said: 'I thought Lady Luck was out.'

'No. She and I have an understanding.'

'It's not an understanding, Michael, it's a mutual dependence.'

Charlie Slipper had no idea what they were talking about. He crouched to get a view of the prawn boat. When he did, he got a bad feeling.

The twenty-metre wooden vessel had not seen a lick of paint in years. Rust stained the edges of the anchor locker. He could see three men. All bearded and potbellied. All tattooed down the arms and neck. All mid-thirties and drinking from beer bottles.

The three, skipper Al Simmer, Bruce Piggott and Willy Luca, had done time together for grievous bodily assault. Their floating wreck nosed closer.

Piggott, sporting a blooming orange beard, called: 'Do ya need a hand?'

Charlie Slipper shouted back immediately: 'Thanks, but we'll be fine. The wind is pushing us into shore.'

Kough looked at Slipper in surprise.

Piggott looked bemused: 'You're still a few kilometres from the shore, cobber. And if you get there in that little blow-up of yours, the surf will tip you all out, the kid and the sheila too.'

Willy Luca laughed: 'And the sharks are feeding along the break line. Staying on your blow-up's not a good option, mate.'

Piggott sounded angry: 'Ya fraid we'll claim salvage rights to ya little floater? Spose it could be worth a few dollars as a big blow-up doll.'

They all laughed and swigged at their bottles. Simmer, who was helming the boat, said something to Piggott, who looked up and said: 'We're comin' to get ya. We'll back up. You can jump straight onto the transom.'

Charlie Slipper yelled back: 'No, we're not coming aboard, thanks. We'll be fine. The surf doesn't bother us.'

The helmsman ignored him and manoeuvred the trawler ahead and then reversed towards the inflatable.

'Why are you refusing their offer?' Kough hissed.

'I have a feeling,' he replied. 'Your Lady Luck, she's taken the rest of the day off.'

'I know they're a pretty rough-looking mob,' said Kough, 'but all fishermen look pretty rough.'

Slipper scratched his grey beard: 'You go, if you want to. I'll take my chances on the beach.'

'You must be joking,' Charlotte said. 'You want to stay out here? What if the wind changes? Or the sea gets up?'

'I'll take my chances, as I said. That boat's a viper's nest. I've come across a lot of scum just like them. Pissheads, bad men.'

The trawler backed slowly up against the inflatable. Two of the crew stood on the transom. They grabbed the ropes that skirted the sides of the emergency dinghy.

'Okay, jump aboard. Hold Bruce's hand. He'll help ya up,' said Piggott.

Kough faced them: 'No, thanks, we've decided to stay. You guys can get on your way.'

Piggott left the transom. He reappeared a moment later, holding a shotgun. 'Enough of this shit. Get yourselves on board. Women and children first.' He laughed at his joke, showing the few remaining yellow teeth he had.

Slipper snarled: 'Just fuck off, ya loser. We're not getting on that floating shit heap.'

Piggott raised the shotgun and fired. Charlie Slipper was hit in the stomach and almost cut in half. He fell backwards and went over the side. He sank without trace. Only a reddish slick stained the surface for a few moments before the waves washed them away. Then there was nothing.

The explosion of the gunshot frightened the baby who began crying loudly. 'Shut the fuckin' kid up and get up here,' Piggott bellowed.

Big Brain said, You go first. If Charlotte goes first, they might shoot you next and she'll be the ship's new entertainment.

Kough eyed Piggott: 'You win. Help me up and then we can both help my wife; she's three months.'

Piggott left the transom to put the shotgun back inside the boat. He reappeared and put his arm out to steady Kough as he stepped aboard. With the baby still in her front pack, Charlotte took Kough's hand and stepped onto the transom.

She was guided up the steps into the cockpit. Kough followed. When he stepped into the cockpit, he felt his head explode. The bottle Piggott had used to hit him clattered onto the deck.

Charlotte gasped. Kough lay sprawled, face down, on the deck, blood blossoming on the back of his white bandaged head.

'Oh my God. You've might have killed him. He's just suffered a brain injury. And you've just smashed him on the head.'

She fell to her knees next to Kough who lay unconscious. She looked about and found a dirty towel that stank of fish. She rolled him over and used it to cushion his head. Michael Chen stopped wailing and held his mother's arm as he stared at his father sleeping but, strangely, not snoring.

The trawler's engine was put in gear and it bumped its way into the waves.

'Do you have a bed, so we can lie him down?' said Charlotte. Piggott gave a drunken leer: 'We've got one for you, darling.'

The beer bottle weapon that felled Kough was rolling backwards and forwards on the deck in time with the swell. Charlotte stood, grabbed the bottle. She spun around quickly and smashed it on

Piggott's nose. He screamed. Blood poured down his chin. He staggered, clasping the boat's rail.

Charlotte went to strike him a second time but his mate, Willy Luca, grabbed her from behind and wrestled the bottle from her. During the short struggle she kneed him in the crutch. He howled but clung on to the bottle and pushed her away. She tripped on her baby son, who was sheltering behind her, and fell heavily to the deck.

Al Simmer put the boat on autopilot and ran to the stern: 'What the fuck is goin' on back here?' He saw his crew bloodied and limping. 'What? You useless bastards can't handle a little Chink sheila like her? For Christ sakes.'

He bent down and helped Charlotte to her feet. He saw Michael Chen close up for the first time. I think we buggered this up, he thought. It was getting too complicated. They would have to kill the baby and the feisty Chink sheila. But not yet. It was a long haul to the Gulf of Carpentaria. Plenty of time for a few parties.

Charlotte recovered her balance and took Michael Chen by the hand: 'Thank you ... er...'

'The name's Allan. Everyone calls me Al.'

'Al, I need to get my husband comfortable. He's just had a serious head injury. He was still recovering and your man hit him on the back of his skull. Where can we lay him down and make him comfortable? Do you have painkillers on board?'

Simmer smiled. Yes, he said, they had a full stock of medical supplies and a comfortable bed for her husband, who was stirring. He ordered Luca to help him take Kough below.

Matty Woods was a radio buff who had never heard a Mayday call. It was faint, but he was certain about it. And he was sure, with his equipment, he could trace it to the northern New South Wales coast.

He reported the incident to the Coast Guard, but no aircraft had issued flight plans or was missing in the area. It was not until the next day he received a call from Border Force. They quizzed him for some time. They thought a learner pilot had been on a solo training flight and got lost. The pilot had not filed a flight plan. This was not unusual in the country areas.

Woods was gratified his wireless hobby had been useful.

A FISHERMAN DISCOVERED an emergency inflatable washed up about fifty kilometres south of Coffs Harbour. Border Force found it was the American model used by Sikorsky. Suspicious, hunting for survivors, the local police reported to Search and Rescue that a family booked into the nearby Coolleegood Peace and Wellness Centre had gone missing. The centre could not raise them on the cellphone number they had provided when they made their reservation. They feared the family had suffered an accident on the area's twisty, narrow dirt roads.

Late in the day the body of an elderly man was found washed up about two hundred metres from where the inflatable was found. But it was almost in two halves. The local cops speculated a shark attack – or a shotgun blast in the guts – had killed the man.

The Search and Rescue exercise was ramped up to a homicide one.

When the discovery of the body made the local news, a fisherman came forward. He had seen a white flash just off the coast. It could have been a shotgun. An old fishing boat had been drifting nearby.

The Sikorsky charter company confirmed their luxury chopper had failed to return to its Sydney base.

FIFTY-ONE

Gary Stone was in a quiet fury over Kough's daring escape. He was following the developments of the chopper's cat-and-mouse chase and then its disappearance. He suspected the Mayday call was another of Kough's ruses.

In what his officials believed was overkill, he ordered a virtual blockade on all coastal vessels coming into any eastern seaport. Elaine had rolled her eyes when he told her Kough had escaped.

'He's just making a mug of you, all of us, actually,' she said. 'And he still hadn't given us the full formula before he flew the coop.'

She began to sit in on the conferences with the heads of Border Force, ASIO, Federal Police and the NSW homicide squad. So did David Hicks, ostensibly as the Border Force Minister.

David Hicks appeared unannounced at the PM's office after the latest Border Force briefing.

Stone eyed him as Hicks fidgeted and exchanged pleasantries.

'What brings you here, Dave?' said Stone. 'Is it this?' He took two scotch glasses from his bottom drawer and walked over to the official bar.

'I thought I should tell you ... I've heard stories whirling about, probably the usual beltway rumour machine, but these ones won't go away.' Hicks took a sip of the offered scotch.

Stone's face fell. What now? he thought.

'Like the new suit, Dave. It takes ten years off you.'

Hicks smiled: 'Flattery will get you everywhere, Gary. But I thought I should give you a heads-up. The wagging tongues seem to have it in for you.'

Stone was struggling to concentrate on what his minister was saying. But then Hicks mentioned the name Horatio Hadley. Stone almost dropped his glass. For the next few minutes, Hicks outlined the story of alleged corruption involving the PM's office, his COS, a senior Force officer and Michael Kough. And the sudden death of the whistle-blower who sparked an Ombudsman's Office inquiry.

'Christ, what are you saying? Do you think I murdered him?'

Hicks' face was expressionless: 'No, of course not, but it's not what I'm saying that matters, Gary. It's what other people will be saying when the Ombudsman's Office releases its report.'

Stone said: 'Fuck.'

Hicks nodded solemnly: 'My press secretary is an old journo. He says a *Telegraph* reporter has been working on the story for a while. No one knows when it'll be published but the best guess is, it'll break in the next few days. Now Kough, the guy in the middle of all of this, has vanished into thin air. And the *Telegraph* guy will be in a hurry because he will lose his scoop if the Ombudsman reports before he can publish.'

Stone swirled his glass and downed his scotch in one gulp.

Hicks was unable to read Stone's reaction so he prodded cautiously: 'We'll be in ... er ... a tight spot politically when all this ... er ... bullshit hits the fan...'

The words hung in the air. Stone squeezed his lips together but said nothing.

He looked at Hicks' glass. Hicks raised and finished his drink. He wiped his lips, but Stone made no offer to refill it and put the glasses back in the bottom drawer: 'Thanks for the heads-up, Dave. I appreciate it. I'll make some inquiries myself now and see if I can get to the bottom of it.' Then added: 'It's all bullshit, as you say.'

Hicks stretched his hand out: 'Yeah, I know it is, but bullshit can cling and smell, particularly in our business.'

The pair shook hands and Hicks left. Stone remained standing alone in the middle of his office for several minutes. He felt he was in injury time, losing a tight game with the clock running down fast. As a coach he would have told himself not to panic. But he felt close to it. It was not the way he ever thought his career would end.

He went to his desk, took a deep breath and dialled the extension to The Lodge's private quarters: 'Hi darling, just trying to find you ... there's another little problem with our friend Kough I've just been told about ... yes, I think we should talk, right now ... oh, stuff the king of Norway ... yes, it is urgent ... well the king is lucky, he can't get voted out ... I'm not being dramatic ... all right, all right, I'll come up.'

MICHAEL KOUGH OPENED HIS EYES. The room was swaying. It was vibrating. It smelled dank. It was dark. He willed his memory to fire up. He felt the top of his head. It was sticky. He looked at his fingers through the gloom. They had dark blotches on them. As he lay injured and traumatised, he willed his memory back to life. And slowly it began to light up.

He was on a pirate ship. They had murdered Charlie Slipper. They had forced him, Charlotte and Michael Chen from the emergency inflatable on to their floating hulk. He had climbed out of the bobbing inflatable first, on to the trawler's transom. But that was it. He could remember nothing more. There was only the frightening sight of the sticky blood on his fingers to provide clues his brain chose not to recall.

He could not see Charlotte or his baby son in the room. He sat up on his elbows very slowly. The pain was not bad. He saw a bottle of painkillers and a glass of water on the bedside cabinet. He shook four of the pills into his hand and swallowed them with a big mouthful of the water.

What do you do with pirates? Make them walk the plank, he thought.

The pirates had a shotgun. He remembered it had been used on Charlie Slipper, almost cutting him in half when he was blasted at close range. He needed to find it.

He heard a key turn and the cabin door opened. 'Hi, I'm Al Simmer, the skipper. Are you feeling better?'

Than what? thought Kough. 'No, I'm feeling stuffed. My head is thumping. Where the hell am I? Where's my wife and son? Who the hell are you?'

'I'm one of the Good Samaritans who rescued you from that little blow-up dinghy of yours,' said Simmer. 'We got you on board before it sunk.'

Big Brain flashed on: Accept the story if you want to stay alive. Kough said: 'Well, thank you for that. We are in your debt. The old bugger with us was crazy. He wanted to stay with that inflatable paddling pool of his. Are my family safe? I can't remember a bloody thing after we got on board.'

Simmer shook his head: 'There's no reasoning with some people, like that old fella. You'd all have been goners if we hadn't come along and got rid of him.'

Kough nodded.

'Your wife and kid? They're upstairs in the wheelhouse. They're enjoying the cruise. We're heading up to the Gulf for the prawn season.'

Simmer paused and looked him in the eye: 'Mate, you need to lie down again. You look like death warmed up. I'll send your lady down to see you and, maybe, get you a feed.'

Kough gave a theatrical sigh and lay down, closing his eyes. Simmers looked at his bloodied, bandaged head. He looked like he would die without any assistance. That would be one less problem, he thought.

FIFTY-TWO

'BUT WHERE IS THE EVIDENCE, SYD? HOW DO YOU BACK UP your claims? How does this old girl Dribble or Tibble or whatever, back up hers? This yarn is all second-hand hearsay.'

Syd Wildboare split his hands in front of him. He was getting hot and bothered. He had been expecting to be profusely congratulated for his sensational scoop and moved permanently from the Sports Section to General or Political Reporting.

Now this bald old duffer, Karl Presson, was berating him for having the best story of the decade. Wildboare knew the editor-in-chief was frightened of a ballbuster story that would bring down the country's most popular prime minister since World War II. His new shareholders were terrified of expensive defamation suits. Their APOLOGY heading was always on call to pacify the egotistical bullies that peopled finance, politics and celebrity shows.

'There is evidence, Mr Presson. We have the body of Horatio. We now have Michael Kough on the run, escaped from a government hospital. We have Horatio's immediate superior who has been found guilty of bullying offences against him. They were trying to shut him up. Intimidate him.' Wildboare helped himself to the chair in front of the editor's desk.

'I didn't say you could sit down, Wildboare. Get up. And get out there in the big, bad world and find some real evidence that Stone and his mob helped Kough, the mad scientist, to smuggle his stolen vaccine into the country,' said Presson. He stood to make clear the meeting was at an end.

Wildboare untangled his legs and stood up. He took the draft printout of the story off the desk and walked out. He strolled back to his Sports Section desk. His so-called colleagues fought to contain their laughter. They were now referring to him as Randy Stone, of the *Night Beat*, a very old American radio drama about a crime reporter; or Bernstein of Bondi.

'Welcome back, Randy. How'd it go down on Mahogany Row? Holding the front page, are they?' said Bob Bottomdrawes, the sports subeditor.

'Any chance of getting a proper story out of ya now? The Stallions are in the crap again; their chairman is up on paedophile charges. Those tossers at the *Herald* got lucky and landed the story before us. So, we need a follow-up story from you that's a scorcher.'

Bottomdrawes saw the look on Wildboare's face: 'I'm sorry, son, it's sex and organised violence on the field the punters want to read.'

Wildboare flopped down on his chair and flung the draft copy at Bottomdrawes: 'No one will remember the Stallions' chairman or his pashing-up of the under-thirteens players.'

'But they'll remember yours? Is that what you're saying?' Bottomdrawes laughed. 'C'mon, we're not covering history, son, we're covering news about today's self-important busybodies who get caught where their hands ought not to be.'

'That's what I'm covering – but the hands in my story are running the country. My story will bring down a government,' said Wildboare.

'Sure, sure. In the meantime, can you get a decent new angle on our paedophile chairman? See if his wife's in on it. They often are, you know? And get a photo of her, anyway. The *Herald* didn't have one.'

Bottomdrawes picked up Wildboare's draft copy and began scanning it. Wildboare watched as the subeditor slumped back in his chair, the way he did when concentrating. After a few pages he was arching his eyebrows. He finished reading and looked up: 'No wonder they won't bloody run it. It's so hot the paper is singed around the edges. Do you think any of it is true?'

'Fuck off, Bottomdrawes. Do you think I'm just making it up. Anyway, Presson has told me to keep digging.'

'That's a good decision from old Presson. Forget about the Stallions, go and find this Horatio's girlfriend or someone he will have talked to. You need more sources.'

Wildboare said: 'You mean it? You'll get someone else to cover the Stallions thing?'

'Yeah. I just said I would, didn't I? Now fuck off and keep digging. You'll give Presson another ulcer and win a Walkley if this is true.'

He looked around at the several sports reporters who had been watching on: 'Now, which of you losers thinks they can beat this Stallions yarn up so it looks like we got it first?'

FIFTY-THREE

AL SIMMER WATCHED THE SWELLS BUILD. AND THE WIND strengthen. The skipper of the *Sarah J* had steered her a hundred kilometres away from the coast – away from police boats and helicopters. But now he knew he would not make it north any further than the Gold Coast. The whole trip was just turning to shit.

They had named her Cyclone Kati. She was off Rockhampton, seven hundred kilometres north. Her winds were already gusting to eighty kilometres an hour and she was powering her way south at a fast clip.

He had not seen Willy Luca or Bruce Piggott for hours, since they stumbled below to their cabins. The pint-sized Chinese chick had crushed Bruce's left testicle. She had also concussed Will Luca after her violent blow to his face had broken his nose, making his breathing difficult and painful.

Simmer was alone wrestling with the steerage system and supping a warming beer. His hopes of a wild romp with the chick were dashed after her attacks on his useless crew. He was now the only able-bodied man left to control the boat.

A freak wave came from nowhere and smashed against the starboard bow. It sent a shudder down the length of the old wooden hull. Kati's howling winds would create even bigger seas in the hours ahead.

He would have to head for Port Brisbane. The *Sarah J* would disintegrate in the jaws of a cyclone. He turned a little to port and activated the ancient autopilot.

He stepped back. Maybe he could have a bit of fun with the woman now *Sarah J* was on auto. He could shag her against the helm, and then sling her and the kid over the side. That meant the trip would not be a total waste. The husband would be no more trouble. One more big whack on the head and he would be curtains.

Simmer opened the gun cupboard. The weapon was not on its mounts. He cursed Bruce Piggott. Where the hell had he put it? He checked the grinding autopilot and went below. There was no sign of the gun. He bashed on Piggott's door and went in. The dozy bugger was flat on his back, mouth wide open and snoring like a truck locked in first gear. He looked around and then closed the door.

Simmer wondered where to look next. He went to Luca's cabin. He was also passed out and pale. He had been seasick on the floor, the pig. There was no gun anywhere.

Finally, he carefully unlocked the Koughs' cabin. There was no one in it. He turned back sharply half expecting Kough to be standing behind him. But there was no one in the rolling passageway.

He raced back upstairs to the wheelhouse. Its door was locked. He hammered on it. He could hear a voice. Two voices. Someone was talking on the two-way radio.

He looked about, hoping there was a fire axe to hand. Or anything heavy to attack the locked door. There was nothing. He steeled himself and smashed his shoulder on it. The thin timber creaked. He did it again. Another creak and it moved off its hinges a fraction. The final assault knocked it down.

He flew bodily into the wheelhouse and tripped. As he went to get up, he saw the Chinese chick. Kough was beside her, bending over, hands on his knees. The tiny chick was trying to hold the heavy shotgun against her shoulder. Then she inexplicably smiled at him. He was suddenly in a titanic rage. He got up and bolted at her.

The sound of the gun was deafening in the small wheelhouse. The pellets from the twelve-gauge cartridge threw up a cloud of confetti when they missed Simmer and struck the mess of paperwork and charts strewn beside the helm. Simmer stood motionless in shock. He waited to feel the pain of a point-blank shotgun wound. He had lost his head. He had not expected the chick to shoot. The gun was so heavy, she had been struggling to keep it on her shoulder. But there was no blood and the only pain was from his ringing ears. Simmer finally shook himself from his near-death trauma and looked up. Kough was now holding the weapon: 'Sit in the helm chair, Simmer.'

Simmer heaved himself on to it.

'No second chances. If you move from there, I'll cut you in half like you did to poor old Charlie Slipper.'

'So that was just a warning shot, was it?' Simmer laughed derisively. He looked over his controls: 'Who were you talking to on the radio?'

'Never you mind, Simmer. All you have to do now is to make sure that autopilot is working. I've already set its new course.'

Kough walked behind Simmer who was hunched over the helm and watching the mounting sea. Without warning he slammed the butt into the back of Simmer's head. Not killer strength, just a warning blow, so the skipper could feel some of the pain he had suffered.

FIFTY-FOUR

Glenda Stropeshire was lying semi-conscious in a King's Cross gutter when the Drug Squad patrol found her. She panicked through her haze when she saw the uniforms. One cop even knew her name.

He eased her to her feet. The second cop looked through her handbag. The usual drug paraphernalia, he thought, till he saw a silver, cylindrical object.

'Is this the heavy stuff, Glenny?'

She began to sob.

'Christ girl, this will put you away, good and proper. What the devil were you thinking getting this trashed on the street? Were you flogging it off?'

They put her in the back of the squad car. They had her handbag, so they gave her a box of tissues to wipe her eyes and nose.

'Car seven five. Our last customer for the night, peddling heavy stuff on the street. She's had a bit too much of it for herself. She'll need a doctor to check her; she's legless.'

The station confirmed the log in and the car moved off.

Glenda sat forward on the rear seat. The driver thought she was going to throw up but she drawled something.

'What's that, Glenny? You'll have to speak up, but don't throw up, okay?'

'I don't want to go back inside. I have something for you.'

She told them her story. They radioed the station again: 'Car seven five. We will need the senior sergeant there when we get in.'

'Wills has buggered off for the night, seven five.'

'Seven five, you better get him back, love, he won't want to miss this.'

'You mean, Control, not love, don't you?'

'Absolutely, Control. Can we trust you, Control, to get Wills out of the Jubilee pronto? He will need to be sober.'

'Yes, you can trust me, car seven five.'

'Thanks, love.'

FIFTY-FIVE

'THAT'S ONE HELL OF A STORY, WILLS.' HERBERT DONKIN, the NSW Police Commissioner, frowned at his Drug Squad chief, Detective Sergeant Will Broadfoot.

'Thank God it's not one of ours who's been caught red handed.'

Broadfoot gave a short laugh: 'My thoughts exactly, sir.'

'So she sung like a canary? You've got the evidence? She won't change her story halfway through cold turkey?'

'If we charge her on this, and with all her previous, she knows she'll get a decent stretch in the pokey this time,' said Broadfoot. 'She's desperate to keep out of jail.'

'Have I got this right? This Border Force guy has been letting her through with bumfulls of coke. The last shipment was late on Sunday. They went home together in his car. The parking lot cams and others en route confirm this. They stopped for petrol in her suburb, and the servo camera confirms they were still travelling together.'

'You got it, Commissioner. And when we searched her apartment, we found articles of clothing that belonged to the guy. There was a belt with the force's logo on it. And then in a drawer, his name tag. The forensics team found plenty of DNA evidence belonging to the guy as well, in the lounge and in the bed. His supervisor confirmed he had arrived without a belt or a name tag on the day he died, and, interestingly, he refused a routine Force drug test.'

Broadfoot laughed and shook his head: 'The clincher, though, is that she videoed them in bed. The poor guy is a real squirt, nothing in the tackle department. In fact, it looks like he got so high, so quick, he may not have got a woodie. The soundtrack gives us all the details we need, of her flying the stuff in from Buenos Aires to coincide with his late shifts.

'They planned a ten-kilo shipment for next Friday. They were going to just leave the gear in her luggage. She was very happy about missing the anal search part of the business. His technique must have been a bit dodgy.

'She says other Force guys are running these rings so we've told her we won't prosecute her if she cooperates and tells the courts everything she knows.'

Donkin said: 'Border Force are going to be pissed big time when this hits the fan. They think Sydney coppers have a monopoly on drugs and corruption.'

'How do you want to handle this public-relations wise?'

'You take the full press conference, Wills. You announce the suicide of the officer led to an in-depth investigation that revealed a major drug-ring operation at the border. You deserve the credit. It's a great score,' said Donkin. 'I'll call our minister directly and he can give Dave Hicks the glad tidings.'

'Are you sure you don't want to take the media reveal?'

'Thanks, I'm sure. I've got something else on. Another diversity and inclusion seminar up in the Blue Mountains with Cindy, I mean Sergeant Blumsford.'

Broadfoot picked up his briefcase: 'No rest for the wicked, then, sir.'

Surrounded by a big desk of page proofs and barking on the phone, *The Telegraph* editor in chief, Karl Presson, waved Syd Wildboare into his office. In the centre of the desk was The Spike.

It was the terminal weapon all reporters feared. He hung the phone up and looked at Wildboare, who began to squirm under the gaze.

'Wildboare, this is your Walkley award story, the one to topple the government.' Presson squared the pages of the hard copy together and then speared them theatrically over The Spike. Modern news organisations had little need for The Spike, but the use of a simple delete button was just too clinical. So, old-school Presson kept one old Spike for special occasions.

Wildboare stared, wordless. His greatest fear was of ridicule, the reaction from the haughty political reporters and the scornful mob in the Sports Section.

'Bad luck, son. Your main man behind all the corruption allegations was – wait for this – just another crook, running his own drug-smuggling operation at Canberra Airport. Coke. Kilos of it. His girlfriend would stick it up her bum and he would do her anal searches and wave her through. A great little gig until she gave him the flick and he jumped in front a train. End of story.'

Wildboare took a seat in front of the editor's desk: 'Un-bloody-believable.'

'I didn't tell you you could sit down. We're not having a meeting, son. This is all character-building stuff. It happens to the best of us. What matters after you get knocked down is how quick you get up again.

'Don't feel sorry for yourself, son. Your source was genuine; she wasn't to know about this Horatio's little sideline.'

Presson came around his desk and gave Wildboare a pat on the shoulder: 'Never mind, while you've been diverted, Stallions has got itself in another scandal. This time it's the coach's wife getting into mischief in the under fourteen-year-olds changing sheds.'

'I know. The punters want sex and organised violence. I get it.' He left Presson's office and steeled himself for a barracking at the Sports Section.

Before he reached his desk, however, he thought of his primary source. The school-mam lady at the Ombudsman's Office. He called her on his cellphone out of earshot of the news room. She answered her direct line immediately.

He told her about the whistle-blower. She had been conned. She had wept over the death of someone who was a corrupt officer himself. She listened quietly, asked a few questions. Finally, as he said his goodbyes, she began sobbing.

FIFTY-SIX

Charlotte listened to the plan, scarcely believing
her husband was serious. She agreed they had to abandon the heaving
hulk and leave its pirates behind. But the cold-blooded murder required
left her shaken.

She wracked her mind for an alternative plan to his but could not
come up with one. She looked at her baby, fast asleep on the wheelhouse
bench seat and oblivious to the danger of the cyclone battering the
Sarah J.

Kough had taped Al Simmer to the helmsman's chair. The shotgun
stood in the corner, no longer necessary in their escape plot.

The boat's radio was broadcasting the latest weather warnings and
tracking Cyclone Kati south-eastward. When Charlotte nodded in
resignation, Kough picked up the radio microphone and broadcast a
Mayday call. Instantly, the Queensland Coast Guard responded.

Kough gave their position, thirty kilometres south of Stradbroke
Island, off the Gold Coast. He said the aged wooden hull of the *Sarah J*
had sprung a leak, the vessel was taking on water and sinking. He needed
a helicopter to winch himself, his wife and baby, to safety.

When Simmer heard the plan, he reared up in a vain attempt to
break the tapes that held him. He went red in the face from the exertion
and his body shook in fear.

He had heard his death sentence in advance, loud and clear, thought Charlotte. It seemed cruel. Did he deserve it? Her moment of remorse passed quickly. Simmer had murdered Charlie Slipper in cold blood, was obviously intent on raping and killing her, and almost certainly, of throwing her baby into the sea too.

Her husband had been battered by this man's crew. It was a miracle Kough had managed to stay alive so far. She still had no idea what the long-term effects on him would be. He had hardly made it to the wheelhouse. He was so weak he had given her the shotgun to hold Simmer off. But the weight was more than she could manage when it mattered, while Kough had mustered his courage and stamina to take the weapon from her after she had fired and missed Simmer.

He then neutralised him with a blow to the head. Charlotte had taped the slob to his chair while he was semi-conscious. Now she knew those tapes would ensure he drowned when the boat went down, along with the two criminal crew members below.

Kough found a large knife in the wheelhouse cupboard. Once the Coast Guard had confirmed they were en route, he nodded to her and limped downstairs to the crew cabins. Both crew members were still laid out on their bunks in a stupor of booze or painkillers. He killed them both quickly by stabbing them in the brain through their eyes.

Kough then dragged himself aft to the stinking-hot engine room. The room was ill lit and the engine ran at such a din it hurt his head. The boat creaked and shuddered violently as the heavy seas rammed into it. The weather report put the swells at five metres. Waves and spray were breaking over the bow but would soon pummel it beam on when the engine stopped and it lost steerage to the gale.

Kough was bruised badly and burned as he brushed against parts of the scalding-hot engine. Driven by thoughts of revenge and anger, he managed to keep his balance long enough to cut into the cooling pump's hose. It was a tough, thick piece of rubber and it took an effort to pierce it and then widen the cut. Water began to spout from it and steam rose from where it hit the labouring engine.

An abhorrent metallic smell filled the room as the engine block began to cook. It would be only a few minutes before it would seize up, Kough thought.

Covered in sweat and filth and burns, he limped to the exit door. He pushed against it. It would not move.

The storm had flexed the boat's structure and the door was jammed ajar. The gap was too narrow for Kough to squeeze through. He felt an icy panic grip him. Big Brain said, Charlotte would not leave the baby to find her way down to the bilges to attempt any rescue. If he was trapped in the doorway, he would drown and Charlotte would be left on a heaving deck, wrestling to hold a helicopter's life rope for her and the infant.

Kough closed his eyes. Big Brain said that if the boat is corkscrewing, wait until it twists the timbers in your favour. Push at the door when you feel the structure creak in a new direction.

Kough tried to sense the hull's movement. He felt the jammed door ease minutely. He waited a few moments for another huge swell to twist the floor and door frame. Then he shoved his body with all his might against it. It gave several centimetres. But not enough. He sucked in hot, fetid air and waited. He sensed his second chance and charged the door again. It sprung back and he was suddenly through and trying to keep his balance.

Above the storm he could hear the loud clatter of a helicopter. Feeling his way down dark passageways, he headed for the wheelhouse. The stairway felt like it had grown longer. And steeper. He heard Charlotte calling for him in a frightened, high-pitched voice.

As he made the wheelhouse, a loud speaker from the helicopter thundered into his consciousness. Bound to the helmsman's chair, Simmer's eyes cast around frantically. Kough held Charlotte's arm: 'Remember what an evil man he is, darling.' She did not reply. Kough grabbed her and the baby she was cradling, and they clambered on to the deck outside. They were instantly drenched and crawled towards the bow.

A man in bright red Coast Guard overalls was dangling above the deck. Kough pushed Charlotte and Michael Chen towards their rescuer. The man strapped them into a harness and they were both suddenly rising in the howling gale.

Kough clung desperately to a deck bollard as the *Sarah J* heeled dangerously against the furious seas. The harness was suddenly swaying near to him. He grabbed it, was harnessed in. The guard said: 'Is there anyone else on board?'

Kough shook his head just as they both heard a loud crack. The pair twirled around on the winch wire rising above the *Sarah J*, and Kough could see inside the wheelhouse. A wave had almost rolled the boat over and its impact had torn the helmsman's chair off its floor mounting. Simmer was still bound and rolling helplessly on the floor. His eyes seemed to stare directly into Kough's.

The guard put a hand by his mouth to shield against the wind and shouted: 'What's that in the cabin? Are you sure we've got everyone?'

Kough turned to look. Simmer was clearly squirming and rolling against the wall hoping some protrusion would jag and break into the plastic tape.

'There's something rolling about on the floor,' said the guard.

'It's an old sleeping bag tied to a kids' high chair we were using,' said Kough. Big Brain said, Not bad but no Kewpie doll.

The helicopter winch line continued to screw its way upward in a tight circle as the machine fought to hold its station. As the winch wire revolved, the guard grew certain the 'sleeping bag' was alive with a mind of its own.

The guard gave Kough a hard look: 'Something's not right, mate. What happened down there?'

'The good guys won,' said Kough.

'What?' yelled the guard. 'What are you talking about?'

'I said: we're all good and done down there.'

The guard shrugged and looked above him as the rescue hatch loomed up.

Moments later a giant wave broke over the wallowing *Sarah J*. She desperately clung to life for a moment before belching up clouds of spray and steam and disappearing below.

FIFTY-SEVEN

The King of Norway had been a boring guest. Gary Stone was tested trying to keep up the idle, inconsequential chatter such diplomatic events demand. Eventually the head of state of one of the smallest European countries had yawned and mentioned the jet lag penalty for visiting the bottom of the globe.

Stone immediately patted him on the arm and stood up: 'I understand, your majesty. I'm sorry for keeping you up so late.'

The king quickly found himself being escorted politely but firmly to his limousine, hands were shaken and he was saluted by the ceremonially dressed soldiers. The vehicle crunched its way down The Lodge's gravel driveway and was gone.

Stone turned to find John Able at his elbow: 'There's been a development with the Horatio thing.'

'Oh, no. Not another one.'

'This one is good news, I think. That little weirdo Horatio Hadley was running his own drug-smuggling ring. The Ombudsman's Office has dropped its investigations.'

The PM's wife, Elaine, stepped between them. She held up her cellphone screen. The *Sydney Morning Herald* was reporting Opposition demands for the Border Force Minister David Hicks to resign immediately. A NSW police report was about to expose the Force's involvement in a drug-smuggling ring implicating senior officers.

Stone whistled.

Able said: 'Hicks is not going to go down quietly, sir. He knows it was you who was named in the Ombudsman's report about Horatio's claims of high-level involvement in the smuggling operations. And named me and Michael Kough as conspirators.'

Stone groaned. Elaine shook her head curtly. Neither said anything. They turned to see off their other VIP guests who had attended the king's state dinner.

By early the next morning, Stone's political crisis had worsened. High-level but unnamed sources said it was the prime minister who should be resigning. Gary Stone had been named in the Ombudsman's inquiries and linked to virologist billionaire Michael Kough's controversial re-entry to Australia after working at an American germ-warfare research laboratory.

Able and Stone's wife, Elaine, waited till the PM had read the news before speaking. Able said: 'We must get our hands on Michael Kough before this gets any further out of control. He's currently being questioned by the NSW Police on the Gold Coast.'

'He won us the last election when he got the Chinese back on side...' Stone muttered seemingly to himself.

'And he's going to lose you the next one,' said Elaine. 'Or force you to retire in the middle of this mess, another Michael Kough mess.'

Stone glared at her. She went on: 'And who is the happy deputy who will take your job?'

'The party would never elect Hicks to be prime minister,' Stone snapped. 'The man's a lightweight. He's such an incompetent I have to write most of his defence-policy speeches for him.'

'He is very ambitious, sir,' said Able.

'He's been busying himself around the backbenchers in his new suit,' said Elaine. 'There's a rumour he may demand a spill.'

Able nodded. He had also heard the rumour. A spill meant an MP of the governing party could call for a new leadership election.

Elaine unfolded her arms: 'It's not all your fault, Gazza. I was the one who wanted Kough locked away in a sanatorium until he recovered from his brain injury and let us have the full anti-viral formula or be handed over to the CIA.'

Stone rubbed his cheek: 'John is right, we have to get to Kough again and end this trail of madness he leads us all into.'

Able said the Federal and New South Wales police had no jurisdiction in Queensland where Kough was being held. It was already a bureaucratic shambles. Kough had not been charged with any crime and was a hero again in the media for saving his family from a sinking rescue boat.

Stone stood up and looked out the window of The Lodge's private drawing room: 'I can make this a national security issue if I want to, particularly with the CIA still chasing him, so access should not be a problem. But I have another idea to bring him to his senses.'

Two hours later, the PM's jet was flying to Brisbane. Its passenger list was short: Elaine, Able and the ASIO boss Frank Church.

Simultaneously the Ombudsman's Office was addressing a media conference. There was no evidence an alleged smuggling ring had any connection to the prime minister. The whistle-blower himself had been a trafficker and had suicided before the Office had completed its inquiries into his claims. The investigation had been terminated.

For the media, the sensational Horatio conspiracy story was imploding. Stone felt a huge sense of relief. His deputy, David Hicks, however, felt robbed. He was watching arch-manipulator Stone shrug off another political crisis which should have destroyed him. Hicks was convinced the Kough-initiated scandal had given off clouds of smoke. And where there was smoke...

In Brisbane, a fuller news story had broken about the Kough family. The scientist and his family had been rescued from a storm-tossed trawler whose crew had murdered his missing helicopter pilot and taken his family prisoner after rescuing them. The crew members were all unconscious, in alcoholic stupors, when the *Sarah J* had finally sunk in the cyclonic seas.

Kough's tale of high drama had not convinced the Coast Guard, which had begun a search for the sunken *Sarah J* and the bodies of the crew as the cyclonic weather eased.

. . .

MICHAEL KOUGH GAVE a look of anguish when the Brisbane Police HQ interview room door opened and a carelessly dressed detective walked casually in.

'Detective Roger Rougess,' said Kough. 'What are you doing here?'

Rougess pulled up a chair: 'Well, well, well ... Michael Kough, as I live and breathe.' He sat back in the chair and removed the fedora that covered his balding head. His brown, misshapen discount suit hung on him loosely as always, the knot of his yellow patterned tie drooped three centimetres below the collar of his brown shirt.

Kough tried to calm his breathing as he faced the old murder detective who tried to arrest him for killing Charlotte's husband.

Rougess slowly took out a notebook and a biro pen and put them on the scarred desk. 'So, up to your old tricks, hah? Can't stay out of trouble, can you?'

Rougess opened a page in the notebook and looked Kough in the eye: 'Husband killer, alleged smuggler, alleged thief, confirmed international fraudster, international drug cartel blackmailer and kidnap target, Chinese flag vandal and the mad scientist who allegedly discovered the cure for the common cold ... and just now a suspect in a multiple homicide case aboard a trawler off the Queensland coast.'

Kough stared open mouthed.

'Did I miss anything out?'

'I thought you were off the beat, promoted to a big anti-crime commission somewhere.'

Rougess smiled: 'I was. I am. But I'm taking a day off. My bosses think I have a better handle on you than anyone else. So, did I miss anything else?'

Kough took a deep breath: 'Yeah, you missed a couple of things out ... like the millions of lives my discovery has saved ... and the fact Charlotte's husband was armed and attempting to shoot me when I beat him to it.'

'Yeah, yeah, always the one with the explanation. And the guy with the friends in very high places to smooth your way.'

'What do you want, Rougess?'

'Now, now. That's not very friendly. Remember, I said you could call me Roger?'

'Just get on with it, Rougess. I'm expecting to be released from here shortly.'

Rougess squeezed his lips together: 'Your mate Gary Stone doesn't run things up here. You'll get released when I've completed my murder investigation. If you told me the truth now, of course, it would save a lot of time. The divers may take some time to retrieve the bodies from the old *Sarah J*.'

Big Brain appeared. You won't beat this wizened-up old murder cop. Play your cards as though you have a royal flush, the highest hand in poker.

Kough sat forward: 'I apologise, Roger. I've been through the ringer trying to keep my wife and baby alive in a living hell. I'm suffering a concussion injury and, I'm afraid, I get short tempered. We had a nightmare time with the *Sarah J* thugs.'

Without missing a beat, Rougess smiled: 'So it'll be another case of self-defence, when we find the bodies, will it?'

Big Brain hovered: Keep calm. Remember, the royal flush.

Kough said: 'I think you know, I'm no killer. But, anyway, you'll never find any of those thugs. Their old crate will be in a thousand pieces spread over the seabed after that cyclone.'

For the first time Rougess paused. He folded his legs. He's buying time, Kough thought. Maybe he thinks I'm holding a royal flush after all.

'Do you still wear orange socks with the suit?' Kough asked.

Rougess' head snapped up. 'What of it?'

Kough laughed: 'Nothing. But it may mean you're determined to be different or noticed.'

The old detective averted his gaze to the pad lying on the table.

'Were you a hippy in the old days?' Kough asked.

'Wait on, wait on. Never mind all this mind shit, I'm the one asking the questions here.'

'Oh, you are? Why don't you ask about what the *Sarah J* crew did to our helicopter pilot? Cut him bloody nearly in half with a shotgun at close range, when he told them to get stuffed. He's the one whose body washed ashore almost in two pieces down off Coffs Harbour.'

Rougess moved on his chair: 'So are you saying we'll find bodies on the *Sarah J* and you killed them in self-defence?'

'No, I'm telling you, you won't find their bodies. They were all in a drunken stupor when I called the Coast Guard to have my family rescued.'

Rougess shook his head: 'No, no. The helicopter winch man saw someone strapped to a broken helmsman's chair, rolling around terrified on the floor.'

'No, Roger, he didn't. He saw a sleeping bag wound around the kids' high chair. The only movement was caused by the to and fro in the swell.'

A constable entered the room and handed Rougess a piece of paper. The detective read it and raised his eyebrows: 'Well, we'll soon see if your sleeping bag story holds up. Divers have located the old boat. She's still in one piece.'

Kough's face went ashen. He was shaking his head when Big Brain said, It's time we mounted up and headed out of Dodge.

Rougess looked pleased with himself as he stood to adjourn the interview.

'I knew the day would come when your slick antics and dubious pursuits would come to a sticky end, and I hoped I'd be there when it happened. Now, it looks like it has happened – despite all your money and political pull.'

Kough said nothing.

Rougess allowed himself another smug smile: 'All right then, I'll be back as soon as the bodies are brought up. Any ideas at this point on their cause of death?'

Rougess turned for the door when it opened and two men in dark pinstriped suits apologised for interrupting.

The older man of the pair nodded pleasantly to Rougess: 'Thanks, Detective, but we'll take the matter from here.'

Rougess drew himself to his full height: 'What? Who are you?'

'Sorry. I don't think we've met. Church, Frank Church. The DG at ASIO. I'm afraid Michael Kough is wanted for questioning on a number of national security charges.'

'WHY AM I wearing leg chains as well as handcuffs?'

Kough stared in disbelief as the shackles were attached to his ankles and belt. His arms were cuffed behind his back, the position preferred by police officers. A falling prisoner lands on their face.

'They asked for the leg chains,' said John Able.

'Who the hell is "they"?'

Able looked at his oldest friend: 'Who do you think, Boffy?'

Able tugged at the cuffs and leg irons, checking they were properly locked.

'Johnny, who is they?' Kough wailed.

'Well, the Chinese for starters; and the CIA. They both wanted you delivered super secure – and I don't blame them.'

Able took Kough by the arm and pushed him towards the door. He staggered a half step at a time against the tight chains.

Kough suddenly stopped and fell to his knees: 'Fuck you all. I'm not going anywhere.'

Able raised his eyebrows: 'Boffy, it doesn't make any difference to me whether you walk out under your own steam or you're carried.'

Big Brain cut through the fog of pain and shock: Stand up and behave. This gets you out of Dodge and away from facing charges for the three murders you committed on the *Sarah J*.

Kough shouted at the guards: 'All right, all right. I'll stand. Keep your hands away from my head, will you?'

Two of the guards helped him to his feet.

Kough shuffled forward and down a narrow Brisbane Police HQ corridor. A few minutes later he was at a rear door and on a loading bay. A big, black, windowless Mercedes van was backed up in the bay, idling quietly.

Kough was helped inside. To his shock he saw Charlotte, and his baby son, seated on one of the two bench seats.

Kough said: 'Char, are you all right?'

She shook her head. She was in a pale blue smock, the sort they hand out to hospital patients.

'What have they done to you?'

'You mean, what have you done to me, Mikey?'

Kough's head slumped forward. The white skull bandage looked grubby and loose. He massaged the side of his head slowly.

Charlotte began crying softly. The baby joined in.

Kough lifted his head and winced with pain from the movement.

He looked at Charlotte: 'Char, I love you. I saved your life on that trawler. And Michael Chen's. I saved you. Both.'

Charlotte shook her head: 'You saved us, but you were the one to put us in danger – and we were nearly killed because of your mad escape scheme.

'That old pilot didn't deserve to die; he was trying to protect us. Sometimes I think you are quite mad, deranged. Now look where we are. Heading to China or America, with you trussed up like a hen.'

The big van began trundling forward. It stopped and started at traffic lights along the bumpy city streets. It was like travelling in a big coffin. There were no windows, the ceiling lights were dingy and the driver's cabin was separated from the passengers by a solid steel wall to complete the near blackout.

After several minutes, Kough looked at Able through the gloom: 'All right, what would I have to do for you to stop all this?'

Able held his palms out: 'It might be too late to do anything, Boffy. We gave you a way out; you only had to let us secure the full Safevac formula and you could have lived the rest of your life in luxury wherever you chose, but...'

The van rolled on for another few minutes. Kough rubbed tired eyes: 'Do you really think Stone will hand me over to the CIA or the Chinks?'

Able took a deep breath: 'I think he's a fair man, but you've played him for a sucker. Now he's fighting for his political life. So, I'd say you've pretty much cooked your goose with him.'

'What about Char and Michael Chen?'

'It's a bit late for you to be worried about them.'

Kough lowered his head and sank back on his cuffed wrists.

Able broke the silence: 'We offered you a perfect solution and you ran. And you made fools out of us in that wild goose chase. Since then, four people have died. What would you do if you were in our position? Give you yet another chance to make us look like the Keystone cops.'

Kough said nothing. Charlotte stood, balanced herself and moved to sit beside Able. She put a hand on his leg: 'Johnny, you know he's not a bad man.'

Able sighed: 'No, he's a dangerous man.'

FIFTY-EIGHT

David Hicks plucked up his courage. It was difficult to do but his political aspirations to live in The Lodge depended on it. He tried to calm his nerves. He felt like a referee scared of using his whistle and handing a foul-play red card to a muscle-bound forward.

Gary Stone had left him waiting sixteen minutes before having him ushered in to the big office, with the national flags unfurled behind the super-sized prime ministerial desk.

Stone had his head down, ostensibly studying some paperwork of urgent, national importance. Hicks stood silently in front of the desk and waited.

Finally, Stone looked up and removed his reading glasses: 'Here to congratulate me, Dave?'

Hicks opened his mouth, but no words came.

Stone sighed: 'That was a narrow escape. Lucky the Ombudsman's Office did the right thing before a full-blown corruption scandal erupted around our government, eh?'

'Well, I'm not sure you or our government have ... er ... escaped,' Hicks began. Before he could continue, Stone said: 'Oh, how rude of me. Dave, please, take a seat, take a seat. Would you like a coffee? It's a bit early for a scotch.'

Hicks cleared his throat: 'I have had two cups of coffee, thank you, waiting outside to see you.'

'What do you think of our coffee?' said Stone, shuffling paper on his desk.

'Gary, I'm not here to talk to you about bloody coffee.'

'Sorry, Dave, I thought you might have an opinion on it.'

Hicks felt his face flush: 'I said I'm not here to talk to you about the bloody coffee.'

'So, you're not here to congratulate me, then?'

Hicks sat on the edge of his chair: 'I'm here, Gary, because it would be in your interests to resign. Today. If you want to preserve the integrity of our party.'

Stone raised his chin. 'At last, you've come right out and said it.'

Hicks shook his head in exasperation: 'Just listen. You're delusional if you think you have escaped.'

Stone nodded slowly and stapled a sheaf of papers together: 'Well, one of us is delusional, I'll grant you that. What is it you have that would make me want to resign?'

Hicks sat back. He said the party's general secretary had agreed to a party caucus meeting to vote on a spill for its leadership. He would show that meeting this afternoon the evidence incriminating Stone. It would show Stone at the heart of a corrupt government.

Stone put the newly stapled papers casually in a drawer.

'Evidence?'

'Yes, evidence. Don't you believe me?'

'Now that you mention it, no.'

Hicks smiled. 'I have all the details of the Ombudsman's Office corruption investigation and you are named, along with your wunderkind, John Able. And the investigation links you directly with that Michael Kough character and his theft and smuggling of his anti-viral drug into the country.'

Hicks began jogging one leg: 'And reports that you hired a Chinese spy that your wonder child was shagging while working in your office.'

Hicks sat back and folded his arms: 'You could never get on top of all that scandal. All the innuendo and sleaze. It would fill the news for weeks and the stench would never fully clear. You know that. It would turn our government into a train wreck.

'Question Time in Parliament would become a circus, with the Opposition in a feeding frenzy. You need to retire gracefully, before this caucus meeting even begins.'

Stone nodded and scowled: 'And where did you get all these details of the Ombudsman's investigation from?'

Hicks shook his head: 'From the horse's mouth, Gary. I'll be showing the caucus the original report I was given.'

'Do you have the report with you?'

Hicks said: 'Yes, but I'm not showing it to you. You can wait to see it at the same time as the rest of the caucus.'

Hicks gave a big sigh: 'Gary, can you just get off your high horse for the sake of the party and admit you've lost, your time's up, your game's up? If you write your resignation letter right now, I'll take it to the general secretary and we'll cancel the caucus meeting. This whole mess will be buried, put to bed for good.'

'You're right. That would be the most efficient way to proceed,' said Stone. He picked up a pen and put two sheets of parliamentary letterhead paper on his blotter. He wrote a few lines on each and signed both with a flourish. He leaned across his desk and pushed his intercom button: 'Ask Sergeant Kilston to come in, would you?'

Hicks frowned.

'While we're waiting for Kilston, this page is for you.'

'For me?'

'Yes. It's formal notice that you've been fired as Defence and Border Force Minister, effective immediately.'

Hicks rose to his feet: 'What the hell? What do you think you're playing at? You can't just sack me.'

The plainclothes sergeant, part of Stone's personal protection team, arrived. He looked at both men with an expressionless face.

'Sergeant, Mr Hicks has told me he has a report from the Ombudsman's Office which is subject to section 718 of the Public Service Confidentiality Code. He has told me he intends to reveal its contents to unauthorised persons later today. Can you ask him for the document or search him, if necessary, please?'

Kilston turned to look at the minister: 'Is this true, sir?'

Hicks looked at the sergeant in disbelief. It must be a practical joke, he thought. But he knew it was not.

'Sir?' said Kilston.

Hicks pulled a long envelope from inside his coat pocket. He stood still, clasping it in one hand and breathing heavily.

'Sir?' Kilston said again. He put a hand out.

'Who are you to say if a document is in breach of the confidentiality laws?' he panted as he wiped perspiration from his brow.

'It will carry a departmental letterhead if it is an official document,' said Kilston. He moved suddenly closer to Hicks.

'All right, take the fucking thing.' He thrust the envelope at Kilston.

He turned to leave. Stone said: 'Where do you think you're going, Dave?'

Hicks swivelled to stare at Stone. 'You can't go back to your office, if that's what you were planning. It's been sealed off, as per the defence protocols. Your personal possessions will be boxed and couriered to you tomorrow.'

As he stood in humiliating confusion, the sergeant said: 'It does appear these are official papers subject to confidentiality provisions, sir. I'll have to ask you to accompany me to my office. There are a few issues to clear up about how they came into your possession and what you intended to do with them.'

Hicks swore under his breath.

Stone said: 'You know what your real crime is, don't you David? Disloyalty. There is no greater crime than disloyalty. As an Australian Army officer and a gentleman, you should have known that.'

The sergeant nodded to Stone and then took Hicks gently by the arm and led him from the office he had so coveted.

When the pair had gone, Stone pushed a speed dial: 'Oh, Steven, glad I could reach you. This afternoon's caucus has been cancelled. Sorry about the short notice...' Stone nodded into the phone: 'Well, yes, Hicks can't make it anyway; he's in custody at the moment being questioned by the police ... it's about a breach of confidentiality provisions in an official document ... yes, it was a shock to me too ... no, I'm advising the Governor-General today to withdraw his ministerial warrant ... yes, I'll be making an announcement on his replacement in a few days ... yes, yes ...very sad ... I'm telling you all of this in confidence. I know you'll understand we wouldn't want this becoming public until

Dave has a chance to resign with a little dignity. All right, I'll leave the caucus meeting cancellation notices to you. Have a good afternoon and thanks for moving that Norway king bore away from me. You should have been a diplomat. Speak soon.'

FIFTY-NINE

Frank Church strode into the ward. The ASIO director-general was a man in a big hurry. He saw through the nursing station's window Michael Kough lying back with new, clean bandages around his skull. He appeared half asleep. He still had the leg chains on. A handcuff fastened one of his arms to the steel bedside railing.

Seated at the foot of the bed, he saw Able, who looked up and waved a greeting.

Grim-faced, Church beckoned furiously at Able, who rushed to the nurses' station.

'We've got to move this boy, fast,' said Church, looking each way down the hospital corridor.

'The doctors are waiting on a new scan. They're worried about the skull flap not healing. It was damaged during his trip on the *Sarah J*,' said Able.

'Too bloody bad,' said Church. 'The local cops are kicking up hell, wanting to keep him right here and charge him. They found two of the trawler crew murdered, stabbed through the eye by what they think was a sharp knife. The third guy was, for all intents and purposes, tortured to death. He was wrapped in masking tape to the helmsman's chair and left to drown after the Koughs were plucked from the deck by the rescue helicopter.'

Able swore and took a glance at the pale figure of Kough: 'So, what's the problem? National security has priority over a murder investigation.'

Church grimaced: 'Maybe, in theory, but the Queensland coppers want to keep Killer Kough, as they're calling him, locked up right where they can see him and interview him.'

'What's behind that little tantrum?'

Church shook his head: 'Truth is, they think he'll escape again if he's left in our hands. They think we're soft and there's a fix in concerning Kough. They can't understand how he sprung himself using a helicopter and then left the Navy and Border Force chasing our tails.'

'So, what are you suggesting?'

Church said: 'The local d's are on their way. We have to move him right now, scan or no scan. I think we need to get him to the airport and on the PM's jet.'

Able looked doubtful: 'That won't work. The locals know about the Merc van; it wouldn't make it halfway to the airport before it was stopped.'

Church was watching the corridor closer than a cat sensing a lurking mouse.

'I've got an idea,' he said. 'A bit of cloak and dagger. You get Kough and Co. wheeled to the ambulance bay. I'll have a little chat with the ambo boss. We'll sneak him out in one of their vehicles with all the sirens and lights clearing the way. The Merc can drive off empty as a decoy.'

Over the protests of the medical staff, Kough was disconnected from various monitors and the bed rapidly trundled to the nearest elevator. It went to the bottom floor and the ambulance bay. By the time bed and patient, and his wife and baby, arrived, Church was standing smiling by the open rear door of a Queensland ambulance. Kough was placed on a stretcher and shoved in. His handcuffs and leg irons were snapped into place as the ambulance pulled out with its sirens wailing.

A motorcycle cop waved them down as the ambulance pulled swiftly out of the hospital driveway. He leaned into the cab: 'If this is an urgent trip, I can clear the traffic for you.'

Church leaned over the driver: 'Yes, it's a matter of life or death. We have a jet waiting for him at the international airport. He needs an urgent operation. It's only done in Sydney.'

'Too easy,' said the cop. 'Just follow me. Be there in no time.' He revved up the big bike and turned on his flashing light. This was much more fun than riding ceremonial escort to the King of Norway.

Both vehicles sped away. On Church's instruction, the PM's jet crew had filed a flight plan, to Sydney. They would alter it to Canberra when they were in the air, safely outside Brisbane tower's controlled space.

The airport tarmac security gate staff saw the ambulance and cycle cop speeding towards them. They waved the tiny convoy to a halt at the gate's barrier.

Able got out. Took the sergeant aside and told him the prime minister's wife had suffered a serious heart attack. The PM's jet was standing by five hundred metres away to take her to a Sydney hospital. They needed access to the tarmac immediately.

The sergeant was Hermaz Gazala, a pretend, civilian policeman, employed three weeks earlier by a private security company. He looked overwhelmed. Driving out on the tarmac was absolutely forbidden, he said. He looked at his other two paunchy security guards. They shrugged at him.

'What's the hold-up here?' Church was out of the ambulance and jogging to the gate.

'We can't let you on to the tarmac, sir,' Gazala explained. 'I need authorisation to do that from the airport police.'

'We have a woman dying here. She needs immediate attention. This is an emergency, man. Don't you understand?'

Sergeant Gazala put his shoulders back: 'What? You think I don't understand? That I'm stupid? You wait here, I'll call the airport police.'

Church waved Able closer: 'Get back in the ambulance. I'll deal with this.'

Church took his identification card out. Gazala sniffed and looked at it. He had no idea what the Australian Secret Intelligence Office was. Had never heard of it. Probably a competing security contractor, he thought.

'Don't know what that card is. I've never seen one like it before.'

Church said: 'Okay, have you ever seen one of these?' He pulled out his Glock and held it against the sergeant's stomach. The man blanched and stepped back.

'Tell your two buddies to open the barrier. Now.' Church watched Gazala deciding whether to tough it out or let them in.

He lowered the Glock and shot a hole in the tarmac beside Gazala's shoe. 'The next one's in your ear. Get the barrier raised.'

Still Gazala paused. He had been a Big Man among his family and friends since he got his uniform. It had given him respect and authority. Something he had never had when working as a migrant dishwasher in Bogota, Colombia's capital.

He gave a smug grin: 'You won't shoot me. This is Australia.'

He felt a shock of pain when Church fired a bullet through his leather boot and into his foot. He fell sideways. When he landed, he saw blood puddling around frayed bootlaces.

Church shouted at the other two guards and waved the gun at them: 'Get that barrier up.' They sprinted to obey.

Then he ordered them to pick up their comrade who was moaning and clutching his boot: 'Take him over to that ambulance. And all of you get in.'

The crammed ambulance drove, lights flashing, to the jet's passenger ramp. Its passengers ran, hobbled and limped up the gangway. The big Dassault Falcon's three jet engines were throbbing and its wheels rolling before the last of the seatbelts had been clasped.

ELAINE SURVEYED the VIP jet's passenger cabin and took in the scene: what a zoo, she thought. A sobbing, shot security guard, his two bewildered colleagues; a scientist in chains, a frightened wife holding her crying baby close to her chest; the country's top spy trying to use his secure satellite phone; and the PM's chief of staff shaking his head and staring grim-faced out the window.

The jet's Royal Australian Air Force steward had taken the first-aid box and was attempting the bloody job of removing the guard's boot, to treat the bullet wound.

ASIO Director-General Frank Church finally made a connection. After several seconds, his hard face lit up. He sat back in his plush seat and pushed a hand through his thin, greying hair.

Elaine sat behind the executive desk, facing aft, watching him and tried to guess why he had suddenly cheered up. Eventually Church broke the connection as Elaine's cellphone lit up with a brief text from her husband: 'Darling, details later, but Hicks now red carded. Ombudsman's probe terminated. I think Kough should stay on the field. G.'

Elaine looked up and smiled as Church walked down the aisle and sat in the seat opposite her: 'You've heard the news then, Mrs Stone?'

'Yes. Gary says now the circumstances have changed radically, the government is not under any threat and we should look at rehabilitating Kough.'

Elaine became aware Able was standing beside her in the aisle. She said: 'But he's facing a triple murder rap in Queensland and he's still the only one holding the total Safevac formula.'

Church said: 'And don't forget his CIA problem. They have long memories.'

The ASIO boss shuffled sideways and Able slid into the seat beside him at the desk. Able said: 'No one will dare indict Michael Kough. You saw those mountains of flowers and cards that piled up by the acre when he was lying unconscious in hospital. And, at the end of this trip, he'll be mobbed by the media as an even bigger hero, having saved his family in the midst of a cyclone from killer trawlermen who kidnapped them and murdered their pilot.'

Elaine nodded but looked unconvinced.

Able said: 'I know he's a wild card but he's not a murderer. He killed those crims on the trawler in self-defence. And don't forget they nearly killed him. They smashed him over his barely healed head flap. I don't know how he survived that. They would have raped Charlotte and thrown the baby over the side without a second thought. There is no jury in the world that would convict the man.'

Elaine looked at Church. The ASIO boss nodded: 'He's right, Mrs Stone.'

Elaine said: 'So, I heard two shots and lots of screaming. What happened exactly at the airport, Frank?'

Church gave a slight sigh: 'There was a misunderstanding, Mrs Stone. The civilian guards refused to carry out a legal command. A gun went off accidently and we've brought the injured guard with us for medical treatment. I'll have a word with Sergeant Gazala in a minute.'

Able chuckled: 'So, he can be an accident victim or a suspect airport terrorist.'

'Yeah,' said Church, 'that sort of thing.'

KOUGH HAD ESCAPED the noose again, thought Able. He went to the rear of the jet and held a small, steel key in front of Kough's bleary eyes. Kough said: 'Is that for me? You think I can't escape because we're at ten thousand metres?'

Able smiled: 'No, I don't. You've probably got a parachute under your shirt.'

Kough laughed. 'Where are you taking me this time? Langley?'

'Boffy, did you ever find the third person to complete the Safevac formula?'

Kough stared at Able for a long time.

'What if I had?'

'Well, it might make quite a difference. The difference between flying on to Langley or stopping in Sydney for a monster ticker-tape parade for a recovering superhero.'

Kough eyed the key. Big Brain said, That's a no-brainer.

Kough said: 'I get to be a hero if I give you the whole formula in writing, is that it?'

'If anything happens to you, the formula would be lost. Millions would die unnecessarily. You know that. That's why you took the precaution of splitting it into three encrypted codes on three cellphones. Your long-suffering first wife, Betty, has one, I have one. Who has the third one? The one that suddenly went missing for some reason. Is that lady of night in the picture again?'

Kough said: 'You don't have to worry who has it. It's back in action. I made sure of that before I went AWOL from the sanitorium. There are no hold-ups in Safevac production.'

Able looked puzzled: 'Then someone who doesn't like you could put a bullet in your head, and the vaccine production would continue?'

Kough nodded.

Able tightened his grasp on the key: 'That was a big call on your part.'

Kough sighed: 'Yeah, it was a big call.'

'So you're not an absolute, selfish bastard.'

Kough laughed quietly.

Able said: 'But the protocol is still not absolutely safe. If any of the three people involved get run over by a truck, the whole system breaks down again.'

Kough shrugged: 'So you do still want me to give the full formula to a single source. That would be a really big decision. I don't think I have enough trust in human nature yet to do that.'

Elaine Stone appeared in the aisle beside them. 'Give me the key, John.'

Able tried to hide his surprise as he passed it to Elaine. She held it up: 'Michael Kough, I'm going to give you this key and your freedom. You are going to publish the Safevac formula and stop your dangerous thirty-day control-freak nonsense. You'll make it available to any pharmaceutical company that wishes to produce it. Each company would pay you a standard royalty.'

Elaine held out the key. Kough stared at it. 'What about the agreement I have with the Chinese? They have exclusive production rights for all of Asia.'

Elaine said: 'The Chinese will still be able to mass manufacture Safevac as they do now. They'll have to pay you a standard royalty and face some possible competition. They'll live with that rather than risk losing their supply of the formula. And the Chinese will have no problem in undercutting any price competition; they're the world's leader at that.'

Elaine stood silently, fingering the little key. She shook her head at him: 'Michael Kough, you have made enough money already to last ten lifetimes.'

Big Brain said, She's right, of course, but your ego is too big to think about it rationally. That formula is you. What would you be without having ultimate control of it?

Elaine raised her eyebrows waiting for a response. I wouldn't play poker with this lady, Kough thought. He stared and was almost certain he spotted a tic, an amused smile playing each side of her lips. Was she a bluffer? He could not decide.

Was he bound for some foreign prison or Woolloomooloo?

He became aware he was breathing too quickly.

The jet hit a small air pocket and jumped a fraction but failed to break the spell. Suddenly Charlotte appeared. She squeezed past Elaine standing in the aisle and sat next to her husband.

She ignored the others: 'Mikey, what's going on here?'

Kough sighed: 'Mrs Stone has offered me the key to my chains and freedom if I publish the Safevac formula on the open market. What do you think?'

Big Brain became distraught. Wait, wait, why are you asking her? Kough opened his mouth to speak but Charlotte turned to face Elaine: 'Can I have the key, please, Mrs Stone?'

Elaine looked uncertain, then handed the key to Charlotte.

Charlotte opened the handcuffs: 'Mikey, you can be such a slow-mo sometimes, for a guy who's meant to be so smart.' She leaned over and unlocked the cuffs: 'You're free,' she said. 'That wasn't so hard, was it?'

Kough looked stunned. She leaned over and kissed him on the mouth. 'Char, I was the one who was going to make that decision.'

Charlotte broke their embrace and bent down to unlock the ankle bracelets. She sat up again: 'You did decide it, Mikey. I just read your thoughts. You know I'm good at that, aren't I?'

Kough sat confused, happy, scared, relieved and in love with this beautiful creature who had seduced him and changed his life three years ago.

Charlotte nodded: 'And my mother will be so happy.'

Kough's smile vanished: 'Your mother...?'

'She always said you were a good man. Well, not always, really,' she giggled. She kissed him on the mouth again and restored his smile.

Able said: 'Thank God Char chose you. You need someone to guide that shambolic mind of yours.'

Kough nodded happily. He had briefly imagined being dropped into the sea from ten thousand metres or being led into a CIA interrogation cell somewhere in Kazakhstan.

Elaine leaned over his seat: 'Michael, Australia will be very proud of you when they learn about this. I'm going to call Gary. He'll be thrilled. Press the call button if you want some champagne. You all deserve it.'

Kough and Charlotte held hands like happy teenagers. Able shook his head and went in search of a seat of his own. Church caught his eye and gave a thumbs-up. Able returned it. A text alert sounded. He looked at the screen. It was an invitation to dinner. From Kough's ex: Betty.

The jet rocketed on at a blistering five hundred knots, more than two-thirds the speed of sound. Its passengers comfortable and relaxed. Except for Sergeant Gazala.

SIXTY

Group Captain Hayden Higgins had joined the RAAF to fly jet fighters. He had not made the cut. His co-pilot, Flight Lieutenant Jessie Waldergrave, suffered the same fate.

There had been compensations, Higgins thought. He was sitting behind the controls of a very big, very powerful prime ministerial jet which flew its VIP passengers very quickly for very long distances. And the Dassault Falcon 7X got to go to destinations a lot more exotic than the jet pilots based on the mainland or the edge of the Far North deserts of Australia.

'We've got an odd-bod mixture of passengers back there today,' Higgins said. 'No names on the manifest, again. One of them was bleeding, left marks on the carpet, I bet.'

'Ours is not to reason why, Higgie.'

'And that trillionaire Kough was in cuffs and iron leggings. What the hell is all that about? I know, I know ... ours is not to...'

They flew on in silence for a few moments. Waldergrave routinely scanned the new state-of-the-art heads-up instrument panel on the glass windscreen: The altitude dial had gone black. He muttered: 'What the fuck?'

Higgins turned to him: 'What, Jessie?' Waldergrave, from his co-pilot's right-hand seat, pointed at the windscreen facing him.

Higgins looked up. He saw his altimeter had vanished. Then both pilots shuddered. The compass and autopilot dials blacked out one by one. Followed by the pitch and yaw indicators. The men watched in silence as the panel of instruments winked and died in a steady procession.

'Jessie, we're meant to have triple backup on all these electronics,' Higgins said.

Waldergrave stared at the black panel: 'Fuck, we're flying on manual but we're flying blind.'

Higgins instinctively looked out the forward window and made out the northern New South Wales coast fifteen thousand metres below. The jet was bolting south on its own, but it seemed to be holding its altitude and speed. No fire warning lights were flashing.

Higgins pressed several switches, hoping to fire up the backup electronic systems. 'Let's go down and try to maintain visuals,' he said.

Waldergrave was on the radio trying to call up Brisbane tower, or any tower. Controlling his fear, he said: 'Radio's out, cap'n'.'

Higgins shook his head and watched the white surf line far below come gradually closer as he manually eased off the power: 'We've been attacked, Jessie, an electronic magnetic attack. Someone's wiped out our systems. We've been jammed.'

'We're blind but the bird on manual is still flying beautifully,' Waldergrave said.

Higgins said nothing. He tried the radio and confirmed it was dead. He checked and discovered the anti-collision transponder had stopped pulsing their position to ground radar stations or other aircraft.

Without an altimeter or an air-speed indicator, Higgins could only make guesstimates of their fall and ground speed as he flew the jet manually. Too slow and the bird's nose would rise or a wing dip; and they would go into a stall and spin out of control. Putting the nose up too far to gain altitude would also cause a fatal stall.

The flight deck door opened. The steward, Sergeant William Billings, put his head in: 'We're losing altitude, sir.'

Higgins shrugged: 'I don't know what we'd do without you, Willy Nilly.'

Waldergrave said: 'Don't worry, we can see the beach down there.'

Billings said: 'Just like driving home blind pissed, then?'

'You got it. Except if we stall.'

'No tarseal under us?'

'Exactly. Hope you can swim.'

Billings said: 'I'd have joined the navy if I want to go swimming.'

Another head appeared in the narrow doorway. Frank Church stood there: 'We're losing height.'

'Yes, our steward, Willy Nilly, has just let us know,' said Higgins. Billings stifled a smile.

'So, why are we losing height?' Church snapped.

Higgins half turned: 'We've been hit by an electronic magnetic attack. We've lost all our instruments. They've been jammed. We're on visual flight status. We can see the coast below us. I'm going down to try to track along the coast and back to Brissie. It's clouding up further south, so I think that's our best bet.'

Church clutched the side of the doorway and said: 'Fuck'n hell.'

Higgins said: 'Well said, sir. Can you check and see if your cellphone works? Bit of a long shot, but you never know.'

Church pulled his cellphone from his jacket, looked at the screen, pressed several buttons and shook his head. 'Nope. No signal.'

Higgins saw Kough join the cram at the doorway: 'I've been timing our descent. We're at about five thousand metres now.'

Higgins spun around to look out the window. The man was right, he thought.

As he went to turn back, his headset radio came to life. So did several of the speakers in the cockpit ceiling. A hollow, electronic voice said: 'Group Captain Hayden Higgins. Your altitude is now five thousand, five hundred metres. Your course is being reset to latitude one-seven-point-six-nine-nine-nine; longitude one-six-eight-point-three-one-nine.'

Higgins looked at the newly lit autopilot panel where the new course was showing as the jet swung gently in a half circle eastward, away from Australia. Higgins pressed his headset transmission button: 'Shark One, alpha five six zero zero two, please identify yourself.'

There was no response.

Higgins disabled the autopilot and began another slow turn until the jet was headed due south for Brisbane.

The cockpit speakers erupted. An urgent voice said: 'Group Captain, your heading is incorrect.'

Higgins pressed his microphone closer to his mouth: 'Shark One: No, it's not. I am returning to Brisbane.'

There was no response.

The Falcon flew on in a tense silence for another minute.

Then the faint noise from the three rear jet engines quietened. The engines' tacho instrument on the windscreen heads-up lit up again. One was flashing a red warning light.

'Jessie, they've knocked out the starboard motor,' said Higgins. 'Willy Nilly, go back and tell the passengers to put their lifejackets on.'

Billing hurried away and Kough squeezed further into the cockpit beside Church. Kough noticed the hands of the ASIO boss were trembling slightly: 'Don't worry, Frank. These things will float for thirty-four minutes once they splash down, if they splash down horizontally.'

Thirty-four minutes? Higgins thought. How would this Kough guy know that detail?

The calm hollow voice from the ceiling speakers said: 'Captain Higgins, use the coordinates I set for you or you will lose the port engine also.'

'Shark One. Go fuck yourself,' said Higgins. 'You won't kill any more engines. I know you don't want us all dead.'

Immediately, the port engine began to lose revs and the jet's altitude started to drop sharply.

The hollow voice said: 'Please re-enter the coordinates I provided.'

Higgins sat fuming. He reached for the autopilot: 'Jessie, what the hell were those coordinates again?'

Kough's voice came from behind him: 'Latitude one-seven-point-six-nine-nine-nine; longitude one-six-eight-point-three-one-nine.'

Higgins thought: How the fuck did he remember that?

Church read his mind: 'Dr Kough has a big brain. He can remember anything.'

He paused and added: 'When he wants to.'

Higgins entered the course and the jet swung away from the Australian coast again. 'Where the hell is this prick taking us?'

Kough cleared his throat: 'Bauerfield Airport.'

Church said: 'Where the hell is Bauerfield Airport?'

Higgins said: 'Port Vila, Vanuatu, sir.'

Church said: 'This is an electronic hijack.'

Kough said: 'Yes, whoever it is, is using directed energy to control our electromagnetic spectrum. He's hacking the jet and controlling us. It's an element of information warfare.'

Church's face lost its colour. Cloud began to envelop the aircraft and it shook slightly. Both silenced engines came back to life and altitude steadily increased to ten thousand metres.

Kough took a pad and pen from the pilots' console. He wrote a few words and passed them to Higgins. Higgins' raised his eyebrows. Kough placed a finger over his lips. Higgins rolled his eyes and nodded.

SIXTY-ONE

A n anguished Prime Minister Gary Stone was alerted just six minutes after Shark One disappeared from Australian radar screens.

The RAAF scrambled several jet fighters from the Amberley air base near Brisbane. They were vectored to the jet's last-known location.

The air force ordered up more aircraft as the time passed and the search area widened exponentially. The searchers found nothing. The big three-engined VIP aircraft had simply vanished.

After a brief knock on the door, Air Chief Marshal Ethan Lewis strode into Stone's office, a cellphone to his ear. He lowered it to his side and saluted.

Stone said: 'Any news?'

Lewis said: 'Some good news, in that we're certain the Falcon didn't crash at the point radar contact was lost. Our pilots report no wreckage floating in the sea anywhere near that. And the Falcon is a big aeroplane – its wingspan's twenty-one metres, almost as long as the fuselage. There would be some debris floating if it had gone in.'

Stone stood up and sighed: 'So what the hell has happened then?'

'We've got a full-scale international search gearing up; all commercial traffic in the area have been alerted. We're putting all our available aircraft up and the navy has some assets in the area, sir.'

'Jets just don't disappear,' said Stone.

'No, they don't, except ... er ... for Malaysian Airlines MH370. But I'm sure there will be some news soon. The pilot, Higgins, is very experienced. Very calm, very professional.'

'It looks like a catastrophic failure electronically,' said Stone.

'We just don't know, sir. It's better not to speculate. I'm sure we'll find the jet – and your wife.'

Stone walked to his office window and looked out. Lewis struggled to find something else positive to say.

Stone said: 'You know, that jet had Dr Michael Kough on board.'

'No, I didn't, sir. There were no names on the manifest beside your wife and John Able. The take-off from Brisbane was, um, rather hurried ... and there was some trouble with the tarmac guards, I understand.'

Almost to himself, Stone muttered: 'There's always trouble if that Michael Kough is around.'

He turned from the window: 'How long can they fly before the fuel runs out?'

Lewis half-smiled: 'No immediate problem there, sir. That Falcon can fly from here to any capital in the world without refuelling. It's got a range of eleven thousand kilometres.'

'So, it can also bloody land at any decent-sized airport, anywhere?'

'Yes, sir. But that's not a bad thing. Whenever it goes to set down, we'll know immediately from the local tower. Everyone is searching for this plane.'

'So, how long can it stay up?'

'It depends on speed and altitude, but it's good for at least twelve hours, sir.'

Stone scratched his chin: 'Twelve hours?'

'Yes, sir, we could be in for a long wait.'

Stone sat behind his desk again: 'So, in the meantime I can take my mind off this and get on with something really interesting, like the Budget estimates then?'

'Absolutely, and while you're at it, if you could put another zero on the RAAF number it would be greatly appreciated.'

Stone laughed: 'Sure, it's just a stroke of a pen. Just the one zero?'

'Well, one doesn't want to be greedy, sir.'

'No, indeed, that would be unbecoming for an officer and a gentleman.'

The Air Chief stood to attention again and saluted: 'Don't worry, Prime Minister, we'll find your wife and the rest of them.'

Stone felt his eyes well up. He nodded and looked away. Lewis turned and strode out, his cellphone going back to his ear.

'Why aren't you in the cockpit?' Kough asked Group Captain Higgins when he appeared beside the VIP desk and nodded at Elaine Stone. She waved him to a seat beside Kough and Church.

'Nothing to do. The bird is flying itself straight and true at Mach point seven two,' said Higgins. 'We're burning more than three hundred gallons an hour. I don't know what the hurry is.'

Elaine said: 'They're in a hurry because they're scared someone will spot us.'

Kough checked his watch: 'It's two thousand kilometres from the Brisbane coast to Bauerfield, so we're about ninety minutes to touchdown.'

Elaine sat up: 'I know it's irrelevant, but why has Port Vila got an airport with a name that sounds German?'

'Bauer was an American marine fighter pilot who lost his life defending Vanuatu against the Japanese in World War II,' said Kough. 'The Japs invaded the Solomon Islands at Guadalcanal, just to the north of Vanuatu. The locals named the airport after him as a mark of respect. Vanuatu needs a Bauer today, now that it's being taken over itself. The place is virtually a colony of China.'

Elaine sighed: 'Is that why we've been forced to land there because China controls the airport?'

'I would say so,' said Kough. 'It means Canberra won't know where we've landed – or if we've landed anywhere at all.'

Higgins clasped his hands together on the desk: 'There will be no radio chatter with the tower radio anyway, even when we're on finals. The autopilot they've programmed will land us on instruments, hands off. This has been so well organised, I'm sure there won't be any other aircraft there to see us arrive.'

Elaine toyed with her necklace: 'What do the Chinese want with us?'

No one said anything. Eventually, all eyes switched to Kough. Elaine sighed again: 'Oh, it's about you again, Michael Kough. And that Safevac formula.'

Kough shrugged: 'They're a bit late though, aren't they? We decided to open source the formula to any pharmaceutical manufacturer.'

Church said: 'We didn't decide that until we were all on board. So the outside world doesn't know. It means we're...' Kough shot a hand out, palm first, to silence Church.

'It means,' said Kough, 'we have a chance to reconsider that decision. I was never in favour of it. It was Charlotte's idea. She's forgotten how wonderful the Chinese have been to us.'

While the others sat confused, Kough took a pad and pen from the desktop and wrote: 'I bet this whole jet is bugged. They can hear everything we say.'

Kough passed it to Church who handed it around the desk.

Church looked at the ceiling as though he expected a microphone to pop out: 'I agree. It was a big step, made in a hurry.'

Elaine sat ashen-faced. The lock on her necklace was threatening to snap as she tortured it back and forth.

Kough looked at Higgins: 'Did you find me that book I asked you for?'

'Yeah, I found it. What did you want it for?'

'As I said, I just enjoy reading all sorts of stuff.'

The Falcon began to steadily lose height. Soon after, trees began to flash past the windows as it gently touched down and reversed its engines to brake. It turned to roll steadily towards the main terminal.

When it came to a standstill, Kough looked at the unruly, gun-toting members of the reception committee. They were not Chinese.

'WELCOME TO BAUERFIELD INTERNATIONAL AIRPORT, Señor Michael Kough.' The figure with the loudhailer stood on the flatbed of a Toyota ute.

Kough was dismayed. Charlotte overwrought. Big Brain said, This figures, the last enemy you made was in Latin America.

The figure with the loudhailer answered the question: 'I am Jose Javas. You knew my father.'

'Fuck,' said Kough. 'Unbelievable. How do these gangsters get to do electronic hijacking?'

Big Brain said, The world's biggest cartel would have no issue in getting any sort of electronic wherewithal it wanted.

'Fuck,' said Kough again. He turned to see Charlotte standing with Michael Chen on her hip. The baby was gooing and stretching in excitement, unaware of the drama.

Elaine took Church by the arm: 'Isn't there something you can do, Frank?'

The ASIO boss looked at his cellphone screen and shook his head. 'All signals are still blocked.'

Kough said: 'It's me they're after.'

A silence fell over the passengers like an invisible black cloud. Charlotte began sobbing quietly. The baby looked at her in surprise.

The airstairs were rolled out and there was a thud when they hit the side of the jet's closed front left door.

'Mr Kough, it is time you disembarked. We don't want any of your fellow passengers to get hurt ... which they will if we have to force our way on board to get you.' Jose Javas chuckled at the end of the threat.

He was having the time of his life. It had been worth the twenty million dollars he had paid to the Chinese officials to use their electronic warfare jamming equipment and to close Bauerfield Airport for twelve hours.

A few minutes dragged by. The fuselage was shaken a second time by the airstairs.

'I'll go and talk to them.' Kough swung around. Hermaz Gazala was upright, leaning on a seat for balance, his wounded foot bandaged tightly.

The bleeding from the bullet Church had fired into his foot had stopped. The painkillers the steward, Sergeant William Billings, had given him, had not worn off. The private security guard limped forward: 'Let me talk to Jose. He's a better businessman than his father was. But he's a cruel man. He was shocked his father got captured and killed by the Americans for kidnapping your wife, Señor Kough.'

Kough said: 'Did you say, Jose? Do you know this gangster?'

Gazala shrugged: 'Yes, I know this man. I work for him. How did you think I got the job guarding the VIP tarmac at Brisbane. Just on my looks?' He burst out laughing.

'Maybe it lucky your Mr Sharkface shot me, no?' He laughed again. He looked at Kough: 'How much this jet worth? Two hundred million?'

'Yes, around about. But I don't think he's here to buy a jet.'

Gazala said: 'I wasn't thinking of selling it to him. I was thinking of letting him have it as a goodwill gesture – when he's finished his business with you, Dr Kough.'

Kough frowned. Big Brain said, Get everyone off. Then we will fly Jose Javas home. I've seen the manual. The instructions are all in my head. Nothing too complicated. It's a fly-by-wire jet. It'll be like a video game for us. It also gets Jose safely home which he'll really appreciate.

Kough stepped forward and shook Gazala's hand: 'Agreed. He gets me and the jet. And we'll supply the pilot.'

Church said: 'Talk to him, Gazala. Say it was Kough who shot you in the foot and you hope Jose deals with him appropriately, but firstly get him to agree safe passage for all the passengers.'

Gazala grunted a nod and moved forward: 'Who can open this door?'

'Willy Nilly does the door opening,' said Higgins. Sergeant Billings went forward and rotated the door mechanism. It opened slightly before striking the airstairs. A rush of hot, tropical air gushed in.

There was some yelling outside and the airstairs were rolled back two metres. The door was pushed fully open. More hot air rushed in along with the sound of boots clambering up the steel steps.

Gazala moved to the doorway and held up an arm. Then he turned to Kough, Elaine and Church behind him. He bent over to seemingly adjust the boot on his uninjured foot; straightened and there was a sharp crack.

Church reeled back and lost his balance. Gazala shouted: 'A tooth for a tooth, Sharkface.'

He turned and placed the tiny gun back in his sock. He filled the doorway and shouted in Spanish: 'Put the guns down. Tell Jose Javas and that his friend Hermaz is here. And tell him I have already shot one of the gringos for him.'

As Gazala made his way down the stairs, Kough and Elaine rushed to help Church back on his feet.

Church broke into laughter: 'I'm fine, I fell over in fright more than anything when I heard his gun go off.'

He lifted his foot up. There was a small indentation on the top of the one of his shoes: 'That pea-shooter's bullet didn't even manage to penetrate the leather on my shoe.'

Able arrived on the scene: 'I heard a shot. What happened?'

Kough said: 'Nothing much. Gazala tried to make a revenge attack on Church's shoe.'

SIXTY-TWO

Jose Javas stared at the fat man coming off the jet in disbelief. Gazala was a low-level operative he had only met briefly, once. But he took a fat Cuban from his mouth and embraced him like a long-lost friend when Gazala reached the foot of the stairs.

The pair walked back to the terminal, arms around each other's backs, chatting excitedly.

Twenty minutes later a bus, with sagging suspension and puffing blue smoke from its exhaust, trundled up beside the Falcon. A small group of swarthy, unshaven men, complete with bandoliers criss-crossing their chests, got off.

Gazala climbed back up the steps puffing and perspiring, and gruffly ordered all the passengers, except Kough and pilots, off. The pilots and the steward had changed clothes at Kough's request. They walked past Gazala, who did not recognise them in their civvies.

Kough kissed Charlotte and Michael Chen goodbye and promised they would see him again very soon. Charlotte gave a slight shake of her weary head and made for the door.

Eventually there was only Elaine and Kough left in the cabin. Gazala looked around in a panic: 'Where are the pilots? Why is she still here?'

Kough said: 'You don't need the pilots.'

Gazala looked perplexed: 'So who flies this posh whorehouse of the air?'

'I do,' said Kough.

Gazala cursed in Spanish. His face reddened in anger. He was being tricked in front of his Big Boss.

'Hermaz, listen, I can fly the Falcon. And I'll take you wherever you want to go.'

Gazala stood, still panting slightly from his stair climb, as he pointed to Elaine: 'And she is going to be your co-pilot, I suppose?'

Kough laughed: 'No, she can't fly. But she knows I can. What more proof do you need that the pilots aren't needed any more?'

'No, no, no. She gets off, with all the other passengers. That's what Javas wants.'

Kough said: 'Too bad. The prime minister's wife has decided to stay.'

Gazala put his hands on his hips: 'Well, she can't.'

'So, what are you going to do? Shoot her? That would certainly bring the hounds of hell down on you.'

Elaine said: 'Hermaz, let's not debate it. I've decided I'll be staying on my husband's aircraft.'

Gazala snorted and swore. He went to the door. The bus had already left for the terminal.

Gazala made his way gingerly down the airstairs and limped painfully to the terminal in the scorching heat. Using binoculars that he found in the cockpit, Kough watched Jose Javas come out of the terminal and confront Gazala.

The two men appeared to exchange heated words. Finally, they boarded a second bus with the rest of Javas's gang and drove towards the jet.

Jose bounded up the stairs. He was brandishing a pistol. But there was no one to see it. The passenger cabin was empty. Kough and Elaine had gone forward to the cockpit.

He pocketed the gun and made himself at home at the VIP desk, facing down the length of the big cabin where his grubby gangsters had begun to plunder the strategically placed cocktail cabinets.

He ordered a perspiring Gazala to bring Kough to him.

Kough put down the flight manual he was scanning and went

through to the passenger cabin: 'Where is it you would like to go, Mr Javas?'

'Ah, Dr Kough. A scientist and a pilot, eh?'

'And a sailor, Jose.'

Jose sneered: 'I'm here so you can sign an agreement to sell me Safevac. My father may have been duped by you, Dr Kough, but I won't be.'

Kough sat himself down at the desk opposite Javas: 'What are you offering for Safevac, Jose?'

The triumphant sneer of a man holding all four aces was stretched across Javas's face: 'I'm offering the life of your second wife and son. My father was sloppy. He kidnapped the wrong woman. But I haven't.' He laughed.

Kough smiled: 'And how are you going to legally acquire Safevac?'

Jose pointed at a small man several rows back. 'My accountant and business manager has the sales contract. It covers everything. You just need to sign it.'

Kough nodded and stared at Jose: 'How do I know my wife and son will be safe?'

'You don't – but they will be. I have no interest in killing them. I do have an interest in killing you if you don't cooperate. It was you who was responsible for my father's capture and death. You do remember that little detail, Dr Kough?'

Kough nodded.

Jose said: 'Of course, I will be keeping hold of you and your family until my scientists confirm your formula is the real thing. If it is another of your scams, like the one you pulled on the greedy Chinese, your wife and son will die. And you'll be happy to die, if we have to persuade you to provide the genuine one.'

The Little Man, with a briefcase and a sheath of papers clutched in one hand, was waved to the table. He slid in beside Kough.

'You realise this formula is worth at least ten trillion?' said Kough.

'Of course I do. Why do you think I'm here. But you have already made billions from it. You shouldn't be greedy, Dr Kough. There is enough for everyone to have a share,' Jose laughed. 'Anyway, I am a real businessman, not a lab rat like you. I will make much more from Safevac than you ever dreamed of.'

Kough raised his eyebrows.

Jose laughed again: 'The current price is too low, señor, far too low. Never mind all that, let's get the paperwork out of the way.'

For the next ten minutes Little Man showed Kough where to sign away Safevac's world rights. When the last paper was inked, Jose said: 'All right, Dr Kough, show us how you can fly this thing.'

'No worries, Mr Javas. There is a small problem about how far I can take you.'

Javas's smirk vanished. His head shot up like a fox suddenly fearing it was inches from a vicious gin trap. He dived into his shoulder holster and produced the pistol: 'What the fuck are you talking about? These jets can fly eleven thousand kilometres without refuelling. Do you think I am as big a fool as my father?'

'What you say is true. But this jet was only fuelled for a Brisbane to Canberra flight.'

A sliver of fear and uncertainty flickered in Javas's dark eyes: 'We can refuel here then.'

Kough nodded: 'Sure. We can do that. But do they have AVOM octane?' He watched Jose. The moustache gave a quiver. Here was a man who had only moments before believed four aces was enough to win this hand, thought Kough. But four aces did not beat a royal flush.

Javas was no mean gambler himself. So he said nothing, waiting for the richest man on earth to speak first.

Kough took a breath. He was holding no cards. There was no such fuel as AVOM. The Falcon's tanks still had nine thousand gallons in them if Javas wanted to check its fuel gauges.

'Jose, this is a military aircraft. Operated by our air force. It runs on very expensive, high-octane fuel. The M in AVOM stands for military. Even if there was AVOM here, there would still be a matter of how long it would take to refuel. When do the Chinese airport operators want Bauerfield back under their control for this evening's traffic?'

Without thinking, Javas snapped a look at his watch. Kough could see the digital cabin clock on the wall at the end of the aisle. He believed the jet had just twenty-three minutes to power up and leave because from five in the evening commercial airliners would routinely be inbound to take advantage of the denser, cooler air that helped them to land and lift off.

That meant the Chinese operators would want their airport back and operational and Shark One gone without a trace in less than half an hour.

Jose began to tap the barrel of his pistol on the shiny mahogany table. He realised Little Man was still present, taking in the drama. He snapped at him to leave. Little Man rose like a jack in the box and scurried away to his seat.

Javas bit his lower lip trying in vain to avoid the next question: 'How much fuel do we have? How far will it take us?'

Kough ignored the question: 'We have enough fuel to easily make it back to Brisbane where this is plenty of AVOM.'

Javas spat: 'Do you think I am crazy? Land in Brisbane?'

'Listen, it wouldn't be a crazy thing to do; it'd be the most sensible thing to do. You have the prime minister's wife as a hostage. No one will come near us, let alone try to arrest you.

'But lot of Asian governments may not give a toss about the fate of an Australian prime minister's wife. They might want to try to shoot their way on board and be heroes before the world's television cameras.'

Jose's eyes went to slits. He hated this too-clever man. He wanted control. He bashed the pistol on the desk, louder and louder, in frustration, denting the polished wood.

'All right, we go to Brisbane, but I don't want this jet ambushed when we land. Any tricks and I'll make sure your lovely first lady gets a lovely bullet in her head.'

Kough leaned forward. It caught Jose off guard. Kough had his hand stretched out: 'It's a deal. I want to see my wife and family again. Do I have your word they'll be safe when this deal is done?'

Jose recovered his wits. He shook Kough's hand: 'Yes, don't worry, they will be safe. Now get this thing off the ground.'

Kough said: 'Where do you want to go from Brisbane?'

Jose scowled.

Kough said: 'I need to know so I can order the AVOM.'

Jose smirked: 'Just fill it up, Dr Kough.'

SIXTY-THREE

Elaine Stone fastened the seatbelt in the co-pilot's chair: 'Where on earth did you ever learn to fly a Falcon?'

Kough pointed to the manual resting in his lap.

Elaine went pale.

Big Brain said, Don't tease her. She's under enough pressure. Tell her handling a fly-by-wire jet is just a form of video game for us. Now, go straight to page fourteen.

Kough pushed several buttons. The three big trijet Pratt and Whitney engines that would hurl the jet down the runway with a twenty-thousand-pound thrust came to life smoothly.

Big Brain said, Now follow the steps on page fifteen and turn to starboard to line up for the main runway.

The jet rolled forward with almost none of the traditional jet-engine roar. Kough tapped the radio, but it was dead. Big Brain said, Don't worry about the wireless. We'll check it out when we're airborne. Set the speed for two thousand feet per second until we get to twenty-five thousand.

Kough tapped more buttons. He reached across and touched Elaine's hand: 'We'll be fine, Mrs Stone. Brace yourself. We'll be doing ten miles per second as we climb out. We need to get out of here quickly, while we can.'

Elaine placed a hand on his and squeezed. She managed a half smile. Pulled her seatbelt tighter. Then crossed herself. I didn't know she was a Catholic, thought Kough. Funny how God emerged in crisis situations.

She released his hand. She could not understand how an aircraft worked without a steering wheel or joystick. She watched as Kough's eyes flickered from his manual to buttons on the dashboard. She saw a weather radar screen light up. It showed a big red patch to the right. She pointed to it. Kough nodded but said nothing.

A second screen flashed on, showing a straight-line course to Brisbane. The screen said home was two hours and forty-seven minutes, and one thousand, nine hundred and sixty-seven kilometres away.

Kough switched on the seatbelt sign. Few of the gangsters saw it and fewer paid any notice. Beer glasses full of tequila were being passed around in a festive atmosphere.

The jet pounced forward. Gangsters, bottles and glasses flew everywhere. Kough could hear loud, angry shouting. Big Brain said, There will be broken bones back there.

The jet only needed seventeen hundred metres to be airborne. At full throttle, it literally blasted into the setting sun. It was exhilarating. Almost like watching a roulette marble jumping into your slot. Big Brain said, This is more fun than yachting. We should buy one of these.

The rear engines' roar shook the Bauerfield terminal but were barely audible in the Falcon. Charlotte heard their roar several kilometres away as she and Michael Chen were driven in a small convoy along dirt roads to a cartel safe house.

The other passengers were left at the airport terminal, to wait for a commercial flight home. Charlotte saw huge thunderstorm clouds billowing up on the western horizon and hugged her baby son.

THE TEQUILA PARTY raged on until supplies ran out, and then became a scotch party. The gangsters sang loudly and danced in the aisles to ghetto blasters they had brought on board in their baggage. Jose sat and watched, nursing a weak scotch.

Several brawls broke out but ended quickly, the fighters quickly exhausted and no one getting badly hurt in the melees.

Towering black clouds loomed to the right of the jet and it began to be jolted in the fringe of the storm. Big Brain said, Don't worry, climb over it.

Kough could not get the wireless to work.

Kough swore. Elaine looked at him. He smiled and looked back at the manual.

Big Brain said, Not a pleasant thought flying into a busy international airport without a radio.

Hermaz Gazala appeared drunkenly at the cockpit doorway, keeping his weight off his bullet-holed foot.

Gazala pointed to Elaine: 'No women. Dull party. You must come … dance with us.'

Kough said: 'Hermaz, get the hell out of here.'

But the private security guard sergeant stumbled forward. He put a hand through hair on the back of Elaine's head: 'Come on, we partying, you must come, dance with us.'

Elaine undid her seatbelt and began to wriggle out of the seat. Gazala beamed. He was always good with the women, he thought, even this posh, snotty one.

Kough said: 'Where the hell are you going? Sit down, for God's sake. You can't go back there with that drunken mob, they're bloody gangsters.'

Elaine grinned: 'Can you do a little lurch to the right with this toy of yours, when I tell you?'

Kough was mystified.

Elaine extracted herself and stood up. Gazala's beam grew even bigger and he took her hand unnecessarily to help her get her balance.

'You want to dance, Hermaz?'

He nodded furiously.

'Okay, Dr Kough. We'll do the lurch.'

She put her arms around the paunchy Mexican and began to shuffle. Big Brain said, Course change starboard for three seconds.

The jet swung to the right. Elaine held fast to Gazala and stamped hard on his wounded foot. He screamed and she pushed him backwards. He landed heavily in the narrow aisle outside the cockpit. She slammed and locked the door. They heard footsteps running forward, then swearing, then loud laughter. Eventually the passageway fell silent.

Elaine clambered back into her seat and refastened the seatbelt: 'That's a little dance step I learned in Lismore. Don't look so shocked, Dr Kough.'

The jet's system had put it back on course after the three-second dance detour. Kough shook his head: 'Mrs Stone, these people are armed. And drunk. If he had a gun and used it, he could have killed you and crashed the plane. A bullet would go straight through the aluminium fuselage. We'd depressurise in seconds and crash.'

Elaine said: 'You men worry too much.'

THERE WAS pandemonium in Canberra when Group Captain Hayden Higgins phoned to report he was in Port Vila while Shark One was being flown home by a man without even a rudimentary student pilot's licence.

Air Chief Marshal Ethan Lewis found the prime minister sprawled and snoring in a big lounge chair in his private quarters. Budget papers were spilled on the floor and a glass of scotch was balanced precariously on his chest.

He walked softly in, accompanied by a household security guard. He lifted the scotch glass gently and shook Gary Stone's shoulder. He woke with start, saw Lewis holding his glass and smiled: 'Don't mind if I do, Air Marshal.'

Lewis passed it to him. 'We have some developments with Shark One, sir.'

Stone took a sip of the scotch and looked questioningly at the air force boss.

'The good news, she is flying home. The bad news, Mrs Stone is on board but pilot is not. He's still in Port Vila,' said Lewis.

Stone took another sip: 'Ha. So, Dr Kough is in the driver's seat.'

Lewis said: 'How did you know that?'

'It's Kough all over. I suppose he learned to fly it by reading and remembering the bloody manual.'

'Well, yes, that is what Higgins understands to be the case.'

Stone nodded and gave an amused grunt.

'I presume Elaine is okay or you would have said. The jet's headed home, so how far are we from full time? What airport is Kough aiming for?'

'Unfortunately, sir, the jet has more than a dozen of the hijack gangsters on board. Its radar signature has it ninety minutes out of Brisbane, but it is not responding to any radio calls.'

'We got the treble with that bloke,' Stone mumbled.

'Pardon?' said Lewis.

'Oh, nothing, just something Frank Church once said about our mad scientist. How best do we handle this ghost flight?'

SIXTY-FOUR

The Falcon was an hour or six hundred kilometres from the Australian coast when the first RAAF Super Hornet jet fighter howled past the cockpit window. The Falcon shuddered in the slipstream.

Elaine gave a gasp and clenched her armrests in fright. Kough swore and checked the dashboard. The Falcon flew on unperturbed after its sudden shaking.

Big Brain said, He's probably been trying to raise you on the radio. So he came by personally to say hello.

A heavy hammering began on the cockpit door.

'Mrs Stone, that'll be Jose. Let him in so he can see he's in no danger. We don't want him panicking and trying to shoot his way in ... but, Mrs Stone, no dancing, please,' said Kough.

Elaine snorted and squirmed out of the big seat again and went to the door she had locked.

Jose stood red-faced in the doorway, brandishing his pistol: 'What the fuck is going on? What's an air force jet doing way out here, buzzing us?'

Kough pointed out the window: 'He's just escorting us, Jose. I didn't know he was coming. Our radio hasn't been working so he's come in upfront and personal.'

301

Jose accepted Kough's explanation but still looked nervous: 'Crazy bastard could have rammed into us.'

Kough said: 'No, no chance of that. We've got the first lady on board, remember. You're quite safe, Jose.'

As they watched, the Hornet showed off its manoeuvrability and flipped around to head back and fly alongside them. They could see the pilot in his cockpit quite clearly.

Kough held up his headset and waved. The pilot gave a thumbs-up and stayed on station. A few, long minutes later he held up a hand with four fingers outstretched. Then a second hand showing three.

Big Brain said, That must be the frequency we need. Kough punched in four point three. The radio came to life.

'Shark One. Thanks for that.'

'Hunter Three. Wilco, all part of the service. We have you inbound Brisbane?'

'Shark One. Roger that. Hunter, be aware we are in a hijack situation. We need to refuel and depart as soon as.'

'Hunter Three. Copy that. Runway One will be cleared for you.'

Kough heard Jose let out a pent-up lung of air.

'Roger that. Please tell ground control we don't want a big reception committee with lots of flashing lights lined up. And we definitely don't want any special-forces types shooting our tyres out,' said Kough.

Jose moved forward and patted Kough on the shoulder: 'Very good, Dr Kough. Very good.'

Kough half turned: 'So far so good, Jose. But put the pistol away. A bullet hole in our pressurised fuselage will blow us inside out.'

Jose put the pistol back in its holster, patted Kough again on the shoulder and left. Elaine immediately relocked the door.

The radio crackled again: 'Hunter Three. Confirming. No big reception planned. Also, the prime minister was asking after his wife; we understand she is on board with you.'

'Affirmative. Please give the PM my compliments. Tell him his wife is fine but risking a red card. Foul tackled one hijacker close to the tryline.'

'Hunter Three. Sorry, what tryline?'

'He will understand, Hunter Three. I have another message for him.

The hijacker Javas has told me my wife and baby son were going to be separated from the other passengers and taken into hiding in a village near Port Vila. This was done to guarantee my cooperation with him. Can the PM please locate and free them? Their lives may be in danger once we've landed in Brisbane.'

They flew on for several minutes in silence. Elaine stole a look at Kough and shifted in her seat: 'What's wrong, Dr Kough?'

Kough said nothing. Big Brain said, Don't tell her anything about the final play.

Kough looked at Elaine: 'Mrs Stone, when we land, I want you to promise you will stay in the cockpit until I come and get you.'

She looked puzzled. And annoyed. She brushed a hair out of her eyes and began twisting her necklace. For Kough, it was a basic tell. She would never make a poker player.

'Don't be upset, Mrs Stone. Your courage is not in question. Please just do as I ask. It's important. You can't unsee things.'

Elaine gave a huff: 'You wouldn't know what things I have had to see, like the irradiated bodies of women and children.'

Kough sighed: 'Please, ma'am, do as I ask. I'll come back as soon as I can after we've landed. And when I leave, lock the door and don't let anyone in except me. Okay?'

Elaine shrugged noncommittally.

Big Brain said, Leave it. She trusts your judgement. She won't quibble or cause any trouble. Now, let's get this done.

Kough leaned forward and carefully stabbed four green buttons, then sat back and prayed for Charlotte and Michael Chen.

PRIME MINISTER GARY STONE had referred to Shark One as a pilotless ghost flight. He would be staggered to learn how right he was. While racing to Brisbane in an RAAF VIP Challenger 604 backup jet, he was organising an operation to free the Kough hostages. He was glad he had taken the role of acting defence minister after sacking David Hicks. It cleared innumerable bureaucratic obstacles.

RAN *Rankin* was carrying a six-man SAS squad it had secretly put ashore on Vanuatu to spy on Port Vila's Chinese military sites. The submarine was now ordered to put the elite SAS troopers back ashore near the capital.

The troopers were to use any necessary means to requisition transport, travel to the cartel's safe house and rescue Charlotte and Michael Chen. Any interference by cartel members, or Chinese officials, was to be dealt with at the discretion of the squad sergeant.

The squad knew the whereabouts of the safe house, thanks to ASIO's boss, Frank Church. He had been left on the island after the hijack of Shark One. He had seen a terrified Charlotte and her baby son bundled into a filthy Toyota Land Cruiser and driven away from Bauerfield Airport.

He found the cartel's safe house was the country's worst-kept secret. Local cops were happy to accept his bribes for an address that was public knowledge.

Stone ordered the Koughs to be freed and taken on board *Rankin*, which would rendezvous offshore with HMAS *Sydney*, now speeding towards the Vanuatu coast.

The RAAF Hornet nudged up close to the Falcon's port cockpit window: 'Hunter Three. I have a message for you. It reads: Flash Frankie has located your personal New Hebrides assets. Arrangements under way to transfer them soonest.'

The Hornet pilot shrugged through his window at Michael Kough.

'Shark One. Understood,' said Kough. He felt tears streaming down his face. He wiped them away with his hand. Elaine handed him a perfumed tissue: 'I presume that was the nickname you used for Frank Church, when he was out of earshot.'

Kough blew his nose: 'Yes, I once called him Flash because he was so slow to lead the cavalry to my rescue. And what kind of tissues are those for a liberated woman?'

'Ones we'll share with the weaker sex,' she said. 'Are you all right now? I hope so because I need the Kough, the macho man, back. You've still got to land this thing.'

Kough laughed and drawled: 'Don't you worry none about that, little lady, I'll be greasing this baby onto the tarmac.'

Elaine laughed and the mood became immediately light-hearted.

They chatted about their families and the trials and tribulations of raising them.

With twenty minutes to run to the Queensland capital, Kough punched the four green buttons again. He got out of his seat. Elaine looked up alarmed: 'Where are you going?'

'Nature's calling. The jet's on autopilot, so no worries. Please lock the door behind me.'

He left. Outside, at the end of the tiny passageway between the cockpit, pilots' toilet and the galley, he pulled open the privacy curtain separating it from the passenger cabin.

He heard Elaine lock the door behind him, then stepped into the passenger cabin and walked quickly up and down the twelve-metre-long aisle. He returned panting, parted the curtain and answered nature's call.

Elaine let him back into the cockpit: 'How's the party going back there?'

'Pretty quiet. Most of them are in a drunken stupor,' Kough said, 'but armed to the teeth. You should go to the ladies while we have a chance. But promise you won't go beyond the curtain and stir them up.'

'The ladies? Where have you been living? All our toilets are sex neutral, or haven't you noticed?'

'Oh, is that what that funny emblem is about,' said Kough. 'I'll come and stand outside them and make sure you're safe, if you want me to.'

'For heaven's sake. No, thank you, Sir Galahad. I'll stay away from those drunken gangsters, don't worry.'

'Promise? I want us all to get safely home now we're this close.'

'Fly your jet, Dr Kough. I will be in and out and quiet as a mouse.'

Kough watched her go. Big Brain said, She'll be fine. She wants to survive and tell her grandchildren about this. Now get on the radio quick while she's gone.

Kough sat back in his seat and placed the earphones over his head: 'Shark One. Change of flight plan. I need to confirm the coordinates for Amberley Air Force Base. That will be our new destination.'

'Hunter Three. Are you seeking permission to land there?'

'Shark One. Negative. That's where I will be landing.'

'Hunter Three. Are you having difficulties with the hijackers?'

'Shark One. I recall the coordinates as twenty-seven point six four seven seven degrees south; one five two point six nine six five degrees east.'

'Hunter Three. Have you landed there before?'

'Shark One. Negative.'

'Hunter Three. Stand by. Checking. Amberley is very close to Brisbane, you know? Only forty clicks south-west. Are you sure you want to land there instead?'

There was no reply.

'Hunter Three. Affirmative your co-ords. How did you know them?'

'Shark One. I just read them somewhere. Now inbound Amberley. ETA fifteen minutes. Please advise traffic control. And the prime minister, if you wouldn't mind. I know Mrs Stone will want to see him.'

He heard the cockpit door close. And Elaine's voice: 'Of course, I'll want to see him. Nice of you, but I'm sure he knows where Brisbane is.'

'I'm sure he does. I'm just being a nice guy.'

Elaine manoeuvred back into her seat: 'This means you're sure Mr Jose Gangster Man will let me go?'

'Definitely. I just had to convince him I could fly this jet. Remember, he's still holding my family so he knows he's got my cooperation right through to Bogota, that's somewhere you wouldn't have quite the same hostage value as the wife of the Australian PM. Most of the population wouldn't even know where Australia is.'

'Bogota? You mean in Colombia?'

'Yeah, the one at four degrees, forty-two forty north; seventy-four twenty degrees west.'

Elaine sighed: 'Dr Kough, you'll wear that brain of yours out if you're not careful.' She sat back, relaxed, and waved to the Hornet pilot flying beside them. He saluted.

SIXTY-FIVE

The intel was good. A muddy Toyota Land Cruiser was parked outside the shabby, two-room hut they had been directed to. Weak light spilled from all its windows.

The face-blackened SAS recon troopers had no way of knowing how many cartel gangsters were inside guarding Charlotte and her baby son. They counted on four or five.

Sergeant Blackie Johnson called his team to a huddle in the bush twenty metres from the hut: 'We can't use flash bangs. There's a baby in there. And a pretty traumatised and pregnant mother.'

The troopers nodded. One said: 'Bloody hell.'

A second one said: 'That means we neutralise the bad guys on sight.'

Blackie nodded: 'That would be the safest way to rescue the hostages. There's also the fact we're not in a position to take prisoners anyway.'

The troopers nodded in unison. Two were assigned to the back door, and Blackie and another trooper to the front. The fifth trooper would stand guard during the raid to deal with any unexpected visitors or any gang members trying to escape.

They moved silently to surround the hut. Two metres from the front door, Blackie snared a trip wire. A series of small explosions were amplified to booms in the still of the night.

The trooper behind Blackie dived behind a clump of bushes.

Blackie tossed his rifle away and laid on the ground in the open. The front door flew open. A gangster, rifle raised, looked out. There was only a figure on the ground, in a foetal position, moaning and crying. The gangster walked forward warily.

'Help me. Help me. I need a fix. Your supply courier never turned up today,' Blackie groaned. The gangster stood over him, shaking his head. The distraught addict in military fatigues was another of the local pisshead militia, he thought.

'No fix here. Get up and piss off before I shoot you.'

Blackie began sobbing. The gangster kicked him viciously in the stomach: 'I said, piss off. Do you want to die?'

Another armed thug came to the door: 'What the hell is going on?'

'Go back inside. It's just another local cop dopehead out for a fix,' said the gangster. 'I'm getting rid of him.'

'Well, don't shoot him. We've got enough trouble with the militia.'

The thug took another look around, turned and disappeared inside, nonchalantly leaving the door open for any ventilation it might provide from the stinking hot, humid night.

Blackie got slowly to his feet. Upright, the gangster realised he was half a metre shorter than the dopehead. His instincts kicked in. Too late. He opened his mouth to shout a warning just as the SAS dagger went through the side of his neck. Blackie jumped clear of an arterial fountain of blood as the gangster toppled into the dust.

Blackie toggled his radio: 'There are probably only four guards inside now. Watch for trip wires. They'll be expecting their mate to return through the front door, so they won't be excited by my footsteps outside. They've helpfully left it open, so you won't hear it being taken down, but you'll hear me once I'm in.'

The squad members all clicked their radio transmission buttons, acknowledging the message.

Blackie retrieved his rifle and strode through the front door. Two men were sitting at a small kitchen table on his left. He shot them both through the head. A third appeared from a side room. The man looked perplexed and was carrying no weapon. Blackie put a bullet between his eyes.

The fourth guard, wearing a grubby red bandana and brandishing a pistol, leapt for Charlotte and grabbed her around the head. The baby on her lap spilled on to the dirt floor and began screaming in fright.

A trooper rushed through the rear door – which had also been left open – rifle mounted for instant action. He saw Mr Bandana holding Charlotte in a headlock and stopped, lowering his rifle. Bandana looked around at his comrades' shattered heads and spilled brains. His red-rimmed eyes wide with shock.

With his free hand he pulled Charlotte to the far wall where he came up against a window ledge.

Blackie sensed Charlotte was not in a panic. A moment later, Bandana gave a piercing shriek. Blackie saw Charlotte had one hand over Bandana's crutch and was twisting her hand savagely. Bandana twisted Charlotte's head in an attempt to break her neck and save his mangled genitals. She made guttural, wild animal growls as she fought for her life.

A single shot rang out and ended her torture. The window behind her blew into a thousand shards. The bullet went through the back of Bandana's head. Blood and brains burst over Charlotte's dress. She looked down at her attacker for a second, and then suddenly booted his corpse. In the crutch. She turned to the troopers. She looks embarrassed, Blackie thought.

Blackie said: 'Mrs Kough. Please come with us. We're here to take you home.' He scooped the wailing baby from the floor and cradled it in his arms, before leading everyone from the blood-splattered hut.

An ancient open Jeep came lurching down the dirt track towards the house just as the SAS squad reached its stolen Ram SUV. Charlotte and Michael Chen were pushed inside. Local police began shouting in their dialect. Blackie put a volley over their heads. Another trooper sprayed the grille and the front tyres.

The militia members dropped their weapons, leapt off the Jeep in terror and fled into the jungle.

Blackie climbed into the Ram next to Charlotte and Michael Chen. Charlotte became aware of the blood on her face. She wiped it with her sleeve.

She looked at Blackie: 'You were very brave. Thank you for saving us.'

He slowed his breathing as the Ram sped off over the rutted dirt track: 'I never thought I'd find a way of thanking your husband.'

Charlotte frowned.

'He saved my life last year, with his miracle pill,' said Blackie.

A dozen emotions swelled up in Charlotte and she burst into a flood of tears. Michael Chen watched, a surprised look on his tiny face. He had rarely seen his mother cry. He let the black-faced man with the gun put him on his knees and joggle him.

The squad met no resistance as it sped to the beach where its inflatable and several submariners were waiting. An hour later they were all safe on the *Rankin*, which invisibly and noiselessly submerged and carried them away from Port Vila to its rendezvous with HMAS *Sydney*.

SIXTY-SIX

'WHY DOES HE WANT TO GO TO AMBERLEY?' GARY STONE
wondered out loud.

Air Chief Marshal Lewis shrugged: 'I'd say he doesn't want a media
circus. He has a gang of very nervous hijackers on board who would get
spooked. Amberley is a secure base and it has fuel.'

Stone saw the tarmac landing lights of Australia's biggest
operational air force base race up to greet them in a blur: 'How far
behind us will they be?'

'Less than five minutes,' said Lewis.

'Kough didn't give us much notice. What the hell is he playing at?'

The pair were pulled forward against their seatbelts as the reverse
thrust braked the Challenger.

Lewis said: 'I think he's been ordered to fly here. The hijackers may
have suspected a trap at Brisbane Airport and told him to change course
at the last minute. He did have the coordinates, so the hijackers must
have supplied them; they must have planned to come here all along.'

Lewis said the Falcon would be directed to the refuelling area. Only
routine staff and fire officers would be there.

'And me,' said Stone.

I knew he'd say that, Lewis thought. 'All right. But we'll have to put you in a set of overalls, for your own safety. A smart hijacker might recognise you. And that's the last thing we need.'

Stone nodded: 'I'm happy to wear the team colours.'

'And we'll get you a bulletproof vest,' said Lewis.

'I am bulletproof. I played rugby league for twenty years.'

Lewis laughed: 'That's a different sort of game. Not too many get shot at.'

Stone said: 'All right, I'll wear a vest.'

'Actually, I'm not sure we've got one big enough for you,' said Lewis.

'Don't worry. I can duck pretty fast. I've been in politics twenty years as well.'

THE FALCON TAXIED to the refuelling area and stopped. Its three jets wound down. A complete silence soon enveloped the area, like a theatre tensed for the curtain to go up. The main passenger door swung open. A lone figure stood silhouetted in the doorway. It was a woman.

The airstairs were wheeled urgently into place. The woman emerged carefully but then hurried to the bottom of the steps, paused, and then rushed into the arms of a burly refueller in tight overalls.

'They're all dead,' she sobbed. 'They're all dead.'

Gary Stone engulfed her in his arms.

'Kough tried to stop me getting off first, but I'd had enough, I just wanted out. So, I left the cockpit and walked straight into it ... the carnage, it's horrible, there are bodies everywhere, on the floor, in seats. And the stench...' Elaine clung to her husband.

The nearby airmen and refuellers caught some of her words and looked on with consternation. Several had not recognised the prime minister, but they had all recognised their Air Chief Marshal.

Lewis looked up the airstairs. There was no sign of Michael Kough. He began to mount them.

Halfway up he heard voices.

He turned and clambered back down. He looked around the small group of airmen: 'Who has a side arm?'

Lieutenant Gordon Riley came forward: 'I have a pistol, sir. I'll go up and find out what's going on?'

'No, I'll go,' said Lewis.

Riley was unmoved: 'With respect, sir, that would not be a good idea. You'd make a better hostage than I would.'

Lewis sighed: 'Okay, okay. Go to the top of the stairs, quietly, and see what you can see. Don't be a hero. Mrs Stone says everyone in there is dead but dead people can't talk. Can you shoot straight with that thing?'

'Sort of, sir. I'm better with missiles.' Riley began to quietly climb the steel stairs. He reached the top, took a deep breath and gingerly peeked inside.

He recognised the famous, tall figure of Dr Michael Kough, standing almost at the far end of the aisle beside a polished desk. A swarthy, red-faced man was talking quickly and pointing a pistol at him.

They were oblivious to him.

He retraced his steps.

'Kough is still in there, I could see him, being held at gunpoint, I assume by one of the hijackers. Everyone else in there seemed to unconscious or dead, scattered about everywhere.'

Lewis said: 'How come the PM's wife got out then?'

Elaine broke her embrace and turned to them: 'I refused to wait until Dr Kough checked things out. I just wanted to get out. So I just left. After I got over the shock at the sight of bodies everywhere, I just walked down the aisle, opened the door latches, and came out.

'I never saw any sign of life. I thought Dr Kough would be right behind me when he finished fiddling with things on the dashboard.'

Elaine held on to Stone's arm: 'I thought we were going to Brisbane. I wondered why the airport looked so dark. Dr Kough never said a word till we were down, and then just "We're here". He flew that big plane after scanning its manual; can you believe that?'

No one said a word.

In the silence, Lewis looked up at the trijet: 'Mrs Stone, we'll have to get you out of here. There's an armed and dangerous thug in there. Who knows what he's going to do?'

Stone nodded: 'However this plays out now, I don't think Kough is going to get off that jet alive.'

Elaine shook her head and blew her nose: 'Don't say that. Dr Kough saved all the hostages. He put the pilots into civilian clothes and smuggled them out with everyone else. Even Frank Church made it out; they obviously didn't know what a prize he was. Then he convinced the thugs he knew how to fly the thing.'

Elaine shook her head and blew her nose: 'They never saw him sitting in the cockpit, sort of talking to himself, with the flying manual on his lap. I've never been so scared.'

Stone said: 'How come all those thugs died?'

Elaine shrugged her shoulders: 'I don't know, I don't know. They were all drunk and partying before we even took off. One of them came into the cockpit and insisted I dance with him.'

Stone said: 'Did you do that Lismore kneecap move on him? Is that what Kough meant in his message?'

'Well, I didn't know what else to do. He was a filthy beast, stank to high heaven and off his chops. Church had shot him in the foot back in Brisbane so when he grabbed at me, I jumped on his bad foot. He let out a huge scream and fell over backwards, right out of the cockpit. So, I slammed the door. Kough told me to lock it. So I did.'

Stone glared: 'Christ woman, you could have been killed if they were all drunk and armed.'

Tears began to run down Elaine's face.

Lewis said: 'Mrs Stone, one of these airmen will take you to the officers' mess. You'll be safe there.'

She stood up straight. Used her tissues to wipe her face. Stone said: 'Do as he says, darling. You've had enough adventures for one night.'

'YOU THINK you're so clever, don't you Dr Kough?'

'I've never met anyone who doesn't need to breathe oxygen, Jose.'

'If you were really clever, you would have known that I don't need much.'

Kough looked puzzled.

Jose gave a smug smile: 'My family lived for years in La Paz.'

'La Paz, in Bolivia?'

'Yes, it's four thousand metres up on the Andes, way up in the clouds. There's hardly any oxygen to breathe up there. People who are not used to it get breathless and feel sick. That's just what I suffered when you pulled the plug on the air supply.'

Kough stared at the cartel boss and shrugged. Finally, he said: 'But the cabin oxygen supply was off for so long ... I just don't get it.'

Jose's smile widened: 'I did have some help to get through.'

He held up several shrivelled leaves: 'This is what the locals chew on to get them through when the air is too thin.'

Kough said: 'They're coca leaves, aren't they?'

Jose nodded: 'Yup. It's what we make our cocaine from.'

Kough smiled at the irony: 'So, you're alive partly because of the coca leaves you distribute to kill off millions of others?'

Jose juggled his pistol in his hands: 'I'm alive, no thanks to you, gringo doctor, but I nearly didn't make it. I was on my last legs when we finally lost altitude to land.

'I played dead when you walked through the cabin before we landed. And stayed dead still when your Prime Minister's snotty wife made for the exit.'

Kough sat back on his seat and folded his arms: 'So, what do you want to do now, Houdini?'

'Kill you, Dr Kough.'

Kough blanched as though he had been hit in the face. After all his ordeals, it would end with a single gangster's bullet. He swallowed and moved on the seat.

'Why are you surprised? You have killed all my men, Dr Kough. What did you expect?'

Jose tapped his pistol on the polished desk top. 'And you caused the death of my father. You have a lot to answer for. While I generously let your wife and baby off the jet.

'But because of your treachery, they won't be safe for long. They will now die as well. I'll personally see to that.'

Jose gave another twisted smile: 'I know, I know, it's a terrible waste of a beautiful woman, but...'

Kough suddenly jerked forward over the desk. Jose fought to remain cool, although the move had startled him. Kough said: 'You seem to have forgotten something, my clever, clever friend. On board here, there is the document I signed, handing you the ownership of Safevac.'

Jose arched his eyebrows.

Kough smiled: 'You said you were smarter than the Chinese who bought a dud formula from me for a billion bucks. But the formula your little lawyer has, back there dead in his seat, has not been tested by your scientists. You have no idea if it's the real thing or just another of my duds.'

'Wipe that smile off your face, Dr Kough. Avenging my father and all my friends you have killed may be enough reason to end your life.'

Kough shook his head: 'No, it isn't. I've watched you. You are a psychopathic, greedy bastard. You crave infamy and power, along with the billions the formula will earn you. I'm right, aren't I?'

Jose's face went a shade of crimson. He raised his pistol only inches from Kough's face.

Kough sighed dismissively: 'Jose, I'm a gambling man. I know when people are bluffing. Like you are right now. Spare yourself any more high blood pressure and put the gun down before you die of a stroke like your father.'

Furious, Jose half rose from his seat, holding the pistol with both hands.

Kough sneered: 'Sit down, Jose. You know you only look out for number one. You don't give a toss for all your dead mates down the back of this jet. They're all just collateral damage to you.'

Jose levelled the pistol at Kough's right eye: 'You are just such a conceited, arrogant bastard, it would be a pleasure to kill you.'

Kough sat back. Big Brain said, Stop, stop, he's losing it, becoming irrational. Find a way for him to save face and put the damned gun down.

Kough said: 'Jose, listen. We're both businessmen. You are, in fact, one of the most successful in the world. We're even both in the drug trade. And we still have business to do. I think we should finish that business.'

Jose took a deep breath. He crabbed further along the bench seat behind the VIP desk. It increased the distance between the pistol and Kough. Just in case Kough made a lunge for it.

'How do you think we should go about finishing that business, clever gringo?'

'I've got a few ideas about how we can finish it,' said Kough.

SIXTY-SEVEN

Jose Javas sat nervously in the co-pilot's seat, headset on, listening to every word between Kough and traffic control. The jet had been refuelled without incident. Some water and coffee and unopened packets of biscuits had been brought aboard. But no food trays. The paranoid cartel boss feared the authorities would attempt to poison him if they were given the chance.

The dead bodies of the gangsters had been removed under cover of darkness. A refrigerated truck acted as a temporary morgue while the government struggled to decide what to do with them.

The Amberley traffic controller repeated the coordinates for the Port Vila flight path. The Vanuatu capital was a friendly destination. The cartel's absurd wealth guaranteed that. And it was where Kough had insisted they fly so he could witness Jose freeing them and giving them safe passage to Australia.

In return he had agreed to remain Jose's prisoner and fly him to Columbia where the virologist would stay until the cartel's scientists confirmed the formula was genuine.

Kough was in a state of quiet despair. He had heard nothing further about his family since the prime minister had relayed a message, through the Hornet pilot escorting them into Australia, saying the family had been located. There had still been no word about the fate of the rescue mission.

The big, French, VIP trijet began to roll smoothly towards its allocated runway for take-off. Jose cowered low in his seat, worried a sniper's bullet through the windscreen could still end his daring financial escapade. He watched wide-eyed as Kough tapped calmly at the dashboard of the state-of-the-art, fly-by-wire, controls.

Kough toggled his radio: 'Shark One, we are lined up, runway two. Before we go, can you seek clarification from the prime minister regarding my private tax treaty ... that my private New Hebrides assets are safe.'

Jose erupted in laughter: 'You have a private tax treaty? Your government is as corrupt as ours.'

Kough said: 'Of course.'

The tower replied: 'Stand by Shark One.'

Jose was gleeful. He slapped a knee: 'I knew it. Holier than thou gringos. My father told me about it, but I was never certain it was true. How much does the prime minister get?'

'Twenty-five per cent.'

Jose whistled: 'You are such a poor businessman, Dr Kough. That is far too much. Unless you cheat him.'

'Of course, I cheat him.' Kough laughed. Jose shook his head. With the prime minister on the payroll, it was no wonder Kough had acted like a wild card with impunity, he thought. Jose relaxed. He suddenly felt safer. The fix was in.

Big Brain sighed. Mr Cartel was, at heart, still just an ignorant criminal. He clearly had no idea Vanuatu's name under colonial rule had been New Hebrides.

The tower broke in: 'Shark One, we are still standing by for contact with the prime minister but, meanwhile, you are cleared for immediate take-off.'

'Shark One. Roger.'

But the jet remained stationary. Jose glanced suspiciously at Kough: was there some sort of trick being sprung at the last minute?

'Jose, just bear with me. I need my tax-treaty arrangements confirmed before I land in Port Vila. You would understand that, yes?'

Jose rubbed his chin: 'Yes, I understand but we can't sit out here for long. I feel, you know, vulnerable. And what happens if he doesn't come back to you? I bet he doesn't want everyone on your open radio to hear what he's saying.'

'You're right. But he will come back to me.'

A slow three minutes dragged by. Jose checked his watch constantly and sat up in his seat to survey the surrounding runway. It appeared deserted. He slumped back down again and paced his breathing.

The tower called: 'Shark One: The PM advises your assets have been safely transferred.'

Kough fought to hold back tears.

Jose said: 'So, good news for you, gringo gangster? What assets is he talking about?'

Kough ignored the question and powered up the jet's engines. The fuselage began to vibrate and the jet strained to leap forward. Kough released the brakes. The jet catapulted away, its engines making an unfamiliar, ungentlemanly, roar as it tore down the runway like a freed cheetah. Jose felt the G forces clamp on his body and the seat belt tighten alarmingly.

'Here we go, Jose, that's what twenty thousand pounds of thrust feels like,' said Kough. 'Only a test pilot ever feels this amount of power. Take your seat belt off. I can see it's half throttling you.'

Jose quickly unclipped the belt and felt the tension on his chest partly subside. His breathing came easier. He sat up on the edge of the seat for a view of the ground whipping past at a hundred metres a second. He gave a whoop and raised a clenched fist: 'Vuela bebé, vuela.'

Big Brain said, Fly baby fly, indeed, punk.

Kough checked his seat belt. He said a silent prayer and abruptly killed power to the engines with the flick of a switch and hit the brakes simultaneously.

Jose gave a grunt as his head snapped forward. Without a seat belt, his face was crushed on the dashboard, splitting his skull. He fell back in his seat lifeless, blood spilling down his chest.

Outside, the Falcon's tyres screamed, smoked and shredded.

Kough hit another button to reverse the jet engines but safety overrides delayed the emergency rear thrust momentarily. When the jets roared to life, they threatened to rip the fuselage apart like a giant Christmas cracker.

The Falcon slalomed down the concrete runway before losing its balance and veering onto the grass verge. The tip of its enormously long port wing brushed the ground because its left-side tyres had fared worse than the starboard ones.

The jet finally lurched to an undignified halt. Kough killed the engines. A putrid stench of burned rubber floated in a low, dark cloud below the fuselage.

The idled jet fans ticked over politely and incongruously in the slight breeze.

Vehicles with flashing roof lights sprung from their garages and stampeded down the runway like freed cheetahs.

Kough toggled his radio: "Shark one. Be advised our flight plan has been terminated."

"Tower. Copy that. Do you have any casualties?"

"One hijacker terminated as well. No other casualties."

Kough shut off the radio and its chatter. In the sudden silence, he sat back and collapsed, succumbing to crushing nervous exhaustion. The flight training manual fell between his legs and landed with a thump on the floor. Pent-up tears cascaded down his face.

As the rescue vehicles reached the Falcon, he took a deep breath and leaned over to Jose's body. He felt through the coat pockets and found a cellphone, its battery long exhausted. He plugged it into the cockpit charger.

He dialled his favourite number and was amazed when Charlotte's voice filled the cockpit: 'Mikey, is that you? Are you safe?'

He was so emotionally overcome he was unable to speak. Big Brain said, C'mon, at least tell her you are safe. But Kough could not find any words.

Charlotte spoke again: 'My darling, we are both safe. Some soldiers killed our captors and we are now on a big, big navy ship heading home.'

Kough wiped his eyes: 'Charlotte, I can hardly believe I'm speaking to you again. I'm safe. I'm safe, too.'

There was a pause. Charlotte said: 'Mikey, I'm so thrilled. I'm sailing home to the man who invented a cure for the common cold and is the world's bravest father. Who is never, ever going to get into trouble again.'

Kough laughed.

Charlotte said: 'Is he?'

EPILOGUE

Six months later: a Queensland cane farmer found a mass grave of illegal migrant fruit pickers. Dental records eventually identified some of them as South American criminals.

The Federal Budget's RAAF estimates allowed for a three hundred-thousand-dollar overhaul of the intercontinental Dassault Falcon 7X in its VIP fleet after hairline fractures were discovered in its engine mountings.

Charlotte Kough gave birth to a baby daughter in Sydney. The godfather was John Able, who had married Kough's first wife, Betty.

Sino Pharmaceuticals undercut the price of every drug manufacturer and dominated the world sales of Safevac. Michael Kough receives a ten per cent turnover royalty based on unaudited Sino profit and loss statements.

Charlotte Kough allowed her husband a hundred thousand dollars a month to play roulette, but casinos everywhere banned him.

Gary Stone won his third successive election victory; Elaine politely refused an invitation to be patron of the Australian Women's Liberation Movement and is writing her memoirs amid fights with government censors.

Charles Henry Daggerell was granted special bail, sponsored by murder detective Roger Rougess. Daggers' tattoos were lasered off and he is now the Kough family head of security. He is paying off a six hundred-thousand-dollar roulette gambling debt to Michael Kough.

The Charles Slipper Advanced Aviation Scholarship Trust is providing funds for student pilot training. It is managed by Michael Kough and also provides an endowment income for the widowed Mrs Slipper.

Suzy Li runs a women's Massage For Health franchise from her Sydney offices.

ALSO BY BARRY COLMAN

AUSTRALIA UNDER ATTACK

Chinese commandos in a lightning raid have seized the vast, under-populated, resource-rich lands of Northern Australia. Thousands of Australian soldiers are held hostage. International realpolitik has left Australia abandoned by its supposed allies and its brittle social fabric is rapidly unwinding as the people panic.

A Chinese ultimatum demands the annexation of the country's top half in ten days, or face a full-scale invasion. As other politicians clamour to sue for peace, Prime Minister Gary Stone, in a desperate race against time and impossible military and political odds, must commit to a risky and radical plan to try to free the country . . .

A Line Too Far *by Barry Colman*

Available from major outlets in paperback, ebook and audiobook formats

www.barrycolman.co

EXTRACT FROM
A LINE TOO FAR

PROLOGUE

IT WAS ALMOST TWO IN THE MORNING WHEN HE SPOTTED
the lights bumping toward the guardhouse.

Sergeant Keith Patterson felt a flash of annoyance. The Sunday
graveyard shift was supposed to be the most peaceful.

The vehicle laboured closer, its engine protesting, as though locked
accidentally in a low gear. Patterson shook his head: it was no Australian
Army-trained driver behind the wheel.

It finally burst from the night into the base's floodlit entrance.
Patterson narrowed his eyes against the glare of its headlights.

He could make out the shape of a bus. A brightly coloured bus. A
garish logo ran down its side: "Happy Tours Queensland".

It shuddered to a halt at the guardhouse barrier.

Patterson sighed, stood and shoved open the guardhouse door. A
thick wall of subtropical humidity engulfed him.

The two privates sharing his shift hardly looked up from their card
game, grateful their cantankerous sergeant had taken it on himself to
leave the air-conditioned guardhouse to deal with the situation: lost
tourists by the look of it.

The last off-duty personnel at Townsville's Lavarack Army Base, the country's biggest, had already checked in as close as they dared to midnight.

The twenty-year veteran sergeant trudged impatiently the few steps to the idling bus as its door hissed open. He sensed it had a full load.

A passenger jumped off. He seemed to be in some sort of uniform — and carrying a weapon.

An instant later Patterson froze as the cold barrel of a submachine-gun was jammed against his hot face. He stared uncomprehendingly at the bright red star on the passenger's cap. Then below it. What the hell? The man was Chinese.

In perfect English Patterson was ordered quietly to turn and retrace his steps to the guardhouse.

Other uniformed and heavily armed passengers swarmed off the Happy Tours Queensland bus.

They pushed in behind their leader and crammed the guardhouse before Patterson's lounging soldiers could spring from their chairs. The bewildered guards were instantly surrounded, their hands clasped behind them and locked together with plastic ties before they were shoved to the floor.

The takeover was rapid and disciplined. It took only seconds and was executed in near silence.

The guardhouse switchboard panel was wrenched open. The entrance floodlights and the guardhouse were plunged into near darkness. The remaining dim light shone mockingly from the guardhouse roof declaring the base's motto: "Guarding the North".

With a submachine-gun pressed painfully into his chest, Patterson was ordered to summon Brigadier Silvey.

The commandant was to be told there was an emergency at the guardhouse. Patterson was then to hang up with no further explanation. The sergeant did as he was ordered. He was then cuffed and joined his hapless squad members sprawled wide-eyed on the floor.

Brigadier Lesley Silvey reached the guardhouse on the run only to find himself surrounded by armed men. Manhandled briskly inside, he was ordered to make a call: to the duty officer, Australian Defence Headquarters, Canberra.

He was handed a written text to read. The grim faces surrounding him made it clear he had no option.

Minutes later a convoy of twenty-two more buses growled up to the entrance. The barrier was lifted. They rolled in taking different internal roads over the sprawling, 750-hectare base, home to more than three thousand Australian soldiers.

Small groups of the raiders were dropped at strategic locations, including each barracks block where they stormed in ordering groggy and baffled soldiers from their beds at gunpoint. Most of the Australians cursed, believing they were part of a surprise attack exercise.

———

DAY ONE

3.42 A.M.

Private quarters, The Lodge, Canberra

It seemed he had been asleep only minutes when a rustling noise outside the door woke him.

He squinted at the bedside clock. Its dull-green digit flicked to 3.42.

A rap on the door sat him up. He heard a murmur of hushed voices. Then a second, firmer knock brought him to his full senses.

Elaine gave a start.

"What's happening?" she said.

The door to the private quarters half opened. A stab of light cut in to the room.

Stone tossed off bedclothes and swung his feet to the floor in a single move.

"Prime Minister. Are you awake?"

The urgent voice of John Able seemed incongruous in the pre-dawn bedroom setting.

"Yes, John." Stone stood up uncertainly. "What is it? What the hell's going on?"

Stone could see the tall backlit profile of the Prime Minister's Department's boss in the doorway. Able hesitated a long second.

"I'm sorry, sir, but we have been unable to find the Minister for Defence and General Thompson needs to talk to you — right now."

"At this hour? What's he want that's so bloody urgent?" Stone turned again to the clock. He hadn't been mistaken. It was only 3.42.

Able didn't reply.

"Come on, John, for God's sake." Stone felt a flush of impatience and the first serious stirrings of unease.

"I'll put the general on your secure line, sir," Able answered. He turned and left before Stone could respond. Stone heard several sets of footsteps retreating down the passageway.

Able had arrived with security guards in tow.

———

STONE SAT ON THE BEDSIDE. Elaine anxiously hurried around to sit next to him. She unconsciously took his left hand, a habit of thirty-two years. They waited in silence for the shrill ring of the secure phone.

When it came, Stone leaned over to push the speaker button. His finger missed. He breathed in deeply, willed his shaking hand to stillness and stabbed a second time.

"General Thompson. What is it?"

"I have some pretty startling news I'm afraid, Prime Minister."

The sentence was left hanging. At sixty-four, General Alan Thompson had just nine months to run as the country's Chief of Defence. He struggled for words to describe his worst military nightmare. And the certain humiliation that would end his career.

Stone waited, slowing his breathing, hoping the general could not hear its raggedness.

"Defence Headquarters took a call from the base commandant at Lavarack, up in Townsville, early this morning," Thompson said. "Since then there's been a steady stream of calls from all our base commanders in northern Queensland, the Northern Territory and the far northwest of Western Australia."

He paused again and heard Stone mutter something indecipherable.

"Forces wearing the uniform of the Chinese People's Liberation

Army have seized all our bases in the Top Half — army, air force and naval — the lot."

Stone said nothing, his mind spinning to grasp the news. He worried Elaine's fingers with one hand, twisting the bed covers with the other till his knuckles went white.

"I know it's a lot to take in, sir," Thompson offered in the silence.

Stone cleared his throat. "The Chinese have just seized all of our northern military bases in the last couple of hours and occupied half of our country?"

Before Thompson could answer, Stone went on: "How the fuck could that happen? It's not possible ... are you absolutely sure, Alan?"

He tried to keep any trace of panic from his voice. He saw Elaine staring at him, one hand covering her mouth in shock.

Thompson named all the bases across the vast northern shores of the world's sixth-biggest country. Teams of lightly armed Chinese had simultaneously seized each one without a fight.

The modus operandi was identical. All base commanders reported their fate directly to Canberra as ordered. The Chinese had descended on their unsuspecting targets in anonymous civilian vehicles, mainly buses, four-wheel-drives and even the odd taxi.

The element of surprise was total. The enemy's strength was still unknown but its control in Queensland stretched south to Gladstone.

"There's more bad news I'm afraid," Thompson said. "Our base commanders say the Chinese regard all prisoners as hostages. If there is any counterattack they will be killed immediately. They are booby-trapping all barracks to guarantee that."

"How many of our people are up there?" Stone realised his voice was a hoarse whisper.

Thompson said there were approximately twelve thousand service personnel and a few hundred civilian contractors on the various bases.

Stone made an effort to collect his thoughts. "If they have Gladstone, are we likely to see them take a shot at Brisbane next?"

"They say not. The message relayed from our commanders claim the Chinese have no further territorial ambitions. This also leads us to believe the actual number of Chinese on the ground is small. I don't think they'd be able to handle a full-scale counterattack from us so the prisoners' lives are a chip they're playing, at least till they get reinforcements."

Before Stone could speak, Thompson said: "The Chinese also say their ambassador wants to meet you urgently this morning to discuss details of a peace settlement."

"A peace settlement?!" Stone exploded. He felt his pulse race.

He knew why the Chinese might possibly be content with the Top Half: it held most of Australia's mining and energy resources.

The most vulnerable frontier on earth had been protecting some of its most valuable energy riches. It had been breached without a shot fired in anger. It beggared belief.

But Australia had always been an impossible land to defend. A mass the size of the United States but with almost 26,000 kilometres of coastline.

Its resource wealth was scattered over enormous deserts with tiny populations. It was an empty land. It had been a sitting duck for determined invaders ever since Queen Victoria's Imperial forces had claimed it as a British colony more than two hundred years ago.

Stone heaved himself to his feet. "Well, what now? And where the hell is Bob Bradbury? Someone must be able to find him."

"Not so far, sir. I'll get the Defence Minister to call you as soon as we locate him," said Thompson. "Meanwhile we are mobilising and putting all our forces on full alert. I'll call you directly if there are any further developments."

He asked to be excused and Stone slowly leaned over to cancel the speaker button. He hit it on the second attempt.

———

ELAINE WATCHED the dawn light beginning to bleed around the edges of the heavy bedroom drapes.

"How could this have happened?" she said quietly. "This is madness."

Stone looked down and shrugged. "This madness happened to the Ukraine. Russia walked in and annexed Crimea," he said. "And got away with it."

Stone put his huge arm around her. They sat motionless, trying to absorb the enormity of the morning's events.

Elaine said, "Do you think the Chinese will get away with it too?"

Stone did not answer. He rubbed his chest and straightened his back.

Elaine shook him by the shoulder. They had to get up. He needed to take charge, she said.

Stone nodded in silent agreement.

He made for the en suite while she went downstairs to stir the rest of the household. But seconds after the shower was flowing the secure phone was ringing again. He trudged naked back to the bedroom while hot water drummed impatiently on the shower box floor.

It was Lindsay Noble who had insisted his call be connected immediately.

The Foreign Minister was in a panic. He had made the first call anyone in his position would after a military attack. To the US State Department in Washington. To invoke the ANZUS Treaty, the cornerstone of Australia's defence strategy since World War Two. Its ultimate security guarantee.

For its part in the alliance Australia had loyally gone off to war alongside America in its battles around the world, including Korea, Vietnam, Afghanistan and Iraq.

As he listened, Stone was alarmed his minister, a former strategic affairs professor with the prerequisite alphabet of degrees, had lost any vestige of his usual urbane manner. Noble had reached the US Secretary of State, Ben Strong.

"Christ, Gary, I got Strong on the line and he already knew what I was going to tell him!"

"For heaven's sake, Lindsay, calm down, man," Stone said, already fighting an icy shiver in his own stomach.

"He knew all about the Chinese. Everything. The Chinese briefed him as the bases were being seized, for God's sake," said Noble.

Stone said nothing.

"Do you realise what this means? They're going to hang us out to dry. We're on our own. We're fucked."

Noble paused to suck in a breath. "Strong said the Chinese had briefed him because they didn't want to risk the shock the Yanks would have if they'd turned on CNN and found out. The Chinese didn't want a macho jerk reaction. They wanted the cool heads in the White House to pacify the big dogs in the Pacific Fleet."

Noble stopped suddenly. There had been something America had offered. Slowly, imitating Strong's southern drawl, Noble said: "Lindsay, rest assured we will call immediately for an emergency session of the UN Security Council to condemn this flagrant act of aggression."

Stone grunted. "Lindsay, they're are not going to risk a war with China for us. Let's not kid ourselves. They never were. Not when it came down to the wire. All ANZUS ever entitled us to do was to 'consult' with America if we were attacked. There was never any guarantee they would gallop to our rescue in a war. Perhaps if we'd picked up some intelligence before the attacks they may have stationed a carrier force off Queensland but ..."

"Fuck, Gary. We're on our own. The Chinese ... I cannot believe we fell for all that hoopla and smiling photo ops with the new chairman. And their Pacific Fleet is off the Queensland coast on its way to Sydney for a goodwill visit, for God's sake."

"Lindsay, settle down, man. You're not helping matters. You're the Foreign Minister, you should know the Yanks and Chinese are the two most interdependent countries in the world. America runs on Chinese cash to fund its economy, China runs on its bullshit undervalued currency and cheap labour to rack up huge trading profits. Neither of them can afford a shooting war with each other."

Stone heard Noble take a slurp of something. He hoped it was only coffee.

Noble said: "The Chinese ambassador has called wanting a meeting. His name is Chen. He's only just been posted here. None of their embassy staff were expecting him. His wife is still in Beijing."

"So we're going to be meeting the next Governor of the Far North," said Stone.

"It's not funny, Gary. But it does look that way if they get away with his ... this ... Christ ... it's unbelievable ..."

Stone told him they would meet the ambassador at The Lodge. Stone was determined not to confront a media pack outside his parliamentary office.

"Lindsay, I really have to go," Stone said.

"But we haven't even begun to discuss our strategy when we sit down with Chen. What's so urgent?"

"I hate cold showers," said Stone.

———

Want to read more? A Line Too Far *by Barry Colman*
Available from major outlets in paperback, ebook and audiobook formats
barrycolman.co

ABOUT THE AUTHOR

Barry Colman is an award-winning journalist and publisher who divides his time between homes in the Gold Coast and Auckland. He is a former staff reporter for the *Courier Mail* and *Sunday Mail*, Brisbane.

A very successful business executive, he founded The Liberty Publishing Company which produced financial and classified papers in New Zealand and he acquired *The National Business Review* from Fairfax.

He has always had a strong interest in geopolitics and his works of fiction are set against realistic political and social possibilities.

He is a recipient of the Queens Service Medal for services to publishing.

www.barrycolman.co

 facebook.com/bccolman